Lohengrin

Antony Melville-Ross

First published in 1986 by William Collins Sons & Co. Ltd.

This edition published in 2017 by Endeavour Media Ltd.

moja kochanka

Table of Contents

For the greater part of the war we did much more than practise a large-scale deception through double agents; by means of the double agent system *we actively ran and controlled the German espionage system in this country.*

The Double-Cross System in the war of 1939 to 1945
J. C. MASTERMAN.
(Yale University Press 1972 New Haven and London)

Chapter One

'Are you a virgin?'

Holding the questioner's gaze with her own the blonde girl shook her head, making her sleek cascade of shoulder-length hair sway like a heavy curtain.

'No,' she said.

She was now more than an hour into her fourth cross-examination by different groups of people in nine days and her only surprise at the enquiry was that it had not been made sooner.

'Are you very experienced?'

This time she looked away and let the regard of her darkly fringed grey eyes rest in turn on the four other men seated behind the long table before looking back at the chairman. Her voice carried a note of bored indifference when she spoke.

'If you're asking me if I'm a whore the answer is no, but I expect you'll turn me into one soon enough.'

'What,' the chairman asked, 'is that remark supposed to mean?'

'Precisely what it says. If that were not your intention you could have no conceivable official interest in my virginity, or lack of it.'

The chairman noted the slight stress she had placed on the word 'official' and scribbled something on the pad in front of him, then stared at her over the top of his glasses.

'I wouldn't put it quite as strongly as that,' he told her, 'but your point is taken and I think we understand one another.' He paused, then added, 'We appreciate your interest in this organization, Miss Helier, and you'll be hearing from us very soon. I think you may assume favourably.'

He watched her incline her head, rise to her feet with sinuous grace, and listened to her saying, 'Thank you. That will be most satisfactory.' She didn't smile.

Claire Helier, a favourite of London society and orphaned daughter of an ancient house, turned her back on the five anonymous men and stalked like a high-fashion model on a cat-walk out of the imposing interview room used by a branch of the Security Service whose name she did not know.

The air-raid sirens began their mournful dirge then, but, conscious only of the pairs of eyes she knew would be following her retreating figure, the sound did not register on her ears.

For a long moment after the door closed behind her there was silence, then one of the men said, 'Exit deathless allure in a cloud of disdain. What is it that makes these empty-headed creatures gravitate towards us? The place is getting to be like an agency for mannequins.'

The chairman smiled briefly and began to transfer his pencilled notes onto a form with a pen before saying, 'Be thankful she didn't pat you on that bald head of yours, Jonathan. But I agree. She did rather overdo it, didn't she? Never mind. She really is ridiculously pretty and we can use her for simple entrapment until she grows up a little. A session or two with "The Puppet Maker" should expedite that process. Agreed?'

He looked left, then right, and having received four nods returned his attention to the form.

*

An escort was waiting to conduct Claire Helier from the building or, he informed her, to the air-raid shelter in the basement if she would prefer that. Only then did she become aware of distant gunfire, but it was not the sounds of battle which made her feel that her legs might fail to support her. She wondered if elation at her success was the cause, or the enormity of the step she had taken, or . . .

'I'd like to wash if I may,' she said.

In the bathroom she supported herself with her hands on the rim of the basin and examined her reflection in the mirror, a little surprised to find it unchanged, not even slightly depraved. The absurdity of the thought came to her then, making her smile, and the smile nudged trepidation aside and let triumph flow into her. Excitement came with it, excitement at the pleasure in store for her when she could tell her beautiful friend Gail of the control she had exercised over her inquisitors. She had been in love with Gail for all of their five years at school together, refused to admit to herself that she still was, but did acknowledge that her approval was of supreme importance.

For a moment she practised her expression for controlling inquisitors, then, 'You mustn't keep that nice young man waiting any longer,' she told her reflection, applied lipstick to her mouth and hurried out to rejoin her guide.

*

10

The *Luftwaffe* failed to press home its assault on London that night and when the nice young man eventually and reluctantly ushered Claire Helier through the main door of the building into the blacked-out street, another man in a room three floors directly above her had not even bothered to move from his desk. He was reading the final report on her and reading it carefully. It wasn't really necessary for him to do so because he knew almost everything there was to be known about this particular applicant, but he was doing it because he was a professional and because 'almost' was not good enough. Others might well have noted what he himself could have overlooked through proximity and affection.

When he had finished he clipped the document to the three interview reports which had preceded it, together with a brief statement from Special Branch, another from the Admiralty where the girl was currently a civilian employee, and a medical report. That done, he lay back in his chair and looked towards the three silver-framed photographs on the mantel above the fireplace at his side.

His wife, killed the winter before when a marauding Me 109 had machine-gunned the mobile canteen she had been running for the troops, held pride of place at the centre. He didn't allow his gaze to dwell on her because the air around him was already sufficiently charged with emotion, but let it settle instead on the frame to the left. Claire Helier looked out of it with a warmth in her smile the camera had failed to freeze and laughter in her eyes that was almost audible.

The man glanced down at the file, then up again. 'Arrogant?' he murmured. 'I only wish you were just a little for your own good in this job, my dear. Don't get hurt by your own play-acting.'

He turned his grave regard onto the third photograph then and, just as gravely, a hauntingly lovely face looked back at him. There *was* arrogance in that look, if only in the certitude of physical perfection. The black and white image could not tell him of the perfect pale skin with its faint under-blush of mauve, of the amber flecks in the slanting green eyes, of the dark red of hair which seemed to float about her head, but then Edward George Mainwaring, Seventh Marquis of Trent, didn't need to be told what his own daughter looked like.

For a few minutes he let his mind drift back in time, remembering the death of Claire's parents in a plane crash just before the war, and his virtual adoption of his daughter's closest friend. He remembered too their 'coming out' together, their presentation at Court together, their London 'Season'

11

together and the joint soubriquet of 'Trent's Transfixers' awarded them by a society columnist. The name had stuck and so had the friendship between the girls.

When he had finished remembering he leant quickly forward and wrote 'Acceptance approved' on the top of Claire Helier's file, just as he had done on his daughter's a few months earlier, wishing very much that he had not had to do so in either case. Only the inescapable necessity of employing so much specialized talent in time of war gave him comfort – that and the guilty knowledge that neither would be aware that he was privy to their secret and had set the official seal of approval on their initiative. So much at least was certain, as each believed him to be involved in the Ministry of Aircraft Production.

He looked up at the photograph of his daughter again and said, 'Take care of her, my old beetroot top. You're much the stronger.' But the likeness of The Lady Abigail Mainwaring had nothing to say.

Chapter Two

The Special Branch men had been careful enough, but still everything went wrong. They had followed the Portuguese from the wine shop in Moorgate, along London Wall to his lodgings near Liverpool Street Station, then waited for an hour before, as their report stated, effecting an entry.

It was Sergeant Newland who opened the front door of the building with his skeleton keys and the door of the bed-sitting room on the second floor with the heel of his boot.

It was Inspector Came who said to the startled man in the only armchair, 'Are you *Senhor* Braga?'

'Yes.'

'*Senhor* Manuel Braga?'

'Yes.'

'We are Special Branch officers and I have here a detention order in your name under DR 18b. I must ask you to accompany us.'

It was *Senhor* Manuel Braga who catapulted out of his chair, struck Inspector Carne full in the face with the crown of his head and kicked Sergeant Newland in the groin.

They caught him. They caught him three hundred yards from his front door. They caught him three hundred yards too late for him to be of any use whatsoever to a branch of MI5 designated B.I.a. because upwards of a dozen people saw them do it. The number could have been thirteen, as it was all very unfortunate for *Senhor* Manuel Braga who had his spinal cord snapped by a hangman's noose on the gallows at Pentonville Prison a few weeks later. The crimes for which he died were spying for Germany and forcing Special Branch to apprehend him in public. The former he might well have survived, but the latter sealed his fate for, onlookers apart, the *Evening Standard* dated 18 September 1941 carried a small item reporting the arrest of a Portuguese wine importer by plain-clothes detectives after a brief struggle in Old Broad Street. The newspaper had even managed to establish his name, and the fact that it was incorrectly spelt was to be of no comfort either to *Senhor* Braga, the Twenty Committee, or B.I.a., its executive arm, as it would have been idiotic to hope that the report would be missed by *Senhor* Braga's German paymasters in Lisbon.

The Twenty Committee took its name from the Roman numerals representing that number. They formed a double cross, which was the Committee's function, a function so ably carried out that somewhat to its astonishment and very much to its credit it found itself in control of the German espionage organization in the United Kingdom. The totality of that control was such as to strain credulity and its maintenance necessitated constant vigilance and a high degree of cooperation between MI5, MI6, the Directors of Intelligence of the three fighting Services and certain highly placed persons from other spheres. Complete secrecy and the ability to adapt swiftly and effectively to rapidly changing circumstances were also paramount, and *Senhor* Braga's short-lived evasion of his arresting officers had militated against both necessities.

An MI6 agent had first recognized Braga for what he was, and for two months, under observation by him in Lisbon and by MI5 in England, he was permitted to pursue his activities and enhance his standing with the *Abwehr* officer to whom he reported at a flat off Praca Marques de Pombal at the end of the Avenida da Liberdade.

Just before the time was thought to be right for an approach to be made with a view to enticing him away from his present allegiance and into the service of British Intelligence, the component parts of a wireless set were discovered in two cases of the wine he imported into England. All such cases had been opened and carefully resealed as a matter of course since his clandestine activities had become known. The discovery painted a different picture, indicating that, if the set was for his own use, Braga had been instructed to cease his journeyings between Portugal and England and establish himself permanently in London as a wireless agent. The code books accompanying the set having been photographed, everything was repacked as it had been and the consignment released to him. Subsequent transmissions from the wine shop in Moorgate proved interesting, and proved too that Braga was indeed the final recipient of the wireless set. That was when MI5, who had no official powers of arrest, sent in Special Branch to take him into custody, where by education, reasoning, persuasion or coercion stopping short only of the sentence of death, it was hoped to obtain his agreement to continuing with his work, but under British control.

The dissemination of misleading information for enemy consumption had almost limitless possibilities and *Senhor* Braga was thought a potentially excellent vehicle, but he spoilt all that when he butted Inspector Carne in the face and rendered Sergeant Newland momentarily incapable with the toe-cap of his shoe. After that there was no alternative but to hang him, to demonstrate to the Germans that his case was closed. It was very annoying from the point of view of B.I.a. in general and of George Pemberton in particular, because Pemberton was to have been Braga's case officer, his mentor, guide, jailer and the repository for his fears during and after the difficult psychological transition from one camp to the other.

George Pemberton was a pleasant-faced man with thinning sandy hair and lazy grey eyes. He was thirty-two years of age and obviously very fit. Because he was thirty-two years of age and obviously very fit, he was required to wear the uniform of a lieutenant-colonel in the Royal Tank Regiment with the ribbon of the Distinguished Service Order on his jacket, as men of his age and condition in civilian clothes could attract unwelcome attention in time of war. Being entitled neither to the uniform nor the decoration, Pemberton had protested, particularly about the decoration. 'Oh, hadn't you heard?' his superior had said. 'You did frightfully well during the retreat to Dunkirk and now you're a tank warfare expert on one of the planning committees. Go away and read up something on tanks in case you're ever asked about them.' Pemberton had done as he was told.

That had been a year earlier and for much of the time since, he had been controlling the life and activities of a captured German agent code-named 'Parsifal'. Living in close proximity to him in the same small bungalow in Hampshire, he had watched with growing alarm the deterioration of the renegade spy from a man content to serve his erstwhile enemies in exchange for his life to a morose being with a reborn conscience. 'Parsifal' became alliterative in his self-condemnation, the words 'treachery', 'treason', 'turncoat' and 'traitor' frequently on his lips. He was given encouragement, assurances, more money, a greater degree of freedom and a pretty girl to take to his bed, but all to no avail. While Pemberton was pondering the alternatives of continued perseverance or a termination of the case, Parsifal settled the matter for him by slashing his own wrists tidily in the bath.

When he had supervised the disposal of the corpse and ensured that it remained anonymous, Pemberton, a case officer without a case and, with the loss of Braga, who hadn't lived long enough to acquire a code name, none in prospect, went to see the Oxford don who was his superior.

Professor Morris had a receding chin which made him appear vacuous, a body which seemed to be composed mostly of skin and bone, and a mind like a rapier. As soon as they had shaken hands, 'I've decided to grow a beard,' he told Pemberton.

Pemberton nodded. 'I'm very sorry about this Parsifal business, sir. I suppose I could have done more. In fact I'm sure I could, but I'm damned if I know what.'

'Thought I'd try disguising this jaw of mine,' Morris said. 'Well, I mean the one I haven't got. Makes me look like one of those Hooray Henry types you meet on shooting parties. What do you think?'

'Good idea. You know, where I might have gone wrong was . . .'

'Oh, do stop drivelling on about it,' Professor Morris broke in. 'Wasn't your fault. You win a few and you lose a few as Shakespeare said, or perhaps it was Milton. I don't have much time for the moderns. Chaucer's my cup of tea. Why don't you take a few days' leave?'

Pemberton sighed resignedly, silently. 'If you say so, sir. I'll go and stay with my folks in Rutland. Am I being fired?'

'Lucky you don't need one,' Professor Morris said. 'Not allowed with that uniform.'

'What isn't allowed, sir?'

'A beard. Only the Navy and pipe majors in some Scottish regiments can wear them. I'll phone you in Rutland when the time's ripe. You'll be wanted in Sussex. Seaford's a nice little town, even if the beach is all covered in barbed wire, mines and pillboxes. Splendid walks on the Downs.'

Thankful that a clear directive had at last emerged from verbal chaos, Pemberton murmured 'Ah', then waited, watching Morris's hand explore the stubble on his chin.

With the operation successfully completed, 'Bloody fool was standing looking into a shop window eating a sausage in his fingers,' Morris said. 'Have you ever seen a citizen of this sceptred isle looking into a shop window eating a sausage in his fingers?'

'No, sir.'

'Germans do it in droves.'

'Yes, sir.'

'All the time in fact.'

'Yes, sir.'

'Intelligent copper saw him at it, followed him home and told the local CID. They told us. I'm setting a girl on him to put him off his guard.'

'How far off?'

'All the way, I hope,' Morris told him. 'Wait until you see the girl. But you'll have to watch your step for all that. We can't afford a repetition of the Braga case, so don't give him a chance to swallow a nasty pill. He might have one hidden inside a sausage.' Morris cackled at his own joke, then added, 'Well, off you go and enjoy your leave.'

'Thank you, sir. I'll do that as soon as I've got some background information on this man. That file you're fanning yourself with has "Seaford" written on it, so I suppose it's relevant.'

Professor Morris stopped fanning himself, looked at the file, muttered, 'Good God! So it has! Bloody poor security!' and savaged the label with the point of a paper-knife. The offending word obliterated, he wrote 'Lohengrin' in its place.

'There you are. Son of Parsifal,' he said and handed the folder across the desk.

*

Claire Helier's transition from her fantasy world to reality was both sudden and unpleasant. The suddenness she resented, because two weeks had been altogether too short a time in which to enjoy the shadow before having the substance thrust at her. The unpleasantness was based both on intense dislike of what she was being ordered to do and of the man who was telling her to do it. From across the desk she gave him a witheringly imperious look. It was one of her better ones, one that she had copied from Gail, but the man appeared not to notice, his own disinterested gaze seeming to indicate that she was a piece of furniture he was considering selling but wasn't sure was worth the effort involved. Angrily she broke the visual contact and stared at his bristly receding chin.

'Is that clear so far?' Professor Morris asked.

She ignored the question and asked one of her own. 'What happens to this man after I've ensnared him, as you put it?'

'We take him from you, expose him to less pleasant pressures and return him partly into your keeping in what I trust will be a sufficiently malleable condition to permit you to continue to manipulate him. You will, of course, be given every assistance in achieving that end.'

'The sort of end that justifies the means, I suppose,' Claire said in a cold voice. 'I think it's despicable!'

'I'm not interested in justifying the means or anything else,' Morris told her, 'and I'm equally uninterested in your opinion. All that is required of you is to perform the tasks entrusted to you. You appear to have all the necessary physical attributes. Kindly employ them as I imagine nature intended and, beyond using your common sense, leave thinking to those better equipped in that department than yourself.'

'What a truly hateful man you are!'

'Oh yes,' Morris said. 'Oh yes indeed. Truly hateful, but puzzled as well. Very puzzled.'

'Puzzled about what?'

'About what put it into your head that you might be of the slightest use to us. The door is still where you left it when you came in. Good afternoon, Miss Helier. I'm sure the Admiralty will be delighted to have you back.'

It was the awful thought of having to tell Gail that she had not so much fallen at the first fence as failed to get onto the course at all which held Claire where she was. The man had picked up a file with the single word 'Lorelei' on its cover and she watched him begin to read from it before saying, 'I'm sorry. I'm behaving stupidly. May we start again?'

'Possibly,' Morris said. 'Let me finish with this.' For nearly a minute he continued to read, then he closed the folder, initialled it and raised his eyes to meet hers. She saw that they were no more friendly than before and that helped to stiffen her newly found resolve.

'You're a charlatan, Miss Helier.'

Claire neither spoke nor attempted to look imperious and Morris went on, 'Save your acting for the enemy. Don't try to inflict it on us. We've seen the play before and there's no part in it for a girl wearing a raincoat and a beret, lounging about in dark bars and waiting to receive the enemy's plans in return for a night of passion. Isn't that how you saw yourself?'

'No, of course not. Well – oh I don't know,' Claire said.

'No, you don't know, do you? What we now have to establish is whether or not there is any point in enabling you to find out. I personally doubt it, but remain open to persuasion that the contrary is the case.'

'I'd like to be allowed to try. I didn't mean what I said before.'

'Don't lie to me, Miss Helier. You meant every word of it.'

'I was – I was shocked, that's all.'

'There's been an administrative error,' Morris said. 'Yes, that's it. An administrative error would explain everything. The female person I'm supposed to be briefing viewed the prospect of becoming a prostitute with equanimity, if the chairman of her selection board is to be believed. I seem to recall that the term "whore" was used by the lady. Obviously she cannot have been you, who balk at forming a liaison with a single male. I apologize for shocking you.'

He began to tidy the scattered papers on his desk, then looked up at the sound of Claire Helier saying, 'It was the singularity that shocked me. Is that the right word? Singularity?' Without waiting for a reply she added, 'It hadn't occurred to me that I would be asked to live with a man for a prolonged period of time. That's an awfully intimate thing to do. I'd expected something impersonal like – well, perhaps you were right about the beret and everything.'

'So?'

'As I said, I'd like to be allowed to try, but I don't want to be a nuisance.'

'You go home and think about this very deeply, Miss Helier,' Morris said. 'Come back here at the same hour the day after tomorrow. We'll discuss the matter further then, but I must warn you that I still doubt your usefulness to us.'

As soon as he was alone Professor Morris made a telephone call.

'Morris here, Lady Abigail. Your protégée has been to see me and . . . Oh, she's not your protégée? I see. I hadn't realized that you sent her to us with great reluctance. Well, I share none of your misgivings. Yes of course she's immature, disarmingly so, and that makes her doubly valuable because she will disarm her quarry. Such lack of guile is rare and should prove a priceless asset in the situation I'm trying to create. No, I've told her none of this. She's on her way back to you under the impression that she's of questionable worth and with orders to return here on Wednesday. What? Oh indeed there's a purpose behind this call. I wanted to ask you to prevail upon her to abandon her chosen role of *femme fatale*. It'll come better from you than me and she'll be much more effective as herself. Yes, I'm sure you'll do your best. Lady Abigail. Goodbye.'

Claire Helier walked home. It was over a mile to Sloane Street and having dressed for effect her high heels and tight skirt hampered her, but she walked anyway. Having to confess almost certain failure to Gail was not a prospect she was relishing and she needed time to think, to decide why it mattered, to understand as well what had really led her to seek entry into such a bizarre world. The realization that she had given almost no consideration to the last point jolted her.

Gail's abrupt change of lifestyle had started it all, of course. Her mixing with people she had not known before and to whom she did not introduce Claire had been both intriguing and hurtful because until that time they had shared so much. Having her questions parried had upset Claire too, as had Gail's unannounced and unexplained absences from home.

Eventually persistence had won and Gail had explained a little of what she was doing. The knowledge that her constant probing having made her a security risk was the sole reason for her being told anything at all had made Claire feel a little guilty, but intense excitement had obliterated the emotion. She knew now what she wanted to do as her contribution to victory and Gail's instruction that she stop being ridiculous went almost unheard.

In her room that night, Claire had consulted her diary to confirm the well remembered fact that she had been in love fifteen times; three of those times very deeply and one of them for nearly a whole month. Even more significantly, she had slept with two men, in both cases without either having any planned intention of doing so or being in love with them. That, she had concluded, indicated a depth of depravity which fitted her perfectly for the career she had selected. Dress after dress snatched from the wardrobe and held in front of her before the long pier-glass while she practised poses and expressions strengthened her conviction that she had found her vocation. She had spent two hours doing that. She had spent another nine weeks arguing her case before Gail had said tiredly, 'All right, darling, I'll give them your name, but they won't take you on.'

Walking through Knightsbridge, Claire mused unhappily on how right Gail had been, feeling miserable at no longer having an important secret she could hug to herself, feeling resentment that her friend should be trusted to do something she was not. When Gail greeted her with a quietly spoken, unsmiling 'Well done', Claire didn't know what she meant.

Chapter Three

Claire Helier paid the taxi driver and made her way onto the concourse of Victoria Station through the jostling mass of humanity which seemed to her to be a permanent feature of railway stations and most other public places nowadays. It was difficult to make progress through the crowds of soldiers carrying rifles, sailors with huge kit-bags and everybody else burdened with something or other. Twice she nearly lost her grip on her suitcase in the press, but eventually reached the side of the man waiting for her under the clock, a heavily built figure with a flat-planed face like a red Indian's and small watchful eyes.

'Hello, blondie,' he said. 'Let's have your case. The New-haven train's at Platform Twelve.'

She surrendered her case thankfully and followed the MI5 man through the ticket barrier to the comparative peace of a First Class compartment.

Before they entered it, 'I'll be doing a lot of leering at you,' the man told her. 'Better get used to it.'

'All right,' she replied. 'Leer away. You probably won't be the only one, but don't call me "blondie". My name's Claire.'

Settled into a corner seat opposite him she crossed her legs to give him something to leer at and tried to concentrate on a magazine, but it held no interest for her. Giles, he had said his Christian name was, and that, she thought, was a caddish sort of name. The black sheep of the family might be called it, the one despatched to Australia to live on a monthly remittance from home. She pondered that for a bit, decided that it was entirely appropriate for what he was going to have to do, then, aware that she was simply avoiding thinking about what she should be thinking about, pushed the fanciful notions from her mind.

An advertising hoarding on the platform caught her attention. The poster on it showed a caricature of Hitler with a devil's horns and tail, the head pressed against the side of a house. 'Walls have ears! Careless talk costs lives!' the caption read and that made her think simultaneously of Gail and Professor Morris. First the former then, at their second meeting, the latter had talked at length to her about secrecy. Gail had done it with calm forcefulness, the professor with a mixture of schoolmasterly irascibility and a hard intensity which had made her blink, but neither had given her the smallest clue about what was so secret beyond the fact that she was involved in a counter-espionage operation. She assumed that Gail had no clue to give and that Professor Morris did but had no intention of parting with it.

When she had been comprehensively briefed, 'Why me?' she had asked the professor, and the question had earned her the first glimmer of approval she had ever seen on his face.

Her gaze still fixed on the Hitler cartoon, but unseeingly now, she heard again the detested voice saying, 'Excellent. Cerebration has begun at last. We are no longer sweeping all before us. We are seeking reasons. Why you, indeed? The answer to your question, young lady, lies in two parts. The first is that females such as yourself do not, as they say, grow on trees. That is a relatively minor matter and one which I would certainly have discounted in your case had it not been for the second part.'

He had paused at that point, murmured 'Certainly discounted' almost to himself, then gone on, 'The second part is that observation has shown us that this man has no permanent female companion, but enjoys the company of women and has a marked preference for those possessing two qualities of yours, two qualities virtually non-existent in this business, the two qualities you are stupidly at such pains to disguise.'

Asked what those were, 'Innocence and gentleness,' he had told her. 'We believe that those, coupled with your appearance, will prove an irresistible combination for him.'

She supposed she must still have looked puzzled because he had added sharply, 'For goodness sake, Miss Helier, can't you see that if we put someone like your friend Lady Abigail on to him he would very probably be frightened to death by her and certainly be put on his guard?'

Claire had made her way home feeling quietly satisfied that she was considered more suitable at least for something than was Gail, and reminding herself to look up the word 'cerebration' in the dictionary.

The train jerking into movement brought her back to the present and she began the process of allowing herself to be picked up by the man from MI5.

*

'Don't be tiresome, Giles.'

The rough fawn tweed skirt Claire was wearing was short, reflecting the wartime necessity to economize on clothing materials, as on everything else. The silk-stockinged legs protruding from it were neither rough nor short and the man removed his hand from her knee with obvious reluctance.

'Just practising,' he said quietly, 'and we have to make sure that the locals get the picture, even if he isn't here.'

'Hmm, some excuse. I don't even believe he's coming.'

'Nor do I. Anyway, we've been here about as long as is reasonable.'

The man stood, helped her from her bar stool and followed her into the street, then took her arm for the short walk to the hotel. They had adjoining rooms there and he stopped outside her door.

'I want to come in for a few minutes,' he said. 'No funny business. It's something I'd like you to try, something which looks very convincing.' He had spoken in a near-whisper and she regarded him curiously for a moment, then shrugged and led the way into the bedroom.

'Come over here, clear of the furniture.'

She did as he said.

'Get down near to the floor. Sit, squat, kneel, anything you like.'

'Look, what is this, Giles?'

'I'm going to show you how to make yourself faint like a Victorian heroine. It won't hurt, it won't do you any harm and I'll catch you when you keel over. It's for our big scene.'

Claire's 'Oh' carried no enthusiasm, but again she obeyed him, lowering herself, feeling her skirt slide up her thighs, until she was resting on her heels.

'If this is just part of your leering routine I'm going to be extremely cross with you,' she said, but he gave no sign of having heard her.

'Breathe in and out very deeply. More. More. Hold your breath and tense your muscles. Good. Now stand up.'

She did so and the room tilted and began to circle about her, then the lights dimmed, went out.

Within seconds, 'All right?' he asked.

He was standing by the bed, looking down at her.

'Yes, I'm all right.'

'Don't move for a moment or two. You're still very white.'

'What a strange feeling, Giles.'

'Yes, the doctors call it hyperventilation. All the blood drains from your head. Can you repeat that procedure when the time comes?'

'Of course.'

He nodded, said, 'Good night, Claire,' and let himself out of the room.

*

It was not until the third evening that visual contact was made and one member each of two couples spoke simultaneously.

'Don't look now, but he's in the far corner with a man wearing a cloth cap,' Giles said to Claire as they entered the bar.

'Don't look now, but a piece of pulchritude the like of which you've never seen before has just walked in,' the man in a cloth cap said to his neighbour.

Two nearly irresistible forces took hold of Claire. One, like a giant hand gripping her skull, sought to turn her face towards the corner. The other, a fast-flowing ghostly tide, impeded her progress across the room, urging her back the way she had come. She fought them both and defeated them, but when she settled herself carefully onto a bar stool she felt drained, very small and not in the least like an exotic temptress. Had it occurred to her that her condition would have pleased Professor Morris she might have felt better. It did not occur to her and she yawned with nervous tension.

'Tired?'

'Not in the least.'

'What do you want to drink?'

'Oh, anything. Half a shandy. Anything.'

Her reflection in the long mirror set in panelling behind the bar was broken by ornamental scrolling and the words 'Tamplin's Fine Ales' frosted onto the glass. Moving her head fractionally gave her a clear view of herself and she was surprised to see that she looked as she normally did, not even slightly stricken. The sight restored a degree of courage to her and she looked up at her companion.

'I wish we could get this over with tonight,' she whispered.

'Well, we can't. We'll do it gradually just as we planned. Anything else would be much too obvious. Drink your shandy.'

A minute later, 'Ah, he's watching you in the glass,' Giles said. 'Act up.' He put an arm around her neck and Claire worked her shoulders irritably, grasped his wrist and ostentatiously thrust it from her saying, 'Don't do that,' in a voice of heavy patience. After that they talked in desultory fashion for a little longer, Claire looking neither at Giles nor at the reflection of the man in the mirror, then she drained her glass, stood up abruptly and said, 'I'm going. Are you coming or not?' Without waiting for a reply, she turned and walked out of the bar. Scowling, Giles followed her.

In the street, 'Did you see him?' he asked.

'Only a glimpse.'

'That's good enough. I'll show you a photograph when we get to the hotel. I didn't want you to see it before in case you gave any signs of recognition. He's a pleasant looking chap, if that's any help.'

Claire made no comment, but looking at the photograph in her bedroom she found herself agreeing with the statement and found too that it *was* a help. The print showed a man at the wheel of a car, his head in quarter profile turned backwards as though he was reversing. Yes, a pleasant face, she thought. Not handsome, but pleasant, with good eyes, a good chin and a gentle mouth, even if the nose was a bit of a blob.

'They've no business taking pictures of people when they don't know it's being done,' she said.

'Don't be silly, Claire.'

'Sorry. Tomorrow night?'

'Yes, if he's there,' Giles replied. 'Be sure to wear a dress that tears easily in case he is.'

*

The pretty blonde girl made a welcome alternative to talking about the war for the bar's regular customers. Male opinion was predictably unanimous, while the views of the women spanned the spectrum from her being no better than she should be to the acknowledgment that a husband who left home for her could almost be forgiven. Only the big man with the good eyes and chin and the gentle mouth said little, confining himself to smiling agreement while his companion with the cloth cap extolled her virtues. He was still doing so when the hum of conversation faded into silence.

'Here she comes now, Frank,' the owner of the cap said.

Without looking round, 'I rather guessed that from the deathly hush,' the man called Frank Pelham replied. 'Is the boy-friend with her?'

'Sssh. She's right behind you.'

'Oh.'

With the noise level back to normal Pelham glanced at the mirror behind the bar. They were both there, the man looking angry, the girl's face obscured by the reflection of his own shoulder, but her voice saying 'Stop pawing me, Giles!' coldly furious. He looked away, embarrassed, picked up his tankard and tried not to listen to the low-toned bitter exchange behind him. It was just as he had decided to leave that everything seemed to happen at once.

Beer slopped from his tankard as the girl's back struck his, and he swung round as the man shouted, 'You prick-teasing little slut!' pushed her again, then ripped her dress from throat to waist.

Pelham didn't remember putting his beer down, but supposed he must have done because he found himself standing between them, both fists clenched, saying, 'Leave the lady alone, you drunken oaf!' Answered only by a rumbling sound from deep in the man's chest and a swinging blow to his left collarbone, Pelham hit him hard on the forehead.

It must all have happened very quickly, he supposed, because the man had crashed to the floor and the girl had flung herself to her knees beside him before the room fell silent again and somebody called 'Hey' rather tentatively as though wanting to register a protest without becoming involved.

People had begun to gather round the small group when the girl gasped, 'Oh my God! You've killed him!' then began to drag great sobbing breaths into her lungs. The barman was coming through the hinged section of the counter calling, 'Get out the way and let me look,' when she reared to her feet, ashen-faced, and toppled sideways like a felled tree. Pelham caught her in his arms and held her, thinking how pretty her breasts looked cupped in a delicate tracery of black lace. He tried to cover them with her torn dress, but could not manage it with one hand.

'Put me down!' Colour returning to her face, eyes open very wide.

'Of course, but take it slowly. You passed out.'

The man on the floor groaned, sat up, and the barman grasped him by the wrist saying, 'All right, you! Get out and stay out! You too, miss! You're both barred from this establishment!'

Nodding, the girl turned and spoke to Pelham through clenched teeth. 'You frightful bastard!' she said, and the sound of her palm striking his cheek was like a pistol shot.

When he had watched the pair hustled through the door Pelham turned back to his companion.

'What was that about?'

'That was about women,' the man in the cloth cap told him. 'You can never tell with them. Have another pint. You spilt most of your first one.'

*

'Was that all right?' Claire asked.

'Perfect,' Giles told her. 'I'll get back to London. It's all yours now. Good luck.'

She watched him walk away until the darkness swallowed him, then retraced her steps to within twenty yards of the door to the bar. There she waited until, half an hour later, the big man and the other she had seen him with came out. Despite the black-out, she had no difficulty in recognizing them by the light of a quarter moon. They turned towards her and she went to meet them, walking slowly.

'May I speak to you, please?'

'Of course,' her quarry replied. 'Provided that you don't want me to turn the other cheek.'

Claire bit her lip and heard the other man mutter ''Night, Frank.' When he had gone she said, 'I'm desperately sorry. Please believe that. I won't ask you to forgive me, because what I said and did was unforgivable. Good night.'

Turning, she walked away, listening to him saying, 'Look, there's nothing to forgive. You were upset, that's all. Won't you let me see you home?'

In a tearful voice Claire said, 'Oh God, don't you start,' and quickened her pace. He didn't try to overtake her and she was thankful for that. Enough was enough for one night and she knew, without turning to look, that he had watched her enter the small hotel. Giles had booked accommodation as close to the bar as possible to make sure of that. At eleven the next morning she had to feign irritated surprise when he fell in beside her almost as soon as she appeared on the street.

'Hello.'

She ignored him and began to walk faster as she had the night before, but he lengthened his stride to keep up with her.

'Go away,' she said. 'I've already apologized to you. What more do you want?'

'To return your apology in kind. I'm sorry I bashed your boy-friend.'

'Ha! That's a likely tale. You're trying to pick me up, that's what you're trying to do.'

'Yes,' he said.

Frowning, she strode on, looking straight ahead. When they reached an intersection she halted abruptly and turned to face him.

'Will you please go away and stop molesting me?' Each word was sharply spoken and isolated for added emphasis.

'Molesting you?' he replied. 'I'm just going in the same direction as you. I'm the one who's been molested. You hit me so hard yesterday that my last deeply entrenched blackhead popped out.'

Claire giggled. The sound burst from her mouth before she was aware of it, bringing momentary confusion to her before she realized that it was the best thing she could have done. Attractive as she might be to him, there was a point at which her repeated rejections could be accepted and she felt that she had made about enough of those now to demonstrate that it was not she who was the pursuer.

'You're funny,' she said.

No, she couldn't lunch with him, or dine. Yes, she supposed she did have time for a cup of coffee. How do you do, Mr Pelham. I'm Claire Helier. It was none of his business who she was lunching and dining with. No, it wasn't with the man who had torn her dress. He'd gone back to London in a huff and good riddance. Yes, he could telephone her tomorrow morning if he wanted to, but she couldn't say what her plans might be by then.

'I must go, Mr Pelham. Thank you for the coffee.'

She left the little tea shop feeling slightly breathless, trying to analyse the sensation. Most of it, she knew, came from relief at a contact successfully made, but not all of it. The good eyes were brown, the thick straight hair the same colour and the fine skin had never known a blackhead. Claire smiled and wished that it wasn't so long until tomorrow.

*

Seventy-two hours later Claire Helier knew that her diary had lied to her about the fifteen times she had been in love, even the one which had lasted for nearly a whole month. That was quite certain because only now had she begun to discover what the condition was, and the discovery dismayed her. There was no blinding flash of insight, no sudden revelation. It came to her slowly as fact after indisputable fact presented itself for her inspection.

Compassion was the first to arrive, compassion for a man who took such obvious pleasure in her company. That was followed by a stronger pity as his pleasure grew into delight. Then came protectiveness, an overwhelming desire to guard her victim against herself, against the power she possessed, against the greater power she represented.

Deeply shaken, Claire looked almost furtively further inwards, frightened by what she might see next, dismayed by what was revealed to her when the liking she knew to be there totally failed to obscure the strength of the feeling behind it. Of all the potential situations she had tried to imagine, being caught in her own trap had not been one, and the reality of it left her directionless for a number of hours.

Without hope she wished herself out of love, so that she might proceed unhampered by emotion with a task she had once thought to be so glamorous. Her wish was not granted and appeals against that judgement based on Frank Pelham's known treachery foundered beneath the knowledge of her own perfidious position in relation to him. To change that position was impossible now, for if he was not seduced literally as a first step towards seducing him from his allegiance, he would die by hanging, and she would be the executioner because the responsibility for achieving that first step was hers alone.

Forcing the unthinkable from her mind, seeking for any source of pride at all, Claire could find only the resolve to hide her love from everyone except her country's enemy, to carry her own cross. That made her feel a little better until she thought of Gail. Keeping anything from her had always been next to impossible, but perhaps she could get away with it by pretending that the object of her affection was somebody else. The colonel who would be joining them eventually would probably do.

Frank took the next important step for her and she was grateful to him for that because, obscurely, it seemed to lessen her guilt. They were having a lunch-time drink at a pub they had taken to visiting when he said, 'Will you let me cook you dinner at my house tonight? I'm really quite good at it considering that there isn't much to cook with.'

Gently amused by the culinary smoke screen which did nothing to hide the longing in his eyes, feeling simultaneously happy, sad, proud and shy, she had accepted the invitation. Now she was back in her hotel making her preparations for spending the night with him.

The looking-glass in her bedroom was small and she had to examine her naked body in sections. Ever since she had reached maturity her figure had pleased her for itself, but it did much more than that this day for she was about to offer it for the pleasure of someone else, not as a chance happening but with deliberation and tenderness. Almost she succeeded in disregarding the reason for its being at Seaford at all.

Her clinging black cocktail dress, velvet choker collar and high-heeled court shoes made her feel sleek, seductive, sophisticated and sure of herself, so she took them all off again, not certain exactly why, only that it was right. A few minutes later, wearing a plain, blue dress and flat-heeled shoes she walked to a house on Southdown Road to join the man who was to be her lover.

Despite chipped plates and wineglasses that didn't match, he had achieved an attractive table-setting with ferns and candles stuck into the necks of two bottles. The food he had prepared was good too, but for all that the meal wasn't a success, with tension present like a third diner.

Towards the end of it, 'Claire, I was wondering – I mean, will you . . .?'

'It's all right, darling,' she said. 'I'll fix breakfast.'

He seemed to expand physically at her words and grinned boyishly before saying, 'No you won't. I'm even better at that than dinner.'

She waited until he was in bed before undressing for him, making it a friendly thing to do, neither hiding herself nor being provocative. Then she sat, took his hand in hers and looked gravely down at him.

'In case you're worrying, I'm not a virgin, but not a lot not.'

For a moment he blinked in perplexity at the convoluted statement before understanding came, bringing a smile with it.

'That makes us equal,' he said. 'I'm not a lot not either.'

*

They had warned her not to use a telephone line that went through a switchboard, or an instrument she could be overheard talking on in any other way, so on the ninth day after her arrival in the little town, Claire Helier walked to Seaford railway station. In the public phone box there she placed a call to London, then stood looking at her reflection in the little mirror fixed to the back of the box. The face that stared back at her was grey under its make-up and she wondered bleakly if she had looked like that when she had done Giles's fainting trick.

When her number answered she pressed Button 'A' and said, 'Hadrian's Wall.'

'Who's calling?'

'Long John Silver,' she told the mouthpiece.

'Hold on.'

For some seconds the line hummed and clicked at her, then Professor Morris's voice said, 'Ah, Miss Helier,' then asked a question she didn't hear because she was thinking dully that they had found common ground at last in disliking silly code names.

'Are you there, Miss Helier?'

'Shut up and listen,' Claire said and told him precisely where and between what hours the arrest could be made. He had begun to ask something else when she replaced the receiver on its rest. Her reflection still regarded her greyly from the mirror, but it had been satisfactory to tell *him* what to do for a change, very satisfactory, satisfactory enough to hold heartbreak at bay for a full minute.

Chapter Four

The small saddle-tank locomotive stopped with a jerk, made a noise like a man hissing through his teeth and emitted a dense cloud of steam from somewhere down by its wheels, as if to make it known that the two coaches in its charge were more than it could reasonably be expected to pull. George Pemberton left the little train, walked through the vapour and surrendered his ticket at the barrier. The RTO sergeant standing beside the railway official there saluted violently at the sight of his uniform, giving Pemberton the impression that he was trying to drive himself into the ground. He returned the mark of respect by touching the peak of his cap with his swagger stick, having long ago decided that his spurious rank was sufficiently exalted to require no greater effort of him.

'Colonel Pemberton, sir?'

'Yes, Sergeant?'

'Transport waiting for you outside, sir, if you'll just follow me.'

'Oh, I think I'll walk. It isn't a very big town, is it?'

The sergeant agreed that it wasn't a very big town, relieved Pemberton of his suitcase, which would be delivered by an army driver to his hotel, saluted again with equal violence and marched away, his free arm swinging to shoulder height. More slowly, Pemberton followed, walked out of Seaford Station and found himself on Broad Street. There he stopped and looked about him, noting the names of shops, some bank premises and a church faced with Sussex flint. The observation was automatic and probably unnecessary in the present circumstances, but habit died hard with him. Pemberton always liked to know precisely where he was.

He sectored much of the town, strolling, recording. It was not, as he and the sergeant had said, very big, nor was it particularly interesting with its prim pebble-dashed houses with their fussily gabled upper-storey windows. Suburban, he thought, those houses and their clipped privet hedges, but home to a lot of people who wouldn't think as he did. Southdown Road he kept clear of. That was home to Lohengrin.

It wasn't until he reached the sea-front that he saw any merit in the place at all. Not that the Esplanade itself held much attraction with its concrete 'dragon's teeth' tank obstructions, its rusting barbed-wire entanglements and sandbagged gun and barrage balloon emplacements. Nor did the beach, several feet below the roadway, look at all inviting, covered as it was with coarse shingle, the tripods of mined anti-landing craft devices and more barbed wire; great thickets of it supporting stalactites of rubbish and seaweed. Even the English Channel looked surly, a slowly heaving expanse of burnished pewter, feathering into dirty white only where it made contact with the long fingers of the breakwaters, the half-submerged tripods and the wire.

But the town's setting was pretty with the Downs climbing away to the east where, over the centuries, the sea's race had sliced them into tall vertical cliffs of gleaming white chalk with undulating caps of turf. 'The Seven Sisters' Pemberton thought they were called, but wasn't sure. Much nearer was the squat shape of a Martello tower, built a century and a half before; one of a chain of strong points set up to repel the Napoleonic armies, armies which never came, many of them now pressed back into service as gun positions to repel another potential invader.

To the north, beyond the town, was farmland dotted with patches of scrub, gorse and pines where the soil above the chalk was too thin to support crops.

Pemberton glanced along the coast to the west and saw, less than two miles away, the stone piers of the port of Newhaven reaching to seaward and a small warship, as grey as the water on which it rode, approaching it, then he turned and walked along the Esplanade towards his hotel. He knew where he was now.

Six hours later he made a telephone call, then left the hotel to apprehend a German spy.

*

Standing in the bar doorway Pemberton remembered Morris saying, 'Wait until you see the girl.' He sighed softly and said, 'I take your point, boss,' but he said it only to himself, then moved slowly into the crowded room, a little disturbed because he had always found such prettiness distracting and could not afford to be distracted now of all times. She's altogether too much he thought. Face, figure, legs, poise, expression. That mouth and those eyes. Or at least the one he could see with her head in profile. Hoping that she had a voice like a corncrake to shatter the image he glanced at her companion, but his back view revealed only the fact that he was a big man with dark brown hair, a fact already known to him from the file.

Within four feet of their bar stools, 'Hello, old thing,' he said. 'How wonderful to see you!'

'George! George darling!'

One sinuous movement had brought her upright and into his arms, her cheek resting against his. He had noted that her right eye was as lovely as her left and that her voice was a caress. Distracting. Her scent in his nostrils simultaneously subtle and heady. Very distracting, but not distracting enough to prevent him from wondering why she was trembling.

Drawing away from him, smiling at him, her hands on his shoulders, the smile too broad, the grip of her fingers too tight.

'What *are* you doing in Seaford, George?'

'Surveying the south coast anti-tank defences. They've got it into their heads that I'm some sort of expert.'

'Good for you, my dear. George, I'd like you to meet a friend of mine. This is Frank Pelham. Frank, this is my cousin, George Pemberton.'

Pemberton shook hands with Lohengrin.

Apart from stolen glances at the girl, the noisy Saturday evening drinkers were engrossed in their own shouted conversations, paying no attention to the two men. It was as good a time as any.

Retaining his hold on the big man's hand Pemberton said quietly but distinctly, 'This building is surrounded. Provided that you make absolutely no scene at all you have an excellent chance of coming out of this war alive, but if you attract any sort of attention to yourself you'll be dead in a week. Don't bother to say that you don't understand. We know exactly what you are.'

The man held his gaze for a moment, then looked at his companion.

'Are you part of this?'

'Yes.'

'I should have guessed.'

'Is the bill paid?' Pemberton asked her.

'Yes,' she said again.

'Right. Take his other arm and we'll stroll out of here.'

It seemed a very long way to the door and relief flooded over Pemberton at the sight of Inspector Came and Sergeant Newland waiting outside it. Why that should have been he wasn't sure, because that was where he had left them only minutes before, but he supposed it had something to do with his doubts about the girl.

The man who called himself Pelham got into the big Special Branch car without comment, nor, after the car had begun to move, did he speak when they searched him for a cyanide pill or anything else unpleasant he might be carrying. Only when Inspector Carne had finished telling him about Defence Regulation 18b did he open his mouth to say, 'You bitch!'

'Yes,' the girl said for the third time and Pemberton marvelled that so much despair could be contained in one syllable.

Claire was sitting in the front seat beside the driver she had heard addressed as Sergeant Newbury or Newstead or something, watching without seeing the hooded war-time headlights illuminating the road little further ahead than the cow-catcher of a locomotive. It was desperately important to get the man's name right, and she hoped it would take a very long time to remember what it was because it was even more desperately important not to think about Frank and what she had done to him. Newcombe? No. Newly? No. Newland? Oh damn, that was right. Now she must think of something else to think about. The other man's name? No use. Nobody had mentioned it. She sought frantically for something to fix her thoughts on, but all that came to her was Professor Morris's voice and that led her straight back to Frank.

'I want him sunk with all hands, young lady,' Professor Morris had said.

That he was indeed sunk in the way Professor Morris had meant it she knew with absolute certainty from the wonderment with which he regarded her, his almost worshipful chivalry and his gentle lovemaking. None of those things were what she would have expected from a German spy, although why that should be she did not know. What she did know was that it was so appallingly hurtful that she was about to lose control and scream against the cruelty of it all, and that gave her something to concentrate on. The journey was only a few miles, but each was a lifetime to her as she sat, hands clenched into fists, concentrating on not screaming.

At the far end of eternity the car turned abruptly to the right off the main road, then stopped, its hooded headlights seemingly cast down before some army insignia on a barrier they were too respectful to illuminate.

'Is this the Maresfield place?' Pemberton's voice coming through the ice surrounding her and the man whose name she didn't know replying, 'Yes, Colonel.'

She jerked convulsively when all four of the car's doors opened without warning, then heard Pemberton say something she didn't catch. The doors slammed shut, the dimly seen barrier rose, the car moved forward, stopped for the second time and again the doors opened in unison as an arc-light blasted the night aside.

'Everybody out!'

A lot of men in the uniform of the Military Police were surrounding the car, she saw, but for once the men had no eyes for her, every pair of them fixed on the figure of Frank Pelham. Two of the soldiers in red caps grasped him and thrust him face first against the back of the car. Instinctively he struggled, so they hit him in the kidneys and smashed his face against the car again.

'Ah don't. *Please* no. *Please* don't.' It came out in a soft wail before she knew that she had spoken.

'Keep your distance, miss!' one of them snapped. Until then she had not been conscious of moving towards them and she stood where she was, biting her lip, watching them handcuff him, watching them hurry him away, his feet barely touching the ground. He was a big man, but then so were the Redcaps and there were two of them. The arc-light blinked out.

'Steady, pretty lady. Steady. He'll be all right just as long as he doesn't make a fool of himself.'

George Pemberton's arm about her shoulder, she turning into his embrace, burying her nose in his coat.

'Shan't.' The word was muffled.

'Shan't what, my dear?'

'Shan't cry,' she said.

'Of course you won't.'

Claire Helier began to sob brokenly.

*

It wasn't a cell so much as a passage three feet wide and twelve feet long leading to nowhere, as though someone had bricked off one end of a room. Someone had. Apart from himself the narrow oblong space was empty, there was no window and the single door was of steel, handleless, its surface broken only by a closed observation port at eye-level. Above his head a single bulb glowed dimly behind thick glass recessed into the ceiling.

They had emptied his pockets and removed his watch, tie, shoelaces and belt. He understood about the watch because it would not have been impossible for him to smash the glass of that and work a shard into an artery. But the other things? There was nothing he could hang himself from even if he could have contrived to position a noose with his wrists still manacled behind his back. The only useful thing his hands could do was hold his trousers up and that they were doing.

Had he thought about it, he might have detected a dull ache in his kidneys and noted the fact that he was breathing through his mouth because his nose had been broken and his nostrils were clogged with congealed blood. He didn't think about those things, for when his confused mind had abandoned the struggle of making sense of the confiscation of objects he was incapable of harming himself with, it settled immediately on the big pain deep inside him, a pain which had nothing to do with professional failure, loss of liberty or his impending execution.

If he had registered the passage of time with any accuracy, they would have been preparing for bed about now, he probably already lying on it watching her undressing. Not just removing her clothes, but undressing for him with that faint, understanding smile on her face which said, 'Am I not beautiful?' It was impossible for him to believe that throughout the happiest week of his life she had only acted that gentle bewitchment and all that followed it. But the facts were staring him in the face because dream had become nightmare. Or were they facts? 'Ah no. *Please* no. *Please* don't,' she had called out when they had treated him brutally and there had been tears in her voice. 'Oh Claire, you're not really just a Delilah, are you?' he said and a soldier in the next room wearing earphones asked his officer how to spell the names, then wrote them down on the pad in front of him.

When an hour had passed without the microphones transmitting any more words, the officer nodded to the two large military policemen.

'Fetch him out and take him to Room Five.'

'Sah!' the one wearing a sergeant's chevrons replied, unlocked the door and shouted, 'Out you come, my lad!' There had been no need to shout with the German standing only four feet away at the precise spot he had reached when they had pushed him inside, a spot from which, frozen with misery, he had not moved for an hour and a quarter.

They released him for long enough to wash the blood from his face and go to the lavatory, their guns constantly trained on him, then handcuffed him again and hurried him to a room with the number 5 on the door. Two officers, a major and a captain were seated behind a trestle table at its centre.

'Stand over there,' the major said, pointing with one hand and dismissing the escort with a flick of the other. He waited for the door to close before going on. 'This won't take long, unless you wish to volunteer information of any sort.'

The major raised his eyebrows as though he had asked a question and gave a satisfied nod on being told by the prisoner that he wished to volunteer nothing.

'Good. That saves us a late night. Your particular Delilah reports that you are a man of integrity and honour. Strange words to apply to someone in your profession, but their use inclines us to the belief that a protracted interrogation would be of little value to us, as we already know virtually everything there is to be known about you.'

Thinking bitterly that he could have done without Claire's character analysis and that it was silly of the major to have let slip that the space in which he had been confined was wired for sound, the prisoner didn't hear the next few words.

'. . . at oh-four hundred hours tomorrow morning,' the major said. He glanced at his watch and added, 'Well, it's this morning now.'

'I'm sorry. I missed that.'

The major's eyebrows lifted again. 'Damn funny thing to miss. I said you will go to the gallows at oh-four hundred hours. What else did you expect?'

'So soon?'

'Well, we aren't sadists, you know. No point in keeping you sweating. Do you want to see the Padre?'

'No.'

He was back in his passage-like cell, but the ceiling lamp had been switched off and there was no vestige of light anywhere. Fear and his inability to use his arms and the lack of any visual reference combined to produce vertigo and he swayed, feeling the fire of friction on palms rasping across the brick wall behind him. The small pain and the tactile contact were enough to prevent him toppling sideways and he lowered himself cautiously until he was squatting on the floor. Then the sweating the major had spoken of started. And the trembling.

'You have an excellent chance of coming out of this war alive,' the colonel whose name he couldn't remember had said. So much for that.

Why hadn't he hit the man and made a run for it? Better to have been shot down by the Special Branch than this. Oh God. Oh Claire. Why you? Why either of you?

Cramp growing in his calves with his feet jammed against the opposite wall. Drawing his knees up to his face. Turning sideways. Falling backwards, striking his head on the concrete floor and producing a sharper stab of pain in his broken nose in front than at the point of contact behind. Strange, that, and what was restricting his legs? Trousers. They must have dropped when he released his hold on them to prevent himself from falling. For a long time he struggled to recover them, to pull them up his legs from behind, failed, tried to be thankful that the cramp had gone and failed in that too. After that he lay still, panting shallowly, his right cheekbone supporting his head on the concrete.

When the door was thrown open and light flooded in, light which made him slit his eyes, he thought that they had come for him, but they only wanted to know what he weighed, how tall he was. Fourteen stone eight pounds and six foot one inch he told them. Get it right for the hangman. For the drop. Fourteen stone eight and . . . The door slammed shut. Nobody had offered to help him with his trousers.

His thumping heart was saying Claire – Claire – Claire, and his mind carried him to her. There he found peace until she drew one of her stockings around his neck, twisting it, twisting it tighter and tighter, laughing happily.

That was when they did come for him and he was almost glad. They were gentle with him now, lifting him upright, pulling his trousers up his legs and guiding his fingers to the waist-band at the back, leading him outside to where a group of four waited, one of them a black-cassocked priest holding an open Bible, another a captain in the Royal Army Medical Corps holding a white cloth hood.

With the hood over his head there was no more light and only the faint sound of the priest's unintelligible mumblings as, with hands gripping his upper arms, he was led away. Once he stumbled and lost one of his laceless shoes, but was propelled forward without pause, faltering again when his feet encountered steps, then being lifted bodily up them. A sudden emphatic halt and the roughness of the noose closing on the skin of his throat. The hands releasing their grip on his arms. Silence and dragging seconds. His own voice booming inside the hood, 'You say you aren't sadists, so get on with it, you bastards!' The hood removed from his head showing him a perfectly ordinary office and a cadaverous man with an unshaven receding chin who said, 'Good morning. How about some coffee with a shot of brandy in it?' The room greying, fading from his sight.

When he recovered consciousness his hands were free and somebody behind him was holding him upright on a chair. The noose had gone from his neck.

'Better?'

He looked at the cadaverous man and nodded.

'All right, Sergeant, you carry on and have somebody bring this gentleman's belongings back to him, will you?'

A bellowed 'Sah!', the stamp of receding boots, a door closing noisily.

'Good gracious me,' Professor Morris said. 'Do they breed them like that in your *Wehrmacht*?'

Nodding again and saying, 'Oh yes. Surely they're common to all armies. You mentioned coffee and brandy.'

'So I did. So I did. Here we are. Here we are. Don't be embarrassed. Grab it in both fists, as you're shaking a bit. Had an unpleasant night, didn't you? Lovely girl one minute and a bunch of raving pongos the next. Enough to make you sign the pledge. Glad you didn't confuse the issue by denying that it *is* your *Wehrmacht*. Saves us both time.'

Feeling the cup rattle against his teeth, but gulping the contents, grateful for the warmth of the coffee and the bite of the brandy, hearing a knock on the door and the strange man saying. 'Ah, here come your things. Put yourself together again, there's a good chap. I want to get you back to Seaford before anybody notices that you've been away.'

Putting on his belt and tie, threading the laces through the eyelets of his shoes while the other talked on, apologizing for his unshaven appearance. 'Growing a beard to disguise this chin of mine, you know.' Wondering if the man was entirely sane, wondering too what was going to happen to him and how they had got on to him in the first place. It alarmed him that he should have been so utterly terrified and so heartbroken as not to have considered that last point before. But the alarm was so much less than the terror and the sadness chat it slipped away from him. He put on his shoes, tied the laces and rose unsteadily to his feet.

'I'm ready.'

'Jolly good show, old boy,' the cadaverous man said.

Chapter Five

It was as though he had been away from the small semi-detached house for months, not hours, and he stood in the middle of the sitting room looking around him as if remembering. They hadn't made much mess, except for levering the gas fire out of the wall with a crowbar to disclose the cavity where the wireless set and the explosives had been hidden. He could have saved them the trouble of doing that, shown them the catch underneath which released it so that it could be lifted out bodily. The set was resting on the frayed carpet now with the sticks of dynamite, the box of detonators and the coil of fuse arranged tidily in front of it like a display in a shop window. Books had been taken from the shelves and placed equally tidily in piles on the floor. Books.

'The code books have gone,' he said.

'You'll get them back as soon as they've been photographed.'

He looked at the speaker in the uniform of a lieutenant-colonel with the tank insignia on his arm. Pemberton. George Pemberton. 'Frank, this is my cousin, George Pemberton,' Claire had said. Her voice came to him clearly, saying it again. Cousin? Bitch. Beautiful, lying bitch.

'*I* don't want them back.'

'You will.'

The words held a quiet certainty but, as though a shutter had dropped, his mind blocked their meaning.

Three men in the room in addition to Pemberton. Two of them the same Special Branch police who had arrested him. Inspector Carne and Sergeant somebody. The third, the thin man with no chin, lounging in a chair looking at the window as though he could see through the drawn curtains. The carpet seemed to be holding the attention of the others. He glanced towards the dining alcove, then moved towards the stairs. Only Pemberton followed him.

The bathroom was a shambles with the bath and the shaving-mirror above the basin torn away from the wall. They must have thought of the gas fire last, he told himself.

'Don't worry. It'll all be put back together.' Pemberton's voice coming from behind him, ignoring it, walking to the spare bedroom, spending several minutes there because he didn't want to see the double room, eventually forcing himself to go to it. Bed upended, mattress slashed and spilling its stuffing, carpeting ripped from the floor, but Claire's things gone from the dressing table, thank God. It wasn't until he turned to leave that he saw the wisp of black chiffon nightdress hanging from the hook on the back of the door.

'Cruel,' he said, and again, 'Cruel,' as though his mock execution had not been so.

'She thought you might like to have something to – to hold onto, as it were. You know, until things settle down.'

'Cruel,' he repeated.

Pemberton saying 'Sorry, I'll remove it,' and lifting the garment from its hook. Snatching it from him with a fierce 'No!' It was so flimsy that it went into his breast pocket with no trouble at all, making only a small bulge. Back in the sitting room he saw that the Special Branch men had gone.

'Sit down,' Professor Morris said. 'Are you hungry?'

'No.'

There was silence for a long time after that, and he sat staring at the pale shaft of morning light in which motes of dust floated coming past one edge of the curtains. He wasn't thinking about anything in particular, nor feeling much except a numbness in his brain until agony exploded in his broken nose. Not knowing how he had got there, he looked up from the floor at the blurred image of the Special Branch sergeant standing over him, not even knowing that the man had come back into the room.

'What an astonishing thing to do,' Professor Morris said. He didn't sound astonished. The sergeant turned and left, walking quickly.

Vision clearing, showing him Pemberton putting the chair back on its legs, feeling himself helped back into it, dabbing with a handkerchief at the new blood pouring down his face, looking at the man with the receding chin, asking, 'Who *are* you?'

'Professor Morris,' Professor Morris told him.

'How did you get onto me?'

'My dear chap, your nose is bleeding! How did that happen?' Morris managed to sound astonished this time. 'Pemberton, get him a bowl of water and something to tidy himself up with, there's a good fellow.'

That done, and as though there had been no interruption, 'Your contact Gustav Froebel told us you were responsible for the south coast from Folkestone to Worthing. He works for us now. Irritating mannerisms, but good at his job. Should go far if – well, never mind about him. That gave us your area. The Navy intercepted your transmissions and they and the Army got directional fixes on them. That gave us your location. Where you went wrong, old boy, was in transmitting so near to the coast. If you'd moved inland a bit you might have gone unnoticed in all the jumble of wireless traffic. Still, you live and learn. At least, I hope you'll live.'

'Sir?'

Morris looked at Pemberton.

'Yes?'

'I thought you told me he was seen eating a sausage in his fingers.'

'No, no, no,' Morris said crossly. 'That was Kurt Sponeck, the bloke we had to hang at Wandsworth Prison last June. Surely you remember. This chap would never eat a sausage in his fingers. Never. Well, only on a picnic. What an absurd notion!'

Pemberton nodded. 'Yes of course, sir. I remember now. This man's too English to do a thing like that. Not like Kurt Sponeck at all. I wonder if he *is* English. He hasn't got a funny accent and he hasn't said "*Heil Hitler*" once.'

Morris slapped his thigh with the palm of his hand. 'Nor he has!' he said. 'Nor he has! Clever of you to notice that, Pemberton. Do you suppose that we've made a terrible mistake? If he was a mining engineer that would explain the explosives. Let's have Sergeant Newland beat him up, then we can ask him if he's a mining engineer. This fellow, I mean. Not Sergeant Newland.'

'Newland's gone to breakfast, sir.'

'Oh. Pity.'

They're mad, he told himself. They're insane, with their childish prattling, their fatuous jokes, their talk of sausages. His head was aching, and that and the numbness made it difficult to follow, difficult to decide whether or not anything of importance was being said. Jokes? There had been nothing at all amusing about going to the gallows. That scene kept replaying itself in his mind as though it were a film, a film with a final frame which froze for long seconds while he stood in darkness with the noose round his neck, waiting for the trap to fall away beneath his feet. Trembling, he put his hand into his breast pocket, seeking comfort.

'What's he holding inside his coat? A gun?'

'No, sir. He hasn't got a gun.'

'What is it then?'

'A nightdress, sir.'

'Oh, he's one of those, is he? Wearing lipstick as well. That's what's the matter with the German male. Did you know they wear hairnets in bed?' Without waiting for a reply to his question, Morris went on, 'There's something pretty telling about him eating sausages in his fingers too. Freud probably had a word for it.'

'Yes, he probably did,' Pemberton said, 'but you're thinking about Kurt Sponeck, not this man. And that isn't lipstick, it's blood.'

With an effort close to physical he shut his ears to the absurd exchange and tried to focus his mind on something – on anything. For a moment it grappled with the name Kurt Sponeck, but found no record of it. With Gustav Froebel it did better. 'To be contacted only in dire necessity and with the utmost circumspection,' the visitor from Berlin had told him a few months before war had broken out. Shrugging mentally, he let his thoughts slip away from unobtainable help and towards imagined sanctuary, but that only brought more tears to eyes already watering from the pain in his fractured septum. She was so desirable, so lovely, so treacherous. The fact of his own treachery to the country in which he had spent most of his life, and the knowledge that treachery begets itself, he was still too shocked to recognize.

A finger tapping his knee.

'Yes?'

'I really must ask you to pay attention when matters of consequence are being discussed, young fellow.'

'Like sausages?'

Morris's frown indicated a lack of understanding rather than annoyance when he said, 'What *are* you talking about? I don't recall any recent mention of food. You did say you weren't hungry, didn't you?'

The shaft of sunlight had changed its direction by several degrees now and he could no longer see motes of dust suspended in it, but the tone of dreary despair in his voice came to him clearly enough when he listened to himself saying, 'If you're going to kill me, just get on with it. I'm tired of sitting at this Mad Hatter's tea party.'

'Tired? Of course you're tired,' Professor Morris told him. 'You've had a trying night. Why don't you nip upstairs and get your head down for a bit while we tidy this place up?'

*

Morris and the Special Branch men had left the house when Claire Helier came silently out of the main bedroom, then stood motionless, watching Pemberton. He had an eye pressed to the keyhole of the smaller room and a hand on the valve at the top of one of two cylinders beside him. Tubes from them led under the door where the landing carpet had been pulled away and up the back of the single bed. She knew that because she had watched Pemberton tape them there while the exhausted spy slept. Now, she guessed, he would be in a deeper than natural sleep with nitrous oxide, heavier than air, forming a pool of gas about his face. Cruel, cruel,' she said, not knowing that she was echoing his own words, but she said it under her breath.

As though feeling her gaze on him, Pemberton straightened, turned, and stared at her, noting her good-looking shoes, her drab raincoat, her make-up, carefully applied but heavy enough to constitute a statement of intent. He noted those things professionally, but felt far from professional because, drab coat or not, she looked alarmingly exotic. When she moved towards him her scent enveloped him, cheap, cloying scent, and that was right too, that was what she had been told to wear to mask the sweet smell of nitrous oxide when the man awoke. Pemberton doubted that he would be able to detect either with his damaged nose, but there were to be no risks taken – no risks at all.

'He's unconscious,' Pemberton said. 'I'll turn on the oxygen as soon as you're inside.'

'Very well.'

'Claire.'

'Yes?'

'It might be a good idea for you to cry when he sees you. Do you think you could manage that?'

'My dear man, I shan't be able to help it.'

She faced the door, her back to him, and unbuttoned the coat. When she slipped it from her shoulders he took it in his hands and watched her walk naked into the room.

Claire Helier positioned herself carefully so as not to obstruct Pemberton's line of sight from keyhole to bed, then stood looking down at the man, waiting. The black-out curtains excluded the day, but the dim bulb of the bedside lamp cast a soft radiance over his face. Such a nice, strong, gentle face, she thought, even with its now battered nose and bruised cheeks. 'Oh dear,' she whispered. 'This is so unkind.'

She could just detect the smell of the gas, but knew that most of it was at bed level and sinking from there towards the floor, propelled downwards by gravity and the oxygen hissing faintly from the second tube.

'Frank,' she said. 'Frank, help me.'

Nothing. His breathing became less stertorous, but nothing else. After half a minute she said it again, a soft wail in her voice.

Brown eyes opening, unfocused, searching.

'Frank. Frank, help me.'

The eyes focused on her now. Tears were welling in her own and a sob escaping from her throat.

'Claire. Oh, Claire.'

Trying to lift his head from the pillow, trying to stretch out a hand towards her, failing because the residual gas in his system was depriving him of all strength. Eyelids fluttering, closing, as the gas came again. 'Claire' – a soft exhalation.

He was fully unconscious when she removed the tubes from the bedhead and left the room. Pemberton was waiting outside it, holding the raincoat ready for her, but she brushed it aside and ran, crying, to the double room and flung herself face down on the ripped mattress. Pemberton followed and covered her with a blanket from the jumbled pile on the floor.

'Cheer up, my dear. It's all going right.'

Claire Helier stopped crying for long enough to say, 'He was hugging my nightdress,' then began to sob again.

Nodding, Pemberton turned and left the room, closing the door quietly behind him.

Chapter Six

With his wife dead and his servants called up for the duration of the war, Edward Mainwaring had relinquished most of the big town house off Sloane Street to a general and his staff and taken up residence at his club. Only the topmost of the house's four floors had been retained to provide accommodation for his daughter and Claire Helier.

At first the two girls had felt uncomfortable at having to run the gauntlet of so much soldiery to reach their apartment, but that had passed quickly because the general's staff did not change and now they knew all the officers and men by name, looking upon them as friends. In return, they were treated with a deference which approached awe and a strong sense of pride of ownership.

It was late evening when Claire, her brief shopping visit in London successfully completed, let herself in at the front door, closed it behind her and pushed her way past the black-out curtain.

'Stone me, Miss Claire!'

The army sergeant behind the desk in the hall had risen to his feet and was staring at her, his eyes wide. She blinked in surprise, then understanding came and she smiled.

'Thank you, Sergeant Watson,' she said. 'It is fun, isn't it?'

'Certainly is, miss!'

It had cost a lot of money and nearly all her clothing coupons, the shimmering silver crêpe de chine dress with its low neckline, showing through the open front of her sable coat. Long diamond earrings sparkled at her neck in harmony with the material. That the garment was 'black market' she was almost sure, but the Service had told her where to find it and that made everything all right. What she was absolutely certain about was that very few other women in an England oppressed by austerity and rationing were dressed as she was and that suddenly made her feel guiltily unpatriotic.

Regretting now the impulse to leave the shop wearing the outfit so that she could show herself off to Gail Mainwaring, 'It's some old stuff a friend gave me,' she lied. 'I had it run up by a little man in Charlotte Street. Is Her Ladyship in?'

'Yes, miss. Leastways, I haven't seen her go out.'

She made her way slowly up the stairs, her thoughts on the dress, hating it and loving it alternately. The hate came from the need for continued deception and lies in which she had been so carefully schooled and of which the garment was a part, but the love was stronger. 'We take him from you, expose him to less pleasant pressures and return him partly into your keeping,' Professor Morris had said and so far been horribly true to his word. But now the time for return had almost come and the gleaming creation represented that too. For that she loved it.

After she had let herself into the flat she stood in the middle of the living room watching her friend through the doorway of her bedroom, thinking how beautiful she was.

'Hello, Gail.'

'Hello, my love. All well?'

'Yes.'

Gail Mainwaring was seated at her dressing table, leaning forward, applying make-up to her right eye, darkening the lashes with a tiny brush and smoothing green shadow onto the lid with a finger as a counterpoint to her red hair and to match the colour of the eye itself.

That done, 'You really must learn restraint, darling,' she said. 'You look like a tart.'

'Oh, Gail. I don't, do I?'

'Not you, silly. Me,' Gail replied and used cream and cotton wool to erase her handiwork. Then the disappointment which had been in Claire's voice registered on her and she lifted her gaze for the first time to the silver and black reflection in the mirror.

'Claire! That's stunning!'

The blonde girl exhaled noisily. 'That's a relief. Sergeant Watson likes it too.'

Gail turned on her stool and looked at her. 'What did he say?'

'"Stone me." He must think I'm Medusa.'

Her voice was thoughtful when Gail said, 'Yes, well, Perseus may have overcome her, but I don't think he would have stood much of a chance with you looking like that. How's it going?'

All the fun of displaying her purchase seemed to run out of Claire and she sounded like a small girl when she replied, 'It's horrible.'

Gail nodded as though that was the answer she had expected. 'Give me a few minutes to get dressed, then we'll go up to the attic and you can tell me about it,' she said. 'I don't suppose any of the soldiers do listen at our door, but I feel safer talking up there.'

The attic was the junkyard of childhood. Hockey sticks shared a corner with broken-stringed tennis rackets and a small saddle. Battered school trunks, a satchel, a tricycle and a chest of drawers papered with photographs of film stars occupied most of one wall. A table provided seating for a row of variously disabled dolls and a solitary teddy bear who regarded them with a malevolent squint.

Claire picked the bear up, looked at it closely and asked, 'Why does Mr Hotchkiss always look so disagreeable?'

'It's the strain of being in charge of all those dolls,' Gail told her. 'Here, this chair's quite clean. I'm so sorry you've been landed with a bastard for your first assignment.'

Mr Hotchkiss continued to hold Claire's attention for a moment longer, then she put him back on the table and sat on the proffered chair.

'He's not a bastard,' she said. 'He's an awfully sweet man and he's terribly in love with me. That's what makes it so horrible.'

'That's what's supposed to happen, darling. That's what we're for. All of us in the "Beautiful Bitch Brigade".'

'I know, but he's got no business being so nice. Spies aren't supposed to be nice.'

Gail didn't speak and Claire went on, 'They took him away from me, beat him up and pretended to hang him. Since then they've – oh, never mind about since then.'

'I can guess,' Gail said. 'It's all standard procedure so far. Are you in love with him?'

'No,' Claire lied. 'No more than fond of him and sorry for him. I'm rather taken with his controlling officer though. He's in love with me too. At least, I'm pretty sure he is.'

Gail made a sound close to a laugh.

'What's funny?'

'You are, Havoc Helier. What are you trying to do? Destroy the whole operation?'

Tearfully, 'I'm trying to do what I'm told, but that doesn't mean I have to like doing it. It just isn't what I expected from my talks with you.'

The tears had gone from Claire's voice when, with a comical grimness, she said, 'I had expected to seduce some frightful German swine, reduce him to putty and mould the helpless creature to my own wicked design. That's what I'd expected to do.' She bit her lip for a second before adding, 'Then he turned out to be a dear, not a frightful German swine.'

'Tell me about him, Claire.'

'What's the point?'

Again Gail said nothing and after a moment Claire began to talk.

'His name's Frank Pelham and he's big and gentle and good-looking without being handsome and . . .' She frowned, a small, quick frown, then went on as though making an official report, 'They showed me the file they've built up on him. He's first generation British. Both parents German. Name, Paulus. They changed that to Pelham when they took out naturalization papers in 1912. Father now believed to have been a "sleeper" during the Great War. Possibly never activated. Frank born 1916. Mother died in . . .'

'Claire.'

'Yes?'

'Do stop barking at me.'

'Sorry,' Claire said. 'I'm trying to be subjective. Or do I mean objective? I'm never sure which is which. Anyway, he's an agro-something or other, which means that he knows about how to grow things, I think, and he works for the Ministry of Food. That's a reserved occupation and he doesn't have to join the armed forces, although I'm sure he would have done if – oh dear.'

Gail Mainwaring regarded her bleakly before asking, 'What's his real job?'

'He's a wireless and sabotage agent. He's been a "sleeper" all of his adult life and the Germans activated him at the time of Dunkirk. We learnt that from the swine who betrayed him.'

The word 'swine' and the reference to betrayal were the last straw for Gail Mainwaring. Rising quickly from the box she had been sitting on, she took two strides forward and slapped Claire hard on the face.

'Gail! Oh, Gail! Why did you do that?'

'Because you're behaving like a stupid little schoolgirl and you ought to have your bottom smacked, not your face!' Gail told her. 'You come here flaunting yourself in that dress and are pleased that Sergeant Watson likes it! Sergeant Watson shouldn't even have seen it! What about your cover?

You're supposed to be an Admiralty clerk and where do you imagine Admiralty clerks get clothes like that from in wartime? Then you go all dewy-eyed about a spy you're supposed to be manipulating! Dear God! Don't you know what he represents? Do you think this is some sexy game invented for your benefit?'

Without waiting for an answer to any of her questions, Gail talked furiously on. 'You'll get sex all right if the Germans ever get here! You'll be put in a farm and be fucked by storm-troopers for the rest of your child-bearing life to produce babies for the Master Race! That is their announced intention, that and castrating our men! How *dare* you let your personal feelings interfere with your work? And Claire, if you cry I'll slap you again!'

'Yes, Gail,' Claire said in a small voice. 'I'm sorry, Gail.' She was trembling, but held back her tears.

'So I should hope. When are you wanted next?'

'Tomorrow morning.'

'In that case, tomorrow morning you will resume the process of reducing this man to putty, as you put it, so that Professor Morris can mould him to *his* design, not *yours*. Is that quite clear?'

'Yes, Gail.'

'Very well. I must go now. I was getting ready to go out when you arrived.'

In a dispirited voice, 'Good luck with your piece of putty,' Claire said.

At the attic door Gail turned and sighed before saying, 'This isn't a putty job. It's a plastering of cracks. He's one of ours, absolutely brilliant they tell me, and his nerves are shot. He's also quite remarkably unpleasant to look at, smells as though he has been marinated in garlic, and I'm going to make all his dreams come true in the hope that I can steady him enough for them to put him back into France. Would you like to exchange jobs?'

'No. I don't think I would,' Claire told her.

When she was alone Claire Helier stood slowly upright, then swung her arm violently at the teddy bear, knocking it into the corner with the hockey sticks and broken tennis rackets. Then she was on her knees, holding it fiercely to her shoulder.

'Sorry, Mr Hotchkiss. Sorry, sorry, sorry,' she whispered. 'Sorry, Gail. Please don't tell Professor Morris. Either of you.'

Chapter Seven

'I don't think the girl can take it, sir,' Pemberton said. 'She's broken down both times she's been in contact with him since the arrest.'

Morris nodded, scratched at the stubble on his face and asked, 'Where is everybody?'

'She's gone, lover boy's asleep upstairs and the Special Branch men are having something to eat in the kitchen.'

'They aren't Special Branch any longer,' Morris told him. 'I've had them transferred to us. Carne will take over from you when you're resting, Newland will be general dogsbody and one of our wireless operators arrives tomorrow. That completes most of your team. Their army uniforms are in that suitcase. Get them all dressed up as soldiers and you can play at inspecting the coastal defences in your spare time.' He cackled as though he had said something amusing and scratched at his beard again before adding, 'Damn thing itches. I think I'll shave it off. What do you recommend?'

Ignoring the question, Pemberton asked one of his own. 'What about the girl, sir?'

'Oh, I don't think she has any particular views on the subject,' Morris said. 'Anyway, I'd prefer a male opinion.'

Pemberton spoke slowly, clearly, not attempting to conceal the tone of heavy patience in his voice. 'If we could postpone judgement on your beard at least for the time being and preferably permanently there is something I'd like to say.'

'Say away, my dear fellow. Say away.'

'Very well. I find it tiresome that you persist with this ridiculous cross-talk when there is no necessity for it. It makes me feel like the straight man in a comedy team on Brighton pier.'

'Oh, that,' Morris said. 'It's called living a role. Good practice for you too. You have the makings of an excellent straight man. Keep it up. What with all the nonsense we talk, the little surprises we've sprung on him, and the pentobarbitone sodium he was given in his coffee and brandy at Maresfield, our friend is rapidly becoming a highly stressed individual.

That's the object of the exercise. Disorientation leading to loss of identity. Have you fallen for Miss Helier?'

The abrupt change of subject and the question itself made Pemberton blink rapidly before saying, 'What on earth put that idea into your head?'

'Your implied suggestion that she be taken off the case because you think she's distressed. Your denying her an identity by referring to her as "the girl". Your indication of jealousy by a sneering reference to our prime target as "lover boy", and now your failure to respond to my query with a clear "no".'

'Don't be silly. I'm not likely to fall, as you put it, for someone who calls me "my dear man".'

Morris made a tutting noise, then went on, 'Resentment too. That's excellent.'

'Meaning what?'

'No matter, no matter,' Morris said. 'But let me make it perfectly clear that there is no question whatsoever of taking her off the case. She's the linchpin of this part of the operation and if she doesn't like it she shouldn't have volunteered. Her emotional welfare is of interest to me only to the extent to which it affects her performance. That, to date, has been very much to my satisfaction and the genuine agitation you say she is now exhibiting is a bonus.'

He paused, then, as though Pemberton had argued the point, added, 'You must see, man, than in his state of infatuation it will have communicated itself to him. That in turn will make him reluctant to cause her more unhappiness by doing away with himself, thus carrying us past the initial suicide phase, and the longer she is capable of controlling his emotions the less likely we are to have a relapse along the lines of Parsifal. God knows it's a tenuous enough hold, particularly if he is the man of honour Miss Helier believes him to be, but it's there and we'll use it. We'll also continue with the ridiculous cross-talk, as you call it, and anything else I prescribe. Now, if all that is quite clear, perhaps you will be good enough to go and wake the tiresome fellow. He's bound to be hungry by now.'

*

'Sit down, sit down,' Morris said, then nobody spoke again until the unpleasant curry prepared by Newland had been eaten. Pemberton was relieved to see the spy finish his portion. The pentobarbitone sodium had been in it. Tinned pears covered in custard, which looked as unpleasant as the curry had tasted, were in front of them when Morris broke the silence by murmuring, 'Delicious. Delicious,' and Pemberton experienced a renewed surge of irritation at the professor's habit of saying things twice.

'When am I to be interrogated?'

Pemberton looked at the speaker, noting that the slightly glazed look was back in his eyes. Morris began to eat his pears. Neither of them spoke.

'I was sick during the night. Are you poisoning me?'

There had been a small pile of vomit on the pillow when Pemberton had awoken him and he had concluded that strain and the inhalation of too much nitrous oxide gas had contributed to that.

Through a mouthful of pear and custard, 'We've decided to make you a knight of the Holy Grail,' Morris said. 'And you weren't sick during the night. It's only evening now. So if you've just been sick it was during today. Tuesday.'

'Today's Wednesday, sir,' Pemberton told him.

'Well, never mind that. He knows what today is. Has to, or he'd never get his wireless schedules right. That's correct, isn't it, Lohengrin?'

'Why do you call me Lohengrin? My name's Pelham.'

'Knight of the Holy Grail,' Morris said. 'Got led to Antwerp by a swan and married Princess Elsa of Brabant. Mozart wrote an opera about it.'

'It was Wagner, sir. Not Mozart.'

Plaintively, 'Why do you keep contradicting me, Pemberton?' Morris asked.

'It's essential that we get the facts right, sir. You know that.'

'Yes, I suppose so, but I don't really care who wrote the damn thing. Whichever one it was, he certainly never wrote an opera called "Pelham", so Lohengrin he is, and I don't want any argument about it. Is that clearly understood?'

'Yes, sir.'

'Good. Why do you suppose he keeps rabbiting on about interrogation?'

'I've no idea, sir,' Pemberton said. 'We've already told him that we've heard all there is to hear about him from Gustav Froebel.'

'Oh, I thought you said it was Kurt Sponeck who . . .'

'Stop it!'

The side of a fist smashing down on the table accompanied the shout. Crockery and cutlery jumped. Custard slopped messily onto the cloth. Newland burst into the room from the kitchen.

'It's all right, Newland. I'm afraid we've been boring our guest. Or perhaps I should say our host, as it's his house.'

Newland shrugged and left without speaking, wondering what had been said or done to produce the wild, hunted look in the prisoner's eyes.

With the door closed again, 'Well, we've stopped,' Morris said. 'Do you want to say something, Lohengrin?'

'Yes, I most certainly do!'

Both Morris and Pemberton noted the first small submission, the trifling point of the acceptance of a name. They noted the onset of trembling too, and the highlights picked out by the overhead lamp on a forehead beaded with sweat.

'Then say it.'

'I . . .'

The face working, then locking into rigidity, the muscles at the angles of the jaw knotting, only the eyes remaining uncontrolled, flickering as he searched for words.

'He's changed his mind,' Morris said.

'Shut up, damn you!'

'Oh, very well.'

Seconds dragging themselves towards a minute, passing it, then: 'There's something I *must* know.'

'Really?'

'Was – was Claire here last night? I mean today.'

'Claire? Oh, Miss Helier. No, certainly not. She's back in Holloway Prison.'

'Prison?'

'That's what I said. She's one of your fraternity, but we've persuaded her to work for us. You know, a job a day keeps the hangman away. Between jobs we keep her confined.'

The eye movements started again, the trembling returned, then Lohengrin had swung his chair sideways and crouched forward, head down, his arms clasping his knees. They had to strain to hear his whispered, 'My poor darling. Naked and defenceless and crying.'

'Now, now,' Morris said. 'I expect you had an erotic dream.'

'No,' Lohengrin replied in a louder voice. 'It wasn't erotic. It was sad. She was calling for my help.'

The Security Service men recorded the fact that the adjective had been challenged, but not the noun. For the time being, at least, Lohengrin had accepted the dream concept.

'Absurd,' Morris said.

Slowly Lohengrin uncoiled from his foetal position and looked at him.

'It isn't absurd. I can see and hear her now. She was trying to tell me what you've just told me. Like in a vision.'

Morris snorted. 'You stick to your fantasies, my dear fellow, and I'll stick to mine. Personally, I've never listened to such unmitigated rubbish in my life.'

'Sir?'

Morris turned to Pemberton.

'Yes?'

'You do realize that she's deeply in love with him, don't you?'

Lohengrin's sudden concentration seemed to Pemberton to wipe the drug-induced glaze from his eyes and he broke the visual contact in case satisfaction at the thrust should be read in his own.

'Of course I do,' Morris said. 'I've never experienced the condition myself, but that doesn't make me incapable of detecting it in others. Does your question have any particular relevance to anything?'

'Well, sir, it's this dream. Accepting the fact that a strong emotional bond exists, it's just conceivable that . . .'

'Oh no you don't,' Morris broke in. 'Not you as well. I'm not buying any of that thought transference nonsense from either of you. If you haven't got anything sensible to say perhaps you'd be good enough to . . .'

'Professor?'

They both looked at Lohengrin.

'Yes?'

'Might I have your permission to go back to bed? I'm feeling very – I . . .'

Morris turned to Pemberton again.

'Do you suppose he wants to parade around in that night-dress?'

'No, he can't actually put it on, sir, it's much too small for him.'

'Then what was all that stuff you were telling me about hairnets?'

'I didn't tell you. You told me.'

Lohengrin had taken the stairs at a stumbling run and they stopped talking for a moment when the bedroom door closed behind him, then Pemberton said, 'There'll have to be an interrogation at some stage.'

'Not at this one there won't,' Morris replied. 'The last thing I want is to introduce normality into the situation.'

*

The hand shaking his shoulder was insistent and Pemberton groaned and opened his eyes. Newland's craggy face was looking down at him.

'The old man wants you downstairs, guv.'

Pemberton groaned again, looked at his watch and said, 'Christ! It's only ten past four.'

He swung his legs over the side of the bed, yawned achingly and went on, 'Listen, Newland. I don't mind you calling Professor Morris "the old man" if that's how you see him, but stop calling me and Carne "guv". I'm supposed to be a lieutenant-colonel, Carne's supposed to be a captain and you're supposed to be an army sergeant now. "Sir" is the proper mode of address while we're playing at being soldiers. Don't let's make any silly mistakes.'

Newland smiled faintly. 'Right, sir. And the time is now oh-four-one-one hours, sir.'

'Christ!' Pemberton said for the second time. 'I'd forgotten that bit. You win, Sergeant.'

He shaved, dressed quickly and joined Morris in the living room.

'Good morning, sir. Is this going to be one of those "darkest hour before the dawn" sessions?'

'No,' Morris told him. 'We'll talk to him again at breakfast. I wanted a word with you first. Shall we take a stroll?'

Without waiting for a reply he picked up an overcoat, put it on and walked to the front door. Pemberton followed, irritated now by the turn of events, tired after too little sleep that night and none at all the one before. The drizzle, invisible in the black-out, which he encountered outside the house did nothing to improve his mood.

'This is a hell of a time to take exercise,' he said, and heard Morris reply, 'Subjective time is a funny thing, you know. We shouldn't let it rule us as we do. It's only thirty-two hours since you picked our friend up at that bar. How long do you suppose he thinks he's been with us? Three days? Four? Five?'

Pemberton didn't speak, but used the sound of the words to locate Morris who appeared to be standing in the middle of the street. He approached him cautiously.

'Ah, there you are, my dear chap. Couldn't see you at all.'

'You mustn't allow subjective time to rule you, sir,' Pemberton told him. 'I was under the impression that it was only me who thought this was the middle of a rainy night in the black-out.'

Morris grunted and began to move along Southdown Road in the direction of the coast and the town's golf course. Pemberton matched his slow progress, smelling the unseen sea, listening to its surge. He was wondering what he was doing there, what Morris wanted of him.

'Halt! Who goes there?'

'Friend,' Pemberton said.

'Approach and be recognized! One at a time! You in the uniform first!'

There were three of them, he saw. The soldier in the centre shone a shielded flashlight straight into his eyes, ruining the small amount of night vision he had begun to acquire, revealing the rain. The two flanking him, betrayed by the glint of their bayonets, thrust forward into the torch's beam. He walked slowly towards them.

'Identity card, please.'

Presenting the card, it occurred to Pemberton that his uniform carried less magic with it here at night than at the railway station during the day.

'Thank you, sir. The other gentleman now, please.'

A pause while Morris was identified as a civil servant employed by the Ministry of Food, then, 'Thank you, sir. Stay right where you are. You, Williams, fetch the officer of the guard.'

One of the bayonets blinked out of existence and there was the sound of heavy footsteps receding, then returning accompanied by others. The second bayonet materialized again.

''Morning, Colonel. Do you mind telling me what you two are doing here at this time of night?'

Just able to distinguish the single 'pip' of a second-lieutenant on the shoulder of the officer's greatcoat in the faint backwash of light from the torch, Pemberton experienced a strong desire to say, 'That's what I want to know,' but suppressed it and said, 'I'm surveying south coast tank defences and some of my recommendations involving farm land have been objected to by the Ministry of Food. Just finished an all-night meeting with them and this gentleman and I needed some fresh air.'

'Then I'd take it in the opposite direction if I were you, sir. Less likely to be ventilated by a rifle bullet. Old Hitler may have packed in his invasion plans for the time being, but there have been a few small raiding parties and that makes my chaps jumpy.'

'Sounds like excellent advice to me,' Pemberton told the lieutenant, then added, 'Come along, Morris.' He enjoyed saying that.

When they were out of earshot of the soldiers, 'Well,' Pemberton asked, 'what *are* we doing here at this time of night?' He enjoyed saying that too, feeling, in some obscure way, that he had snatched a little of the initiative from his superior.

'It's about Miss Helier,' Morris said.

'Oh? I thought we had covered that ground pretty comprehensively.'

Morris made no comment on the remark and half a minute of slow pacing passed before he spoke again. He did it in a near whisper.

'Pemberton, I want you much closer to Lohengrin than you ever were to Parsifal. If we succeed in turning him I want you inside his head. I want you to feel empathy, to rejoice at his successes and deeply regret his failures. I want you to share his loneliness, his anxiety, even his panic if he experiences it. In fact, I want you to be his emotional *doppelganger*. Only by being him can you hope to out-guess him, to anticipate his every move, to control him.'

'I'm familiar with the technique,' Pemberton told him, 'but employing it is something else altogether. You're asking a very great deal.'

He glanced to his left in time to see the pale blur of Morris's head nod its agreement and heard him say, 'Yes I am, aren't I? And you are the man to deliver the goods. There are marked similarities between you and him which go beyond the tendency for spies and counter-espionage agents to complement each other with their blend of the practical and the romantic.'

'Ah, I was wondering when you'd get around to Claire Helier,' Pemberton said and heard the reproof in Morris's voice when he replied, 'Come now, I didn't use the word "romantic" in any such narrow sense. Nevertheless, she is the main topic of this conversation.'

Whether it was the early hour, the rain saturating his trousers and making them cling unpleasantly to his legs below the hem of his greatcoat, or the feeling of amused superiority the brush with the army sentries had provided which made him abandon all deference towards his senior, Pemberton did not know. He only knew that it was immensely satisfying to say, 'That's funny, I thought *I* was, but I understand now. You got me out of my nice warm bed to walk around in the cooling rain so that I wouldn't get too excited at the prospect of experiencing Lohengrin's sexual ecstasies at second hand. You must have taken leave of your senses if you imagine that my taste for the vicarious stretches that far.'

Expecting a sharp rebuke, he felt cheated when Morris murmured, 'Dear me, we are prickly this morning, aren't we?'

They reached the house, but Pemberton did not attempt to turn in at the gate, much as he would have liked to have done, because Morris obviously hadn't finished yet.

'George.'

It was the first time that Morris had called him that, and Pemberton wondered whether it was a warning or an attempt at friendliness. He decided he didn't much care.

'Yes?'

'Despite what you said yesterday, or even because of it, I believe that I am correct in inferring that you find Miss Helier attractive.'

'Oh for God's sake,' Pemberton said. 'Of course I find her attractive. She's the prettiest thing I've seen in ages, but that doesn't mean that I've fallen for her as you suggest. I'm not an impressionable schoolboy. You infer away to your heart's content, but leave her out of your "meeting of minds" equation as far as Lohengrin and I are concerned. You'll be offering me a half share of her body next.'

'That could be arranged. Probably *should* be arranged.'

Pemberton stopped walking and took Morris by the arm with just sufficient force to halt his progress. 'Those statements were in the worst taste I have ever encountered,' he whispered. 'You will kindly never repeat them.'

Just as quietly, 'As long as you remember them there will be no necessity for me to repeat them,' Morris replied. 'Now kindly let go of my arm.'

He turned away then and walked on, moving more quickly. His anger growing, Pemberton overtook him, then matched his stride.

'You listen to me, Professor . . .'

'Be silent,' Morris said. 'I'm not interested in your protestations. You are valuable to me because you are quick-witted, because you toss the ball back to me and say the right things at the right time when we are engaged in confusing an enemy of this country. You have great potential, but have not yet realized it to its fullest extent, as was demonstrated by the Parsifal case. I told you at the time that that failure was not your fault. Nor was it, for the error lay with me for crediting you with a better technique than you possessed. That mistake will not be repeated.'

Pemberton walked on, furious with himself for inviting the lecture, furious with Morris for being right. He didn't speak.

'George.'

'Yes?'

'You don't like me, do you?'

'There's nothing personal about it,' Pemberton said. 'I just don't like puppet makers.'

'Well, you had better understand that other things I am simply not interested in are . . .' Morris stopped then – both talking and walking, faced Pemberton and asked, 'Who told you I was called "The Puppet Maker"?'

'Nobody. I didn't know you were. I was making a general observation. What other things had I better understand?'

Morris grunted again before saying, 'That personalities mean nothing to me. The brief given to me by my superiors is explicit and, within its context, the emotional wellbeing of those who work under my direction does not qualify as a consideration. You will all do whatever I require of you. Is that clear?'

'I hear what you say.'

'Good,' Morris said. 'And, as our American cousins are fond of remarking, you had better believe it, too. We will now return to the house and indulge in a little more of the cross-talk you dislike. After that, we shall continue with the process of increasing Lohengrin's dependence for sanity and life itself on Miss Helier. She should be back from London by now.'

Chapter Eight

Waiting for a cue which never came, Pemberton wondered sourly if Morris was including him in his confusion tactics, because rhetoric seemed to have replaced cross-talk at breakfast that day, and he listened while Morris explained the origins of the Great War of 1914–18 to Lohengrin. They lay, he learned, in the imperialistic, economic, nationalistic and militaristic rivalries between Germany, France and Britain and between Russia and Austria-Hungary. He learned, further, that the war had been unavoidable but not ideological, and that who bore the main responsibility for starting it was still a matter debated by historians. The dissertation lasted throughout the meal's sole course of porridge; porridge which had been over-sweetened by syrup to disguise the taste of yet more pentobarbitone sodium in one portion of it.

When Lohengrin asked why he was being subjected to a history lesson, Morris ignored the question and continued his monologue, saying that there was no shadow of doubt about who was responsible for the present conflict or who had right on their side. He added that the war might go down in history as the first truly just one that Britain had ever fought.

'Propaganda,' Lohengrin said.

'No, no, no.' Morris sounded put out, as though an intelligent companion was being deliberately obtuse. 'The facts are plain to see. Your pre-war purges of your own people, your rampant nationalistic hysteria, your fawning on that frightful shit Hitler, your genocidal approach to what you describe as the "Jewish problem", your slaughter of innocent civilian refugees on the roads of Europe, your unrestricted U-boat warfare and the bombing of – but there's no need to go on. The list is too long, and growing longer with some very sinister tales reaching us of unspeakable things happening inside Germany.'

The look Lohengrin gave Morris was long and hard but, Pemberton guessed, it indicated more an attempt at understanding words spoken than at refuting their message. When the stare ended with a confused fluttering of Lohengrin's eyes and the statement 'I don't know what you're talking about', Pemberton knew that he had been right. The drug was already at work.

'It's really perfectly simple,' Morris told him. 'I'm trying to demonstrate that you have espoused an unholy cause. Once you have accepted that indisputable fact it should not be difficult for you to arrive at the conclusion that your sole hope of salvation lies in transferring your allegiance away from the powers of darkness and joining us in our march onwards and upwards towards the light.'

For a moment Pemberton watched the spy grappling with the verbiage, then he glanced at Morris, noting incongruously that the professor's lengthening stubble was multicoloured, resembling the fur of a tabby cat. He looked back at Lohengrin just as he asked, 'Are you suggesting that I work for the British?'

'That,' Morris said ponderously, 'is the general drift of the idea I am endeavouring to convey. Do you find it difficult to grasp?'

Lohengrin swung his head slowly from side to side and Pemberton wondered if the movement was a denial of difficulty, a refusal to cooperate, or an attempt to rid his brain of the blanketing drug. He thought it was probably the last and again had his impression confirmed when Lohengrin broke a full minute's silence by saying, 'Well, this charade had to have some point to it.' There was another long pause before he added, 'What makes you think you could persuade me to do that?'

'I imagine we could persuade you to do virtually anything we put our minds to except possibly levitate,' Morris replied, 'but we aren't aiming as high as that. All you will be required to do is to carry on as you have been doing, but under our control.'

A look of intense concentration appeared on Lohengrin's face as though he were considering the merits of an interesting proposal, then his expression cleared and he said, 'You're too late. All the wireless schedules I've missed recently will have alerted them. They'll know by now that I've been arrested.'

The statements gave him obvious satisfaction and the satisfaction seemed to increase when he heard Morris say, 'That *is* a nuisance. How many schedules have you missed?'

'As many as the days you've been holding me for.'

Suspicion replaced satisfaction at the sound of Morris's amused cackle, then grew into disbelief when he was told that he had been in custody for only thirty-six hours.

'So,' Morris went on, 'they won't be getting all fidgety and impatient yet. You might have missed your train or had a motor accident or – or . . .' He waved his arm about, then let it drop to his side again as though unable to conceive of what else might have happened. 'Anyway, I know you're only teasing. You have never transmitted daily, nor would you dream of doing so. What's more, your wireless set is out of action. Very shoddy equipment, they tell me, but don't let that worry you. They'll fix it in a jiffy. I expect you've written to Germany for new parts, haven't you?'

Lohengrin didn't reply, but Morris said, 'I thought as much. We'll talk about how they're to be delivered later, but for now I really must caution you against telling naughty fibs. We *would* look silly if we let you go on the air with a set your friends know doesn't work, wouldn't we? Still, it was very brave of you to say what you did.'

'Brave?'

'Sacrificial then.' Morris jerked his tie above his head and contorted his face into a grotesque mask, eyes crossed, tongue protruding. Pemberton winced in embarrassment at the sight and unknowingly joined Lohengrin in wondering if Morris was entirely sane.

'I see,' Lohengrin said.

'I'm sure you do, my dear chap. Had I believed that you were truly of no use to us, I'd have been left with no alternative but to put you down. Most distressing for me, but quite inevitable.'

'I see,' Lohengrin repeated. 'In that case you had better prepare to be distressed, as you've been wasting everybody's time. It's a simple matter of honour and if that word forms no part of your vocabulary your Army friend here can probably explain it to you.'

'Oh I know what it means,' Morris said. 'Just because I don't possess any myself you mustn't think me ignorant.' His voice suddenly becoming excitedly enthusiastic, he added, 'To prove that I do know what it means, let me tell you about honour which transcends patriotism, a sense of decency which can save humanity from the rabid dog of Nazism.'

'I'd sooner you saved your breath.'

'Oh, pity. I was rather pleased with "the rabid dog of Nazism". It not only sounds good, it's also extremely apt and I'd have liked to have developed the theme, but I mustn't bore you. The last time I did that you upset the custard. You upset Newland too. We'll have to liven things up a little by killing your father, if that isn't a contradiction in terms.'

Admiration for the stand Lohengrin had taken had been growing in Pemberton. At first he had been unsure if the man's drug-confused mental processes had allowed him to see where his talk of missed wireless schedules was leading him, but his subsequent ready acceptance of death by hanging had erased that doubt. It had brought dignity too, and that only made the sight of resolution slipping away again the sadder. That it would so slip away had been next to inevitable because MI6 had made certain enquiries in Portugal and a fully briefed Claire Helier was waiting in the wings further to undermine Lohengrin's resolve. For all that, the sadness remained and irritation touched Pemberton with the knowledge that the empathy Morris had spoken of was developing in him as if by osmosis.

'My father died years ago,' Lohengrin said, but neither the words nor his eyes carried conviction.

'You're full of crap, as our American cousins are fond of saying,' Morris told him. 'Full of crap. He's living with a woman in Putney under an assumed name. Now that's a very serious offence, living under an assumed name with a woman in time of war for the purpose of avoiding National Service.'

Pemberton watched as Lohengrin's shoulders relaxed and saw his eyelids droop, close. He supposed that a combination of relief and the pentobarbitone sodium winning its fight against consciousness had brought that about and he wished several things. He wished that Morris would stop repeating himself, particularly about American cousins and what they were fond of saying. He wished too that Morris would stop raising his victim's hopes for little more than the pleasure of dashing them again. Above all he wished that Carne and Newland were not waiting in the kitchen. The sound of Morris slapping his own thigh brought him out of his pointless reverie.

'My word no, that's wrong!' Morris announced. 'I'm thinking of Gustav Froebel's old man, not yours!' Then he brought Pemberton into the conversation for the first time by asking, 'Where did you say Lohengrin's dad was now, George? Ireland, was it?'

Tonelessly Pemberton said, 'He's reverted to the family name of Paulus and lives at 145, Rua Alexandre Herculano, Lisbon, Portugal. It's handy for the *Abwehr* office he works in near Praca Marques de Pombal.'

There was no sleepiness about Lohengrin now, and so preoccupied was Pemberton in meeting his intense stare that he barely heard Morris's 'Well, in that case you'd better alert Standish. He may have to arrange an accident. Very good at arranging accidents Standish is.'

'Leave him alone!' It was a fierce whisper, rising to a near shout when Lohengrin added, 'The British don't go around murdering old men!'

'His life is in your hands,' Morris told him, then turned his head towards the kitchen and called, 'Carne! Newland!'

The two men burst into the room. Carne tall, lanky, bald. Newland stocky, thick-chested, rock-like. It was Carne who dragged Lohengrin off his chair, an arm around his neck, a hand clamped over his mouth. It was Newland who kicked him on the inside of each knee, first the right, then the left, and Pemberton who, for the first time ever, heard a man screaming through his nose.

'Medial condyle of the femur. Hurts, doesn't it?' Newland's voice was conversational. 'Let's see what we can do to your elbows.'

Arms and legs paralysed, his whole weight supported by Carne, Lohengrin whooped his message of pain through nostrils still partially blocked by blood, while Newland stabbed rigid fingers at pressure points, then delivered heavy clubbing blows to his chest and stomach. For a few moments Pemberton watched the writhing figure, listened to the thuds and the gradual lessening of the muted trumpeting; then he stood up, walked to the downstairs lavatory and brought his breakfast up into the bowl.

When he returned Lohengrin was lying on the floor semiconscious, twitching, and Morris was saying, 'That's something else that the British don't go around doing, young fellow.' Then to Carne, 'Get him into bed and sedate him. You know the dose. What's the matter with your hand?'

'He bit it, sir.'

Morris made a tutting noise.

*

He was floating on a cloud of pain, supportable pain now that they had injected some drug into his arm, but ever-present nevertheless, reminding him constantly of the sudden, savage, inexplicable assault. It seemed utterly incredible to him that it was possible to be so badly hurt by only a man's hands and feet, that it was possible to be so badly hurt without dying. He had moments of clarity when he could see one of the soldiers sitting near the foot of the bed, watching him. It was the colonel, he thought, but the next time he looked it was the captain and that confused him because the change had seemed to take place in the flickering of an eye. A sense of cunning came to him and he watched the seated figure from under drooping lids, waiting for it to change back into the colonel again, or perhaps to become the sergeant who had hit him. But doing that, he found, called for awareness and with awareness came the return of pain, so he stopped doing it and let his eyes close and his mind drift.

The time factor worried him, although what was important about it was no longer clear. Very little was clear, beyond the ache which moved about his body and limbs as though seeking somewhere to settle. Occasionally something pricked the inside of his elbow, but the little pain was too insignificant to investigate, and after it the ache diminished. Sometimes it withdrew from him entirely, but he knew that it hadn't left the room because he could see it through his closed eyelids, a black blob hanging in the air to the left of the curtained window.

'Black blob,' he said, and Sergeant Newland recorded the words on the card where the times of the injections were written, then added '1708 hours'.

Memories began to come then, as if the act of speaking had partially withdrawn a veil surrounding the brain cells containing them. The man with a face like a goat whose name he couldn't remember, saying 'Mozart wrote an opera about it.' Another man asking if he wanted to see the Padre. No meaning. No contact between recall and reality. Somebody talking about the Holy Grail. The Padre probably. What Padre? 'Kill your father.' Who had said that? Whose father? Hands on his arms propelling him, guiding him because he couldn't see with the hood over his head. Losing a shoe, lurching up steps and – *Nightmare*!

'Jerky body movements at 1957 hours presumably indicate Subject regaining consciousness,' Carne wrote on the card. He stood up and went quietly out.

Mental pictures forming in brilliant primary colours, to be replaced before their message had been comprehended by others in monochrome. Kaleidoscopic images of horror swiftly changing; then isolated frames freezing momentarily for his recognition, producing a blurred overall understanding, a certainty that he was going to die, but not why that should be. A period of undirectional blind groping, a questing until, quite suddenly, he had it. He was to work for them against Germany and if he did not his father would be killed.

The sense of cunning returned because they had overlooked something. He would pretend to agree and kill himself at the first opportunity, an opportunity that was bound to come as it was impossible for them to watch him for every minute of every hour of every day. That was the solution, for with him dead there would be no point in their harming his father. With the taking of this decision, Lohengrin passed through the door Professor Morris had opened for him into the suicidal phase from which earlier he had been barred.

Revulsion and fear came quickly. Revulsion at the thought, fear of the act; his mind recoiled from it, seeking sanctuary, finding it at once. 'Oh, Claire.' A just audible sigh of longing.

'I'm here, darling,' Claire Helier said.

Hazy. Ghost-like. Shimmering. Vision clearing to show him unbearable beauty.

'Oh, Christ,' Lohengrin whispered and turned his face to the wall.

Gentle hands, cool hands, on his cheeks, turning his head back.

'Frank. Frank, they said you needed me, my love.'

'Claire, is it you? Is it *really* you?'

'Of course it's me. Don't I look like me?'

'The last time you came you weren't here.'

A faint smile and Claire saying, 'I expect you were dreaming. It's rather flattering for a girl to be dreamt about.' Saying it calmly because she had to with the hurt of that visit still in her. Because she mustn't make a mess of this. Because Gail had been so angry. Because Gail had been so right.

'I can't believe it's you!'

'I'll prove it to you, darling.'

The gleaming silver dress dropped away to form a shining pool at her feet, shoes were discarded, stockings stripped off to lie like two wisps of smoke, a black slip drawn over her head ruffling the burnished helmet of her hair, the bedclothes were sliding down his body.

'Oh my God! The bastards!' Claire said.

Lohengrin looked down, and for the first time saw the red, blue and black bruising covering him from shoulders to solar plexus; he was startled by its extent and severity, but the surprise faded before the embarrassment of his sexual arousal. He reached for the blankets.

'Don't you dare move! Not one inch!'

His hand dropped to his side and he watched with trembling urgency as she straddled him infinitely gently, upright, not touching his injured torso, only her hips moving.

Release immediate and violent, clouding his brain. He drifted out of mist to find his head softly cushioned and her lips murmuring endearments into his ear. Almost at once the urgency returned.

'Sorry. So sorry.'

'It's all right, darling. It's the fear. All perfectly natural. I know. I know.'
Gentler pleasure and sleep.

It was two o'clock in the morning when he said, 'They make you do this, don't they?'

'Yes, darling. They do.'

'One of them said you were in love with me.'

'He was right. We're two of a kind.' It wasn't difficult for her to say that.

'I love you so, Claire.'

'Rest, darling. Don't talk.'

'I must. They're going to kill my father if I don't do what they want.'

'I know. They told me.'

'Do they mean it?'

'Oh, they mean it all right.'

He was silent for several minutes before he began to talk again.

'The day I was taken to the Army place, just before they pretended to hang me, I had a dream about you.'

'Another? Was it a nice dream?'

'Not very,' he said. 'You were strangling me with a silk stocking. But if you could do it now, I wouldn't struggle at all.' He felt her stiffen beside him and added quickly, 'I know you can't, but it would have been better. Much better than killing myself.'

'What are you saying, Frank?' An anguished whisper.

Fairly levelly, 'With me dead there would be no point in harming my father,' he told her. 'The British are hard people, but they aren't vindictive.'

'Oh my God!' Claire said for the second time.

'Don't worry about it, my dear. Just the fortunes of war.'

For several minutes she lay still, cradling his head, then asked drearily, 'Do you know that I'm in prison when I'm not working for them?'

'Yes. That professor man told me. He said you were – well, like me. You're not of German extraction, are you?'

'No. I got involved with Oswald Mosley and the Fascist Party. They seemed to have everything so right and – and then I went to the German Embassy to ask if I could help. I – I even met von Ribbentrop, and he said – he said I was the most perfect Aryan specimen he had ever seen and they taught me things so that I could help and gave me a man to contact called Kurt Sponeck and then the war started and Kurt Sponeck got caught and he told them about me before he was executed and I was arrested and . . .' The stream of words ended and she began to cry softly.

'Don't worry, Claire darling. If they intended to harm you they'd have done it by now.'

Her voice quiveringly taut, 'No, it's not like that,' Claire said. 'The day you die, either at their hand or your own, I hang. That's the price I have to pay.'

*

'I'm glad you've decided to do the honourable thing, and I'm sure your father and Miss Helier will be pleased too.'

It was mid-morning and Lohengrin looked at Morris out of exhausted, red-rimmed eyes, hating him.

'"His honour rooted in dishonour stood and faith unfaithful kept him falsely true,"' he quoted in a voice of quiet venom.

'Ah yes. Shakespeare.'

'It was Tennyson, actually.'

'Oh, was it?' Morris said. 'I don't have much time for the moderns. Chaucer's my cup of tea.'

Professor Morris enjoyed saying that and said it often, despite the fact that he had never read Chaucer and had no intention of doing so. His professorship was in applied psychology, not the arts.

Chapter Nine

The sun was rising on a Berlin covered in a light dusting of snow when *Abwehr* Major Ernst Dressier turned on to Unter den Linden. He had set himself the task of walking to the Brandenburg Gate and back before breakfast, both to clear his head and to give himself time to relish his good fortune at having got to the Belgian before either the *Sicherheitsdienst* or the apes from the *Geheime Staatspolizei*. His branch of Military Intelligence had never been on good terms with either the SS Security Service or the Gestapo, but his satisfaction at having forestalled any action on their part went deeper than professional rivalry and was much more personal.

To his left Dressier could see several distant columns of smoke rising above the buildings in the early light and assumed that the English terror flyers had been over the city again during the night, although he had been unaware of that in the deep cellar in which he had carried out his nocturnal interrogation. It had, he supposed, been more of a prolonged execution than an interrogation and he strode on, enjoying the tingling of his cheeks in the cold air and marvelling at the Belgian's reluctance to die. He had died eventually, of course. It was quite essential that he should have done so because he was trying to tell Dressier things he did not want to hear, things that it had been absolutely imperative that neither the SD nor the Gestapo should hear.

Obviously the man, employed as a courier by the *Abwehr*, had had self-interest as his motive in travelling from England to neutral Portugal and thence to Germany to deliver the warning that an agent of the Reich had not only been liquidated by the English, but that the latter were continuing to operate his wireless transmitter as though he were still alive. What made the notion so unacceptable was that the agent with the code name of *der Eingang* in Germany, and, although Dressier had no way of knowing it, of 'Parsifal' in England, was one of what Dressier liked to call his 'stable'.

There were six agents in that stable, each one a source of prestige for Dressier, who could now consider his promotion to lieutenant-colonel at the age of twenty-eight a certainty. They were a source of financial benefit too, because whenever they asked for funds he doubled the amount and kept the extra money for himself. That was why he had screamed, 'Liar! Liar! Liar!' and beaten the Belgian about the head and body with a rubber truncheon every time the man tried to explain how he had acquired the knowledge.

Fleetingly Dressier wondered if perhaps he should have listened to what the man had to say, then shrugged, knowing that to have done so could have undermined his confidence in himself, as well as his future standing, had he passed the information on to his superiors. No, he thought, the action he had taken had been right. His stable was one of the best, the reports of each agent confirming in large measure those of the others, and valuable reports they were. To have them placed in question by a Belgian renegade would have been unthinkable.

The Twenty Committee in London would have been pleased but not surprised by Dressler's conclusions, and intensely relieved at his night's work. They had a file on him, but he knew nothing of that, or of them. Unaware that he had just made a significant contribution to his country's defeat. Major Ernst Dressier turned and began to retrace his steps. Looking up to his right through the bare branches of the linden trees he saw that only three of the fires started by the English bombers were still burning. By the time he had breakfasted they too had been extinguished.

'Good morning, Ernst.'

Nodding at his desk, Dressier hadn't heard the colonel come into the office. He jerked himself to attention and said, 'Good morning, *Herr Oberst!*'

'Sleeping on duty, eh? Been womanizing again?'

'No, *Herr Oberst*. I was interrogating a prisoner all night.'

'Ah. Anything interesting?'

'No,' Dressier told him. 'It was that Belgian courier. I've had my doubts about him for some time and had him arrested as soon as he arrived from Lisbon yesterday. He confessed to being in the pay of British Military Intelligence, but died under questioning before I could establish who his contacts were.' The rehearsed lies came out easily enough.

'They have an irritating habit of doing that,' the colonel said. 'Well, sit down and show me what you're working on.'

For half an hour they examined reports relating to British aircraft production received from a number of sources, by radio, microdot and secret writing hidden between the lines of papers ranging from private letters to cargo manifests. The estimates varied widely, but all showed a rapidly increasing upward trend for both bomber and fighter planes to which a growing flood arriving from the United States of America had to be added. When averaged out the trend was impressive to the extent of being alarming. It was meant to be; it was reasonably accurate although somewhat optimistic from the British point of view and it had been carefully computed by a single group in London for dissemination through a number of controlled agents.

Two of the reports, one tentatively and one positively, suggested that much of this upward trend, while existing, could be largely discounted as a military factor because of a very high rate of aircraft losses brought about by inexperienced RAF student pilots on training flights. This information also originated with the same London group, was designed to encourage, and was quite untrue.

The British were in fact still probing, still practising, still not quite able to believe that they controlled most, if not all, of the German espionage organization in the United Kingdom. If the enemy made use of the item about training losses in a psychological warfare broadcast, they could be just that much more certain.

'Ernst, I think you'd better send a memorandum to the Ministry of Propaganda about those student pilot crashes. Dr Goebbels might be able to use it.'

'*Jawohl, Herr Oberst,*' Dressier said.

A messenger arrived then, placed copies of the day's newspapers on the desk and went wordlessly out. The colonel glanced at the front page of the *Völkischer Beobachter* and said, 'I see we've sunk their aircraft carrier *Ark Royal* again. That's about the eighth time, isn't it?'

Looking up from his own paper, 'It says here that the English have admitted it,' Dressier replied.

'Ah well. Let's hope it's the truth this time. That ship has been a damned nuisance. Put paid to *Bismarck* and was part of the force which scuppered the Italian Fleet at Taranto, wasn't she?' Without waiting for an answer, the colonel went on, 'Talking of ships, you're landing a man in England by U-boat tonight, aren't you?'

Dressier nodded. 'A courier with radio parts for *die Brücke* and money for *der Eingang*. He'll be met by *die Brücke* and return to the U-boat. The money will be left at a "postbox" by *die Brücke* for *der Eingang* to collect when he can.'

'Good,' the colonel said. 'I'll leave you to it.'

*

The Marquis of Trent was short, dapper, slightly built, and had sparse red hair which was a carroty version of his daughter's. He had none of her good looks, and if he possessed any of her striking personality he kept it well hidden.

Peter Clayton, his chief assistant, wore thick-lensed spectacles which, when removed, made his eyes look bald; was inclined to perspire freely and had a figure like a tired pear which no tailor had ever been able to disguise. They were an oddly matched couple, but shared a mutual respect, a certain diffidence, brilliance of intellect and middle age.

'Appalling!' Clayton said and stabbed his forefinger at the front page of the 15 November 1941 issue of the *Daily Express*, which shortage of newsprint had reduced to a single sheet of paper folded in two.

Mainwaring looked at it. 'Yes, pity about that, but I doubt many ships paid such good dividends before going down.'

The remark seemed to startle Clayton, who removed his glasses and polished them vigorously before saying, 'You mistake my meaning. Look at this headline. "*Ark Royal* went down like a gentleman." I think I'll write to the editor.'

'Why?'

'Because they should have put "like a lady." That's why. Ships are always feminine.'

'Bad case of transvestism if you ask me,' Mainwaring said, 'for merchantmen and men-of-war.'

Clayton looked startled again, sighed and muttered, 'What a ridiculous language we do have,' then, as though anxious to change the subject, added, 'I'm having a little trouble with the Navy wanting to attack the U-boat bringing in Lohengrin's wireless spares. After they've been landed, of course.'

'You mean you're having trouble with Rear-Admiral Dunne, surely. He can't have been such a bloody fool as to mention it to the Admiralty.'

'Oh no, he wouldn't do that, but he's arguing a case that we're putting thousands of tons of shipping at risk by letting her – er, it – go.'

'Damn the man,' Mainwaring said. 'I'm afraid we'll have to let *him* go. He seems to have no sense of priorities, no real grasp of the colossal potential of this deception operation. Can't he understand that the Germans must not be given the slightest reason to suspect that we might have had advance knowledge of their intentions?'

Clayton, who could recognize a rhetorical question when he heard one, didn't answer and after a moment Mainwaring went on, 'All right, Peter. Leave it with me. I take it that you'll be at the rendezvous.'

'Yes,' Clayton said. 'I shall be there. This first contact with the other side in his new role is going to be a somewhat traumatic experience for Lohengrin. He'll be bound to be feeling rather bitter and may try to test us, so I've ordered that Claire be taken to Holloway Prison.'

The Marquis of Trent nodded and Clayton left the office, feeling renewed satisfaction at having a chief who didn't need to have a thought process explained to him.

*

Built in 1934 by *Deutsche Werke* at Kiel, in defiance of the Treaty of Versailles, the Type 11A U-boat was small, cramped, slow and inadequately armed, but it was admirably suited for clandestine operations over the short sea passage separating Germany from the coast of England. It surfaced, clear of the end of the great mine barrier, into a night of patchy mist four nautical miles to the east of Deal in Kent. The commander ordered an officer and four look-outs to join him on the bridge.

That made it very crowded on the narrow conning tower, but as many pairs of eyes as possible were needed to watch for hostile patrol craft. They would have to go below quickly, those men, if the enemy was sighted, because the little 250-ton submarine could submerge in less than half a minute.

There were no patrols to be seen and the commander was thankful for that, but nervous about what might be concealed by the banks of drifting moisture. He was anxious, too, about his ability to make a precise landfall in the shifting visibility, with the total black-out ashore depriving him of any guidance. It was essential that he launch the rubber dinghy at exactly the right spot, at exactly the right time to enable it to reach the shore and return during what passed for 'dead water' in this place where the tides streamed rapidly around the corner of England. Somewhere ahead the bell of a buoy set up a desultory clanging as it rocked on the slight swell, but that didn't help him because it was impossible to gauge its bearing within fifty degrees and there was no certainty about which buoy it was. Deciding that the depths to the sea-bed marked on the chart were his only real source of possibly reliable information, 'Start the echo-sounder,' he said.

He didn't like having to say that, because the noise of the electronic depth-measuring device could be readily detected by enemy destroyers and the depths recorded could mean nothing in an area where the sandbanks were forever on the move, but he had little choice.

'Engines ahead. Half speed.'

A belching cough from astern, then a steady rumbling, water churning and the stench of burnt diesel oil drowning the clean smell of the sea.

'Steer due west.'

The U-boat forging purposefully ahead, accelerating, sliding into a bank of fog, visibility zero, the diesel stink fading, gone.

'Listen when you can't see,' the commander said to the men on the bridge, and the fog seemed to make his voice boom in his ears. The fog thinning, clearing. The sequence repeating itself constantly. Tension mounting as the distance to the shore decreased.

'Line of soundings indicates we are half a mile south of our track, *Herr Kaleun*.' The navigator's voice addressing him by his unofficial title. It was quicker than saying '*Herr Kapitanleutnant*' every time.

'Very well. Steer fifteen degrees to starboard.'

The bows, dimly seen, swinging to the right, steadying. The curve in the wake astern quickly lost to view. The clang of the bell away on the port beam now.

'Ship bearing fine on the starboard bow!' An urgent shout.

'Stop engines. All of you down below.'

The rapid shuffling of shoe leather on steel, muttered imprecations.

'Wait, *Herr Kaleun*. I think it's only another buoy.'

'I see it. Stay where you are, everybody. Weber, keep your eye on it and try to read the number as we go by.'

The buoy passing rapidly along the starboard side and another voice calling, 'Land Ahead! I think I can see buildings!' Weber saying, 'I'm sorry, *Herr Kaleun*. I can't read the number. It's covered in seaweed and barnacles.' The commander replying, 'No matter. That's the town of Deal ahead. We know where we are now,' pausing then adding, 'Steer sixty-five degrees to port, warn the civilian and stand by to launch the dinghy through the torpedo supply hatch.'

*

Die Brücke, 'The Bridge', who was Pelham, who was Lohengrin, stood just above the high-tide mark mid-way between Deal and South Foreland, waiting to receive wireless parts for himself and money for *der Eingang*, 'the Entry', who was Ulbricht, who was Parsifal, who was dead. The mist swirled around him and under its blanket the almost flat sea hissed softly, snake-like. He had never felt so lonely, so isolated, yet he was not alone.

A tubby man whose name he did not know lay amongst rocks fifty yards to the south. A machine-gunner was with him. Pemberton and a second machine-gunner were hidden a similar distance behind his back. Both groups of men had a small search-light. Further inland and well out of earshot, an arc of soldiers waited to keep the curious away, although away from what they had not been told. The night was mild, but Lohengrin was shivering, a combination of shame and fear producing the physical reaction. He steadied himself with slow, deep breaths and by concentrating his thoughts on Claire Helier. To allow his mind to focus on the girl, either by intent or by letting it drift to her, was becoming a commonplace for him. Because he was by no means a fool, he recognized the loss of personal identity this indicated, but had neither the will nor the wish to make it otherwise.

Lohengrin had been standing statue-like, unmindful of anybody or anything else, for almost a quarter of an hour when the dip of paddles brought him back to himself. He didn't immediately identify the sound, but softly spoken words with a German cadence and the rasp of something being drawn across gravelly sand some way to his left told him that the courier had arrived. Tense again, he walked stiff-legged towards what he had heard, then jumped at the suddenness of the materialization of a figure out of the mist. It had a case in one hand, a gun in the other.

'Ich bin "die Brücke",' Lohengrin said.

'Gott sie danke! Auf Wiedersehen.'

Those were the only words spoken. The courier lowered the case to the sand and backed away, his gun still pointing at Lohengrin. A gap in the curtain of mist opened then and Lohengrin saw the dinghy with two men in the uniform of the Kriegsmarine standing beside it, saw them replace it in the water, saw all three of them climb cautiously in and paddle out to sea. The courier's gun remained trained on him until the little craft was swallowed by darkness and mist. Only then did he pick up the case.

Two minutes later, 'Here's your fucking delivery,' he told the man whose name he didn't know.

'I say, that's very colloquial. Rather rude, but colloquial,' Clayton said. 'But of course you were born here, weren't you?'

'I want to talk to you.' Lohengrin's voice was as taut as a violin string.

'Please do.'

'Alone. Away from these people.'

'Very well. Let's walk.'

They had covered seventy yards before Lohengrin said, 'You're somebody senior, aren't you?'

'Yes, reasonably so.'

'Then you'll have the authority to take me to London. I must go there and Colonel Pemberton is to come with us.'

'Why must you?'

'I'll tell you that when we get there.'

'And if I refuse?' Clayton asked.

'If you refuse you'll have a suicide on your hands.'

'And if I agree I may have a bomb victim on my hands. London isn't a healthy place to be these days, although it's better than it was last winter.'

'I'll take my chance with the bombs,' Lohengrin said. 'We get them on the south coast too, you know.'

Clayton murmured, 'As you wish,' and turned to retrace his steps.

*

The big government car ran out of the mist near Canterbury, back into it again at Chatham, and it was dawn before it reached Greenwich.

'Where do you want to go?'

Half asleep between Clayton and Pemberton on the back seat, Lohengrin jerked up his head and said, 'What?'

Clayton repeated the question.

'Oh. King's Cross first.'

Visibility had increased with the coming of day and Lohengrin sat dispiritedly looking at the damaged streets, scarred and pock-marked buildings, buildings supported by great balks of timber, buildings covered in scaffolding and screened by hoardings, buildings that were blackened skeletons and gaps where buildings had once been. The grim evidence of aerial bombardment gave him no satisfaction. Occasionally he raised his eyes to the countless barrage balloons, their silver-grey flanks and undersides tinged pink by the rising sun. Most were now being winched towards the ground by uniformed girls. After a little he let his eyes close, tired of looking at what might be his last day on earth.

Just when the suspicion that he had been tricked had begun to grow in him he was unsure, but he knew that suspicion had become conviction during the past night. Now he was seeking final proof of cruel deceit, proof that would kill him because it would leave him with no desire to live with his own double treachery as his only companion. He sought relief in sleep, but sleep wouldn't come to him.

'Where now, sir?'

Lohengrin opened his eyes and surveyed the drab façade of King's Cross railway station. He doubted that the driver had been addressing him, but replied anyway.

'Go to Holloway Women's Prison. I think it's near the top of Caledonian Road.'

Clayton sighed gustily, as though some mystery had been explained to him, as though he had not anticipated his prisoner's suspicions.

'Do as he says, driver,' he said.

At the gate-house Clayton asked diffidently if it would be possible to see the prisoner Claire Helier, and the identity card he proffered for inspection with equal diffidence guaranteed the possibility. He and Lohengrin were ushered inside. Pemberton had elected to remain in the car.

Suspicious, puzzled, Lohengrin stood just inside the door of the visitors' room, a small bleak space containing two plain wooden chairs separated by an unpainted table. His body jerked visibly when Claire Helier came through an opposing doorway, followed by a wardress.

Beauty. Even in prison uniform, without make-up, with her light golden hair drawn back into a severe bun. Beauty. Not, he thought, that her skin needed any make-up, and her eyebrows and lashes possessed their own natural mascara, but – but she did look awfully pale, awfully tense, her eyes seeming to ask questions her parted lips could not form.

'Oh Claire.'

Her lips moving. 'Did you do it?' A whisper only just heard.

'Did I do what?'

'Whatever you were supposed to do last night. They're going to hang me today if you didn't.' A voice already dead.

'Yes, my darling. I did it.'

Claire swaying, straightening, stumbling towards him, the wardress barking, 'Helier! Stand where you are!', grasping her by the shoulders, then, in contravention of her own order, propelling her to one of the chairs and forcing her down onto it. Slowly Lohengrin sat on the other and stretched out his hand.

'You may not touch the prisoner,' the wardress said.

'Forgive me, Claire. I had come to believe that . . .'

'Believe what, my dear?' Her voice tremulous with relief now.

'Nothing.'

There was no way, he knew, that they could have guessed his destination, no way that they could have planted Claire in this awful place just to deceive him. He felt disgust at himself for his disbelief of what she herself had told him, and love and sorrow for her. They exchanged soft endearments until the wardress told them to speak clearly. At that Lohengrin stood up, smiled wanly at Claire, and left, walking quickly.

When the door closed behind him, 'That was well done,' the MI5 operative dressed as a wardress said.

Self-revulsion flooded over Claire Helier and the chair toppled backwards when she leapt to her feet.

'Oh, go to hell!' she shouted, then threw her arms around the woman and burst into tears.

*

There was no sign of the tubby man when Lohengrin was escorted to the car. He got into the back beside Pemberton, settled himself in a corner and closed his eyes. Not a word was spoken throughout the two-and-a-half-hour drive to Seaford.

He spent that time trying to reassess his situation. Whether or not his father was indeed in Portugal and consequently within reach of British assassins, he did not know, but thought it likely as the older man had been employed by the German firm of Marcus & Hartig on Lisbon's Rossio before the outbreak of hostilities. It seemed natural that his knowledge of the Portuguese language would have led to his continued employment in a different capacity in that city where hostile and neutral Intelligence agencies rubbed shoulders. Lohengrin had concluded that he had no choice but to accept Pemberton's words as the truth.

It had taken him long periods of agonizing to decide that if he was prepared to commit suicide in order to deprive the British of an instrument which could do incalculable harm to the Reich, his father could hardly object to dying himself. The thought of some man called Standish 'arranging an accident' had come to him repeatedly, postponing the moment of decision, but he had eventually suppressed the mental images that invoked by recognizing that, unlike his own, his parent's death would come without the agony of anticipation.

It had taken him even longer to convince himself that Claire Helier was nothing more than an accomplished man-trap who had worked her magic and woven her spell with cynical amusement. Had he been asked how he had arrived at such a conclusion he would, he knew, have found it difficult to answer, beyond saying that her explanation for her arrival as a blackmail victim in his life was simply too apposite to be true. With so much so suddenly going so terribly wrong with an always hazardous but carefully nurtured career, the sheer openness of what she had told him made her doubly suspect. It had angered him that it had taken him so long to grasp that obvious point and he had experienced a perverse sense of satisfaction in the calling of a bluff which, had it succeeded, would have ensured his extinction. It hadn't succeeded because she had been where he had satisfied himself she could not be. His suspicion of her died and with it his resolve.

Rationalization took hold of him then. To drag down with him two people, one of whom he respected and the other of whom he loved, was something not even patriotism should require of him. In addition, he told himself, he had not yet committed a positive act of treachery, unless to accept money and wireless spares from the courier, thereby saving the man's life and the lives of the U-boat's crew, was treachery.

Those thoughts stayed with him for almost two miles before they collapsed under the weight of their own fallaciousness and, when no others came to fill the vacuum they had left, he resolved to do nothing for the time being. His chance to redress the balance, he assured himself, would come.

Lohengrin had sunk further into submission.

Chapter Ten

The memorandum was fifty-seven pages in length and Edward Mainwaring picked it up, balancing it on the palm of one hand as though judging its weight. It made a fat plopping sound when he let it drop to his desk and he sat, looking down at it, smiling faintly at the opening words. 'Oh so very secret,' they read. 'Your eyes only. No copy exists. Typed by me. Forgive errors. Suggest you destroy after perusal. P. J. Clayton.'

The marquis turned his head towards the window framing a tiny portion of a London made sallow by an anaemic November sun, but his eyes registered none of it. They were turned inwards onto a vast canvas his mind had been roughing out over a period of weeks, a canvas Clayton had now blocked in for him. Some of it was in bright colours, some in pastel shades. There were grey areas too, but he found nothing to quarrel with in that because there were always grey areas. Contentment grew in him, both at thoughts clearly set down and at thoughts shared. Had Clayton not anticipated him, the proposals he himself would have put on paper would have differed little from the document before him. He had hesitated about setting it down at all because the entire concept was, as Clayton had written, 'Oh so very secret', but now it was done and very satisfactorily so. His gaze returned to the thick pile of papers and he began to leaf through them, reading paragraphs at random. Then there was only one page left and that he read again in full.

'I suppose it was that frightful fellow "Lord Haw-Haw's" sneering references on Radio Berlin to bad RAF training techniques and the consequent heavy loss of planes and their student pilots, which finally persuaded me that the enemy is swallowing the information we feed to him. On the basis of that incident alone my position would not be tenable, but there have now been too many cases as recorded above, in several of which the enemy has reacted to his own disadvantage, to permit me to believe that we are having our own bluff thrown back at us. Therefore I submit that, be it only temporarily, we control the German espionage organization in this country in its entirety.

'If one is to accept this hypothesis, one must also accept that we have in our hands a weapon of incalculable value, a weapon we must clutch to our bosom like misers, eschewing the blandishments of the armed forces and the civilian authorities alike demanding its use for tactical gain. The weapon is strategic in its potential and, while we should be unflagging in testing and honing it, in my opinion its proper function is long-term deception on a grand scale. Wishful thinking it may be, but I have in mind great enterprises, like our eventual return to mainland Europe in force, when confusion in the enemy camp as to our precise intentions could result not only in the saving of tens of thousands of lives, but in the saving of humanity itself. As islanders we are uniquely well placed to safeguard our secret, as the absence of a common land frontier makes it close to impossible for the enemy to establish what is taking place.

'If you agree that we should adopt this stance we shall, of course, come under intense pressure to abandon it for short-term advantage and, no doubt, powerful arguments will be advanced to that end. It is my contention that we must be prepared and able to educate our peers and masters alike to – I think the expression is "go for broke". What say you? Peter Clayton.'

Having decided that eyes other than his own should read the submission too, the marquis opened a drawer, took a red telephone receiver from it and held it to his ear.

'Douglas, I need to see him for half an hour. Not urgently, but soon. Yes, two thirty a.m. tomorrow will do very well. Thank you.'

He replaced the receiver and closed the drawer.

A man with a briefcase chained to his wrist was waiting for him when he arrived back at his office the following morning. He accepted the contents of the case, signed a receipt and waited until the man had gone before breaking the seals of the thick manila envelope.

On the top page of Clayton's memorandum was written, 'Let it be so. Winston S. Churchill.'

With the document in his hand he walked along the passage to Clayton's room.

*

'I do believe I'm beginning to look less reptilian. I really do believe I am,' Professor Morris said and angled his head from side to side, admiring the reflection of his emergent beard in the glass of a framed print of Dover Castle on the living-room wall. Pemberton, lounging in the only comfortable chair, watched him morosely, not speaking. After a moment Morris turned to him.

'George.'

'Yes?'

'You know the next step, don't you?'

'Yes,' Pemberton said. 'Sprinkle salt on it before you go to bed, let it suffer all night, then hold a glass of water near it when you get up. It'll be so frantic for moisture it'll grow anything up to three inches trying to reach the glass. Works every time.'

'Most amusing,' Morris told him, 'but I wasn't talking about my beard, I was talking about Lohengrin. You'll have guessed what happens now, no doubt.'

Pemberton shrugged. 'Not precisely, but I expect you'll think up something suitably nauseating to put him through.'

'Wrong, my dear fellow, wrong! *You* will put him through something suitably nauseating, if that's how you like to describe it, whenever it appears to be necessary. You will also dangle the delectable Miss Helier in front of his nose when that seems more appropriate. I'm leaving Seaford this morning.' Morris sounded like someone delighted at the success of a carefully prepared surprise. 'Stick and carrot,' he went on. 'Ice cream and hot chocolate sauce. You know the routine now. If you can't change their ideological outlook, keep them confused with sensations pleasant and unpleasant, and individual loyalties of a more immediately personal nature. In Lohengrin's case we were very lucky to have his father to add to Miss Helier. Got him skewered with two prongs there.'

'Unbelievably lucky,' Pemberton said.

'What do you mean by that?' Morris's voice was sharp.

'Just what I said. It's unbelievable because it's just too convenient. I've been thinking about that MI6 report and I don't believe it. I don't believe that his father is in Lisbon and I don't believe that we have the remotest idea where he is.'

Morris moved away from the picture of Dover Castle and sat on an upright chair, facing Pemberton and staring at him for a long moment before saying, 'Don't be too clever for your own good, George. Lohengrin believes that his father's in Lisbon because it's logical that he should be there. I want you to believe it too, so that you can worry about his welfare as Lohengrin will and – oh, surely I don't have to go through all that again, do I?'

Ignoring the question, 'So he's not in Lisbon,' Pemberton said.

'I didn't say that.'

Pemberton made a noise somewhere between a sigh and a groan, then began to speak slowly, clearly. The words came without emphasis, almost without punctuation, and, paradoxically, that gave them added strength.

'You listen to me, Professor Morris. You live in a world of fantasy and for reasons which I accept you have drawn part of me into that world, but I must keep one foot firmly planted on fact. The Germans may summon Lohengrin to Lisbon for consultation, or it may become desirable for us to send him there ourselves. I must know if his father is only notionally there because if that is so I may have to have him notionally transferred elsewhere at very short notice. It's unthinkable that Lohengrin would not seize the opportunity of trying to see him, and you even told me to quote that address on Rua Alexandre Herculano. Forget about your meeting of minds concept. You've already achieved enough of that by making me thankful for Lohengrin as well as for myself that you're leaving. I'm sure I speak for both of us when I say that we shall be glad to be spared any more of your squalid presence. Now is his father in Lisbon or is he not?'

Morris sounded not in the least put out when he replied, 'No, he is not and, before you ask, we don't know where he is, but I do know when I'm *de trop*, so I'll leave you two together. If I haven't fully achieved a meeting of minds, as you put it, at least I appear to have effected a satisfactory introduction.' He stood up then and added, 'If you need me, I shall be at The Patriotic School.'

'At the what?'

'That requisitioned building near Wandsworth Prison they use for screening people who escape from Europe. Surely you know of it.'

'Oh yes,' Pemberton said. 'I just didn't know they had given the place such a ridiculous name. As to needing you, I don't think that is very likely, so off you go and concentrate on turning somebody else.'

He got to his own feet then and stood facing Morris as if to emphasize the instruction, but the professor stayed where he was, frowning slightly.

'George.'

'Yes?'

'I don't like that word "turn". It's a hazy abstraction, not susceptible to quantitative appraisal. You must realize that Lohengrin is as turned as a snake in a pit, or a bull in a field which has been prodded with a pole.'

'Like all analogies those are dangerous,' Pemberton said. 'They are also inaccurate. With the pressures you have put on him he's more under control than that.'

'They'll do as long as they serve to remind you how potentially dangerous he is,' Morris told him. 'Never forget that.' He had spoken reprovingly, but his tone changed when, as if in anticipation of his own joke, he cackled and went on, 'Stay close to him, George, prod away, keep him on the straight and narrow and we'll turn the Wilhelmstrasse into a garden path for leading the Nazis up.' The absurd rattle of mirth came again.

Pemberton watched sombrely as 'The Puppet Maker' left the room. He heard him call for his driver, heard too the sound of a car engine starting, then fading with distance. For a moment he stood, thinking about that abrupt departure and how typical it was of the man to do the unexpected thing even when it was manifestly unnecessary. Irritation at being left with no instructions other than to stay close and prod rose in him before subsiding under a renewed wave of release. It was good to have him out of the house. Already the place felt cleaner.

*

The car was approaching Newhaven when the driver drew Professor Morris's attention to the planes approaching the harbour from seaward.

'They're German I think, sir.'

'Very probably. Very probably,' Morris said.

'Shall I head for an air-raid shelter, sir?'

'No, get on, man. Get on.'

To Morris, the visible side of war was an irrelevance, an inconvenient irrelevance which all too frequently interfered with his carefully planned schedules and disrupted his train of thought. It had done so now, and he experienced resentment, not so much towards the enemy as towards his driver for reminding him of it.

'They're Heinkel IIIs with an escort of Me109s, sir. Must be thirty of 'em.'

'Kindly spare me a running commentary,' Morris said. 'I am simply not interested.' But he turned his head towards the advancing formation nevertheless.

As the driver had told him, it appeared to consist of bombers with fighter cover above them, two long straggling lines of planes silhouetted against the bright winter day. Somewhere close at hand an anti-aircraft gun began to bark, others followed its example and puffs of black smoke pock-marked the sky. The small aerial armada seemed to hang motionless in the air, unnoticing.

'I didn't hear any sirens.'

'They sounded as we were leaving Seaford, sir.'

'Oh.'

Morris tried to concentrate his mind on the strange ménage he had just left, although, being only one of many that he had organized, it held no strangeness for him, but a series of heavy thumps and the roar of engines distracted him. He glanced out and up as the eighth pressure wave shook the car, just in time to identify the roundels of the RAF on the wings of fighters climbing to intercept the advancing enemy.

'Ah, Spitfires,' he said.

'They're Hurricanes actually, sir. Those are Spitfires coming in from the direction of Brighton. Old Jerry'd better run for it!'

As though the words had been heard and accepted as good advice, the bombers turned back, dense forests of splashes marking the fall of the bomb-loads they jettisoned to achieve greater speed. Four taller splashes followed as planes trailing shrouds of smoke struck the water. High above, most of the fighters drew white arabesques against pale blue until, as one, pursuers and pursued streaked towards the coast of France. Soon they were only dots above the hard line of the horizon.

'What a poorly planned operation,' Morris said. 'That cost them four planes to no purpose.'

'Three, sir. One of them was ours,' the driver told him, and added knowledgeably, 'That will have been a feint. They've drawn off our fighters so their main strike can go in somewhere else.'

Morris scowled. He did it not so much because he found the unsolicited explanation of the tactics employed a little too plausible to bear close scrutiny, as for the reason that he didn't like to be contradicted except by prearrangement, least of all twice in succession. The driver saw the facial contortion in the mirror and smiled. He didn't like his passenger.

Seaford was ten miles behind him before Morris succeeded in coaxing his brain back to the task of preparing an estimate of the reliability of the Pemberton – Lohengrin combination. That was one of the first things that the marquis or Clayton would ask about. It should do well, he thought; the teaming of two men of similar character, both intelligent, both too gentle for their own good in time of war. The manipulation of Lohengrin had been simple as far as it had gone, but would inevitably be a continuing process for Pemberton. In the case of Pemberton himself, it had been necessary only to induce an attitude of mind, and Pemberton had contributed unconsciously to the achievement of that goal.

His flat refusal to witness Lohengrin's mock execution had encouraged Mojris in the belief that he had chosen the right man, and that belief was strengthened when he had noted that Lohengrin's distress at the use to which the Helier girl was being put was mirrored in Pemberton. That had been intensely gratifying, as had the man's finding Lohengrin's beating sufficiently distasteful to make him vomit. But most pleasing of all had been watching Pemberton's attitude towards authority as personified by Morris himself change from formal respect to outright impertinence and finally unqualified insubordination.

What had he said? Oh yes, the 'squalid presence' outburst. Excellent. Truly excellent. There could be little doubt that Pemberton had been driven emotionally close to the spy in his charge, and whether or not he realized the fact was neither here nor there. Morris cackled.

'Want to share the joke, sir?'

'Oh no. Oh indeed no,' he told the driver. 'It's much too good for you.'

*

Pemberton watched the brief aerial combat too. He did so through the living-room window of the house on Southdown Road, Seaford, and it startled him. The encounter was no more than minor and commonplace, but for him the abnormal had become routine and the normal had sunk below the level of consciousness taking the real war with it. Astonished at his lack of awareness of the outside world since Lohengrin and Morris had come into his life, he tried to remember how long it was since he had read a newspaper or listened to the BBC News, but could not number the days with any accuracy. 'Subjective time,' he muttered to himself and that made him think obscenities about Professor Morris.

When the battle had disappeared from his field of view, Pemberton took an envelope from his pocket, rested it on the window ledge, fumbled for a pencil stub and wrote:

'Get "L" back in circulation in local community.

Get "L" back on his Min of Food job.

Get "L" operational!!'

He noted the two exclamation marks he had put after the word 'operational' and added a third, then, as though having done so constituted a major step forward, he began to pace around the room, impatient for the return of Carne and Lohengrin from the spy's daily exercise outing.

*

Although he knew him as *die Brücke*, Major Dressier was also most anxious that Lohengrin should become operational again. It had been several days now since the U-boat courier had reported the success of the rendezvous with him on the coast of Kent and he knew that the man had spoken the truth because forty-eight hours later *der Eingang* had acknowledged by radio the safe arrival of the two hundred pounds sterling he had asked for. It followed, therefore, that *die Brücke* had received his radio spares, but no message had been received from him despite three transmitted requests that he report on his circumstances. Dressier frowned at the thought of the drop in his personal income which would result from the loss of *die Brücke*.

'You are preoccupied tonight, *liebling*.'

'It's nothing of consequence,' he said.

The girl was a member of the office staff and it had been the colonel himself who had encouraged him to take her as his bed-mate. The colonel had been rather more than simply persuasive, pointing out that what he described as Dressler's womanizing was a risky off-duty occupation for an Intelligence officer and that he would do better to sleep with a woman having a high security clearance within the same organization.

Dressier hadn't liked the thinly veiled order too much. Ulrike had a superb body which did something to compensate him for having to look at her gleamingly healthy stupid face with its baby-blue doll's eyes, button nose and small round mouth, but it was her obtrusive healthiness which he found aesthetically offensive. It smacked of Hitler Youth camps and fifty-kilometre hikes through the mountains, as did her 'sensible' clothes and 'practical' underwear. She wasn't wearing either at the moment and he concentrated on her body, pretending that she was one of the colonel's glamorously decadent women. He had two; one of them his wife, the other his secretary who spent an hour in his office every afternoon, but never did any typing when she came out. Dressier sighed.

'Tell Ricky, *liebling*. It's not good for you to worry alone,' Ulrike said. 'It'll make you all thin and scrawny. I hate scrawny men.' She laughed and began to stroke Dressler's protruding belly, on which his walks to the Brandenburg Gate and back had no effect whatsoever.

'One of my agents in England has been silent for too long,' he told her. 'There may be a perfectly good reason for it, but it's unusual.' That was another compensation, he thought, being able to tell her some of his worries. She knew that the purpose of the section for which they both worked was to run agents in the British Isles, so he wasn't divulging anything of a secret nature by talking about it, but on this occasion there wasn't a lot to be said and he soon tired of the exchange. Her caresses reinstated decadence at the top of his list of priorities.

The demands he made of the girl were unusual and unpleasant for her, but she closed her mind to them, thinking instead of the *Führer*, with whom, along with thousands like her, she imagined herself to be in love. When Dressier tired she lay with her head on his fat paunch, waiting for him to fall asleep, allowing her mind to settle on the payment she would soon exact from him. The anticipation of that brought her such exquisite pleasure that she had to force herself to lie very still in case it should communicate itself to him.

Chapter Eleven

Lohengrin turned towards the entrance to the public bar of the 'Anglo-Saxon Arms', then stopped at the touch of Pemberton's hand on his sleeve.

'This one,' Pemberton said and pointed to the saloon-bar door.

'Why? That would be out of character. I always used the public. Are you a snob or something?'

Nervous about this first re-exposure of Lohengrin in a place he had frequented, Pemberton snapped, 'Keep your voice down. No, I'm not a snob, but you're with two men dressed as Army officers and your bar will be full of soldiers, matelots and airmen. What do you expect the poor bastards to do when a colonel and a captain walk in? Drink their beer standing at attention?'

'Oh yes, I see,' Lohengrin said. 'I hadn't thought of that.'

Pemberton relaxed and smiled faintly. 'Neither had I,' he confessed. 'It took Sergeant Newland to tell me the correct procedure.' It touched and saddened him when Lohengrin returned his smile. He was not to know that a large part of that smile signalled Lohengrin's intense relief that he now need not enter a room in which he had spent so much time with Claire Helier, a room in which the life he had built for himself had ended.

A moment later, 'Well, if it isn't Mr Pelham! Welcome back, sir. I thought you'd left the town. The regulars say the Army has taken over your house.'

Lohengrin shook hands with the landlord across the bar. 'So it has, Mr Brent, and here are two of them. Colonel Pemberton, Captain Carne, this is Mr Brent. He's the boss here.'

'Welcome to the "Angry Saxon", gentlemen,' Brent said. 'That's what the locals call the place. What'll it be?'

They asked for beer and Brent looked relieved. Rationing had left him with a small supply of gin and he would happily have served Mr Pelham with that, but not the Army officers if he could help it. They had yet to qualify as regular customers. Hardly anybody even bothered to ask for whisky any longer because it was generally known that most of that was exported to the United States to help pay for arms. Bloody war, he thought, then said it out loud.

Pemberton agreed that it was a bloody war, invited the landlord to have a drink with them, then, the tenseness of his muscles belying his casual stance, propped himself languidly against the bar. Conversation became general.

Eventually, 'Where're you living now, Mr Pelham?' Brent asked, and ridiculously Pemberton found himself holding his breath.

'Same place,' Lohengrin said. 'The Army just moved in on me. You know how they are. Requisition anything at the drop of a hat.'

'Go on. You're pulling my leg!'

A watchful Pemberton saw Lohengrin smile and heard him say, 'Yes, of course I am. It's just that there's a conflict of interests between the War Office and the Ministry of Food. The military have a remarkable aptitude for selecting all the best bits of arable and grazing land for turning into airfields, or gun positions, or something. There have been so many arguments about it that it was decided to form a liaison committee. We're it. I provide the accommodation and they pay the rent. Suits me.'

Brent grinned and said, 'It's an ill wind, as I always say. Now then, gentlemen. How about one on the house?'

Relaxing, Pemberton thought that Lohengrin had even improved on the briefing he had given him for surmounting that particular hurdle. He wondered if the subject of the beautiful girl who had been Lohengrin's companion would come up, but it did not. He was thankful for that.

*

The four hours since they had returned from the pub had been bad ones for Lohengrin. He had scarcely touched his lunch, then had retired to his room and thrown himself fully dressed onto the bed to fight an adversary he could neither see nor grasp. It was too deeply inside him for that.

After the small nervousness over the exchange with the landlord he had been coached in had subsided, he had almost enjoyed the quiet hour of beer drinking. Perhaps, he thought, 'enjoyed' was too strong a word, but he had achieved a degree of tranquillity, something he had forgotten existed. Walking back to the house he had asked Pemberton if it would be possible to repeat the visit. 'Of course, my dear chap,' Pemberton had replied. 'Any time you like. Go by yourself if you want to. In fact, you're free to go anywhere as long as you do your job.'

The satisfaction he had felt at the words had lasted a full twenty seconds before their implication struck him like one of Newland's blows to the body. Were they that sure of him? The unspoken question had answered itself immediately. Naturally they were. That was when gloom had taken hold of him again, tightening its grip, becoming the all too familiar despair against which he had no antidote. Not even the building of fantasies around Claire Helier helped him any longer because that was so obviously what they were and to indulge in them only added to his emotional malaise. For that reason he had hidden her nightdress.

Perversely, Lohengrin found himself resenting the departure of Morris, who had at least served as a focus for all his hates and fears. Deprived of it he felt a greater sense of loss of direction than ever, something he would not have believed possible but now found to be so. Moving restlessly on the bed, turning a pillow which had grown too warm against the back of his neck, he tried to engender hatred for Newland who had beaten him so severely and cracked three of his ribs in the process. It didn't work. The best he could achieve was a momentarily satisfying picture of himself confronting Newland on equal terms without Carne holding him from behind. Recognition of the childishness of the thought coupled with the almost certain knowledge that the outcome of any such encounter would be the same as before cleared the imaginary scene from his mind.

Carne? Nothing there. Carne had a grey aura, neither likeable nor dislikeable, a faceless man with a face, who rarely spoke; the only noticeable things about him, brown eyes which never stopped watching and a bald head which glistened in the light.

Pemberton then? Nothing there either. He actually *liked* Pemberton and that was very disconcerting. Under different circumstances he was virtually certain that they would have been friends and felt even now that there was an affinity between them which . . . Lohengrin pulled himself up sharply, dismayed by this latest demonstration of his inability to control the course of his own thinking, his failure to prevent his mind reaching thirstily for the mirage of some small comfort.

Not for the first time he wondered if he was being drugged. Not today, he decided. He had drunk coffee for breakfast out of the same pot as the others and eaten only toast. That couldn't have been tampered with, nor could the beer at the pub. Lunch had been one mouthful of plain boiled potato. No, not today, but there had been times when his behaviour had been totally uncharacteristic. Uncharacteristic? Pathetic! The memory of his breakdown in front of Morris and Pemberton after the dream about Claire made him sweat with embarrassment, as it did whenever he recalled it.

His pillow was damp as well as too warm now He turned it again, wondering why, if he had not been drugged, he was incapable of coherent constructive thought, why it appeared necessary for him to waste time in trying to identify somebody to hate. The knowledge that that was all he had left to him rose towards the surface of his consciousness and was registered before he could force it down again.

Carne found him asleep two hours later with his cheek resting on Claire Helier's nightdress. This he found of sufficient interest to report to Pemberton, because periodic searches of Lohengrin's room had revealed the garment consigned to the bottom of a drawer over recent days.

*

'I'm nervous,' Lohengrin said and held out a hand on which fingers quivered.

'Hardly surprising,' Pemberton told him. 'If it's any consolation to you, so am I. Would you like a drink? I've got half a bottle of Scotch somewhere.'

'Yes, please.'

Pemberton found the whisky, poured a strong measure into a glass and watched Lohengrin sipping it. The nervousness had been growing in Lohengrin by the hour as this moment approached and Pemberton knew the reason for it. Of the series of small submissions forced on the spy, none had had the slightest effect on the conduct of the war, but now the time for positive treachery had come and Pemberton felt extremely sorry for him.

'Don't stare at me! It makes it worse!'

'Sorry,' Pemberton said and lit a cigarette, his eyes on the smoke drifting almost vertically upwards in the still air. Beside them Harry waited impassively, his hand resting beside a Morse transmission key, the twin of the one in front of Lohengrin.

If Harry had another name nobody seemed to remember it and Pemberton knew only that until bomb splinters had ended his naval career, he had served as a leading telegraphist in a destroyer commanded by Lord Louis Mountbatten. MI5 had taken him on then because he shared his famous ex-captain's uncanny ability not only to identify the sender of Morse transmissions by their style but to duplicate that style. He had watched, listened to and copied Lohengrin's technique for a total of nearly four hours and now it would have taken Mountbatten himself to tell the difference between them.

His voice strongly cockney, 'Like me to do it, sir?' Harry asked. He called everybody with an educated accent 'sir', on the grounds that the speaker might be an officer.

'No, I'm all right now,' Lohengrin replied, breathed in deeply and took hold of the key, forcing himself to keep his touch light. The contacts began to click rapidly.

'*Die Brücke*,' the numbers spelt out to the ionosphere, and the ionosphere deflected them to the radio antennae on top of Berlin's *Rundfunk* building. '*Die Brücke*. Acknowledge.'

Lohengrin pressed his headset to his ears. So did Harry. Morse chattered briefly.

'They've acknowledged,' Lohengrin said, saw Pemberton nod encouragingly and began his main transmission. It spoke of a fall, of cracked ribs, of time spent in hospital. It asked for instructions and for 150 pounds sterling.

'They've acknowledged,' Lohengrin said again. 'Now we wait for half an hour precisely. The message goes from the *Rundfunk* building to *Abwehr* HQ by land-line immediately, but Major Dressier, or whoever's on duty, will need time to encode a reply.'

Yes, Pemberton thought, he is nervous and talking for the sake of talking. The entire procedure had been gone over several times not only with him, but with Came as well. He felt his own anxiety increase on a sympathetic as well as a professional level and experienced renewed anger that he was so readily falling into the role of *doppelgänger* that Professor Morris had cast him for.

'More whisky?'

'No, thank you.'

Pemberton lit another cigarette and was lighting a third when, with Germanic precision, Berlin came on the air again, half an hour to the second after the last transmission had ceased. He stubbed the cigarette out. Lohengrin began to scribble numbers on a pad. So did Harry, but he did it automatically, almost absent-mindedly, most of his attention concentrated on the transmitting technique of the man far away in Germany. You never knew, Harry told himself, with peculiar people like his new employers. They might want him to replace that man. He was working on the problems of mastering the German language, gaining access to Berlin and related trifles when the message ended.

Alone together, Pemberton and Lohengrin set about decoding it. A number of minor errors impeded them until they switched to Harry's copy. After that it was perfectly straight-forward. Unable to read Morse himself, Pemberton mentally excused Lohengrin's poor performance on the grounds of lack of practice, nervousness and unfair competition. Anybody who had served under Lord Mountbatten was bound to have an unfair advantage and . . .

Sudden embarrassment at his unspoken defence of his protégé stopped the line of thought, but it took effort to exorcize the apparition of 'The Puppet Maker' he could feel in the room. For a moment he imagined he heard it cackle.

*

By any standard guilty of double treason now, Lohengrin added fear of his own people to fear of his present masters. The amalgam released adrenalin into his blood and forced his limbs into action, his legs taking him from end to end of his bedroom, one hand manipulating the knuckles of the other in a series of staccato cracks. After a little he stopped maltreating his finger joints, but his legs continued their frantic pacing as though striving to carry him away from the chilling knowledge that Berlin was now in possession of proof that he was operating under British control. He found no comfort in the knowledge that the proof was not yet recognizable for what it was. It would very rapidly become so when the German army landed in England. Apart from extorting money under false pretences, his signal had been innocuous enough, but it would become his death warrant as soon as Pemberton was interrogated.

For long minutes he indulged in thoughts of what might have been, remembering the summer of the year before when the vast *Luftwaffe* air fleets darkening the sky had signalled his imminent release from his under-cover existence. Then he had seen those fleets decimated by planes of RAF fighter Command, planes which appeared as if by magic where no planes should have been. He knew something of that magic now and had himself reported to Berlin the appearance of strange towers along the long stretch of the coast of southern England which he was required to keep under observation. Those structures, with electronic eyes which watched and gave warning, often as soon as the German aircraft lifted from their bases in France, had indefinitely postponed his escape from duplicity.

Thwarted in his ambition immediately to crush his country's traditional enemy, the *Führer* had turned east and struck at Russia. Knowing that his leader had done that not out of pique but because the Third Reich needed the Russian granaries and the Rumanian Ploesti oil region to feed the war machine, Lohengrin had still doubted the wisdom of the move. He had been happy enough to have his doubts dispelled when, after a brilliant, savage campaign, German mechanized divisions had destroyed a large part of the Russian Army and now stood before the gates of Moscow.

Admittedly, appalling winter weather had brought the *Wehrmacht* to a halt, but the coming of spring would see a Russian capitulation and then Britain would be faced with the impossible task of fighting against the reserves of nearly all of Europe and vast tracts of Asia.

Lohengrin's mind jumped back fifteen months to an urgent notice addressed to people in the south-east of England, a message he and, he guessed, his unknown colleagues had despatched to Germany. 'Temporary Transfer of Population', he remembered it had been headed, and it had gone on to say that to enable the Army to operate more effectively, all those whose duty did not require them to remain where they were should leave the area, taking with them their National Registration Identity Card, passport, ration book, gas mask, a rug or blanket, and food for twenty-four hours. London was to be avoided, as were the coastal regions of East Anglia, Kent and Sussex. Those who had no friends to go to elsewhere were to leave for Gloucestershire by trains specially provided for the purpose on specified dates in September 1940. He had supposed that huge camps had been set up to receive the evacuees in that county.

They had gone, the mothers with children, the aged and the infirm, the majority of them to return when the threat of that invasion had receded. Within a year, Lohengrin calculated, the threat would return and the fact with it. He supposed that they would run again then, the mothers, the children, the aged and the infirm. He supposed too that he would try to run with them, but doubted that there would be anywhere to hide.

*

Edward Mainwaring put Dressler's signal to Lohengrin down on the desk and looked at Clayton.

'Identical, isn't it, Peter?'

Clayton removed his glasses and began to polish them on his tie. 'Word for word,' he said, 'to Wotan, Tristan, Parsifal, Lorelei and Brunhild. They're Dressler's mob. Messages coming in from other *Abwehr* controllers are couched differently, but the content is . . .' For a moment he seemed at a loss for the right expression, then added, 'the same,' sighed contentedly and replaced his spectacles on his nose. Mainwaring smiled, wrote rapidly on the top of the signal and handed it across the desk.

'Do me a note to the PM, will you?'

Clayton glanced at the pencilled jottings. 'Preoccupation with food,' they read. 'Defensive posture? Attrition. U-boats. RAF. Min of Aircraft Prod'n. Home Forces to 8th Army.' He got to his feet, nodding, not asking what the jottings meant. He didn't need to ask. Exactly the same points had occurred to him.

Back in his own office he pulled a typewriter towards him, expertly inserted a piece of paper, then inexpertly poised his two forefingers above the keys. After a moment he began to stab at them.

'Enemy signal traffic to "his" agents in this country,' he wrote, 'shows a present preoccupation with food production, imports and storage locations to the exclusion of much else which has previously engaged his attention. It could be argued that this information is required to enable an invasion force to live off the land, but this is considered to be a non-starter because (a) Germany has never achieved parity, let alone superiority in the air since the Battle of Britain, (b) she is too heavily committed on the Russian front at this time and (c) the reports asked for cover the whole nation and the enemy would not risk the loss of inquisitive agents in areas where there is no possible point in attempting to invade.

'It is suggested that this Intelligence completes the strategic jig-saw puzzle to show positively that Germany is now resigned to a defensive posture and a war of attrition vis-à-vis UK and that the current investigation is to establish our ability or otherwise to withstand the U-boat blockade. Instructions to certain agents to run no risk of discovery seem to bear this out, the inference being that they may be of greater value prior to an armed assault on this country at some unspecified future date.

'If this argument is thought to be sound, the Ministry of Aircraft Production and the RAF may wish to give thought to increasing the output of bombers and long-range escorting fighters at the expense of home defence. Additionally, the release of troops and aircraft by Home Forces for service with 8th Army, or elsewhere in the Middle East theatre, becomes a practicable proposition.'

Reading through what he had typed Clayton wondered if it presented too sketchy a picture, then, remembering the Prime Minister's preference for reports and recommendations limited to one side of one page, decided that it did not. He reloaded his typewriter and tapped out an instruction to the officers controlling 'turned' agents that their replies to the questionnaires should indicate the food situation as being much worse than it was. To be misleading and to give 'Lord Haw-Haw' something else erroneous o sneer about was too good an opportunity to miss, particularly when it might provide further evidence of the strength of the chain linking MI5 and Admiral Canaris's *Abwehr* organization.

The astounding concept of two hostile Intelligence departments being in daily wireless communication with one another and only one of them being aware of the fact caused Clayton only mild surprise, but then he was a mild man not given to extravagant emotions.

*

In Berlin, relieved at the regaining of contact with *die Brücke*, Major Ernst Dressler sedulously hammered another nail into his own coffin by becoming expansive and taking Ulrike Ebernach to dinner at the latest of the fashionable nightclubs to spring up on the *Kurfürstendamm*. Its prices were high, Ulrike was not the companion he would have chosen to be seen with, but very senior officers and other people of influence frequented the place. To be seen there at all was eminently satisfying.

Chapter Twelve

There had been no pre-dawn knock on the door, no demand that he identify himself, no charge; just men debouching from a black car. It had drawn alongside him as he approached the Brandenburg Gate on his daily walk and they had grasped him by the arms, thrust him into the back of the car and down onto its floor. One of them had placed the heel of a boot on his neck to keep him there.

Apart from that, he had not been handled particularly roughly, even when they had stripped him, but already, in this terrible place they had brought him to, Dressier was screaming. The sounds burst from him in regular whoops which seemed to proclaim a monotony of agony as his testicles contracted under the freezing contact of the bar of ice they had made him straddle. At its first searing touch he had tried to rise, but his naked skin had frozen to it instantly, holding him where he was. Then the pain had come and grown like an expanding balloon, filling his universe.

When the balloon began to deflate as the intense cold applied its own anaesthetic, they struck him repeatedly over the kidneys with rubber truncheons. Nobody asked him anything. Nobody spoke at all. He felt his skin rip as his body toppled sideways and tore it from the bar.

He recovered consciousness lying on the stone floor, his groin, burning now, rejecting the comfort his hands sought to give it, as though their touch completed a high-voltage electric circuit. When the ability to focus returned to him he looked up at the four black-uniformed figures of the Gestapo agents standing in an arc in front of him, the three men he had never seen before, and Ulrike Ebernach, her eyes and mouth forming little circles of delight like a child's at a surprise party.

'For the love of God! What do you want of me?' His voice a panting whisper.

'God? Surely you can't be a Jew as well.' The shortest of the three men.

'Not a Jew. Not a Jew.' The same gasping speech.

'Oh good,' the man said. 'In that case you won't have any objection to telling us which Jews you have been using to change the pounds sterling you steal into Reichsmarks. Let me advise you to tell us quickly and to tell us the truth. Your little friend here was given the task of proving the existence of a link between your English transactions and your periodic bouts of extravagance. She found it remarkably easy to do so. You are a very stupid man, Ernst.'

His whole being a welter of despair, confusion and pain, Dressier lay seeking for words, finding some, but the order in which they should be spoken eluded him. He whimpered.

'Ulrike, I think he wants you to play with him. You know what he liked. Let's see if he still likes it.'

'*No!*'

'Then talk to us,' the man said, and Ulrike Ebernach drew back, pouting.

The words came then, breathily, as though forced out of him by the air that carried them. At first they made little sense, but he became repetitive until, slowly, a pattern emerged and they heard about the numbers underlined on a certain page of a certain telephone book in a certain kiosk. These indicated the amount of currency to be exchanged and the time and date for the transaction when two men would meet at a café and leave with each other's copy of the *Deutsche Allgemeine Zeitung* with the money inside its pages. No, he didn't know the other man's name or anything about him. Yes, he could describe him. Forty, medium height, stocky, thinning brown hair, blue eyes. They wouldn't have any trouble picking him up. Just mark the numbers in the phone book and keep the café under observation. Yes, of course there was a charge. The contact took fifty per cent, deducted before the meeting. Yes, he could tell them how he had heard of the criminal organization. It had been from a man accused of dealing in stolen army stores who had died under interrogation. No, he did not know if any of his fellow spy controllers were doing what he had done.

The men left, doubtful about his last two answers, then accepted them as the truth when Ulrike Ebernach joined them twenty minutes later to report that the prisoner, unconscious now, had not changed his story. She was no longer pouting and one of the men felt his flesh crawl at the sight of her contented expression.

Dressier was delirious for two days after Ulrike's ministrations before he came to himself in a prison hospital to find a young man in civilian clothes sitting beside his bed. He peered at him vacantly.

'Ah, Dressier,' the man said. 'Can you hear me?'

'Yes.'

'Good. There are some questions I want you to answer.'

'I told them everything. Everything.' A flat, dead voice.

'Oh, I'm not interested in your pecuniary peccadilloes,' the man replied. 'Beyond the fact, that is, that they led us to look deeper into your activities. My present preoccupation is with a Belgian courier who failed to survive a night in your company. I've formed the impression that he told you rather more than you mentioned in your report, which seems to confine itself to his claim to have been in the pay of British Military Intelligence.'

'He told me nothing more.'

'Well, that is strange,' the man said. 'The guard outside the interrogation room states that he could hear you repeatedly shouting "liar". That went on for a period of some hours. If he was simply denying your accusation that he was working for the English, and it took you all night to make him confess that he was, doesn't that cast a shadow of doubt on your findings? Most people would confess to anything after that time.'

'Perhaps, but that's all I got out of him.'

'What made you suspect him in the first place?'

Dressier tried to think about that, but the reawakening of pain which had been dormant opened a blurred window in his mind, letting in a shaft of memory so brilliant that it blocked his mental processes and drained his face of colour. The ice! The ice and Ulrike! Unbelievable spasms of agony interspersed by the distant sound of happy laughter! Sweat broke out on Dressler's forehead, formed into globules, hesitated, then ran down to lodge in his eyebrows, glistening there.

'My question seems to be causing you some concern,' the man said.

'What? What question?'

Patiently, the man repeated it. 'What made you suspect the Belgian in the first place?'

'Oh. I – I . . .'

'Yes?'

'I noticed – I noticed shiftiness in his manner. Yes, shiftiness. One develops an instinct for that sort of thing in my job.'

The man nodded. 'I'm sure one does, and I can't imagine anything shiftier than denying being an enemy agent after you had told him that that's what he was. Why, it's almost evasive. Indeed, I'd go further and say it's downright deceitful. Now, suppose you stop talking nonsense. All I have from you so far is that this unfortunate fellow was unable to meet your regard squarely, so you took him down to the basement and beat him to death. He must have been quite put out at that, having taken all the trouble to travel voluntarily to Berlin to see you. It would certainly have upset me if I'd been in his shoes.'

New terror took Dressier by the throat, immobilizing his vocal cords, then spread down his body to join the pain there. This exchange, in which he had played so small a part, was going all wrong. No, worse! It had already gone completely wrong, because the man had asked a question to which his lurching brain was incapable of formulating a logical answer. Bluster, then. Bluster! His organization carried prestige with it, prestige and power. He swallowed repeatedly to recover his ability to speak.

'Who the devil are you to cross-examine me? I'm a major in the *Abwehr*!'

'No you're not. You're a prisoner in a prison bed.'

The feeble defiance evaporated. 'Can't this wait? I'm unwell!'

'I'm afraid it can't wait. You have an appointment this evening. Still, as you appear to find it difficult to articulate, let me paint the picture for you. The Belgian came to you with urgent news, news that you did not want to hear, so you killed him. What, I asked myself, can that news have been?'

'That's not true,' Dressier said. 'That simply isn't . . .'

'Oh, but it is,' the man interrupted him. 'I clearly remember asking myself that very question and I also remember concluding that the answer lay close to the connection your Gestapo friends had already made between your misappropriation of funds requisitioned for operatives in England and your liking for the good life. Of course, they are very limited people and didn't know what they'd got hold of. It has long been my conviction that petty theft is about as far as their abilities stretch, so it was fortunate for the Reich that I was able to extend their researches to include the Belgian. Don't you agree?'

Dressier didn't speak, but as though he had done the man went on, 'I knew you would. No doubt you find it a little ironic that, but for your dedication to improving your standard of living, nobody would have given the Belgian a second thought.' He paused for a moment before adding sharply, 'Now tell me what he told you! Was it that some of your agents in England are no longer operational?'

'No,' Dressier whispered.

'Did you silence him so that you could continue to collect their pittance for yourself? Did you sell your country's Intelligence Service for the thirty pieces of silver the Christians talk about?'

'No!' The whisper more urgent now.

The sharpness had gone from the man's voice, and he sounded merely curious when he said, 'I suppose you're one of those masochists. If that's the case just tell me. Your mistress could be here in fifteen minutes to change your bandages for you. I gather she'd enjoy that.'

The silence was little more than measurably long before it was broken by Dressier saying, 'He told me that *der Eingang* was dead and that his *Stelle* is being run by the English as though he were still alive.'

He had spoken barely audibly, but the man heard the words, made a soft hissing sound and murmured, 'Thirty pieces of silver.' Then he moved a cupped hand up and down as if judging the weight of the metal.

'There was nothing more! Nothing at all! I swear it!'

The man stood up abruptly, looked down at the sweating face on the pillow and said, 'I believe you. I wouldn't want that ugly woman of yours touching any parts of me, public or private, either.' He took an envelope from his pocket, dropped it onto the blanket, and added, 'Your engagement for this evening I mentioned. Don't be late.'

Dressier watched him leave the small room, close the door, heard the key turn in the lock. His hands were shaking when he picked up the envelope, but he got it open eventually and withdrew a single page of thick paper. The print blurred continually on the quivering sheet and it took him a long time to register its full message. When finally he had done so he began to shout hysterically, but no nurses came running.

*

Almost at the precise moment when the blade of the guillotine severed ex-Major Ernst Dressler's head from his shoulders, simultaneous raids were carried out on the homes of employees of branches of the *Reichsbank*, the *Dresdener Bank* and the *Deutsche Kredit Gesellschaft*. It had taken the Gestapo forty hours to set up the rendezvous with the man who read numbers in telephone books, but almost no time at all to extract from him the information which enabled them to spread their net. A currency ring was broken.

The *Abwehr* came under close Gestapo scrutiny too, which led to angry exchanges between the two powerful organizations. The personal intervention of the *Führer* saw to it that the Gestapo prevailed and changes took place in that section of counter-espionage handling agents in the British Isles. Because it was in the nature of the Gestapo to over-react, the changes were more extensive than was logical, and stretched to include radio telegraphists in the *Rundfunk* building and other transmission centres.

In the higher echelons the colonel with two decadent beauties at his beck and call was amongst those who escaped suspicion, for it was he who had put the Gestapo onto Dressier in the first place.

*

Harry noticed it first.

'This ain't any of the blokes what usually sends to us, sir,' he said to Pemberton.

'Are you sure?'

''Course I'm sure, sir. Much better than them, this one is. Matelot, probably.'

Pemberton smiled at a pride of Service which could cross frontiers, but when the message had been decoded and Lohengrin said, 'This isn't Dressler's style,' he became thoughtful. Two hours later he was shown into Clayton's room in London.

*

It was on the day following the meeting between Clayton and Pemberton that the *Abwehr* colonel was summoned to the presence of the head of German Military Intelligence. His department in a shambles, its continuity disrupted, its English end suspect, he went with some trepidation.

''Morning, Frischauer,' Admiral Canaris said. 'How's that pretty wife of yours?'

The colonel relaxed. 'She's well, sir, thank you.'

'Good. Give her my regards. Now, what are we going to do about this bloody awful mess?'

Colonel Frischauer had thought of little else since the news about *der Eingang* had been relayed to him and the conclusion he had reached was as inescapable as it was risky.

'We'll have to put a man into England to confirm this tale about *der Eingang*, sir. Somebody who knows little or nothing about the extent of our organization there, to minimize the danger to us if the English take him alive. He'll have to be an extremely talented individual with a complete command of the language and . . .' Frischauer stopped talking, smiled ruefully, then went on, 'I beg your pardon, sir. You know better than I what he must and must not be. More to the point is the fact that I'm having difficulty in locating such a person.'

'I may be able to help you there,' the admiral told him, picked up a telephone and said, 'Bauer, I want to know the present whereabouts and occupation of *Freiherr* Wolfgang von Neustadt. Quick as you can, now.'

Quick as he was, it still took Bauer twenty-five minutes to obtain the information, then Frischauer heard his voice coming distinctly from the receiver held to the admiral's ear. 'Sir, the baron is currently a *Waffen SS Sturmbannführer*. His unit was last reported as being in action to the south-west of Moscow. Anything else, sir?'

'Yes,' the admiral replied. 'I want him in this room within forty-eight hours.'

Chapter Thirteen

'Sod it!' the man said, dropped a spanner into the snow and pointed a gloved finger at a tool box. 'Give me that something-or-other-millimetre one, Kurt. The one with the blue paint on the handle. That might fit.'

The soldier grinned, gave it to him and asked, 'Why don't you let me have a go, sir?' His voice was muffled by the cloth covering his mouth and nose, his shape unrecognizable under layers of non-regulation clothing.

'Because I don't want to deprive you of the golden opportunity of watching a mechanical genius at work. That's why.'

An artillery shell whimpered overhead and burst fifty metres away, dissipating its violence in a snow bank, bringing more snow down from the branches of trees. It filled the tool box and covered the damaged track of the Tiger tank the man was working on.

'Sod it!' the man said again. 'I'll say one thing for Ivan, he's an obstinate bastard. I thought we had knocked out that battery last night.' He began to scrape the fallen snow off the metal track.

'Which one of you is *Sturmbannführer* Neustadt?'

He paused momentarily at the sound of the unknown voice, then went on scraping snow when a sideways glance showed him that Kurt had spun round, Schmeisser automatic pointed at the stranger.

'That's me,' he said, 'but don't be formal. Just call me Baron.' He glanced up at another shapeless figure crouching on top of the tank's turret. 'What's all this, Hans? Aren't you supposed to be on sentry duty?'

'Sorry, sir. He came out of the wood just about where Heinrich had gone for a pee. I thought he *was* Heinrich.'

'I see. Well, if he isn't Heinrich I wonder who the sodding hell he is. Ask him, somebody.'

'*Geheime Staatspolizei*, Hofacker!' the stranger announced, and von Neustadt turned to look at him for the first time.

'Christ,' he said, 'if we need the Gestapo poncing around here we must be in a bad way. What do you want, Hofacker? If you've come to arrest Stalin he's about a hundred kilometres in that direction.' He waved his spanner vaguely towards the north and east, then resumed work on the tank track, adding, 'Just ask for the Kremlin.'

Another shell erupted, closer this time, and a tree fell tiredly over, filling the air with drifting snow.

'I'd move along if I were you, sonny,' von Neustadt told the man from the Gestapo. 'Ivan knows we're in this wood and, as I had occasion to remark a few moments ago, he's an obstinate bastard. Persistent too.'

'I have orders to take you to Berlin, *Sturmbannführer*!'

'Really? I have orders to take Moscow. I'll come with you as soon as I've done that. Now sod off. We're busy.'

'By force if necessary, *Sturmbannführer*!'

Without looking at Hofacker, 'Don't be ridiculous,' von Neustadt said. 'Lay one finger on me and my boys will nail your ears to a tree and leave you for Ivan to use for bayonet practice. Ah, that's better. I've shifted this sodding nut at last. Unscrew it while I start on the other one, Kurt.'

'The orders come from Admiral Canaris himself, *Sturmbannführer*!'

Slowly von Neustadt turned to face him again. 'Then why didn't you say so in the first place? Let me see them, and stop yelling at me. I'm not one of the *Führer*'s public meetings.'

He took the proffered paper and read it, conscious of Heinrich approaching, fumbling with his trousers.

'All right. How do we get there?'

'There's a *Fiesler-Storch* light aircraft waiting the other side of this wood. It'll take us to the nearest *Luftwaffe* field.'

There were eight tank silhouettes painted on the side of the Tiger's turret. Rising from his crouching position von

Neustadt patted them and murmured, 'Sorry, old girl. I'd meant to get you into double figures at least.' Then he looked round at his men.

'Can you silly sods get "Gerda" moving and rejoin the others without my help?'

They assured him they could. He nodded, undid the top buttons of the three coats he was wearing, lifted the ribbon supporting the *Ritterkreuz* over his head and handed it to Kurt.

'Here. Hang this inside. It really belongs to you people anyway.'

'It's not going to be the same without you, Baron,' Kurt told him and the others muttered their agreement.

'Sod it!' von Neustadt said and trudged into the wood with the man from the Gestapo at his heels.

*

'Hello, Uncle Willi.'

Admiral Canaris looked up from his desk at the big man, his eyes taking in the crumpled grease-stained uniform, the scarred boots and the week-old growth of beard on the tired, handsome face. He smiled.

'My God, you're a mess, boy.'

Turning his hands palms forward in a gesture of resignation, von Neustadt said, 'I know. Fifteen hours ago I was building a snowman in this wood near Moscow and some sod from the Gestapo arrived with your orders. My feet haven't touched the ground since.'

The admiral nodded. 'Yes, I had a phone message to say that they had to pull you out in the middle of a battle.'

Von Neustadt blinked. 'Battle? What battle? That was the day before. There wasn't an Ivan in sight.' He paused, then added, 'Oh, some local yokels did poop off a couple of shells in our general direction, but *battle*? Sodding Gestapo!'

Canaris smiled again.

'Sit down, boy. Cognac?'

'It's eight in the morning, uncle.'

'I'm aware of that.'

'Yes please, I am a bit shagged.'

'That's what I thought. What's the situation on the East Front?'

When ten seconds had gone by with no reply from von Neustadt, the admiral put down the brandy decanter and looked over his shoulder to find the other man staring pensively out of the window. Accepting the glass held out to him seemed to bring him back to himself.

'I don't think it's all that good, uncle.'

'Explain that.'

'Well, I'm not the General Staff, but as I see it we've lost momentum. Lost the initiative too. Brilliant campaign to start with, of course. Rolled them up like a carpet nearly all the way to Moscow. Then the winter stalled us. That's the official line anyway, and it's true to a large extent, but nobody seems prepared to admit that Ivan stalled us as well. His armies are smashed or scattered, useless as fighting formations. Everybody knows that except Ivan. He just keeps coming back for more; there's millions of him and the weather doesn't seem to bother him a lot. I think we've got a fight on our hands.'

Canaris watched him sipping his brandy. He didn't speak and after a moment von Neustadt went on, 'Remember how old fatty Goering was going to flatten the RAF last year, uncle? Ten days was all he needed, wasn't it? Sweep them from the skies was what he was going to do, but their sodding fighters kept right on chewing up our formations even when we knew they hadn't got any left. It's like that in Russia, only more so. Kill an Ivan and ten more crawl out of the woodwork.'

Von Neustadt sighed, drained his brandy glass and said, 'You'll have me arrested for defeatist talk if I keep on like that.'

'I think that was an unpleasantly accurate appreciation of the situation,' the admiral told him. 'Still, to business. How's your English?'

'As good as my German. Remember? Eton and Cambridge, no less.'

'Good. How would you like to take a trip to England?'

'Sod it!' von Neustadt said. 'I was afraid you might be going to ask me to do something silly.'

*

'Lohengrin's case officer noticed it first,' Edward Mainwaring said. 'Or, more accurately, his wireless operator did by identifying a previously unknown hand on a Morse transmission key. The case officer took note of that fact and subsequently found that the style of the decoded message was also unfamiliar. He decided that this was sufficiently interesting to travel up to London and tell Peter Clayton here about.'

He was sitting at the head of a long conference table with Clayton at his side. There were places for forty people in front of him, but only ten of them were filled. With the exception of Clayton, staring vacantly at the ceiling, all eyes were on him.

'We alerted all the other case officers,' the marquis went on, 'and eight of them have now reported similar changes in pattern. That is a large enough proportion to indicate that a major reorganization has taken place in Berlin. Just why that should have been undertaken we had no idea at all until today. Read out the relevant part of that signal to Parsifal, will you, Peter?'

'What? Oh yes, indeed,' Clayton said. He picked up a piece of paper and read, 'Regret inform you your sister Ilse killed in English terror raid on Stuttgart.' He put the page down and added, 'Quite clever. It doesn't require an acknowledgement, you see. Not, that is, unless you never had a sister called Ilse, or any sister at all for that matter.'

'Which applies in Parsifal's case?'

Clayton looked at the speaker seated across the table to his right and nodded. 'That's what I was endeavouring to imply. Parsifal has now transmitted a message denying his possession of a sibling of either sex and asking if the message is in a code he has no key to. I expect they will reply that the message was intended for someone else but, whether they do or not, I think we must assume that the deliberate mistake gambit has been employed to test Parsifal's bona fides, as it were. The question is, why?'

'Parsifal is one of the dead ones, isn't he?' the same man asked.

'Yes he is, Grant.'

'Then perhaps whoever is controlling his ghost has made a mistake.'

'Perhaps, but a study of all recent wireless traffic has failed to reveal one.'

'Well,' Grant said, 'we were very lucky to be able to spot the trap.'

His tone slightly pompous, 'Luck is not the word I would have chosen,' Clayton told him. 'We do our prep with great care. It may interest you to know that the carpet in the living room of the house in Osnabruck where Parsifal used to live has a rather objectionable brown and black zig-zag pattern, his dog was a dachshund called "Pretzel" and . . .'

Clayton stopped talking, gave a small self-deprecating smile and went on, 'I'm sorry. I don't carry these facts in my head, you know. They're all on file and I looked those up because, with two new members present, I thought some such point might be raised.'

Grant smiled back at him and said, 'Please don't apologize. I, for one, am impressed. Do we have that much background material on all "turned" agents?'

'Yes, with the exception of Lohengrin. He's our latest acquisition and, according to Professor Morris, still too emotionally disturbed to be interrogated under Pentothal, or any other way, without running the risk of further upsetting his balance and destroying his usefulness to us. We shall get around to him in due course.'

'Thank you, Clayton,' Grant said. 'I'm afraid I've taken us a long way from the point under discussion, the link between this German reorganization and their setting up a skittle for Parsifal to knock down. Have you a theory on that?'

Clayton glanced sideways at Mainwaring and returned contentedly to his survey of the ceiling when the marquis began to speak.

'None at all,' he began. 'But we must assume that the link exists and examine the possible consequences. As I see it, these are as follows. First, the receipt of additional trick questions. We shall do our utmost to deal with those in the most logical ways as they arise. For example, a show of indignation on the part of the recipient at being required to make unnecessary and potentially detectable transmissions could well be appropriate. Second, agents trained in sabotage may be instructed to blow something up, something verifiable by *Luftwaffe* aerial photography, something sufficient to arouse the interest of our national press. If such orders are issued we shall, of course, give the agents concerned every possible assistance.'

'You would actually go so far as to destroy some of our own installations?' Grant asked.

'Certainly we would.'

'Even at the risk of killing people?'

Mainwaring, his expression thoughtful, lowered his gaze to the table for a long moment, then looked back at the speaker.

'Even,' he said, 'with the *certainty* of killing people, although we should try to avoid that.' He paused then before adding, 'This isn't a very pleasant organization you have been invited to join, Grant. We believe that we have a war-winning weapon in our hands, but it's about as easy to hold as quicksilver. We cannot afford half-measures. If the enemy calls upon one of what he believes to be his agents to attempt to sabotage an aircraft factory, that attempt must be sufficiently effective to convince not only the Germans but our own press and most of our masters. In the very unfortunate event, from our point of view, of the agent being apprehended during his mission, his death would follow automatically and we wouldn't lift a finger to help him beyond ensuring that his execution was given due prominence in the press. Is that clear to you?'

'Absolutely.'

'You're not developing moral scruples?'

'None whatsoever,' Grant said. 'I'm glad to know precisely where we stand. It makes things simpler.'

As though there had been no digression, 'Third,' Mainwaring went on, 'we should be prepared for certain agents being summoned to Portugal for consultation with *Abwehr* contacts there. This procedure is obviously extremely dangerous, but the almost insurmountable difficulties connected with foreign travel in time of war permit us to pick our own time for the meetings without arousing suspicion. More often than not it is we who suggest them and have used them in the past as a confidence booster and as another method of handing over information. Such information is almost invariably genuine and, for the most part, capable of being rapidly checked, thus ensuring the return of the agent to these shores with a feather in his cap and his standing enhanced.'

Mainwaring paused for no longer than was necessary to indicate a change of topic before saying, 'The fourth possibility is that we may receive a visitor. I think, in Admiral Canaris's shoes, I'd put somebody into Britain if I had reason to suspect that anything was amiss with my organization. It's unlikely that any such infiltration will be attempted through a neutral country. Too much risk of exposure at immigration, without the sort of elaborate cover they can't afford to give themselves the time to contrive. So I suggest we assume a U-boat landing, or a parachute drop, and assume further that we shall have no prior knowledge of the person's arrival or, chance apart, be aware that we have a visitor at all until he or she attempts to make contact with any of the agents we control.'

He looked around the table then and said, 'I'm sure you gentlemen will forgive me if I enlarge on that a little for the benefit of Grant and Hutchinson by explaining that new enemy arrivals have normally been given the name and address of one resident agent as a contact. In the past the resident agent has also been forewarned of the newcomer's arrival which, for obvious reasons, has enabled us to provide a reception committee. It is, however, highly improbable that any forewarning will be available for the visit I am adumbrating now. Do I make myself clear?'

'If I understand you correctly,' Grant replied, 'we are faced with the possibility of a spot check being made on each and every one of the German agents in our hands.'

Mainwaring nodded. 'In essence, yes. I doubt they would entrust this hypothetical visitor with the identities of more than two in case he should fall into our hands, but as we have no way of knowing which two, it amounts to the same thing.'

'Parsifal for one?'

'I refuse to speculate,' Mainwaring said. 'We must take appropriate precautions for all of them.'

*

The shock of the body landing on his, jerking him out of sleep, was appalling. Squirming, he fought to regain his breath and his scattered wits, then lay very still when something sharp pricked him under the chin.

'Not one move, or this goes in all the way to your brain.' The German words carried a quiet venom.

Sweat breaking out on his face and under his arms, heart pounding, but air returning to his lungs.

'Who the devil are you?'

'*Abwehr*, and we'll speak in German.'

'What do you want from me?' Obediently speaking German.

'Answers. I may or may not permit you one lie, one mistake. Two and you're certainly dead.'

'Answers to what?'

'What's your name?'

'Lamprecht! Hans Lamprecht!'

'Place of birth?'

'Berlin! Konigin-Luise Strasse, 17!'

'What is written on the portico of the Reichstag?'

'"*Dem Deutschen Volke*"!'

'Where exactly is the *Führer*'s Reichskanzlei?'

'Wilhelmstrasse, 77!'

The questions followed no logical sequence. The replies were yelped. The man pinned to the bed tried to move his neck away from the probing knife.

'What's the name of Julius Streicher's newspaper?'

'*Der Stürmer!*'

'Your date of birth?'

'14 July 1915.'

'Where does Dr Goebbels live?'

'Near the Tiergarten!'

'Be precise! The Tiergarten's a big place!'

All the man on the bed could see of his questioner was a black shape silhouetted against a shaft of light coming through the partly open door of the room. The point of the knife pricked his neck again. He winced and the sweat came faster.

'You don't know, do you?'

'Yes – yes I do! Just north of Unter den Linden! Near the Adlon Hotel and the Propaganda Ministry!'

'What's your code name?'

'It's *der Eingang*!'

The knife left his throat and a knee lifted from his chest. The bedside lamp was switched on. The man on the bed raised himself on his elbows, shaking his head violently as though trying to dissipate a nightmare.

'You're a bit free with that knife of yours, aren't you?' he said in English. 'For a moment I thought all that was real.'

'That,' the other man told him, 'was the general idea. You'd better get dressed now. We leave for Hampshire in half an hour. Incidentally, you did well, Stafford. Just never forget one thing until this operation is over. You *are* Hans Lamprecht. You *are der Eingang*. Even if he *is* dead.'

*

In a labourer's cottage overlooking the Thames estuary in Kent, the plump, motherly woman in tweeds with the badge of the Women's Voluntary Services on her hat stopped pointing her gun at the elderly man sitting opposite her and put it away in her bag.

'Fair enough, Christopher,' she said. 'Fair enough. You'll get by.'

'I only wish I could second that vote of confidence,' he told her. 'Was that gun loaded?'

The woman blinked, took the automatic out of her handbag, looked at both ends, then handed it to him.

'I don't know. Where do you put the bullets in?'

'Dear God,' he said, ejected the magazine, worked the slide action twice, clicked the magazine back into place and returned the gun to her. 'It's empty, Maude.'

'Oh, that's nice. What aren't you confident about?'

He picked up a poker and began to prod at the innards of an ancient coke-burning stove. It crackled apathetically and emitted a cloud of evil-smelling smoke through its iron grille.

'Blasted contraption. If it goes out I'll never get it alight again, it's December and you say I may be here for weeks waiting for some Jerry who may never turn up.'

'There, there,' Maude said. 'You can always keep warm by working on your market garden. In fact you must, to get your hands roughened up and your nails chipped. You look as though you've come straight from the manicurist. Don't shave too often, either.'

'All right. Look, are you really sure the locals aren't going to notice that I'm not O'Hara?'

'Virtually certain. He was very unsociable, never had anything delivered and never went near the village. In fact the only time he ever left here was to go to Margate to make the daily letter drop on shipping movements that you'll be doing now.'

'Don't tell me again,' the man called Christopher said. 'Let me relish the thought. I spend all day staring at ships through these excellent Zeiss binoculars, multiply by two, divide by three, subtract the number I first thought of, put it all down in secret writing and stick the result to the back of the cistern in the third cubicle from the left in the public conveniences near the Catholic church. Couldn't I indent for a wireless set and buy myself a Boy Scout's diary with the Morse Code in it? Save me a lot of travelling back and forth in this nasty weather.'

She smiled fondly at him. 'No you couldn't, you silly old man. *Der Schlüssel* isn't a wireless agent. Just act as you've described it and make your reports fairly accurate. It's a pity about the accuracy. We had hoped to start some mild deception soon, but we must allay any more suspicion than we're already under until this panic is over. You understand that, don't you?'

He ignored the question, prodded the fire again, waved the resultant smoke away and muttered, '*Der Schlüssel*. The key. Now if I actually had one, I shouldn't have to part with a penny every time I go to that public lavatory. Where's *der* blasted *Schlüssel* now? Have you slit his jugular and rendered him down for soap?'

'Nothing so dramatic. We've put him in Maidstone jail until it's safe for him to come back here.'

'Good thinking. Tell me, Maude, how is my German?'

'I've heard better,' Maude said, 'but it's good enough for somebody who isn't supposed to have been in Germany since before the last war. That's your strong suit, you know. Now I must go before you talk any more nonsense.'

She rose, kissed him on the top of the head and walked out of the cottage, leaving the substitute for the spy the Service called Wotan to his own devices.

*

The after-image of Claire Helier's flashing smile of happiness seemed to Clayton to linger on the retinas of his eyes as he watched her swinging stride carry her towards the door of his room. He wondered if she might skip. The fact that she did not do so failed to cheer him, and when the door closed behind her he sat for almost a minute staring at it, then reached for the telephone.

'Please get me Lady Abigail Mainwaring,' he said.

*

Bubbling with excitement, longing to share it, the lipstick scrawl on the mirror she and Gail used as a message board in the house off Sloane Street made Claire frown in quick disappointment. 'Back about 9' it read, and nine o'clock was three hours away. She went up to the attic to tell Mr Hotchkiss all about it but, with the teddy bear continuing to look as cross as it always did, she soon tired of the game.

When the hours had dragged themselves away and another half hour had followed them, not even the sight of Gail Mainwaring looking as cross as Mr Hotchkiss could hold the words back.

'Oh, Gail darling! I was sent for by the dearest little fat man this afternoon and . . .'

She stopped talking when Gail snapped, 'I know! I've just had dinner with him. Sit down and *shut up*!'

Startled, Claire sat abruptly, as though she had been struck behind the knees, then watched her friend striding angrily about, disposing of hat, coat and gloves as if they were missiles and the chairs she threw them at targets. She wondered if she was going to be slapped again.

'Claire!'

'Yes, Gail. That's me,' Claire said miserably. 'And I've done something awful. Again.'

'You most certainly have! Your dear little fat man is somebody terribly senior in our organization. Who the top man is I have no idea, but I'd lay long odds that the man you made an utter fool of yourself in front of today is number two!'

'Why did I make a fool of myself, Gail?'

'God may know. I don't!'

'I meant "how".' Voice flat now in the knowledge that the evening had been spoiled.

Gail continued to scowl furiously for countable seconds, then, as though a switch had been turned off, the anger flowed out of her and she too sat down.

'All right,' she said. 'We won't have another scene like that one in the attic, but you had better listen to me very carefully indeed.' She hesitated and shook her head before going on, 'No, first you tell me what you think you have been ordered to do.'

Suddenly stubborn, 'I know what I've been ordered to do,' Claire told her. 'It isn't a question of thinking.'

'Well?'

'They're withdrawing Colonel Pemberton and his men from the house in Seaford because Frank may have a visitor from Germany who mustn't see them there. My job is to be with Frank as his temporary case officer. There won't be anything suspicious about that because I shall pretend to be his mistress.' Claire dropped her eyes when she added, 'Well, perhaps not pretend. Then I'm to watch him and take care of him and make sure he doesn't do anything foolish.' She looked up again.

'Is that all?'

'No, I'm to deliver the messages he receives to Colonel Pemberton at a boarding house in another part of the town and take back whatever is to be transmitted. That's about all, really.'

'Your cover?'

'I'm an Admiralty clerk again, spending my leave with Frank and, before you ask, I think all he does is work for the Ministry of Food and don't know anything at all about what he's really doing. I'm not that stupid!'

'My host at dinner will be delighted to hear it,' Gail said. 'He was so alarmed by, in his words, your girlish and starry-eyed reaction to resuming your liaison with an enemy agent that he almost took you off the case there and then. He told me that the only reason he decided to talk to me first was his awareness that you have far more influence over the man than anybody else and that to devise some other form of control in the time available would be impossible. Do you follow me so far?'

Ignoring the question, her voice resentful, 'Why couldn't he have told me all this himself? Why have you to do it?' Claire asked.

'I think he underestimates himself, but he claims not to be very good at understanding women, so he has left it up to me to decide if you are capable of continuing to exercise the influence he spoke of. That means in the national interest, not your own. The next few days or weeks are absolutely vital, Claire. Do you think you are up to it?'

'Yes, I do.' The answer came quickly, too quickly, Gail thought, and the resentment was still there.

'You two are very much in love, aren't you?'

The words, as much a statement as a query, had the intended effect and Claire's voice had softened when she replied, 'Yes, Gail. I think he was almost from the start. I knew for certain after they hurt him so badly.'

'Are you sure you aren't confusing compassion and love?'

'Yes, I'm sure. I did think about that, but I'm quite sure.'

'In that case I'm authorized to give you this,' Gail said. 'It could save him a much bigger hurt if things go wrong.'

Claire gazed wide-eyed at the small automatic resting on the palm of Gail's hand.

'What's that for?'

'For protecting yourself, for protecting Lohengrin or, and you'll know if it's necessary, for killing him with. You weren't taught to use one for fun.'

The gentle ticking of the French travelling clock on the mantelshelf sounded loud in the silence of the room, as though suddenly called upon to emphasize the passing of the seconds. Twenty of them had gone by before Claire stretched out her hand.

'So you've decided to let me carry on.'

'I think you made the decision for yourself when you accepted that gun,' Gail Mainwaring said.

*

Across the length and breadth of Britain the people working under the direction of Edward Mainwaring, Marquis of Trent, continued to take what he had described as appropriate precautions.

Chapter Fourteen

They had been told it over the telephone many hours before, but the news was so momentous that their eyes kept turning to the pile of newspapers on the corner of Edward Mainwaring's big desk. On top of the pile the issue of the *Daily Mail* for Monday, 8 December 1941, shouted at them:

JAPAN DECLARES WAR ON BRITAIN AND AMERICA

HEAVY BOMBING OF HONOLULU AND GUAM HUNDREDS DEAD

'I'm finding it difficult to concentrate,' Clayton said, picked the paper up and began to read what he had already read in different forms a dozen times. After a moment he added, 'I wish they wouldn't print things like that.'

'Bit difficult to keep it secret.'

Clayton looked confused, then his expression cleared. 'Oh, I meant this bit in the lead article where it says that people cheered as the Fleet steamed out. Out of Pearl Harbor that is. I wish it *had* steamed out and I wish the Americans could spell "harbour" properly.'

Knowing that Clayton rarely attempted levity unless he was distressed, Mainwaring didn't speak, and Clayton went on, 'This is going to make a big difference, you know.'

At that Mainwaring said, 'What's the matter with you, Peter? With another hundred and eighty million people on our side, of course it's going to make a big difference.'

'Apart from the difficulty I am experiencing in concentrating,' Clayton replied, 'I appear also to have lost any ability I may previously have had to make an intelligible remark. Please accept my apologies, Edward. My inadequately voiced thought was that this development is going to have a direct bearing on this organization of ours and on all our Intelligence Services. It cannot fail to do so because, having no conception of Intelligence work themselves, the Americans will have to rely entirely on us. I see that as becoming an intolerable burden and a very grave security risk.'

Smiling, 'You appear to have recovered your powers of speech,' Mainwaring told him, but the words served only to make Clayton frown and set in motion his spectacle polishing process. When he had completed it he continued.

'They are not a naïve people and that makes it doubly difficult for me to understand their total neglect of one of the most essential weapons in the military armoury. For them to have done so on the grounds that it is un-American is puerile beyond belief and I can only thank God that we have never been afflicted with such short-sightedness.'

Still smiling, 'Admiral of the Fleet Sir Arthur Wilson,' Mainwaring said.

'Eh? Who's he?'

'He's dead, Peter.'

'What are you talking about, Edward?'

'I'm talking,' Mainwaring said, 'about the fact that at the turn of this century we were falling behind in the development of the submarine because Admiral Wilson maintained that it was "underhand, unfair and damned un-English". How does that square with your conception of the excellence of British vision?'

'I must confess that it does not.'

'We all have our blind spots.'

'So it seems. Well, let us hope, in this instance, that the Americans will listen to us and learn.'

'They are already doing just that,' Mainwaring said. 'Some are already here to study our methods. You must have come across them. There'll be a flood of them now and they're very fast on the uptake.'

Clayton nodded, but failed to look convinced.

*

'This should bring the war to a satisfactorily rapid conclusion,' Colonel Frischauer said.

Von Neustadt nodded. 'Inevitably. I shall assassinate Churchill as soon as possible after my arrival, then occupy Bognor Regis. That'll bring the English to their knees.'

'Bognor Regis?'

'Yes, it's a small seaside town on the south coast. King Edward VII, or it may have been George V, was always being dragged down there on holiday. He hated it. In fact I'm told that his dying words were "Bugger Bognor".'

'I was talking about the Japanese declaration of war on Britain and America, *Sturmbannführer*.'

Without looking up from the forged British documents he was examining, 'I wish you'd stop calling me that,' von Neustadt said. 'My inability to spell it has automatically blocked my promotion to *obersturmbannführer* and I dislike being reminded of that. Oh, and don't bother me with trifles about the Japanese. I had enough trouble with the Ivans and now I've got the English to contend with.'

'You're incorrigible, Baron.'

'It runs in the family, and my name's Wolfgang. Were you able to fix that practice parachute drop for me tomorrow?'

'Yes, all arranged. You take off from Gatow at oh-eight-hundred hours and jump over open country somewhere to the east of the city. There'll be a car to bring you back. The *Luftwaffe* has the details for that and for a night drop later.'

'Hmm. Look, if you were me, of the two chaps you've given me, would you visit the suspect *der Eingang* first and risk walking into a trap, or would you start off with *die Brücke* and possibly prove nothing?'

'If I were you I wouldn't go in the first place, Wolfgang. You'll have to make your own decision on the basis of what you find when you get there. It's your neck.'

'You're so right, sod it,' von Neustadt said. 'Let's go and have a drink.'

*

With his country pitchforked into war, a lot more people were suddenly prepared to talk with General William Donovan despite the suspicion with which his responsibilities as coordinator of Intelligence information were regarded. That fact helped him greatly in his preparation of a memorandum for the eyes of the President of the United States, a memorandum which had brought him a summons to the White House.

'Sit down, Bill.'

'Thank you, Mr President.'

The president nodded dismissal at his aide and waited until the door closed before saying, 'This makes for depressing reading. Tell me frankly where we stand in the league table.'

Donovan glanced down at the document he had prepared on which the president's fingers were playing a gentle tattoo.

'We aren't even in the ball park, Mr President. Leaving aside the FBI's counter-espionage role, it's barely an exaggeration to say that we haven't had anything resembling a professional espionage agent since Nathan Hale in the Revolutionary War, and look what happened to him. We've relied on embassy reports, travelling businessmen, newspaper correspondents and suchlike. No agents in place, no radio intercepts, no nothing. Compared to the Krauts and the Nips we don't know we're born yet. Both of them have established widespread sophisticated nets and have used them to considerable effect, as we now know to our cost.'

'And the British?'

'I hate to say it, but I also thank God for it, they're the masters, Mr President.'

Roosevelt nodded again. 'So I understand. There used to be a saying that the world was run by the White House, 10 Downing Street, the Vatican and the British Secret Service.' He paused, then added, 'I'm still trying to forget that the British sent us a warning of the likelihood of an attack on Pearl Harbor which some idiot filed behind the office radiator. It was ignored, just as we ignored the evidence of our own radar sets on Hawaii. You probably know that they detected the first strike of Jap planes way out to sea and persuaded themselves they had a malfunction in their equipment. Well, that's water over the dam. Blood-stained water. We must never again permit loss of American blood by neglect. Tell me more about this organization you're proposing.'

'It's going to cost us, Mr President.'

'Let me worry about the funding.'

'Yes, sir. First, I see it as an autonomous government agency answerable to your office, capable of acting independently of the military, the FBI or any other body, for operational and security reasons.'

'But staffed by military personnel?'

'No way, Mr President. I don't rule them out, but my aim would be suitability of the individual. The Limey pattern makes good sense. There's nothing military about MI5 or MI6. The initials are misleading and the numbers used to be those of rooms in some building. They recruit from the universities, the law, big business, medicine, any darned place where they can find brains, and the word "amateur" doesn't signify with them. It's the grey matter they look for. I'd like to do the same.'

'Do it. What contacts do you have with them? The British, I mean.'

'William Stephenson, for one. As it happens he's a Canadian, but he heads that British outfit in the Rockefeller Center, New York City. Its front is "British Passport Control". Maybe they have a clerk or two dealing with passports but basically it's an MI6 set-up handling disinformation and propaganda. Quite a bit of that goes out over some of our own radio stations, courtesy of financial contributions from the British government. Then – Sir, you maybe know all this.'

'Stephenson's the guy who gave us the map showing how the Nazis figure on rearranging South America,' Roosevelt said. 'That much I certainly remember, but keep talking. I'd like to know what else he's done.'

'He's done a lot, sir. His people came up with a load of embarrassing information and passed it to us in the hope that we might do something about it. It was political dynamite, particularly in the mid-west and California. Not the kind of news we wanted to hear.'

Donovan paused, noted the look of patient impatience on the president's face, chided himself for imagining that political embarrassment any longer meant anything to this man, and hurried on.

'Mr President, they claimed that German money was being channelled through the Italian and Vichy French embassies to the "America First" movement and the "Moral Rearmament" organization for purposes of sabotage and the creation of industrial unrest in armament factories producing weapons for Great Britain. When we expressed doubts they handed us the proof, chapter and verse.' He thought he heard Roosevelt murmur 'Damned Republicans' then, but wasn't certain because he was already saying, 'Then they have this team on Bermuda, sir, intercepting transatlantic mail, including our own. Some of it they just copy, some they tinker with. I think they're engaged in phone tapping and other forms of surveillance in this country too, plus espionage, military, industrial and counter. Support reaches them from London through Canada and their agents have spread all over, like from the 49th parallel to Tierra del Fuego.'

'You've been busy, Bill,' Roosevelt said.

'I haven't needed to bust a gut, Mr President. Stephenson handed most of it to me on a plate. I just had to add the relish. He's been – well, I guess plain helpful is the word.'

'Continue to cultivate him. Learn everything he's prepared to tell you about systems and techniques. Now, how about the London end?'

'We have men attached to various agencies there, sir. They're treated well, even helpfully, but I wouldn't say they were taken seriously. Mr President, they're too polite to say so, but I truly believe the British think we're quaint and, goddammit, in this particular regard they're right.'

Roosevelt smiled, the movement of the facial muscles forcing his long jaw forward until his cigarette holder was almost vertical. He took the holder from between his teeth.

'Polite, eh? "Cock the gun that is not loaded, boil the frozen dynamite, but, oh, beware my country when my country grows polite." Rudyard Kipling wrote that about England and it was an acute observation, but I guess the last thing we need out of them right now is a courteous kick in the teeth. Leave Whitehall to me for a while and you concentrate on getting this show on the road here. If you run into opposition you can't handle you'll find my door's open. My mind too.'

'Thank you, Mr President,' Donovan said for the second time.

Donovan's car was half way along Pennsylvania Avenue before Roosevelt took his eyes from the doorway through which the general had left and looked down at the folder in front of him. 'To the President of the United States of America. Proposal for establishing an agency to be known as the Office of Strategic Services,' the label gummed to the cover read, but his mind did not register the words. It was occupied by the picture of the map of South America he had spoken of, a map which changed the face of a continent and which if put into effect would have placed *Luftwaffe* bombers within range of the southern United States. Argentina and Chile had doubled in size, swallowing their smaller neighbours, Brazil remained, but, as a sop to the defeated French, France was to acquire both British and Dutch Guiana. Finally, Ecuador, Colombia, Venezuela and, with stunning emphasis of German intent, as if emphasis were needed, Panama also were to be given to Spain. *Neuspanien*, the legend had proclaimed in bold lettering across the entire north-west corner of South America.

For that offering, Roosevelt had assumed, the quid pro quo of opening his country to the free passage of German armed forces for an assault on Gibraltar would have been required of the Spanish dictator Franco. The president had wondered if that would have been given and had concluded that it was unlikely. Both the Spanish and the Portuguese had been impressed and disturbed by the near contempt with which the British General Wavell had treated their fellow Latins in destroying the Italian armies in North Africa. That had not augured well for conflict with the United Kingdom, its Commonwealth and Empire.

The map had augured even less well for the United States, and Roosevelt recalled his almost instant decision to use it as a tool against his country's Neutrality Acts. The tool had been effective and within days of his broadcast revelation of the map's existence the previous autumn, first the Senate and then the House of Representatives had repealed the Neutrality Acts in the face of outraged American public opinion. Without a declaration, and before ever the Japanese had launched their assault in the Pacific, America had gone to war with Nazi Germany.

Relaxed in his wheelchair, Roosevelt thought again of his doubts about the map. The British claimed to have stolen it from a German agent and Donovan and other experts believed them. Roosevelt, keeping his own counsel, remained unconvinced that it was not a British forgery, and a man called Edward Mainwaring could have told him that his suspicions were well founded; that it was indeed forged. The fact that he had never heard of Edward Mainwaring made no difference. The ruse, if such it had been, had worked, and while the possibility existed that the British Secret Service had achieved such a coup in covert grand strategy, it was obviously necessary to maintain the closest contact with that organization.

President Roosevelt leaned forward and picked up a telephone. 'Please find out if it would be convenient for Prime Minister Churchill to talk with me today,' he said.

Chapter Fifteen

The chalk cliffs to her left and the port of Newhaven to her right were hidden from Claire Helier by the moisture-laden wind driving from east to west along the English Channel. In front of her the grey-brown sea churned in angry confusion about the rusty barbed-wire entanglements as though uncertain whether to obey the dictates of the tide-race or the growing storm. Occasionally a more directional wave struck one of the breakwaters and threw parts of itself petulantly skyward like dirty white arms flung up in exasperation. It was very cold.

Blonde hair plastered across her face, toes working inside sodden shoes, Claire hugged herself beneath her cloak. It was a lovely, lovely day and the dull little town of Seaford at her back was the most exciting place on earth.

She had been shopping. Really shopping. Not just ordering things at Harrods, or in Bond Street, or at her dressmaker, but going from small shop to small shop to find one that had things left on its shelves, things that she and Frank could eat together after she had cooked them. Not that she was much good at cooking, but he didn't mind about that at all. It had been such fun, the shopping and pretending to be a real wife. Dealing with 'points' and ration books had been confusing as all that had always been done for her, but it hadn't mattered. The shopkeepers and the people in the queues had helped her and smiled at her because she was pretty and so obviously happy too.

At the last stop the little old woman who owned it had covered the purchases in her basket with a sheet of greaseproof paper to keep them dry, so she hadn't had to worry about them and could walk the long way home by the sea to give Frank more time to sleep. He had been up half the night waiting for wireless conditions to improve so that he could transmit a signal Colonel Pemberton had authorized him to send to Berlin about troop movements. Now he was resting, and she didn't want to go home quite yet because ever since the arrival of a visitor from Germany had become a possibility he had taken to waking instantly at the slightest sound within the house.

A group of soldiers came marching down Southdown Road in double file, then followed the track bordering the golf course towards Hawks Brow where she stood, passing the Club House and the signs with a painted skull on them and the words 'Danger! Mines! Keep Out!' Behind the men a corporal barked, 'Lep! Right! Lep!' in metronomic monotony like an excited sheepdog.

They were almost abreast of her when the chant ceased and he shouted, 'Platoon, you lucky lads! Eyes right!'

Grinning faces snapped in her direction and the corporal saluted.

''Morning, Miss!'

Claire laughed happily, returning the salute as though she were an officer, until she was looking at their retreating backs. The lovely day had even given her own parade.

Five to twelve, her watch said. She could go home now, change her clothes, wake him and they could have a drink together at the 'Angry Saxon' before lunch. Stooping, she lifted her handbag from its resting place on top of the shopping basket and the weight of it swung it against her leg.

Suddenly the day wasn't lovely any more. It was just driving rain and the tortured sea. And the weight of the gun.

*

Lohengrin twisted and turned on the rumpled bed, not sleeping. Sleep, never easy to come by since his arrest, had become increasingly elusive after he had been told of the interrogation he might have to undergo at the hands of some individual connected with German Intelligence. They had done what they could to prepare him for that, to the extent of staging a dress rehearsal, when a large aggressive man had questioned him, threatened him and accused him of treachery, all in faultless German and at knife-point. It had been an unnerving experience both physically, with a hand dragging his head back by the hair and a knife probing at his throat, and mentally, because of the confusion in his mind about which loyalty he was supposed to be declaring.

That experience had alerted him to one of a number of variations of what might occur, but did nothing to ease the agony of anticipation. Deep inside him foreboding had blended with his ever-present crippling shame, to fester and spread outwards to his nerve ends. For Lohengrin tranquillity had become a virtually unobtainable state.

He did approach it at times, at least closely enough to drift into the shallows of sleep, but those times were dependent now on Claire's presence beside him, on her loving, her touch and the sound of her heartbeat when she held his head to her breasts. Deeply grateful as he was for the relaxation of stress she could induce in him, his dependency only served to make him feel more ashamed because it reduced him or her, he wasn't clear which, to the status of the ridiculous teddy bear they had allowed her to bring with her from Holloway Women's Prison to share their mutual incarceration.

It was, he conceded, an absurdly idyllic confinement, despite the heavy irony of each prisoner's continued existence hanging by the thread of the other's good behaviour, but, pettishly, he felt it would have been better still without the bear. He scowled at it, squatting above him on the chest of drawers. In the dim daylight filtering through the closed curtains he couldn't see its grumpy expression, but the black of Claire's nightdress draped over its shoulders stood out against the pale wallpaper. She hadn't taken the flimsy garment from him, but had said that it was in Mr Hotchkiss's charge as long as she was there. Mr Hotchkiss! Of all the stupid names for a toy!

Had he known that its presence had been decreed by Professor Morris, the person he most hated, to ignite in him a small flame of jealousy at Claire's apparent need of it, he would have acknowledged a subtle, if minor, touch. He didn't know that, or recognize the thing as a beneficial outlet for some of his tensions.

At the sound of a key in the lock Lohengrin stiffened and cast the bedclothes aside, then relaxed, smiling, when Claire's 'It's only me, darling,' reached him from downstairs.

*

''Evening, gentlemen,' the landlord of the 'Anglo-Saxon Arms' said. 'What'll it be?'

Pemberton and Carne ordered beer.

'I've got some gin, if you'd like it.' The two officers were regulars now, so he could afford to offer them something from under the counter.

'No, beer's fine, thanks.'

Holding a pint glass beneath the tap with one hand and drawing back the pump handle with the other, 'The locals tell me you've left Mr Pelham's house, Colonel,' Brent said. 'You been quarrelling with him about who has which bit of land?'

It was a question Pemberton had hoped would be asked. It was more convincing that way than if he had raised the topic himself, but he managed a look of mild annoyance when he replied, 'As your customers are so damned observant they may have noticed the reappearance in this town of a stunning blonde girl. Mr Pelham thought it would be rather nice if we went somewhere else while she was on leave. You shouldn't have too much trouble making the connection.'

'Ah. Getting married, are they?'

The query disturbed Pemberton, bringing to the surface a nagging worry he had kept mainly submerged over recent days. He had grown to like Lohengrin, to pity him for what he knew he must be suffering, to admire him for the way he carried a cross of almost insupportable weight. But he had found Claire's attraction for him increasing as well, to the extent that he experienced anxiety as well as disappointment when she failed to appear at his boarding house with one of Lohengrin's incoming signals. The fact that this meant only that no signal had been received reduced neither his concern nor his discontent. But it was not until he began to see through the veneer of sophistication to the child beneath that he realized that he was falling in love with Claire Helier, that the substance was so much more endearing than the shadow, that he was jealous. For all those things, as though the man were a wizard, he blamed Professor Morris.

'You'd better ask Mr Pelham about that,' he said, and that set him wondering if marriage *would* be possible for them. The obvious answer that almost anything was possible, if the Service deemed it necessary, depressed him profoundly.

The taciturn Carne watched Pemberton's prolonged absorption and read him like an open book. He thought that his superior officer and Miss Helier would make a handsome couple once the German was out of the way.

*

As the Germans meant them to do, RAF night-fighters scrambled from airfields in the south of England to intercept a number of enemy probes which radar had detected. Locating, attacking and repulsing assorted groups of Ju88s and Me110s took time and nobody paid any attention to a solitary plane crossing the coast to the east of Selsey Bill. Ten miles inland and two thousand feet above the South Downs, *Sturmbannführer* Wolfgang von Neustadt fell out of it into the night.

The biting cold of the slipstream snatched at his face and clothing, producing the now familiar momentary disorientation. He felt his cheeks vibrating and snapped his mouth shut to exclude the man-made gale. Then came the very welcome violent jerk of his harness which told him that his parachute had opened and he was swaying in still air with only the receding drone of the plane for company. There was no sensation of dropping. 'So far, so good, as the man said when he stepped over the edge of the cliff,' he announced to the darkness and began dragging at the cords above him in an attempt to stop the swing. Slowly the pendulum motion of his body eased, he sighted the ground for the first time and the impression of speed returned as England rushed up to meet him.

The pilot had promised him open country and had kept that promise. Von Neustadt landed heavily on grass and patchy snow, bending his knees and rolling forward, as he had been taught to do. A gust of wind caught the deflating canopy of the parachute, filling it again, dragging him along the ground until he remembered to hit the release catch at his waist and the movement ceased. Apart from an ache in his ankles he seemed to be unhurt and he began at once to fumble with the fastenings of the long tubular canvas bag which had been suspended from his left leg. It came open eventually and he unpacked it, arranging its contents on the parachute. He stiffened when somewhere behind him a dog set up a desultory barking, then, as though some private duty had been accomplished, it fell silent and there was only the intermittent hiss of the breeze. Relaxing slightly, but still wishing that he was back with his tank squadron on the East Front, von Neustadt stripped off his flying suit.

Within less than three minutes, a heavy overcoat covering his civilian clothes, a flat cloth cap on his head, he began to distribute the remainder of the bag's contents about his person, trying to avoid over-filling any pocket. The clothes would withstand the closest inspection. They bore Savile Row labels which he knew to be genuine because he had bought them there himself before the war. His papers were proof against all but the most expert of scrutinies. It was the other things he was carrying that worried him. In wartime England it would be difficult to explain the possession of concentrated foods, let alone a *Luger* pistol. He was pleased to have thought the word 'difficult' as it demonstrated the ease with which he had slipped back into the British habit of understatement. That could be important if he was to survive the eight days separating him from the rendezvous with the U-boat which would take him home.

Where did one put a clean shirt without reducing it to a crumpled wreck? Shrugging, he double-folded it and stuffed it into the breast pocket of his overcoat. Spare socks and underwear presented a lesser problem. His disposal of articles completed, he put his flying suit and the parachute into the canvas bag, picked it up, turned his back on the pole star and walked south. The dog began barking again.

Dawn found von Neustadt at the junction of two country lanes, peering at the pointing fingers of a signpost. The paint was peeling from them and it was difficult to decipher their message in the early light, but he was grateful for any sign as most, he had been told, had been removed. 'East Dean, West Dean, Singleton', one read, and the other, 'Chichester'. Distances were not recorded. Two miles from where he stood, his canvas bag, weighted by pieces of flint, lay at the bottom of a reed-clogged pond. He had nearly fallen into it in the darkness, cursed it, then blessed it as the perfect hiding-place for objects which could betray him. Without its bulk he could move more easily too, but was not yet ready to go further until he knew with greater certainty where he was. There were gaps in the hedge at the roadside and he forced his way through one of them to wait in a field until day came.

Except for the birds there was no sound and no movement until the morning's aerial activity began with the drone of high-flying fighter aircraft, their condensation trails tinted pink by a sun he could not yet see. It was his first sight of the English as an enemy and although the planes represented no menace to him, he yawned in nervous reaction. Then the cows came down the lane, a more immediate enemy because they were accompanied by a small boy calling, 'Hiyup, Bess!' and repeatedly whacking the rear animal across the rump. Bess didn't seem to mind but, von Neustadt thought, it was rather unjust that she should be made to suffer for the ambling progress of the whole herd. He recognized the mental levity as a symptom of his own anxiety and stayed very still as the creatures passed almost within touching distance, their breath forming white plumes on the cold air, his eyes never leaving their escort. Small boys were observant and inquisitive. Small boys were dangerous. Imagination had this one asking, 'Why're you hiding behind that hedge, mister?' but all the child said was 'Hiyup, Bess!'

It was full daylight by the time he was alone again and he took a handkerchief from his pocket, spread it on the ground, urinated on it, then watched a map released by the acid come into being like a developing film. There was no mention of the first three signposted names on the map, but Chichester was clearly marked, as was the line of the South Downs, and with those rolling hills already behind him he knew that the drop had been a good one, that Chichester and the public transport it would provide were not more than ten miles away.

He had covered one of those miles, striding openly along the lane now, swinging a walking stick he had cut from the hedge, when he met the policeman, an elderly stout figure breathing heavily from the exertion of pushing his bicycle up the slope to the corner von Neustadt had just rounded.

'Merry Christmas, sir!'

'A merry Christmas to you too, constable.'

'Thank you, sir. Cold one, ain't it?'

Von Neustadt agreed that it was a cold one and strode on, shaken by the harmless encounter, furious with himself for having forgotten a date and a greeting which was as good as a password for the next fifteen hours.

*

Across the Hampshire border near the town of Emsworth to the west of Chichester, the man called Stafford had forgotten about Christmas too. As he had been doing for days, he continued to act the part of a German agent, persuading himself that he *was* Hans Lamprecht, that he *was der Eingang*, deceased as that person might be, just as he had been told to do. He neither huddled in his bungalow, nor travelled far afield, but limited his journeys to vantage points from which he could overlook Portsmouth Harbour and the warships it contained. That, at least, would be expected of him. Above all he never stopped looking, and it was on Boxing Day that he saw the same man three times at three different locations.

'Probable contact,' he said into the telephone that evening. 'If he passes this dump once more I'll be virtually certain. Big handsome chap, very well dressed, except that his shoes are badly scuffed. He looks so like English gentry that he has to be something else. What? Yes of course I'm serious. You know the Germans. They get every item right, then add the sum up wrong. He's over-dressed for these times by about two years. In addition, he seems interested in me and I don't think it's lust. Keep your fingers crossed.'

The man did not pass the bungalow again, but shortly before midnight he walked openly up the garden path and knocked on the door. Stafford did nothing until the knock was repeated, then he shouted, 'All right! All right!' opened the bedroom window he had been watching through and asked, 'What the hell do you want?'

'Police, sir. I have some questions for you. Would you be good enough to let me in?' English perfect, educated, upper class.

'Can't it wait? It's the middle of the bloody night!'

'I'm afraid not, sir.'

Muttering angrily to himself Stafford closed the window, patted the Webley .38 revolver in his dressing-gown pocket and crossed the sitting room to let the man in. When he had done so he shut the door, drew the black-out curtain across it and switched on the light.

'Well?'

'I'm Inspector Arnold of Special Branch,' von Neustadt said.

'How nice for you. No doubt you have a card to support that claim.'

Von Neustadt nodded, reached inside his coat and Stafford found himself staring at the barrel of a *Luger* automatic.

'Sit down over there, Mr Lambert.'

Stafford looked at the chair, back at the gun, then did as he was told before saying, 'What the blazes is all this?' He felt nervous, very nervous, so it wasn't difficult for him to let the emotion sound in his voice.

'I have reason to believe,' von Neustadt told him, 'that your name is not Lambert, but Lamprecht, Hans Lamprecht, and that you are an enemy alien, spying for the Germans.'

'You must be out of your tiny little pointed skull!'

As though the other had not spoken von Neustadt went on, 'And for your sake I very much hope that I'm right. If I'm not, you're going to be awfully dead within the next few seconds.' He extended his arm until the gun was almost touching Stafford's forehead.

'Put that damn thing away,' Stafford said. 'Of course I'm Hans Lamprecht and I don't much relish the thought of having my head blown off by some bastard from the Gestapo. Put it away!'

The gun didn't waver.

'What makes you think I'm German? Answer in that language.' Stafford did so.

'Firstly, you've just told me so yourself. Nobody in this country knows me, or has ever known me, as Hans Lamprecht. Secondly, the English Special Branch don't carry *Lugers* and would never send only one man to arrest a spy. There's only one of you. I've been watching you all day. Thirdly, your clothes. They're too good for wartime Britain. You'd better mess them up a bit before you call on whoever's next on your list. Fourthly, I've been expecting you.'

'Expecting me?'

'You, or somebody like you. A few weeks ago there were changes amongst the telegraphists at home. I know that because I'm good at Morse and can tell one man's transmissions from another's. That didn't mean much until I realized that the contents of the messages were not in Major Dressler's style. Putting the two things together I concluded that there had been some sort of palace revolution inside the *Abwehr* and wondered why.' Stafford shrugged, then went on, 'Trouble over this side was one distinct possibility and the only way that could be checked would be by sending someone across.'

Still the gun didn't move.

'Describe Major Dressier.'

'Porcine.'

The brevity of the description and its accuracy made von Neustadt smile faintly. He had never met the major, but had heard him and his habits described by Colonel Frischauer.

'Dead pork now,' he said. 'It was he who believed you were dead yourself and your *Stelle* under British control.'

'Reports of my death are both premature and vastly exaggerated,' Stafford told him. He felt rather silly saying that. It wasn't even original, but it was the sort of joke an anxious man might make.

'Who was Dressler's immediate superior?'

'Colonel Frischauer.'

'Describe him.'

'I can't. I've never met him, but he has a glamorous wife and secretary. Dressier told me that when we met in Lisbon last year. I think he lusted after them.'

That seemed satisfactory enough, von Neustadt thought. Dressler's name, rank, appearance, sexual appetites and the Lisbon meeting. Frischauer's name, rank, wife and secretary. They were definitely not details the British could know about. He lowered the *Luger* slowly and Stafford was thankful for that. The information he had gleaned from the file on the dead Lamprecht, the dead *der Eingang*, the dead Parsifal, as well as from those on others still alive, was sketchy on that section of the *Abwehr* hierarchy.

Von Neustadt looked thoughtfully down at the automatic resting against his leg, then put it away inside his coat. 'Incidentally, I'm nothing to do with the sodding Gestapo,' he said.

'I believe you,' Stafford replied. 'You're either British, or a bumbling amateur, or both. Take that gun out again, using the forefinger and thumb of your left hand, and drop it on the sofa. I recommend that you do it very carefully.'

In his turn von Neustadt found himself facing a gun barrel and, also in his turn, did as he was told.

'Flat on your back on the floor and put your hands behind your head!'

His eyes moving from the Webley .38 revolver in Stafford's right hand to the *Luger* in his left, von Neustadt lowered himself to the carpet. Then the catechism began, the questions much the same as those that Stafford had had put to him by the man with the knife. All von Neustadt's answers were correct, except that he could not remember what was carved on the portico of the burnt-out shell of the Reichstag.

'"*Dem Deutschen Volke*",' Stafford told him. 'Here, catch.'

Von Neustadt removed his hands from behind his head in time to field the *Luger* lobbed towards him. He put it on the floor beside him, sat up and crossed his forearms on his knees. His expression was simultaneously rueful and enquiring.

'You're not very good at this game, are you?' Stafford said.

'No, I'm not, sod it!'

'Ah well. You're obviously German. I suppose they picked you for your command of English, gave you a book on how to operate in enemy territory in ten easy lessons, told you next to nothing in case you were captured and put you ashore from a U-boat.'

'Something like that. I'm really a . . .'

'Shut up!' Stafford said sharply. 'I don't want to know what you are, or who you are! Don't you understand anything? They could pick me up tomorrow! Then where would you be?'

'You're right, of course. Could I possibly spend the night here?'

'You *must* spend the night here. Go wandering about at this hour near a major naval base and they'll pick you up at once. You can have the bed. From the look of you you could use it. I'll work on that suit of yours to make it a bit less fancy. Now, is there anything you would like me to do?'

Von Neustadt said, 'Yes. End your next transmission with the sentence "*Der Eingang ist noch offen*". Sign it "*Neffe*".'

'It'll be done,' Stafford told him.

*

A few minutes over two hours after his visitor had left the bungalow, the Royal Navy Walrus amphibian carrying Stafford had splashed rather heavily down onto the flat water of the River Thames near Tower Bridge and taxied to the bank. Another police car had been waiting for him there and now he was shaking hands with a small, tubby, bespectacled man he didn't know in a room on the top floor of a building which he did.

'Good of you to get here so quickly, Stafford. Most helpful. Do sit down.'

'Thank you, sir,' Stafford said. He had no idea who the man was, but something about him made the use of the term of respect natural.

'The Portsmouth police phoned to say that you made them stop at the railway station on your way to the harbour. I take it you were trying to establish where our friend had gone.'

Stafford's eyes turned towards the woman sitting in a far corner of the room holding a pad and pencil on her lap. She smiled, showing large, very white, very false teeth, and patted the grey hair at the side of her head coyly. He saw that she had a spare pencil piercing the bun at the back of it.

'You can talk in front of Miss Crabtree, Stafford. She knows more about this business than I do.'

Looking back at the speaker, 'Yes, I was, sir,'. Stafford said. 'He bought a ticket to Brighton. The ticket clerk recognized him at once from my description. Obviously that's no guarantee that he went there.'

'Obviously.'

'But I think he probably did, sir.'

Clayton's eyebrows lifted slowly above the rims of his spectacles and Stafford answered the unspoken question by saying, 'He's just a boy. A big, enthusiastic kid without an ounce of subtlety in him, who doesn't know his arse from his elbow.' He glanced at Miss Crabtree in apology, then quickly away before she could show him her teeth again. 'He even tried to tell me who he was. I stopped him, of course.'

'Of course.'

'Dressler's dead, sir. Executed after interrogation, at a guess. Apparently he had come to suspect the truth about *der Eingang*. I can't tell you how.'

Clayton nodded but made no comment, and Stafford went on, 'Whoever is ghosting for Parsifal is to end his next transmission with the message that *der Eingang ist noch offen* and authenticate it with the word "*Neffe*".'

'The way in is . . .?'

'The way in is still open, sir, and *Neffe* means nephew.'

137

'The message could have a negative meaning,' Clayton said.

'Yes, sir.'

'But you don't believe it has, for reasons you have already stated. Is that correct?'

'It is, sir.'

Turning to Miss Crabtree, Clayton said, 'Obtain a detailed description of his guest from Mr Stafford, Jane, and pass it to Sussex, warning them that they may receive a visit at any time now. Also, kindly arrange for the transmission of that signal and for a note of commendation to be entered in Mr Stafford's file.' To Stafford he added, 'We must get together one day so that you can tell me the details,' then stood up and hurried out of the room as though embarrassed by his own effusiveness.

Chapter Sixteen

Lying, lounging, squatting, many of them bandaged, all with faces still blackened, the throng of commandos looked like some remnant of a defeated army. Around them the steel walls of the speeding liner's saloon thrummed, rattled and creaked to the urging of the propellers as, flanked by destroyers, the ship raced through the night.

A lieutenant-colonel, muddy, wet and with blood seeping slowly from beneath a field-dressing taped to his right forearm, from which the sleeve had been cut away, came in through the main door of the saloon and began to thread a path amongst the figures on the deck towards one of the dining tables. Normally a dapper man, the only dapper thing about him now was his green beret, its leather band a regulation one inch above its wearer's eyebrows, the bulk of its material drawn rakishly down one side of his head to the ear. It looked incongruous above the smeared facial camouflage and the rest of him.

Halfway to his destination he paused, looked around him and said, 'Christ! What a derelict shower of slobs!'

Men grinned at him. Some said 'Sir', a few, 'Colonel', and an Australian voice added, 'Too right'. Nobody stood. Nobody moved. They knew the colonel wouldn't want them to.

When he reached the table he sat on it and added, 'Not bad, Badger Force. Not bloody bad at all.' Then he lay back and composed himself for sleep.

*

It was 4.18 a.m. when Mainwaring walked into Clayton's room and said, ''Morning, Peter. What's up?'

Although it was he who had telephoned his superior twenty minutes before and apologetically asked him to come to the building, Clayton still managed to sound surprised when he replied, 'Oh, hello, Edward. It's you. I'm glad you're here. I think we've got the makings of a useful piece of deception at last, but we'll have to act quickly. No time to mess around and discuss it in committee.'

'Yes?'

'Yes.'

Mainwaring sat down and waited without impatience. Clayton, he knew, would get to the point in his own good time.

After a moment, 'This arrived from the Admiralty half an hour ago. It's about a sizeable commando raid on the Norwegian coast earlier tonight. They – well, read it.'

Taking the sheet of paper from him, Mainwaring read, 'From Commanding Officer Badger Force. Double landing to south of Alesund successfully accomplished. Assault groups re-embarked and now withdrawing having destroyed enemy ammo dumps, oil tanks, food stores, plus 2 factories. 4 enemy ships sunk at anchor. 98 German prisoners taken and their dead estimated at double that. Also have on board 200 Norwegian civilian volunteers. Our dead limited to 3 officers and 17 men.'

'Highly professional,' Mainwaring said, 'but they've hardly re-taken Norway. I take it that you want to create the impression that the raid was a prelude to our doing just that.'

Clayton smiled shyly, feeling, not for the first time, that it really was very pleasant working for someone it was unnecessary to explain one's thoughts to.

'Yes,' he replied. 'We know from the War Cabinet that there is no serious intention of invading Norway, at least while so much of our military effort is centred on North Africa, but by persuading the Germans that the contrary is the case we might achieve a welcome useless dispersal of their forces. Tonight's endeavour was a pinprick within the overall context of the war, but they used a big pin to considerable effect and I doubt it will have escaped the attention of the German General Staff.'

'It's good, Peter. We'll do it, but why the haste? Of necessity it will have to be a lengthy and carefully nurtured deception, almost certainly backed up by similar military operations.'

There was a brief period of silence with half of Clayton's mind considering the desirability of polishing his glasses and half on what he was going to say. The decision to leave his spectacles alone and the form of words he wanted came to him at the same moment.

'Edward, I would like your permission to have someone forewarn the enemy of that raid, um, in retrospect, as it were. You will argue that if we send them intelligence obtained by hindsight we destroy the credibility of the organization we have set up, and I would counter by saying that, in this instance, hindsight has had no opportunity to function yet. "Badger Force" won't reach a home port for another sixteen hours or so, which rules out any possibility of an agent having learned what they have done. That being so, he can strengthen his own position, obtain kudos in Berlin's eyes, if he transmits now. Tonight.'

Clayton paused as though to give his totally unaccented words time to acquire an urgency he had failed to impart to them, then went on, 'In their shoes you, of course, would be suspicious, but you have seen the hand of cards and you are not a German. They have seen nothing and have a national tendency to believe what they want to believe. Such a coup as I am suggesting should serve us well while we are under scrutiny by this visitor as well as being beneficial in the longer term.'

Folding his arms above his paunch Clayton frowned in anticipation of the destruction of his argument.

'All right,' Mainwaring said. 'You've told me everything I would do and be. Now tell me what you want to transmit and put me out of my misery. I've only just got up. That piece of paper you were fiddling with probably has your message on it.'

Looking as though he had been caught out in something underhand Clayton picked the sheet up and read aloud from it.

'Talked with drunken farmer yesterday who stated his son, a private in Royal Engineers attached to commando unit, visited him some weeks ago on short leave from amphibious training west coast of Scotland. From type of equipment issued son believes sea-borne landing on Norwegian coast planned. Area and scale of operation, if any, not known. In view of source, reliability this information questionable. Shall I pursue enquiry?'

'Who would you have send that?'

'I thought Lohengrin. It'll give him something to brag about if he does receive a visit.'

'Do it,' Mainwaring told him.

*

A restless night spent at a small Brighton hotel, a brief train ride and a briefer survey of Seaford on foot was all the time von Neustadt needed to realize that if he were to complete his assignment he must act before his remaining courage ran out of him. He had never thought of himself as a nervous man, but the awareness of inimical authority first represented by the country policeman with the bicycle had grown to include everybody in his field of view, while his imagination peopled places he could not see with additional pursuers. Even the glances of women, and he received many of those, seemed to carry menace.

Except at its seaward end where the soldiers stood, Southdown Road was almost deserted. Automatically, he turned away from the group as he came out of a side street and now he could feel their eyes on his back like a physical touch. Countless other eyes watched him from blank windows. Moving his shoulders in irritable self-contempt lessened the illusion, but did not entirely dispel it. 'You're not very good at this game, are you?' Hans Lamprecht had said. He had agreed at the time and did so now with greater conviction, wondering bleakly what had induced him to play it. Being *Sturmbannführer Freiherr* Wolfgang von Neustadt, holder of the *Ritterkreuz*, no longer seemed the obvious explanation it had once been.

There it was, across the road to his right and slightly ahead of him: the house where Paulus, called Pelham, called *die Brücke*, lived. No cover anywhere from which he could keep it under observation without being himself observed. A lone man sitting at a desk seen indistinctly through the dirty glass of a ground-floor window. Now? Or lie low until it was time for the rendezvous with the U-boat? There was no third option. It wasn't cowardice considered and rejected but the memory of his tank crews burning and dying in the white vastness of the East Front which carried him to the opposite side of the road and along the short path to the front door. A little to his surprise it wasn't locked.

'You're home early, darling,' the man said and swung round on his chair.

His back to the closed door, the *Luger* in his hand, 'Who,' von Neustadt asked, 'is "darling"?' But all the man replied was, 'What the devil?'

'What the devil?' von Neustadt repeated. 'I've never been sure whether those words constitute a question or an exclamation. So very English, aren't they? They mean nothing and ask everything, but, for the moment, let me do the asking, there's a good chap.'

It didn't take long, the game of questions and answers. For Lohengrin, with at least his more distant background genuine, forewarned and coached, the encounter was less alarming than he feared it would be. For von Neustadt, with the matter of the suspect Hans Lamprecht satisfactorily disposed of and wanting to believe, belief for the taking was an offer to be grasped. Almost as though it would make the grasping easier to accomplish, he put his gun away and said, 'Add to the end of your next transmission the words "*die Brücke ist unbeschädigt*". Sign the message "*Neffe*".'

Lohengrin nodded and sighed softly before saying, 'I'm extremely thankful to be undamaged, as you put it. Living amongst the English is enough of a strain without people like you walking in waving *Lugers* around. I nearly died of fright.'

'I'm sorry, but it was necessary.'

'No doubt, but what possessed you to make contact in the middle of the day?'

Relaxing now, 'I'm trying to become a legend in my own lunchtime,' von Neustadt said and smiled. It was a relief to make a joke. Then, in case he should be thought guilty of irresponsible levity, he added with a touch of sententiousness, 'The straightforward thing is often the safest in this game.' That, he felt, made him sound experienced and, on reflection, was probably true. He followed it up with, 'Incidentally, we have no record of your being married.'

Grateful for a topic on which a lapse admitted was hardly a matter of life and death, Lohengrin had opened his mouth to explain the absence of marital status when Claire Helier entered the room from the street.

Recognition between her and von Neustadt was mutual and instantaneous. She was back at Cambridge on a lovely summer's night, just before the war, dancing with the handsome, aristocratic German youth who, a few hours later, was to become the first man she ever slept with. He vividly remembered the pretty blonde child he had been introduced to at the annual university dance which, although it took place in June, the English perversely called 'The May Ball'. Just as vividly he recalled the name of her titled guardian, a name he had been reminded of a few days earlier in Berlin when Colonel Frischauer had told him a little of the hierarchy of the British Secret Service. The man whose ward she was held high rank in it and that made total nonsense of everything he had come to believe since his meeting with the first of his contacts in England. So *der Eingang* was blocked, *die Brücke* was broken and from that it followed that the entire organization was suspect. His duty to alert Berlin was as clear as the first step in that direction was distasteful.

'What a pity,' von Neustadt murmured and took the *Luger* from inside his coat.

The seven gunshots followed each other in rapid succession, loud in the small room, but lacking sharpness. The first bullet tore a furrow across Lohengrin's chest, laying the flesh open to the ribs. The second smashed the glass of the print of Dover Castle on the wall. The remainder, widely spread, found their target.

'Sod it,' von Neustadt said quietly, stood slowly upright, gazed curiously at the smoking, tattered end of Claire Helier's handbag and added, 'One might have thought that being shot by a pretty girl would be preferable to having an Ivan do it. It isn't really.'

Blood poured over his lower lip then, fanning downwards to blend with the red flowers blossoming on his Savile Row jacket. The *Luger* clattered when it struck the floor, making more noise than his body subsiding back into the chair. Claire Helier began emitting sounds like an Arab woman's lament.

*

'Steady, pretty lady. Steady,' Pemberton said. He had said that to her once before, he knew, but couldn't remember when it had been, only that her face being buried in his shoulder was somehow a familiar experience. She was trembling so violently that his own body shook in sympathy with it and to his dismay he found himself experiencing sexual arousal. Self-disgust and a flood-tide of protectiveness dispelled his involuntary reaction to close physical contact and he increased the pressure of his arms until she moaned in grateful protest. The trembling eased, stopped.

'Did I kill him?' The words muffled.

'What did you say, my dear?'

She drew her head back and he saw that his jacket and the medal ribbon to which he was not entitled were smeared with lipstick. It would be nice, he thought, if he could keep them like that.

'Did I kill him, George?'

'Comprehensively,' he said and winced, wondering why he had to be flippant in the face of adversity, particularly somebody else's. Quickly he added, 'You did what you had to do.'

'No, not him,' she whispered. 'I meant Frank.'

'Good Lord no. You creased him a bit. That's all. They've taken him off to hospital to stitch him up. He's not seriously hurt. Just a bit sore.'

'I'd be a bit sore too if I'd been shot by mistake. That's what the Americans say, you know, when they mean "cross".' Claire giggled and then began to sob gently, her face sinking back onto his chest.

'So much blood.'

'What, my dear?'

She shook her head, not repeating the words, and Pemberton continued to hold her, relieved for her that relaxing tears had replaced the high-strung quivering of over-stretched nerves, relieved for himself that his own chief emotion was now restricted to overwhelming pity.

When the crying stopped he found that he was supporting her whole weight. He lifted her, carried her up the stairs and put her on the bed she shared with Lohengrin. She showed no sign of awareness either then or when he tucked the covers round her as he had done once before. Temporarily Claire Helier had withdrawn from the world.

Chapter Seventeen

Little more than a mile from the old county town of Lewes where the anonymous black car had met Pemberton, it drew off the road and stopped beside an inn. He looked out and upwards at the almost vertical walls of the chalkpit quarried out of the side of the hill, its top invisible, mist-shrouded.

'Most apposite,' Clayton said, then added in an apologetic voice, 'Driver, I wonder if you would mind forsaking us in favour of an alcoholic beverage. Half an hour should suffice.' As if to soften the blow he took a pound note from his wallet and held it diffidently forward across the front seat.

The man saw the gesture in the rear-view mirror, smiled and got out of the car saying, 'Don't you worry about that, sir. If it comes too expensive I'll charge it under "Exigencies".'

When the door had thudded shut, 'What's most apposite, sir?' Pemberton asked.

Clayton gestured towards the pub sign, not speaking. 'The Chalkpit' the legend read, and Pemberton grunted indifferently. He was tired after the events of the day before and the night which had followed it, disturbed by the sudden summons to meet the grey eminence from London at his side, distressed by the shocked condition of Claire Helier.

Seconds dragged before Clayton spoke again, then, 'I've read your report, Colonel, and must confess to a certain degree of disquiet at what you neglected to write.'

'Oh? I made no intentional omissions, sir.'

Nodding his head in emphatic acceptance of the statement, 'I'm sure of it,' Clayton told him. 'It would have been better had I said that I was worried by what you had failed to see. Listen, my dear fellow, this is really Professor Morris's territory, not mine, but I am aware that you dislike him and a conflict of personalities in what is already a precariously balanced situation must be avoided. You are not, I should add, alone in your dislike, and I only hope that it will not extend to include me if I don his mantle for a few minutes.'

146

Before Pemberton could comment, Clayton hurried on as if to counter any charge of disloyalty. 'He's quite invaluable, of course. Having assisted him in his work, I'm sure you will bear me out.'

His voice cold, Pemberton replied, 'If you set great store by injecting insanity into verbal exchanges, and an aptitude for both physical and mental sadism, I'd be bound to agree with you. Personally, I see him as someone with not the slightest conception of teamwork. In one breath he speaks of the need for empathy and in the next says that the emotional wellbeing of the parties concerned is of no consequence. The statements are contradictory and the second of them absurd. All that I can handle, but when he sets up shop as a procurer I draw the line.'

While he was speaking Pemberton had begun to despise himself, but seemed incapable of stopping the flow of words, and it surprised him to hear Clayton saying mildly, 'I'm glad you mentioned that. It's really the reason I'm here with you now, sitting in this extremely cold vehicle. You see, I suspect that your reaction to Professor Morris may have its origin in the misconception that your colleagues are gentlemen. Be assured that, apart from yourself and one or two others who also cause me some concern, none of us merits that description.'

Pemberton didn't speak and Clayton went on, 'Let me give you an example. The best outcome of the visit by the man Miss Helier has identified for us as Baron von Neustadt would have been for him to have returned safely to Germany, satisfied that all was well here. I take it that you agree.'

'Of course.'

'Good. What other result do you consider would have best suited our purpose?'

'The one that was achieved,' Pemberton said. 'We still have Lohengrin, thanks to Miss Helier.'

'Are you sure of that, Colonel?'

The day outside misty, the windows becoming opaque beneath a film of condensation, the interior of the car was dim, making it difficult for Pemberton to discern any message in the bespectacled eyes of his companion. He was aware that he himself had spoken foolishly, but had scarcely been rebuked for that, and Clayton's last question had been asked diffidently, as if coming from a man seeking reassurance.

'I can't think of a better,' he replied.

'Can't you?' Disappointment in the voice now.

'No.'

'It's those honourable instincts of yours clouding your vision,' Clayton told him. 'The point is entirely hypothetical, but imagine the benefit to us if von Neustadt had succeeded in shooting Miss Helier before he died. That would have bound Lohengrin to us with bonds of hate for the man who had killed the woman he loved and who had just saved his life. It's Lohengrin's services we require, not Miss Helier's.'

Staring at him incredulously Pemberton opened and shut his mouth twice before managing to say, 'God! You really have got a twisted mind!'

'Indeed yes. It's most infernally bent, but it's bent on victory at the least possible cost in Allied lives. That's what this exercise in deception is all about and I'll go to any lengths to make it a successful one.'

'I think you're trying deliberately to shock me.'

Sounding irritable for the first time, 'Of course I'm trying to shock you!' Clayton said. 'I'm trying to shock you into constructive thought. If I have succeeded you may now be able to rectify the omission we referred to at the beginning of this conversation. What else should have appeared in your report?'

'From what you've been saying, some comment to the effect that, regrettably, Miss Helier failed to get herself shot would have been appropriate.'

'Do you wish to resign, Colonel? I shall not stand in your way if you feel that a genuine military career would be preferable to what you are now doing. I'm afraid overseas service could not be permitted because you know too much, but I'm sure the War Office would be glad to employ a man of your undoubted ability.'

Pemberton broke the visual contact he seemed to have been holding for so long and looked morosely about him at the grey cocoon of condensation limiting the world to the confines of the inside of the car. Trying vainly to remember what, after the arrival of the black-out had enabled him to supervise the removal to London of a corpse, a wounded man and an hysterical girl, he had or had not written made him chew his lip. It was a relief when Clayton began talking again.

'I seem to have confused you,' he said. 'Perhaps it would help you to make a decision if I explained what is in my mind.'

'Perhaps. It might have helped even more if you had started that way.'

'Hmm. In your report you dwelt at some length on the suffering Miss Helier was undergoing as a result of her action. I have no quarrel with that as it was necessary for you to assess both her immediate and long-term usefulness. That you did. What you did not do was give Lohengrin the same depth of consideration. To state baldly that he had a superficial bullet wound from which he would soon recover seems to me to be glossing over the facts.'

Still angry, still distressed, but with the merest inkling of what was coming stirring in his tired mind, Pemberton bit down on a sarcastic reply.

'I would put it to you,' Clayton went on, 'that the first tangible evidence of his own treachery being presented to him in the form of a fellow countryman gunned down in front of his eyes by an enemy alien, constitutes something of a traumatic experience. The fact that the enemy alien in question is dearly loved by him is likely only to increase the trauma. In short, I question the rapid recovery you forecast and anticipate withdrawal into himself and withdrawal to an unknown degree of the cooperation he has so far been persuaded to give. Can you understand my fears? Can you divorce your thinking from the gentlemanly delusion that women have a monopoly of emotional ills, while men need only a period of convalescence to recover from physical mishaps?'

Requiring no time now to answer the questions, Pemberton still remained silent for a long moment before saying quietly, 'Somebody ought to kick me, sir. I really am the most unutterable fool.'

Clayton noted the return of the term of respect with satisfaction; a term which had been markedly absent since Professor Morris's name had been mentioned. 'Yes and no,' he murmured.

'Sir?'

'Yes, somebody ought to kick you. No, you are not a fool. Do I take it that you do not wish to resign?'

'I'd be glad if you would keep me on, sir.'

'Then that's settled. Now let's discuss the immediate future,' Clayton said and wiped clear a section of the window beside him with the back of a gloved hand as if to give himself a view of what the future held.

*

'You're back quickly.'

Pemberton nodded at Carne. 'Yes. I only had to go as far as Lewes.' He looked around him at the room they had shared since relinquishing the house on Southdown Road to Claire Helier, frowned and added, 'Look, would you mind coming for a walk? I want to think and to bring you up to date. I'm not sure in which order.'

'I'll get my coat,' Carne said.

They walked south and east, leaving the town behind, climbing towards the cliffs, neither man speaking. Carne concluded that thinking had taken precedence over briefing in Pemberton's mind and occupied himself by returning the salutes of passing servicemen to which Pemberton seemed oblivious.

Pemberton wasn't thinking, he was feeling, just as Professor Morris had wanted him to do, but which it had taken that morning's meeting with the tubby man from London to achieve. As if he had been in the room at the time, he felt Lohengrin's startled apprehension when, at the sight of Claire Helier, von Neustadt had drawn his *Luger*. He felt the shock of a bullet laying open the flesh covering his ribs like the lash of a bull-whip, the cringing anticipation of more shots striking him and confusion when they did not despite the continuing gunfire.

Realization of who was firing at whom would have come next, Pemberton knew, accompanied by relief and gratitude. All those sensations came to him readily and without conscious effort, but he had to apply his mind to what emotions would have gripped Lohengrin when immediate danger was past. A reluctance to accept, perhaps, that a girl so gentle, so child-like, so very feminine, could, however inexpertly, shoot a man to death? Probably, but that phase would not have lasted long with the evidence before his eyes, the handbag-muffled shots hardly faded from his ears and the smell of burnt cordite still in his nostrils. What then? Revulsion? Unlikely, with love so strong.

Jealousy stabbed at Pemberton with the last unspoken thought and subjectivity returned, bringing with it a *mélange* of awe, bewilderment coupled to a sense of emasculation and reborn fear. Distrust of those around him and disdain for himself followed so readily that Pemberton had to remind himself that he was not Lohengrin. Of what the tubby man had said, of how right he had been, he did not need to be reminded.

High above the sea now, the wind flapping the tails of his army greatcoat about his legs and dispersing the day's mist; the setting sun painting the undulating chalk cliffs to the east pinkly white, 'One, two, three, four, five, six, seven,' Pemberton said.

'Yes. They're called "The Seven Sisters".'

Pemberton looked at Carne as though surprised to see him there. 'Oh, I thought we were standing on one of them.'

'No, this is Seaford Head. Those are the "Sisters". That's Birling Gap and Beachy Head at the end.'

Following the direction of Carne's pointing finger, Pemberton said 'Oh' again, then turned his attention to a squadron of tanks churning the green turf of the Downs into a muddy morass half a mile away. The constant whinnying sound of their tracks reached his ears faintly. When he had finished looking at them he turned his gaze seawards to watch two small coasters escorted by an armed trawler with a barrage balloon floating above it making their slow way down-Channel. Beyond them, below the hard line of the horizon but clearly visible to his imagination, lay occupied Europe. Icy fingers prodded his stomach to remind him that he would almost certainly go there soon and probably to Germany itself.

'They've decided that Lohengrin should recruit me into the German Secret Service,' he said.

'Really?'

Carne didn't sound particularly interested but Pemberton didn't mind. That was just Carne's way.

'Yes. It will involve a trip to Lisbon with him for vetting by the *Abwehr*. Unless they have a team there senior enough to handle that, which is unlikely, I'll probably be taken to Paris. Berlin even.'

'Rather you than me.'

'Travel broadens the mind.'

'I'm perfectly content for mine to stay narrow,' Carne said, but the words were lost in the scream of four Hurricane fighters passing low overhead towards the south and some airborne targets that only radar could see. The grass about the two men flattened in the wash from the propellers and both clutched at their uniform caps.

When the sudden squall had abated, 'What did you say?' Pemberton asked.

'Nothing important. When's all this supposed to happen?'

'That depends on two things. Lohengrin's fitness and his obtaining an invitation for him and me to take a holiday abroad.'

'Well, he'll be fit enough quite soon. He wasn't badly hurt,' Carne said and Pemberton experienced mild satisfaction that his was not the sole case of mental myopia. He was still enjoying the sensation when Carne asked, 'Is one permitted to ask what this is in aid of?'

'The von Neustadt tour of inspection,' Pemberton replied. 'He checked on somebody in Hampshire before coming here. That went all right and our visitation would have gone off well too if he and Claire hadn't recognized each other. Now London is arranging for him to have been killed somewhere else. With suitable newspaper publicity, naturally. It may be enough, but they aren't prepared to bet on it.'

'I see. By using you we hope to avoid a repeat visit and persuade old Jerry that his network here is not only flourishing but expanding. Right?'

'Right.'

'Funny,' Carne said thoughtfully. 'I never took you for a bloody fool before.'

Pemberton shrugged and started back down the slope towards the town. Carne fell in beside him and they continued to talk in low tones. When they were near the bottom the Hurricanes came in from the sea, turning over and over in victory rolls, but there were only three of them now.

*

Softly, to the tune of 'Colonel Bogey', Harry sang,

'Hitler has only got one ball.
Goering has two but rather small.
Himmler has something sim'lar,
But poor old Goebbels has no balls at all.'

Then he began to sing it again.

'Shut up, Harry.'

'Aye aye, sir. Sorry, sir,' Harry said and began to clean his fingernails with a match.

They were back in the house on Southdown Road; Pemberton, Carne, Newland and Harry. Newland was in the kitchen admiring a simmering concoction of brawn, potatoes and beetroot he had prepared for the evening meal. It had reduced itself to the consistency of lumpy porridge. The others were sitting round the small table in the living room with the transmission key on it. Pemberton was looking at his watch. When the hands indicated 8.30, 'Off you go, Harry,' he whispered as though there was a risk of his being overheard in Germany.

'Aye aye, sir.' Harry put down his match, took hold of the key with a feather-light touch and Morse stuttered, Morse which an educated ear would have vouched for as Lohengrin's. Pemberton watched him curiously, wondering if Harry's fingers possessed a mind of their own, as the words coming from his mouth told of a brain preoccupied by the reproductive deficiencies of the leaders of the Third Reich. This time he made no attempt to silence the singer.

The coded signal spoke of changes in the disposition of troops near the south-east coast and of new divisional and regimental insignia identified. It told of the construction of a factory near Brighton, its purpose not yet established, and of concrete emplacements around the port of Folkestone which appeared to be intended to support anti-aircraft guns. It complained of a risky contact made by an unknown German agent, described the man in detail and requested that his bona fides be confirmed. It ended with the words '*die Brücke ist unbeschädigt*' and the signature '*Neffe*'.

'They've acknowledged, sir,' Harry said.

Forty-one minutes later, Pemberton and Carne had finished decoding the reply. 'We'll eat now, please,' Pemberton called towards the kitchen, but the expression on his face when Newland set his offering before them made Carne smile and say, 'It hasn't been your day, has it?'

*

'I've been in touch with Eton and King's College, Cambridge,' Mainwaring said. 'The Canaris family paid von Neustadt's fees at both. That, and the signature *Neffe*, leads me to suspect that he was at least an honorary nephew. I also think it's reasonable to assume that he was hand-picked for this job by the admiral and brought back from the Russian Front to do it. There's his reference to Ivan just before he died, recently healed bullet wounds in addition to those that killed him and even more recent evidence of frostbite on the tips of his ears. Can you finish it for me, Peter? If so, I'll know I've got it right.'

'Yes, I can finish it,' Clayton told him, 'but only because I know you and what you have come to suspect. You believe that von Neustadt was selected by Admiral Canaris because he didn't want the mission to succeed. I'm inclined to agree with you. Even allowing for *Abwehr* complacency it still makes no sense to put a young man into a field for which his only qualifications are courage and a perfect command of the English language. Stafford described him as a big, enthusiastic kid. Well, we know the Germans can do better than that.'

Clayton moved his buttocks restlessly from one side of his chair to the other and back again before adding, 'All of which supports your theory that, while Canaris may not be actively on our side, he still does not want Hitler's Germany to win this war. In view of his known conservatism, and sundry straws in the wind such as this one, I'm prepared to accept that as a working hypothesis while never losing sight of the . . .' Clayton waved his small hands around like a man dispersing a cloud of smoke from somebody else's pipe, then subsided against the back of the chair, his proviso made to his own satisfaction.

'Quite,' Mainwaring finished for him. 'We could be utterly wrong. I take it the necessary arrangements have been made to explain away von Neustadt's death.'

'You can read about it in tomorrow's papers,' Clayton said. 'I'd like to talk about Norway if you have a few minutes to spare. Berlin is very interested in that Alesund commando raid. Lohengrin in the person of Pemberton made contact yesterday asking for an assurance that von Neustadt was what he appeared to be. That was provided, but the bulk of the reply referred to his earlier signal and was devoted to a demand for the immediate transmission of any information which might indicate that an invasion by us of any part of Scandinavia was imminent. Two other agents under our control have received the same instructions and I expect the rest will too when they are next in communication.'

'Well done, Peter.'

'It was just a passing thought,' Clayton murmured, looking embarrassed, and added, 'I have some suggestions to make for capitalizing on it if you'd like to hear them.'

Twenty minutes later Mainwaring replaced a telephone on its rest and looked at Clayton.

'Could you hear that?'

Clayton shook his head. 'No, only your end.'

'Two of your requirements are already met. There's a commando raid scheduled for tomorrow night on a coastal airstrip near a place called Manda to the west of Kristiansand at the southern tip of Norway. Ostensibly the target is *Luftwaffe* installations, but the real object of the exercise is to divert attention from some of our fast patrol boats coming out of the Skagerrak with cargoes of Swedish ballbearings.' Mainwaring smiled faintly and added, 'When I asked them if they could make the whole thing as noisy and impressive as possible, they wanted to know what I thought was usually done on a diversionary raid. Oh, and the second thing which may help to provide a bit of local colour is that a cruiser squadron lobbed a few salvos of shells onto Stavanger airfield last night. Just a hit and run job.'

'How very fortuitous,' Clayton said. 'Of course they may recognize the Manda raid for the diversion it is, as opposed to a probe, but – well, let's take it step by step. I think our most telling card will be leaving evidence around that we have tested Norwegian beaches for load-bearing properties. Would you like me to liaise with the Army to establish logical sites for that?'

'Yes, please. As soon as you've done that we'll get a signal off to Knut Larsen. It should be simpler for his people to handle it locally than to involve the Navy.'

Rising to his feet Clayton turned to leave, then faced Mainwaring again before saying, 'Edward, we both realize that all this is only window dressing. We shall need to mount a probe in considerable strength if we are to hoodwink the enemy and, as that will require some intensive lobbying of the armed forces, the support of the full committee will be essential.'

'I entirely agree with you,' Mainwaring said.

Over the necessity for an additional display of force to influence enemy thinking both men were quite wrong; jointly wrong for the first time since the formation of the Twenty Committee had brought them together. Their fault lay in their disregard of the intuitive powers Adolf Hitler believed himself to possess.

Chapter Eighteen

'I don't imagine you'll be particularly interested in my condolences, sir, but you have them for what they're worth.'

'On the contrary, Frischauer,' Admiral Canaris said. 'I take it kindly that you should trouble to voice them in these terrible times with so many dying every day. I shall miss the young man.'

'As long as you don't blame yourself, sir. Life expectancy on the East Front isn't very high either at the moment.'

'Yes, there's always that way of looking at it, but I shan't waste time blaming myself anyway. I sent him to do a job and he appears to have done it well. How was he killed?'

'I've got the English press cuttings with me, Admiral. They arrived from Lisbon this morning. Would you like to see them?'

Canaris waved the proffered strips of newsprint away. 'No. Just tell me.'

Intensely disliking his role of bearer of ill tidings, the colonel began pacing rather jerkily back and forth across the admiral's room, his hands clasped behind his back. 'It was the purest bad luck, sir,' he said. 'The baron bought a bicycle in a town called Eastbourne. That's very close to Seaford where he had his meeting with *die Brücke*. I imagine a lot of bicycling goes on over there as it does here because of petrol rationing, and he thought it would be an inconspicuous way of making his rendezvous with the U-boats.'

'Frischauer.'

'Sir?'

'Do stop perambulating, sit down and get to the point.'

Frischauer shrugged, threw himself onto a chair and went on, 'He set off on the wrong side of the road, sir. Wrong for the British that is. It's a very easy thing to do if your concentration lapses for a moment. Anyway, he corrected the error after fifty metres or so, but a passer-by had seen him do it and that made him suspicious enough to raise the alarm. Von Neustadt tried to run for it and was shot by an army patrol. It's hardly surprising. Most of the south and south-east of England is a very sensitive defence area, as you know.'

'Yes. Was he identified?'

'Only by the name he was using, Admiral. There may be a lot of Michael John Taylors in England, but it won't have taken them long to establish that he wasn't one of them, and close examination of his papers revealed them to be forgeries. The inevitable conclusion was drawn.'

Frischauer glanced down at the sheaf of clippings in his hand. 'Alert Civilian Fingers German Spy,' the headline read, followed by the words, 'Visitor to Eastbourne, Mr Thomas Braithwaite, described today how . . .' He sighed and put the pieces of paper into his pocket.

'So you're satisfied that there is nothing sinister behind all this?'

'If you mean could they be holding him alive, I don't think there is, sir,' Frischauer replied. 'We have learnt to suspect anything put out over the BBC, but the British press is a different matter. It can have a "D" Notice forbidding publication applied to it, but I doubt there is the machinery to enforce the printing of misleading information. Their reporters are too curious and freedom of the press still means a great deal to the British, even in time of war. It's almost an article of faith with them.'

'Yes, you're right,' Canaris said. 'I think we can safely assume that *der Eingang* and *die Brücke* are still secure and, by projection, the rest of them as well.'

A number of people in England would have been glad to hear the admiral's words, including some junior operatives of MI5 who had staged von Neustadt's posthumous death. One had bought a bicycle and ridden off on it keeping to the right-hand side of the road. Another had watched him curiously for a moment, then broken into a run, shouting. A group of soldiers who were not soldiers had tried to bar the cyclist's way, but he had evaded them and pedalled furiously on, ignoring both calls to halt and warning shots. Finally he had gone down under a hail of blank-cartridge fire, and the force of his rolling fall had burst the small bladders of pig's blood taped inside the lining of his coat.

A local chief superintendent of police had been briefed on the charade, and it was he who ordered the few onlookers to stand back and waved down a passing army truck which was not an army truck. Two minutes after the gunfire had ceased, of the actors only he and the man calling himself Thomas Braithwaite remained. The crowd grew rapidly, but by then there was only the fallen bicycle and a pool of blood in the gutter to look at.

When the press arrived the chief superintendent had referred them to the area army commander and then stood patiently listening to the temporary Mr Braithwaite enjoying his role of sharp-eyed patriot.

*

Of those women who worked for Clayton in the capacity which had led them to style themselves 'The Beautiful Bitch Brigade', some had glamour, some were pretty, others handsome, a few highly intelligent. He intensely disliked the collective title they had chosen, on the grounds that it was cheap, self-deprecating and, to the extent that his dinner companion was the only genuine beauty amongst them, inaccurate. She not so much diminished other women as extinguished them, doing it without intent and, remarkably, without attracting resentment to herself. The explanation, he supposed, lay in the pointlessness of competing with perfection, for she was not only lovely to look at, she possessed poise and presence beyond her years, a quick mind and a rare gift for friendship which knew no favourites.

'It's kind of you to give up an evening to dine with me again, Lady Abigail,' he said.

The slanting green eyes laughed at him, but the wide mouth did not. 'No it isn't, Mr Clayton. I enjoy it but, you know, you don't have to feed me to brief me. I can always come to your office.'

'Put it down to selfishness,' he told her. 'There's been a lot to do and this is the first time I've visited a restaurant since last we met. In addition, I find you comfortable to be with.' He paused, looking first startled then annoyed, before adding, 'Oh dear. I really must learn to think before I speak. That's not the sort of thing one says to an elegant female companion. What I meant was . . .'

'Don't spoil it,' Gail Mainwaring broke in. 'It was a very nice thing to say. At least to this elegant female companion.'

Overburdened as she was by compliments of a kind more suited to an allure of which she was well aware, the word 'comfortable' had touched her. Many men were drawn irresistibly to her, some she frightened away without meaning to do so, nearly all desired her, but never before had one sought her out for comfort in the way Clayton had meant it. The laughter gone from her eyes now, she regarded him gravely, remembering how the small, tubby man had impressed her at their first meeting, finding, at their second, that she liked him.

He smiled quickly, shyly, then hid behind his menu as though he had inadvertently overstepped some marker on the road to intimacy and did not know how to withdraw.

'It's a poor choice,' he said. 'I'm awfully sorry.'

Gail glanced at her own menu. 'I must remember to hold you personally responsible for the rationing. May I have the boiled mutton without spinach, please? I know that spinach is good for you, but I've always hated it and as I don't want muscles like Popeye it would be a waste.' She continued to talk amiable nonsense throughout the meal, leaving him with no effort he need make, pausing occasionally for long enough to let him voice what she knew was in his mind, but it was not until they had been served with coffee that he told her there was a matter of some delicacy on which he would be grateful for her advice.

Without waiting to have the matter explained to her, 'If your requirements are still the same,' Gail said, 'I think you had better let them get married. It's the only thing likely to induce a sense of responsibility in Claire. At the moment she's turned right in on herself and is wallowing in anguish. I don't suppose that he's feeling too good either, for quite different reasons, but if they had each other to rescue and a life together to look forward to . . .' She lifted her shoulders in a small shrug and let the rest of the sentence go.

Clayton sat staring at his coffee cup, remembering his conversation with Pemberton outside the pub called 'The Chalkpit' in Sussex. After a trying exchange Pemberton had seen and understood the problem, while this woman had recognized its existence and provided a possible solution before it had been directly mentioned. He found it remarkable too that she had considered it from the male as well as the female point of view and that she could change so swiftly from playing the geisha to being an adviser with something positive to recommend.

His eyes were still lowered when he said, 'Thank you for that. I'll ponder it,' but he raised them quickly to meet hers when she replied. 'Don't ponder too long. She's just stupid enough to try to kill herself.'

'Ah.'

Neither spoke after that for almost a minute. Clayton peered around him at the restaurant's other guests, as though, Gail thought, surprised to see them there, then, 'Lady Abigail?'

'I'm still here.'

'You spoke of inducing a sense of responsibility. Would you enlarge on that? It doesn't automatically come through marriage.'

'No, but achieving this particular marriage will demand it from both parties. He'll have to convince her that she's not the murderess she has persuaded herself she is, and she'll have to entice him away from the sense of newly recovered patriotism he's probably experiencing. The fact that they want each other may not be a sufficiently volatile mixture to overcome the degree of manic depression Claire, at least, is suffering, but if you added a catalyst like hope for the future . . .' Gail shrugged again.

'I'm impressed that you should have pin-pointed the man's problem without even knowing him,' Clayton said.

'You get to know a lot about men's reactions to situations when you're a government harlot,' she told him, then, at the sight of sudden pain in his eyes, added quickly, 'I'm sorry. That was a tasteless thing to say. Have I helped at all?'

Clayton snatched gratefully at the question. 'Yes, very much. I have – er – pondered, and think we should follow the course you suggest, or perhaps I should say attempt it, although by what means I've no idea. One can hardly walk in and say . . .' It was, Clayton decided, his turn to leave a sentence unfinished and he did so.

Elbows on the table now, chin resting on the heels of her hands, she gazed sombrely, unblinkingly at him for what seemed a long time before saying, 'It'll have to be something official, something in the line of duty. She's too frightened to go to see him of her own accord, despite asking me if he's all right ten times a day.'

'And despite having saved his life?'

'Yes. That's a very unimportant part of the script. At the moment she's a penitent who must suffer the consequences of taking a human life and sees him as the stern, unbending figure who would never associate with a vile killer. It's – it's – Oh, I'm very fond of her, Mr Clayton, but she does make me so cross at times. Still, never mind about that. Can you invent something that might persuade her to change roles?' Gail Mainwaring sat upright and dropped her hands to her lap.

'Fortunately, I don't need to tax my imagination,' Clayton said. 'I require something of her, something which will sound little enough to you, but which is of paramount importance to an operation I am engaged in. Please listen carefully and interrupt me if anybody comes within hearing distance behind me.'

Nobody approached Clayton's back and in under four minutes he had finished what he had to say, ending with, 'Do you think she could be prevailed upon to do those things?'

'I don't think that "prevailed upon" is the right expression,' Gail replied. 'It's more a question of convincing her that the situation isn't bad enough to prevent her doing what she wants to do anyway, or at least trying to do it.' For a moment the long sleeves of her sober pale grey woollen dress seemed to engage her attention. She smoothed one and then the other before looking up at Clayton again. 'Given that, and a favourable reaction from the man, she's certainly capable of speaking her lines. After all, being the truth, they aren't difficult to remember and she's very much the frustrated actress.'

Clayton nodded. 'So the selection board reported, but she wasn't acting when I instructed her to return to him. She was elated. You will remember that I had to call on you to calm her, to remind her that she was on duty.'

Nodding in her turn Gail said, 'Oh, she's in love with him all right. She has an almost limitless capacity for being in love. She even is with me.' At the sight of Clayton's quick frown she smiled and went on calmly, 'Don't worry. There's nothing lesbian about her. It's just a schoolgirl crush she's never grown out of and that gives me a lever. The trouble is that it's all tied up with her need to be loved in return and if she receives a rebuff she may go to pieces.'

'That's a risk I must ask you to join me in taking, Lady Abigail, and perhaps I should add that we shall have no further use for the man if she should fail.'

There was, Clayton felt, something hypnotic about the brooding regard of her green eyes. It induced uneasiness, but he made no attempt to look away even when she said in a toneless voice, 'I think I'll spare her that euphemism. Saving his life by instinct and being required to do so under duress are not the same thing.'

'I entirely agree. When will you speak to her?'

'Tonight. In fact I should go soon. I gave her a sedative before I came to meet you, but she'll be coming out of that before long.'

A few minutes later he stood watching her leave the restaurant, aware that the many eyes which had repeatedly turned towards his companion during the meal were now following her progress towards the door. When she had gone he sat down again, gestured to a waiter and made writing motions with one hand on the palm of the other to indicate that he wanted the bill.

*

A start of bewilderment at the first sight of the handsome face, surging alarm when full recognition came and mirrored itself in the man's eyes, a silent scream of terror exploding in her brain when a gun grew out of his hand. Her own hand taking on a life of its own, plunging into her bag, grasping, jerking, jerking, jerking. Sounds like doors slamming punctuating the scream in her head, Frank twisting sideways, toppling, glass splintering, the man rising, towering over her, saying something she didn't hear, shapes like Armistice Day poppies growing on his coat and a terrible red tide flowing from his mouth, obscuring his chin. The pressure of the scream increasing, becoming unbearable, forcing its way past her clenched teeth in an ululating wail, her body quivering, one shoulder shaking violently.

'Wake up, darling! Wake up! It's only the dream!'

Claire Helier opened her eyes, eyes that were unfocused, flicking from side to side, horror-filled. Gail Mainwaring shook her by the shoulder again, fiercely, urgently.

'It's only me, Claire! Me, Gail! Wake up!'

Slowly Claire came back inside herself and the wailing sank to a whimper. Gail sat down on the bed and took one of her hands in both of her own.

'That was a bad go, my love.'

'Horrible,' Claire whispered and her teeth made tiny clattering sounds.

'The same as usual?'

'Yes. It's always the same. What am I going to *do*, Gail?'

'You're going to get up and have a bath while I make you some supper. There are things I have to tell you. Important things.'

'I don't want a bath.'

'But you must. You're streaming with sweat.'

'Am I? Oh, I do so wish Mr Hotchkiss was here.'

'Well, he isn't, darling. You took him to Seaford. Come on. Up you get.'

Her face suddenly wooden, 'I wish you didn't always talk to me as though you were my mother,' Claire said. 'You're only a few weeks older than me. It makes me absolutely livid!' When she was answered with a flashing smile and the words 'That's more like it', she flung angrily out of

162

the bed and walked naked to the bathroom, one hand trailing a dressing-gown across the carpet.

When the door closed behind her, 'I'm centuries older than you, little one,' Gail whispered to the empty room.

It was cold in the attic amongst the discarded school trunks and broken-stringed tennis rackets, but Gail, watching elation and trepidation alternating on Claire's face, knew that her friend was unaware of the fact. She pushed the small discomfort out of her mind, knowing that assurances already sought would be asked for again.

'This isn't another cruel trick, is it, Gail? I mean, after the war they won't send him to prison, will they? They won't take him away from me?'

'He'll only be taken from you if the Germans win the war,' Gail said. 'You have your dear little fat man's word for that, which makes it very official indeed.'

'Do you *really* think there is any chance of Frank marrying me?'

'I can't answer that, Claire, but Havoc Helier always gets her man, doesn't she?'

It went on until two o'clock in the morning, then, 'Gail.'

'Yes?'

'I'm awfully scared. May I sleep in your bed tonight?'

'Who wants Mummy now?' Gail asked herself, but all she said aloud was, 'Yes. Just this once.'

*

'In there, miss,' the stocky man with a gun under his coat said to Claire Helier. There was no sign of the holstered gun beneath his armpit, but she was sure it was there because she knew all about guns now and the people that carried them. In this case she was even right. She went into the small lobby leading to the private room in the private clinic on Wigmore Street, found the door slightly ajar and stood, looking in, her lower lip caught between her teeth.

Unaware of her presence, Lohengrin was sitting fully dressed on the side of the bed staring at something which was probably a window because the eye she could see was slitted as if against the light. Either that or he was concentrating, or perhaps crying. He looked awfully pale too and his hair was getting too long at the nape of his neck and he hadn't bothered to comb the rest of it properly and his clothes were crumpled and when he turned his head slightly she saw that his face was drawn and thought oh my God I'm going to cry, but bit harder on her lip and did not. When she was almost sure that she had herself under control Claire tapped on the door and pushed it wide.

'Hello,' she said.

He got up slowly, stiffly, stooping slightly forward, favouring his wounded chest. She could see the outline of the bandages beneath his shirt.

'Does it hurt awfully?'

Lohengrin smiled bleakly and shook his head. 'The old pectoral muscles took a bit of a hammering, but they're healing.'

'Oh, that's good.'

He made a half-gesture with his arms towards her, then dropped them to his side again, but it was enough and Claire moved forward, reached up and cupped his face in her palms.

'Poor chest,' she said.

They stood motionless for a long time, eyes locked unblinkingly, then, by unspoken consent, sat side by side on the bed and held hands like children.

'I had decided by this morning that there was no hope of ever seeing you again,' Lohengrin said.

It *was* a window he had been staring at, a window with a metal grille inside it to prevent him either escaping or injuring himself with the glass, she supposed. She took her eyes from it, turned her head and looked up at him.

'I was afraid to come to you.'

'Because you hurt me by mistake?'

'No, because I killed that man.'

'You saved both our lives by doing it,' Lohengrin told her.

Refusing to be comforted, 'I liked him,' Claire said.

'How could you possibly know whether you liked him or not?' The first hint of amusement in Lohengrin's voice.

'Because we met at Cambridge before the war. That's how. We recognized each other at once.'

'I see,' Lohengrin said. He didn't see, but her words had fanned some ember of memory which had been almost extinguished by sudden fear and the shock of pain lancing across his chest. It had all gone so well, the meeting with the visitor from Germany in which he had been coached. He had even told him about the girl he was living with. All perfectly natural and perfectly acceptable. Then she had walked in, which should have been all right too, but the man's face had changed and he had said 'What a pity' and drawn his automatic again. Gunfire had accompanied the action and he had known that he was dead when a stunning impact hurled him sideways, until the sound of Claire sobbing incomprehensible words into the telephone had told him that he was not dead at all. That was clear enough in his mind now, but it still didn't make sense, still didn't explain the connection between recognition and instant tragedy. A soft sound beside him made him turn his head and meet Claire's wide-eyed gaze. She was crying softly, almost silently, tears forming above her lower lashes.

'Now you listen to me,' he told her. 'I don't care whether he was likeable or not. It's ridiculous to blame yourself for his death. All you did was shoot by instinct when he pulled that gun.' He released her hand and put his arm around her, but the action was nothing more than brotherly.

'You don't hate me?' Her voice tremulous, the tears spilling over and trickling down either side of her nose.

'Hate you? You are a silly. You know exactly how I feel about you.' Lohengrin took a handkerchief from his pocket, dabbed at the tears, then held it to her nose. 'Blow,' he said.

For long seconds there was silence between them until Claire asked, 'Do you still want to marry me?'

'Yes.'

'Then let's do it.'

'No, Claire.'

'No?'

Lohengrin shook his head. 'I couldn't do that to you. You see, you didn't kill that man, I did. I killed him by being what I have become and I carry the mark of Cain to prove it.' He touched his shirt where it covered the bandages. 'That scar will always be there to remind me. It would remind you too.'

'Cain?'

'Cain killed his brother Abel.' He moved irritably and added, 'I'm making the kind of melodramatic noises I particularly dislike, but that doesn't alter the sense of what I'm saying. Treachery is bad enough, but to have your nose rubbed in the evidence of it – is . . .' The handkerchief in his hand caught his attention and he put it back in his pocket, then went on. 'No, that's nonsense. Treachery is treachery. Whether or not you can see its effects makes no difference. I won't taint you with it.'

'You *were* born here, Frank. Couldn't you just think of it as making amends for before?'

If Lohengrin heard her he gave no sign of it when he said, 'I think they drugged me on and off for quite a long time. It was difficult to think and I was terrified of that Professor Morris. Then there was you and my father. I didn't know which way to turn.'

His tone of voice, stating facts, not making excuses, his ignoring the dubious mental escape route she had offered, his refusal of a proposal of marriage he wanted to accept and his attempt to shift her burden onto his own shoulders affected Claire deeply. She felt both pride and gratitude as well as a longing to take him in her arms, but the memory of Gail Mainwaring's words of the night before held her motionless at his side. 'Don't smother him with sex appeal, darling,' Gail had said. 'It's all too serious for that now. Make him come to you. That way you might succeed in doing your job and achieving happiness at the same time.' Taking three slow, deep breaths to steady herself, Claire assembled in her mind the words, part truth, part lies, she had been authorized to speak. They *might* make him come to her. They *would* give him the freedom either to take his own life or have it taken from him.

'Frank.'

'Yes, Claire?'

'I've got things to tell you.'

'Yes?'

'You needn't worry about your father any more. He isn't in Lisbon. I don't think he has been for a very long time. Anyway, we can't harm him. They just made that up to frighten you.'

'Ah.'

Claire read relief in his face, but not much surprise and less reaction of any sort than she had expected. His arm had gone from her shoulder now and his hands, fingers interlaced tightly, were gripped between his knees. She waited.

'That must be true,' Lohengrin said, 'otherwise there would be no point in telling me, and as there is a point in telling me it must mean that Pemberton wants me to go to Lisbon. He couldn't afford to wait until I got there for me to find out that they'd lied about my father. That's right, isn't it?'

'Yes, Frank.'

'When?'

'I don't know. Not soon. Colonel Pemberton wants you to take him with you as a – as a recruit for the German Secret Service.'

'Oh Christ,' Lohengrin whispered, then added in a louder voice, 'That means Germany for processing.'

'For him, yes. For you, possibly. Oh Frank, I'm so frightened.'

Lohengrin looked squarely at her. 'Do you know something, Claire? We seem to be on remarkably formal first-name terms this morning. You haven't called me "darling" once and you nearly always do. Have you got another bombshell for me?'

Claire imprisoned her lower lip with her teeth again and nodded.

'Well?'

After a long pause, 'There's something else that isn't true,' Claire told him. 'I never was a Nazi sympathizer, I never had anything to do with Oswald Mosley and his British Union of Fascists, I never met von Ribbentrop and I never was in prison. Well, only that once for a few hours when they guessed that you might want to check on me.'

She watched him in an agony of suspense, noting again his apparent lack of surprise, of reaction. Apart from heightened colour in his cheeks his expression spoke only of calm thoughtfulness and that increased her anxiety nearly to screaming point.

'Very clever of them, that prison bit,' Lohengrin said. 'They must have read me like a book. Well, now I know what you're not, it's obvious what you are. Do you charge by the hour, or the night?'

Without thought of the consequences, without any thought at all, Claire Helier hit Lohengrin full in the face. She didn't slap him, she drove her fist straight onto his nose. Seated beside him as she was, the blow carried little of her small weight, but despair, misery and shame compensated for the lack. Lohengrin gave a sharp bark of surprise. Claire hurled herself at him and the man with the gun under his coat materialized in the doorway.

'Hey! What the – Oh, sorry,' he said.

Only the lower legs of the spy he was guarding were visible under the girl and his head seemed to be buried between her breasts. He listened to the girl saying, 'I love you, I love you, I love you, I love you,' in a low growl like a cat with a bird in its mouth, saw the spy's arms go about her, grinned to himself and retreated to the end of the lobby.

With difficulty Lohengrin turned his face to one side. 'I can't breathe and you're hurting my chest,' he said.

'Bad luck. You shouldn't have gone away from me like that.'

'My nose is bleeding onto your dress.'

'Mmm.'

'Claire, darling.'

'Mmm?'

'Why did you let me know you're with British Intelligence? It doesn't make sense.'

'Because I couldn't live a lie with you any longer and I told them so and they said all right tell him if you want to it won't make any difference if he loves you as much as you say.' It came out like a single sentence, without punctuation. Although that was the untrue part, she didn't mind too much because, she told herself, it would have been true if she had thought of it herself.

'Oh Claire.' A hesitation, then, 'What am I going to do?'

'Not go away from me again,' she said.

Tension and consciousness slowly slid from Lohengrin, but Claire did not. Emotionally drained, she fell asleep sprawled on top of him.

Chapter Nineteen

February advanced towards March and bore witness to the words Wolfgang von Neustadt had spoken to Admiral Canaris. With casualties past the million mark, its combat divisions mauled beyond both recognition and cohesion, its panzer groups shattered, the German army ground to a halt in the Russian snows. Having appointed himself Commander-in-Chief of the Army, as well as Supreme Commander of the Armed Forces, Adolf Hitler flew to the East Front to organize the summer offensive. While he was there he sent for Grand Admiral Raedar, Commander-in-Chief of the *Kriegsmarine*.

Puzzled by the sudden summons, tired after a long, cold, bumpy flight in the belly of a rattling Ju52 transport, Raeder was in an irritable mood when he was summoned into Hitler's presence.

'*Mein Führer*,' he said. He liked to get that mode of address done with at the outset and dispense with it thereafter.

'Come in, my dear Raeder, and welcome. I've just been explaining the basic principles of strategy to my generals. Look, I'll show you.'

Raeder's irritation increased as he followed Hitler to the big map on the wall, knowing that this affable greeting meant that in due course he would be ordered to do something either ill-considered or patently stupid. He glanced at the group of senior army officers, but their faces told him nothing.

'The broad-front concept had its advantages,' Hitler began. 'Personally, I was against it, but I mustn't quibble because it very nearly took Moscow and Leningrad. Now, however, we must adopt a more surgical approach and, to that end, we must take Stalingrad as a matter of priority.'

At Raeder's abrupt nod, 'I knew you would get the point,' Hitler went on. 'The key lies in the Caucasus. I must have the oil from Grozny and Maikop, or at least deprive the Russians of it, and Stalingrad controls the main route via the Caspian Sea and the Volga River by which the oil can reach central Russia. So, as soon as the snow has melted and the mud dried, we shall strike and then – no, no, I mustn't take up your time with these local problems. What I wanted to tell you is that the British are about to invade Norway. No doubt you will wish to make the necessary naval dispositions to frustrate that design.'

'*Norway? The British?*'

The sudden total silence in the room was an almost tangible thing then, slowly, the sound of breathing and the faint rustle of material returned to dispel it.

'Are you doubting my word, Commander-in-Chief?' Hitler's regard was fixed, simultaneously blank and intense, affability gone from him as though it had never been.

'Far from it. I was surprised, that's all,' Raeder lied. 'It hadn't occurred to me that the British were in any position to contemplate an operation of such magnitude.'

The eyes seemed to flare briefly, a thin smile forming, and Hitler said, 'The evidence is all there for those capable of interpreting it. I take it that certain recent savage assaults by their commando troops on the Norwegian coast and bombardment from the sea of airfields have not escaped your notice.'

Raeder felt it wise to set his preference aside. 'They have not, *mein Führer*,' he said.

'Excellent. That being the case you will also be aware of the continued enemy U-boat activity in that area.'

'Indeed. Our coastal shipping has been under attack ever since our invasion and occupation of Norway.'

Hitler sounded infinitely patient when he asked, 'Is there not a connection to be made between the sighting of those U-boats and the poorly concealed evidence discovered at a number of locations of beaches tested for their load-bearing qualities? For their ability to support heavy armoured vehicles?'

'With respect, I doubt it,' Raeder said. 'If the position was reversed and I wanted to create the illusion of an imminent invasion I too would order U-boats to show themselves, but I wouldn't bother to land men from them to probe the beaches and collect samples of rock and sand. I'd get the Norwegian underground to do that for me.'

'Illusion? Did you say "illusion"?' Hitler's voice was silky.

'Perhaps, "impression" would have been a better word.'

'Perhaps, but I'm not dealing with words, I'm dealing with facts, facts supplied by our agents in the British Isles.' Affability returned and Hitler smiled broadly before saying, 'The latest intelligence summary won't have reached your office before you left to come here. No matter, I can save you the trouble of reading it. Briefly, no less than nine of our agents have passed information to us which, when considered as a whole, provides inescapable proof of what I have told you.'

'That's most interesting.'

'I thought you would find it so,' Hitler said. 'Listen well, my dear Raeder. Troops in significant quantities are being withdrawn from key defence points on the southern and eastern coasts of England and sent to the west of Scotland for mountain training on a rota system. They have been observed in transit and positively identified by their divisional insignia. Canadian ski-troops, trained in the Rockies, have been arriving at the port of Liverpool with full mountain warfare equipment. Passenger liners are being camouflaged in winter colours and certain shipyards are directing their attention exclusively to the construction of landing-craft. Now, be honest with me, Raeder. Can you believe that all this activity is directed at – shall we say Holland? No? Northern France? Belgium perhaps, or even Denmark? Mountain troops with skis? I ask you! Or perhaps you think they're bluffing!'

'If it's a bluff, *mein Führer*, it's certainly a complicated one, and pointless at that, as the British cannot know that we would ever hear of it. Such information cannot all be acquired by aerial reconnaissance.' For the first time Raeder sounded as though he *was* interested.

'Precisely. I shall be addressing *Wehrmacht* and *Luftwaffe* commanders on the subject as soon as I return to Berlin, something you may warn them to expect, but I am giving you this advance notice as your dispositions will require the longest time to make.'

Hitler turned abruptly back to the army officers, taking up his briefing as though there had been no interruption, at the point where he had ended it. It was unwise to leave until told to do so and Raeder stayed where he was, listening to Hitler saying, 'As you gentlemen will know, General Keitel here has been in Budapest and Bucharest this winter obtaining the services of Hungarian and Rumanian divisions for our summer offensive, and *Reichsmarshal* Goering has informed *Signor* Mussolini of our need for Italian troops. I shall be speaking to the *Duce* myself in that regard. Meanwhile, for our part . . .'

He broke off there, turned back to Raeder and said, 'Oh, I mustn't detain you any longer, my dear fellow. Please feel free to return to Germany and to organize your reception committee for the British in Norway. They have had insufficient time to equip their armoured divisions with the tanks and personnel carriers they lost to us at Dunkirk, but in a land such as Norway where armour is of limited value, their lies their greatest opportunity. Believe me, Raeder, I have a feel for such things. Deploy our heavy naval units and at least twenty U-boats.'

'Twenty U-boats? Admiral Dönitz isn't going to like that!'

'And why not, may I ask?'

'Because, *Führer*, he needs every U-boat he can lay his hands on to reap the astonishing harvest the Americans are making us a gift of. Not only have they withdrawn most of their effective escort vessels to the Pacific, but their coastal lights all the way from New York to Florida are still burning as if there was no war. Apparently the tourist industry in places like Atlantic City and Miami takes precedence over victory. Dönitz's U-boat commanders are extremely grateful for the present at night of ships unescorted and silhouetted against the lights, particularly along the Florida coast where the loaded oil-tankers pass.'

There was a long pause before Hitler said, 'A few minutes ago we spoke of bluff, Raeder. America is a big bluff. Concentrate your thoughts on Norway.'

The irrelevance of the remark, its disregard of overwhelming proof that the United States had yet to awake to the realities of war, its failure to acknowledge the existence of the golden opportunity which that lack of awareness presented for the destruction of shipping bound for the British Isles, silenced Raeder. Having just completed one of the longest uninterrupted statements he had ever made to the *Führer* he knew that he would not be permitted further argument. Clicking his heels together he inclined his head in abrupt acceptance, but Hitler had already turned his back to him.

*

'Come in, Peter,' Edward Mainwaring said. 'I wanted you to be the first to know the outcome of your passing thought and to congratulate you on it.'

Clayton, looking first puzzled, then mildly irritated, shuffled across the room, sat on the edge of a chair and folded his hands on his lap.

'What are you talking about, Edward?'

Mainwaring looked at him affectionately for a moment before saying, 'Not long ago you had what you described to me as a passing thought about Norway. Since then your people have been transmitting a lot of nonsense to Germany about our troops undergoing intensive mountain training and Canadians arriving with snow on their boots or skis on their backs, and so on and so forth.'

'That is so,' Clayton said. 'Has there been some development?'

'You could say that,' Mainwaring told him. 'According to Knut Larsen the *Wehrmacht* has been moving formations around the country in significant numbers and has been strengthened by two brigades of *Waffen* SS from Russia. In addition, the *Luftwaffe* has been reinforced by three ground-attack fighter squadrons, also from Russia.'

'Pity we can't tell the Russians. They might make us Heroes of the Soviet Union.'

Mainwaring heard the tone of disinterest in Clayton's voice, made a mental note of it and said, 'Quite, but that's only the beginning. There have been extensive naval movements too. The *Tirpitz* has been stationed at Trondheim since 16 January, the *Prinz Eugen* and *Admiral Scheer* followed her to Norway and they have now been joined by the *Lützow* and *Hipper*, together with eight Fleet destroyers and a considerable number of U-boats. Taking the surface ships alone, Peter, that is virtually every heavy unit the Germans have left to them, with the exception of the *Scharnhorst* and *Gneisnau*. Probably they would have gone too if they weren't in dock as a result of mine and bomb damage since their escape from Brest.'

Clayton nodded. 'Good. I'm glad it worked.' He half rose to his feet but subsided again at a gesture from Mainwaring.

'Peter.'

'Yes, Edward?'

'I don't need to tell you this, you of all people, because you're the chief architect of the plan, but I'm going to tell you anyway. This is a stunning achievement and I intend to draw our part in it to the attention of the full committee and the Prime Minister. We have now unquestionably demonstrated our ability to manipulate the enemy, to move his forces uselessly about on a large scale, by remote control as it were. It's a stunning – well, I've just said that. If we can maintain that capability the future benefits to us are incalculable.'

'Indeed, yes.'

'You don't sound exactly overcome with delight,' Mainwaring said.

'I'm glad, as I've already told you. The capacity for delight has deserted me since I discovered that I was no longer at ease in your presence. I think it would be best if you were to look around for a new chief assistant. Hyatt is an excellent man.'

'It's my two girls, isn't it?' The words were more statement than question and Mainwaring saw Clayton's eyebrows lift above the rims of his spectacles in two arcs of comical surprise, then slowly subside again.

'You're very quick,' Clayton said, 'but then you always were. What brought you to that conclusion?'

'The fact, as you put it, that you are no longer at ease in my presence, a condition which has been apparent for some time now. Are you in love with Gail? I know it can't be Claire. She's not of your metal.'

'No, no, no, no.'

Mainwaring smiled and said, 'That's very encouraging. It must bring the number of men who are not almost to double figures.'

Finding himself again indulging in the habit he had been trying so hard to break of polishing his glasses Clayton made tutting noises before saying, 'I find Lady Abigail quite delectable and an all round extremely – er – good number, as they say nowadays, but that, and taking pleasure in her company, is as far as it goes.'

'She detests being called Lady Abigail, Peter, and I doubt she'd enjoy being described as an all round good number, even an extremely good one.'

'Oh, do be serious, Edward. I'm not enjoying this at all.'

'Very well. Then suppose you tell me what the trouble is.'

For almost a quarter of a minute Clayton lost himself in reverie, then blinked and said, 'Because he's very much a key figure, some time ago I intervened at a personal level in the handling of Lohengrin. It's something I have never found it necessary to do before and I quickly found myself wishing that I had never left the rarefied atmosphere of these offices. I am not without imagination, but I rarely give it free rein because to do so would be inhibiting.'

He stopped talking then, clamping his lips together as if he had already said too much and Mainwaring asked encouragingly, 'You don't imagine that you're alone in employing that form of self-protection, do you?'

Clayton shook his head vigorously. 'No, but I do imagine that I'm alone in instructing the very beautiful daughter of my friend and master to control the activities of his pretty child ward. Had the identities of the girls been different, and the activities less painful to contemplate, it is possible that I would have been less affected. In fact it is certainly so, but all this is too close to home and I find it difficult to face you knowing what you must be suffering. That reduces my efficiency, which is why I think I should go.'

Speaking very deliberately, Mainwaring said, 'I fervently hope that you will do no such thing, Peter. It would greatly increase my burden. In the first place, while it is true that no man is irreplaceable, you are close to it. I don't want Hyatt or anybody else that I can think of. Secondly, in these bizarre circumstances, it's a great comfort to me having you to exercise even a modicum of control over the girls. Suppose it were Professor Morris, as it was when they started. It hardly bears thinking about, does it?'

Without waiting for an answer, Mainwaring went on, 'Finally, while we both know that such young women are potentially more dangerous to the enemy than a battalion of infantry, and that not to employ them would be an abdication of responsibility, the fact remains that I have morally forfeited all parental rights by authorizing their enrolment. Patriotism says otherwise, of course, but that's small consolation on a personal level. Add to that the anonymity required of me, and the silence required of them, precluding any conversation between us of a professional nature – well, let me put it like this. I'm pretty useless to them and, even if *in loco parentis* is scarcely the appropriate expression, it's good to have you holding a watching brief.'

'Touched,' Clayton murmured.

'What, Peter?'

'I'm very touched.'

'And you'll stay?'

'It's blackmail, of course but, yes, I'll stay. Gladly, now that the matter is out in the open.'

Mainwaring smiled his thanks, wondering why a situation of which Clayton had been aware for months should have come to a head at this time. He concluded, correctly, that the two meetings with Gail had had a greater effect on Clayton than he would admit to, but that only served to deepen his liking for the strange, brilliant little man.

'Well,' he said, 'now that you have manoeuvred the United States prematurely into the war and succeeded in transferring a large part of the German Navy quite unnecessarily to Norway, do you have any more passing thoughts?'

*

175

On the day, in St Peter's Church, Seaford, when Claire Helier became Mrs Frank Pelham, a lieutenant-colonel of the Royal Tank Regiment who was not a lieutenant-colonel in any regiment, stood as 'best man' to a German spy.

Although he had acceded at once to the request, Lohengrin's diffident, embarrassed approach had released in George Pemberton a flood of emotions which drove him striding for miles across the Sussex Downs by day and destroyed his ability to achieve more than snatches of sleep at night. Shock that such a marriage should have received official sanction marched hand in hand with an intensity of jealousy far outstripping the envy the unofficial liaison had caused him. That that was now to be blessed by Church and ratified by State hit him hard, holding up to his face proof of how shallowly he had buried the hope that at some magical time when all this was over Claire might become his wife.

For a while he persuaded himself that the union would be illegal and could be dissolved when Lohengrin's usefulness came to an end, then cast the thought from him for the illusion it was. Lohengrin was a British subject, charged under the Defence Regulations, but tried and convicted of nothing. As if that were not enough, Claire's open adoration of the man made any thoughts of dissolution absurd, and his own violent desire to protect her laughable.

Pemberton's suffering was of too high a degree to support itself for long and, collapsing under its own weight, left him embedded in a confusion of splintered shards of dead dreams, which emitted nothing more than the smell of irony. Bleakly, he wondered if, as was customary, the bride would kiss him after the service. The indication of just how alone Lohengrin must be to have asked his controller to stand at his side at the altar, and how much that would please Professor Morris, escaped him.

Carne, who said little but saw much, noted Pemberton's turmoil, accurately identified its cause and thought it of sufficient importance to inform London. His message reached a man called Clayton, of whose existence he was unaware, and the reply to it instructed him to observe and report.

Three people enjoyed the small reception enormously. Mr Brent, landlord of the 'Anglo-Saxon Arms', because it was being held out of licensing hours in his saloon bar and that meant money in his pocket; Sergeant Newland, because there were quantities of free beer to be drunk; and the bridesmaid, because she enjoyed parties and didn't get invited to them very often. She was a tall angular girl called Alice who had a capacity for aggressive friendliness and for sustaining conversation in a high-pitched screech.

Two people quite enjoyed it. One of them, Lohengrin, in a bemused haze of pleasure at his acquisition of a lovely wife, but the haze repeatedly ripped by shafts of conflicting loyalties which, even on this day of all days, refused to leave him at peace. The other, Claire, happy and excited, but disappointed too. 'His Lordship will not be able to attend,' the voice on the telephone had told her. 'He has flown to the States on Ministry of Aircraft Production business.' Then when she had asked Gail to be her bridesmaid she had been gently reminded that members of 'The Beautiful Bitch Brigade' only mixed in public when it was absolutely necessary, so she had had to settle for Alice, who lived not far away in Kent.

The remaining three people didn't enjoy it at all. Pemberton who couldn't wait for it to end, Carne, because he was worried about Pemberton and because Alice's voice was giving him a headache, and Harry. The couple were to spend their honeymoon at the house on Southdown Road and Harry was to go with them. He didn't like the thought of that. He didn't like the weight of the gun in his pocket either. If while he was monitoring a wireless transmission to Germany, Lohengrin should attempt to overpower him, Harry had been ordered by Carne to shoot him dead.

Chapter Twenty

'We've had a request from *die Brücke* for a Lisbon meeting, sir,' Colonel Frischauer said. 'He claims to have recruited a disaffected British Army officer and wants to take him with him for vetting.'

Admiral Canaris nodded. 'I see. Who's this Army man?'

'A lieutenant-colonel who's considered an expert on tank warfare and serves on one of their planning committees. He's said to be violently anti-Russian and would be prepared to work for an English surrender if the armistice terms were lenient and included a requirement that they join forces with us in defeating the Soviet Union.'

'I see,' Canaris said for the second time. 'You know, Frischauer, I get quite remarkably nervous when our people in Britain become involved in recruitment. The potential benefits are great, but so are the risks. Do I take it that this fellow is not aware of our agent's true function?'

'That's correct, sir. They're simply long-time acquaintances with a shared fear of Soviet world domination. I understand that that fear is much more widely spread in Britain than is generally recognized here and that our 1939 non-aggression pact with Russia was a contributing factor in bringing them into the war in the first inst . . .'

'Yes, yes, yes,' Canaris broke in. 'You've answered my question. I don't need a lecture. Wasn't *die Brücke* one of the two cleared by von Neustadt?'

'Yes, he was, and he appears to be extremely angry about having his position jeopardized by what he describes as an amateurish approach.' As though regretting having mentioned something the admiral might take as a criticism, Frischauer added quickly, 'Incidentally, he was slightly injured in a *Luftwaffe* attack on Folkestone the other day. A cannon-shell splinter across the chest. Nothing serious.'

Apparently interested neither in *die Brücke*'s anger nor his physical condition, 'There's always the possibility of this being a British plant,' Canaris said, 'but I can't see the logic of their attempting it this way. Firstly, it presupposes that *die Brücke* has been compromised when all the evidence indicates that that is not the case. Then, even assuming that knowingly or unknowingly he *has* been, the last thing they would do would be to expose him to interrogation by us by sending him to Lisbon. No, it makes no sense.'

Canaris shook his head as if confirming the accuracy of the conclusion he had arrived at and added, 'Let them travel to Lisbon and arrange for this anti-Russian to be brought to Berlin. He'll come readily enough if he's genuine. If he's reluctant, have him put under restraint and flown here anyway. It shouldn't take long to establish what he's about.'

'And *die Brücke*, sir?'

'He's to be held by the Lisbon *Stelle* until we've read their report on the Englishman,' Canaris said. 'I'll decide then.'

*

'I think you must assume that they'll take you to Germany,' Clayton said. 'Indeed, it would be most disappointing if they failed to do so.'

Pemberton agreed that it would be most disappointing and his tone of voice made Clayton glance questioningly at him.

'Are you nervous?'

'Scared stiff would be a better description, sir.'

'Good. This is no job for mindless heroes. Don't be afraid to let a little of it show. They'd expect that. You might convert some of it into anger when the opportunity arises. For some reason I have never been able to fathom, the Germans seem to appreciate being shouted at. It'll be good therapy for you too.'

'Yes,' Pemberton said, 'I thought a spot of hectoring might be in order, so I've been practising in front of the bathroom mirror.'

They smiled faintly at each other and Clayton went on, 'Whether or not they will want Pelham with you in Berlin I cannot say, but my guess would be that they will. By the way, I hope you have accustomed yourself to thinking of him by that name. It's vital that you put code names, ours or theirs, out of your mind until your return.'

With the wedding still a vividly unhappy memory and hearing Claire, hurtfully for him, referred to as Mrs Pelham several times a day, 'I'm quite used to it now,' Pemberton told him. 'Why do you think they'll want him in Berlin?'

'To cross-check your stories. You see, I shall be instructing him to express doubts about you to the enemy.'

'Thanks very much.'

'Oh, nothing specific, my dear chap,' Clayton said. 'Just natural caution on his part. After all, he wouldn't expect them to take you on trust and has to protect himself against your being found to be other than he has come to believe. His accompanying you to Lisbon, instead of simply arranging for you to be smuggled aboard the ship, fits the picture too. Suppose you were unmasked, as they say – well, when you failed to return, he wouldn't want to be still in England, would he?'

'Hmm.'

'Yes, it does sound risky, doesn't it? The thing to bear in mind is that the Germans will find it logical when he has told them his motive for absenting himself from these shores and they're demons for logic. It's very fortunate for us that they experience great difficulty in matching it with an equal degree of imagination. But, be that as it may, his attitude is likely to increase their trust in him without adding to their suspicion of you. You'll have all of that anyway, but I think that they'll find even the remotest prospect of having somebody in their pay on one of our military planning committees hard to resist.'

Already lying back in an armchair, Pemberton crossed one leg over the other, let his chin droop to his chest and contemplated the sharp crease in his khaki uniform trousers. He stayed like that for almost a minute before raising his eyes to Clayton and saying, 'Okay, sir, I'll buy it as far as I'm concerned, although I admit to a certain disquiet at placing my life so completely in Pelham's hands.'

'In his wife's, I think.'

The words had been no more than a murmur and Pemberton said, 'What, sir?'

Clayton fought and won a battle against his spectacle-polishing habit, then began to speak slowly. 'Look at it this way, Pemberton. We manufactured two imaginary holds over him in the form of threats to his father and the girl he had fallen in love with. At that time he was too confused by fear and drugs to guess at their unreality, even if his German background, and the ruthlessness that implies, and which he would attribute also to us, had permitted him to do so. Then, when we became aware of the depths of his affection for Claire Helier, we removed those holds, choosing a time when he was again in something of an emotional turmoil over the shooting of his compatriot, von Neustadt.'

Frowning as though he had lost the place in his measured monologue, then his face clearing as if he'd found it again, Clayton went on, 'I was advised by your *bête noire*, Professor Morris, that this relaxation of our grip would confuse Pelham further by its apparent illogicality, but that his overriding emotion would be gratitude for burdens eased, rather than resentment at our deceit. In addition, it was thought likely that he would turn even more to Claire Helier as a source of stability and comfort and the suggestion was made that they be permitted to marry. You know the outcome.'

'Yes? What about it?'

'Well, surely the rest is obvious. The strains on his German loyalties are greater now. I shall be giving him the choice of an unpleasant death which his countrymen will certainly arrange for him on receipt of his file, which I shall ensure gets into their hands if he betrays us, or of returning to his pretty wife.'

'All right,' Pemberton said. 'I know which I'd choose, but then I'm not very brave, which brings me to my final point. If this goes wrong and they produce the red-hot nutcrackers, what do I do? I have no illusions about my ability to remain silent. It doesn't exist.'

'You blow Pelham,' Clayton told him. 'You tell them everything you know about the Lohengrin-die *Brücke* case in isolation. You tell them he is the first and only German spy we have been able both to uncover and turn, and that we were using him in an attempt to infiltrate you into their Secret Service. Much of what you would be saying would be true, Pelham would be unable to deny it, and the consensus is that they would believe it because they would want to believe it. That is thought to be the case after close study of the German character and for the reason that anything remotely resembling the whole truth they would find unbelievable.' He hesitated, then added, 'None of which will save your life, but I think they'll put the nutcrackers away.'

*

The rollers advanced on the freighter with mindless obduracy, lifting the bow and dropping it, lifting the stern and dropping that too in a constant see-saw motion. Lohengrin huddled in the corner of the bridge, staring gloomily at the grey-green walls of water streaked with white like veined marble, hating them for the unremitting physical discomfort they caused him, hating them more for the submarine menace, both German and British, they concealed. Nausea, never quiescent for long, surged in him and he retched violently, but nothing came up. There was nothing left *to* come up. At the sound, the ship's mate said something in Portuguese to the helmsman, they both laughed and for a moment Lohengrin transferred his hatred to them, then went back to hating the sea.

When he had gone aboard in Cardiff the sight of the large Portuguese flag painted on the side of the hull with the name *Estefânia* above it and *Lisboa* below had given him some comfort. The markings had served well as talismans against marauding warplanes of both the RAF and the *Luftwaffe*, but he doubted their efficacy in warding off torpedoes when, in such seas, a periscope might reveal nothing more than the masts, funnel and bridge of the rusty old ship. Lohengrin, a courageous man out of his element, was afraid, and, with Lisbon only hours away beyond the *Estefania*'s rearing, plunging bow, a new fear awaited him. He was vaguely grateful that he appeared capable of thinking of only one at a time.

Much more positive gratitude enfolded him like a warm blanket when he opened his mind to his wife's existence. The very thought of her brought tears of happiness close. That they were also tears of weakness he knew, but no longer resented. They came closer still, the tears, when he recalled her urgent whisperings during their last night together. 'Don't come back, darling,' the breathy voice close to his ear had said. 'Don't do anything to hurt that nice Colonel Pemberton, but stay away and be safe. I'll be waiting for you when the war's over, however long it takes.'

He loved her for that; for her concern, for her naïvety. The appeal to him had been spontaneous, not relayed, and he thought that apart from her ability to swamp a man's critical faculties she must be a truly disastrous Intelligence agent. He loved her for that too.

When the mate spoke to the helmsman for the second time, the *Estefânia* turned across the swell onto a direct course for the mouth of the River Tagus and her pitching changed to a corkscrew motion. Claire fled from Lohengrin's mind, and after a minute he retched again.

*

Somewhat to his surprise and vastly to his relief, Pemberton had been unaffected by the weather. His main preoccupations during the three and a half days it had taken the *Estefânia* to cover six hundred miles of sea had been endurable claustrophobia and a small diesel-generator. The generator had shared the large crate in which he had been smuggled aboard and, although shackled to its container, it had shown an alarming tendency to lurch in sympathy with the ship's movements. Even now, in the calm waters of the Tagus, his imagination replayed to him the harsh screech of protesting metal. He took positive pleasure in the knowledge that it was only imagination for, of all the possible fates in store for him, being mangled by a piece of errant machinery was not one he had considered.

Twice a night, with only the bridge watch awake, Pelham had released him from his wooden prison on the after well-deck so that he could relieve himself and stretch his aching limbs and back. It had amused him that the spy should be travelling openly and in comfort as a representative of the Ministry of Food while he himself was so confined. That he, with plenty to eat and drink inside the crate, had fared much better than Pelham, to whom the sight of food had become anathema, he was unaware.

*

'That's the one,' the man in blue overalls said in bad Portuguese, and pointed at the last in line of four crates secured to the after well-deck of the *Estefânia*.

The customs officer grunted and shouted up at the crane driver. He guessed from his accent that the man beside him was German and he didn't like Germans, but he did like American dollars and the man had given him a lot of them. Keeping his hand on the thick wad of bills in his pocket he watched while the slings were attached to the crate, saw it lifted, swung towards the jetty and lowered onto a Ford truck. He took his hand from his money for long enough to make a chalk mark on the crate, then strode away.

Although he had been expecting something of the sort, the pendulum-like swing from ship to shore made Pemberton gasp and clutch the diesel-generator for support, only to have his grip broken when the crate thudded heavily onto some surface which oscillated momentarily under him. He cursed softly.

For a little while after that there was stillness and silence, then came a sharp rapping and a voice saying, 'You are there, Colonel Pemberton?'

'Yes,' he said.

The sound of an engine starting, a jolt and the beginning of swaying, juddering progress across cobblestones which lasted for seventeen minutes before stillness and silence returned. A creak of hinges and sunlight stabbing at his eyes, the first full light he had seen for eighty-five hours.

'Welcome to Portugal, Colonel Pemberton.'

He squinted at the man in blue overalls, nodded and eased himself to the ground, then stood beside the truck, swaying slightly, looking around him at the courtyard of a house. A big solid wooden gate stood open to the street showing him people passing on the pavement outside, an occasional car on the road.

'Come!'

Ignoring the summons, Pemberton walked to the gate.

'Where you go?' Sudden alarm in the voice.

Ignoring that too, he looked across the road for a street sign and saw one. 'Rua Braancamp' it read. He glanced to his right at a tall pillar resembling a stocky Nelson's Column with an heroic effigy of a man with a lion lying beside him at its summit. As always, Pemberton liked to know exactly where he was and now he knew. He had studied a map of Lisbon before leaving England, memorizing salient points together with the major streets surrounding them. The statue he was looking at had been raised in honour of the Marques de Pombal and stood at the centre of the great traffic circle bearing his name, staring over the city spread out below it. And that, Pemberton concluded, meant that he was almost certainly at the *Abwehr* house he had spoken of to Professor Morris when they were tormenting Lohengrin.

'You come! Now! *Schnell!*'

The man in blue overalls was tugging at his sleeve, but he jerked his arm free and closed the big gate before turning to face him.

'Are you in charge here?'

'No, not in charge.'

'Thank God for that,' Pemberton said in a fierce whisper. 'Clear all that food and stuff out of the crate. Get rid of everything that shows I was ever in it and bring my suitcase indoors. I'm going to find somebody who knows what he's doing!'

He had gone into the house through a side door leading to a flight of stairs when the man caught up with him, shouting in German and trying to free an automatic from a pocket in his overalls. Pemberton hit him hard in the solar plexus, then brought a knee sharply up into his face as his body jack-knifed.

Writhing, trying to drag air back into his lungs, blood pouring from his mouth and nose, the man lay across the threshold. Pemberton dragged him inside and picked up the discarded gun.

'Drop it.'

The voice coming from the stairs behind him carried quiet authority and he put the automatic carefully back on the floor then turned round in obedience to a second command. He made both movements very slowly.

'You are Pemberton?'

He looked at another gun and at the man holding it, a dapper figure in a pale grey lounge suit, shiny black shoes, white shirt and blue tie.

'This place is like a bloody arsenal,' he said. 'Yes, I'm Pemberton.'

'Then perhaps you will be good enough to tell me what it is you think you are doing.'

The gun was still pointing at him and the man holding it had not moved from the top of the stairs.

'I'm trying to save myself from the attentions of this idiot,' he told him. 'Somebody ought to lock him up out of harm's way.'

'That is so? Why, please?'

'Stop pointing that thing at me and I'll explain,' Pemberton said, saw the gun lowered until it was resting beside a grey-trousered leg and went on, 'His first piece of idiocy was to hammer on the crate when we were still in the dockyard and address me by my name and rank. He did it again when we got here. Is the bloody fool trying to get me interned by the Portuguese?' Without waiting for a reply he went on, 'As if that wasn't enough, he hasn't got the sense to shut the gate and I climb out in full view of the public. Well, perhaps people in filthy clothes with three days' growth of stubble on their faces are always emerging from crates in Lisbon. Never having been here before I wouldn't know, but it strikes me as the sort of behaviour likely to attract attention. Christ, it would make a retarded ape think!'

'And this makes you strike him down?'

Pemberton shook his head. 'No, that was when he tried to pull a gun on me. I get frightened by amateurs with guns. What's he carrying one in public for anyway?'

The man walked down the stairs then and stood looking down at the overalled figure, sitting now, back to the wall.

'*Der Englander hat recht. Du bist ein Dummkopf,*' he said without venom, and equally passionlessly kicked the other's thigh before adding something that Pemberton didn't understand. The overalled man got to his feet, wiped blood from his face with a handkerchief and went out into the courtyard.

'What's he going to do now?' Pemberton asked.

'I tell him to clean out your transport box. Come. You will wish a bath and a shave before we eat and talk. I am Horst Eckart.'

The German turned abruptly away and Pemberton followed him up the stairs, glad that he had not been offered a hand to shake, hoping that he had not overplayed his own.

While Pemberton lay luxuriating in a bath, Eckart, under orders to attempt no interrogation in case it should prejudice the chances of the experts in Berlin, wrote out a radio message giving his first impressions of the man who might or might not be an English renegade. It informed Colonel Frischauer that, in the sender's opinion, Pemberton was the run-of-the-mill regimental officer he claimed to be. In substantiation of that view, he reported that while Pemberton had noticed the various deliberate mistakes in basic procedure made for his benefit, he had also attempted to establish his whereabouts in an openly clumsy fashion before assaulting his escort in a virtually purposeless display of nervous hostility. His actions, Eckart ended, were more in keeping with those of a man playing a part he had cast himself in than of an Intelligence operative with even minimal training. Frischauer's reply reached Lisbon before the two had finished a late lunch.

'They wish you in Berlin,' Eckart said. '*Herr* Pelham also.'

'When?'

'Tomorrow. You will travel by *Lufthansa*, dressed as airmen.'

'Very well. Where's Pelham now?'

'He stays at the Avenida Palace Hotel. As an official of the English Food Ministry, it would not be logical for him to be seen here.'

'Quite,' Pemberton said. 'I'll go and see him this afternoon, just to make sure he's all right.'

Eckart frowned at him and Pemberton went on, 'Look, I've been shut up in that blasted crate for days and I need to get out and about. I know I haven't got any papers, but according to our press neither have half the people in Lisbon, all of them refugees trying to get away from you people.'

'Like the English army at Dunkirk perhaps?'

A faint smile had replaced the frown on Eckart's face and Pemberton experienced unreasoning anger at the taunt. The lifting of a third of a million men off the beaches and their safe return to England had become part of British folklore. Some saw it, perversely, as a victory, the majority as a miraculous deliverance, a few realists as a crushing defeat. Those in the last two categories were both right, for it had been both of those things and Pemberton had to remind himself of the fact; remind himself, too, that he was supposed to have taken part in the retreat and the evacuation which followed it, and that he was also supposed to be an admirer of the German military machine.

'At least we fought the best army in the world and didn't surrender,' he said coldly. 'Where is the Palace Hotel?'

Eckart told him.

*

The Avenida da Liberdade ran broad and straight from the heights of Praca Marques de Pombal down the long sloping hillside towards the River Tagus, before losing its sense of purpose and its identity by colliding incongruously with the unimposing hotel which was Pemberton's destination. The Avenida Palace stood half astride the great thoroughfare from which it took its name, blocking its progress into the vast square of the Rossio beyond, and Pemberton wondered, without any particular interest, what thought processes had resulted in such poor planning. It made him think of building a pier, starting to seaward and abandoning the work before the structure reached the shore. Shrugging, he went into the hotel and walked to the reception desk.

'No,' the man behind the desk said, '*Senhor* Pelham is not in the hotel. His key is on the board. You leave a message, please?'

'I'll wait for a little,' Pemberton told him.

It was good to sit down in the comparative cool of the foyer after what he thought must have been a two-mile walk down the Avenida. Not that two miles was anything, but it had tired him after his long incarceration in the crate aboard the *Estefânia*. That and the heat and the teaming masses of people, many of them the refugees he had spoken of to Eckart, milling apparently aimlessly about on the broad pavements inlaid with never-ending mosaics of black and grey.

They were of many nationalities, the people; only the Portuguese themselves readily identifiable, small and dark-skinned, most of the women of child-bearing age pregnant, most of the men spitting frequently, making paving stones slippery with slime. Pemberton grimaced and stared through the open doorway of the hotel at the long vista of the Avenida da Liberdade, stretching upwards, losing itself in distance and a haze of heat, its triumphal proportions made ridiculous by the unimposing buildings lining its sides.

Finding himself guilty of dismissing Lisbon out of hand on the basis of small evidence, Pemberton called on his memory, summoning up the points of the city he had imprinted on his brain. The Praco do Comercio, reputed to be one of the most beautiful squares in the world; the Castelo de S. Jorge in the Alfama district overlooking the river; the Rossio with its . . .

The Rossio, immediately behind the hotel he was sitting in! That was where Lohengrin would be!

Pemberton stood up and left the hotel, not hurrying. He turned right and right again into the big square, looking for the store of Marcus & Hartig where Lohengrin's father had once worked. It wasn't difficult to find, a small crowd standing in front of the display windows looking curiously at the blown up photographs depicting a mixture of German military might and German youth at play. Of the two he found the latter more disturbing than the massed tanks, the goose-stepping soldiers, the bomber formations. They looked simultaneously idiotic and sinister, the hand-picked, fair haired, laughing boys and girls in their lederhosen and dirndl skirts. Lohengrin was sitting at a pavement café table within a few yards of the place, staring morosely at nothing.

'Hello, Pelham,' Pemberton said.

'Oh, hello. Like a beer?'

'Yes, please.'

Pemberton sat down, facing the way he had come, waiting for the fat man to arrive. In less than a minute he did so, sitting down himself at the next pavement café, unfolding a newspaper.

'You're being followed,' Lohengrin said. 'The tubby bloke in the striped shirt, reading a paper just along the street.'

A waiter brought their beer then, and Pemberton waited until he had gone before saying, 'Yes, I noticed him at Praca Marques de Pombal and saw him again hanging about outside your hotel. How did you know?'

'I had a visit from a chap from the German Embassy. He told me I was to fly to Berlin with you tomorrow morning. That man was driving the car.'

Pemberton nodded, relaxing, sipping his beer. 'Oh, that's all right then,' he said. 'Just as long as he isn't Portuguese. I couldn't believe that MI6 could be stupid enough to come within a mile of us.' He paused, looked at Lohengrin and asked, 'Are you nervous about tomorrow?'

'Of course I'm bloody well nervous. Aren't you?'

'Yes, you could say that.'

Neither spoke again until Pemberton felt something touch his knee under the table.

'Take it,' Lohengrin said. 'It's from Claire. I was to give it to you when we got this far. You're to read it and destroy it at once.'

The fat man was engrossed in his newspaper and Pemberton took the envelope, glanced down at it. There was no inscription. He tore it open and looked at the single line of handwriting on the sheet of paper it contained. 'Please, oh please bring him safely back to me' it read. Each word was heavily underlined. There was no signature. Pemberton looked at Lohengrin.

'Do you know what this is?'

'No. I was going to steam it open aboard the ship, but I was too seasick to do it well enough for you not to notice.'

'It's a love letter to you,' Pemberton said. 'Here. Read it and destroy it yourself.'

He watched Lohengrin look down and read the message below the level of the table, saw him crumple the paper and thrust it into his trouser pocket, heard him say, 'Was she instructed to write that so you could show it to me?' There was a fixed, falsely bright smile on Lohengrin's face.

His eyes locked on the other's. 'No,' Pemberton told him. 'Think about it. Do you really imagine the Service would be a party to such a blatant breach of security? The inference . . .' He didn't bother to finish the sentence, but went on, 'Quite apart from that, we aren't stupid enough to kid ourselves that we any longer have control over your wife as far as you are concerned. She loves you, man.'

The fixed smile softened, faded. 'As you love her,' Lohengrin said.

From its beginning the exchange had been in low voices, but Pemberton's sank even lower when he replied, 'As I love her. I suppose it was inevitable that one or the other, or both of you should notice, although I've tried hard not to let it show.'

'You tried too hard.'

Pemberton shrugged. 'Well, I'm sorry, but you've got nothing to fear from me. I promise you that.'

'I'm sure of it. Rotten for you, though.'

'Christ,' Pemberton said in a louder voice. 'This is a weird conversation to be having in the middle of Lisbon. I only came down to see if you were all right. It's time I took my fat friend for a walk back up the Avenida. See you at the airport.'

He stood up, murmured, 'Destroy that note', saw Lohengrin's emphatic nod, and walked away, thinking a little bitterly that Claire's breaking the rules could have done nothing but good. After a minute the fat man folded his paper and strolled after him.

Dusk overtook Pemberton on the Avenida da Liberdade and night had come before he had completed the long climbing walk to Praca Marques de

Pombal. The lighted streets and buildings confused him with their unnaturalness and he found himself glancing nervously, ridiculously, at the sky. It was a long time since he had seen a city illuminated by anything other than fires, anti-aircraft shell bursts and searchlights.

It was stranger still the next day to be sitting in a *Lufthansa* plane, dressed in *Lufthansa* uniform, beside Lohengrin similarly attired; two airline pilots returning to Germany on leave.

With the narrow strip of land which was Portugal soon left behind, the tri-motored Ju53 bumped its slow way through the convection currents rising from the sun-scorched land of Spain to Madrid. Both stayed in the plane there to avoid the unnecessary risk of exposing themselves to the scrutiny of yet more neutral officialdom.

Unaffected as he had been by the sea, Pemberton came close to vomiting during the soaring plummeting progress between the rocky crags of the Pyrenees and he stumbled thankfully out onto the tarmac at Toulouse in Vichy France. At Paris the might of Nazi Europe enfolded him like a shroud and he began seriously to doubt his own courage. His tension increased at Frankfurt, but it was not until the plane's tyres squealed their protest on contact with the dimly lit runway of a Berlin airport that Pemberton's doubts were swept away by the certain knowledge that he was deeply afraid. Whether he was at Gatow, or Tempelhof, or some other aerodrome, he did not know, nor did he greatly care, as his liking for precisely establishing his whereabouts seemed to have lost all relevance.

Two cars waiting near the foot of the aircraft's steps, he being urged into one, Lohengrin into the other. A fast drive along blacked-out, unidentifiable streets. Some bomb damage visible against the skyline. Not as much as London, but there. Thinking, you wait, you bastards, it's coming. The officer beside him with the double lightning-flash of the SS on his collar saying 'Look forward only, please.' Ignoring him. The second car turning off towards some different destination, carrying Lohengrin away, increasing his loneliness, his fear. The officer repeating his instruction. Telling him to drop dead. The car slowing, stopping. Being guided by the elbow into a large building, along passages, into a small room. A very pretty girl at a desk giving him a mechanical smile. Not returning it. A second, larger room beyond. Two officers standing at its centre. The one extending a hand, saying, 'Welcome to Berlin. I am Colonel Frischauer.'

Chapter Twenty-One

Almost the whole Committee was present and the main item on the agenda had been the subject of files, a matter so prosaic as to be boring, so important as to command no less a classification than 'vital'. The problem had been growing for eighteen months now, expanding as the files filled and multiplied, burgeoning into volumes, into shelves, into libraries of chronicles containing information which must never be overlooked. Every questionnaire from Germany, be it on food production, bomb damage, civilian morale, shipping losses, the specifications of a new fighter aircraft, the movements of troops both internally and from across the Atlantic, any of the multifarious matters of urgent concern to the German High Command, was meticulously recorded. So too were the replies of each and every double agent to his *Abwehr* spymaster, whether passed by radio, invisible writing or any other means, for never must the fallible memory of a case officer allow the spy under his control illogically to contradict a statement he had made a year before.

Conversely, for him not to modify his earlier assessment of some situation which had manifestly changed would be equally damaging to his credibility, as would something as simple as a failure to ask for money after sufficient time had elapsed since his previous payment to make him theoretically in need of it.

All such information, indexed, and cross-indexed to cover those agents notionally in contact with one another, made up a volume of paper it was becoming increasingly difficult for a case officer to encompass. The drastic pruning of non-essential material had become a prerequisite of continued efficiency and, after some hours of discussion, a sub-committee had been elected to deal with the matter, its terms of reference clearly defined.

No lover of administrative work, Edward Mainwaring was both tired and anxious to return to his own desk when somebody asked, 'Before we disperse, is there any news of our two tourists?'

'Yes,' he replied. 'Beresford saw them board a *Lufthansa* plane at Lisbon this morning dressed as pilots.' He glanced at his watch and added, 'They should have reached Paris by now and be in Berlin by tonight, if that's where they're being taken.'

'Good luck to them!'

Mainwaring smiled, nodded, and was gathering his papers together when another voice said, 'Sir?' Looking to his left, diagonally across the long conference table, he identified the speaker as Grant, one of the most recently appointed members of the Committee. He raised his eyebrows questioningly, not speaking.

'I wasn't present when the decision to mount this operation was taken,' Grant told him, 'and I'm very unhappy about it. You explained to me when I first attended one of these meetings that it was not uncommon for a turned agent to make contact with his original masters in a neutral country, but it is surely beyond all reason to send his case officer with him. The next twenty-four hours may well bring the entire house of cards we have constructed tumbling about our ears. I doubt it will take the Gestapo longer than that to discover everything Pemberton knows and I can see no possible justification for our taking such a risk.'

Disliking people who raised objections to matters which had already passed beyond anybody's control, disliking being addressed as 'sir' as though he were a schoolmaster and having no particular fondness for Grant, Mainwaring sighed inaudibly. Already working for eighteen hours out of every day, he resented this additional call on his time, but unanimity of thought, of purpose, had to be maintained and he nodded again.

'Come with me,' he said. 'You too, Peter, if you wouldn't mind.'

In his room he gestured towards chairs, sat behind his desk and looked searchingly at the palms of his hands as though something might be written there before saying, 'The position as I see it is this. We have now passed through the formative stage and arrived at a point where we have reason to believe that we control the German espionage system in this country in its entirety. That there may still be spies at large operating independently of those in our hands is a possibility we must never lose sight of, but the likelihood of that being so decreases with the passage of time and with the continued lack of any evidence of their existence. New arrivals being promptly apprehended because the enemy obligingly forewarns us of their coming is additional proof that he still believes his own organization to be inviolate.'

Grant moved uneasily in his chair, opened his mouth to speak, but closed it again at the sight of Mainwaring's raised hand.

'Bear with me,' Mainwaring said. 'I know you didn't ask for a history lesson, but it's important that you should see the overall picture so that you may understand why I have taken what you consider to be an unjustifiable risk. All right?'

'Of course.'

'Very well. So far we have done little more than test the water with our big toe, but for all that we have achieved several successful deceptions, two of them of considerable significance. First, the luring of a large part of the German Fleet to Norway, where it remains to this day ready to oppose a non-existent threat. Second, the forging of the map of South America, so deftly handled by William Stephenson in New York. That led directly to the abandonment of United States neutrality after President Roosevelt apparently accepted it as genuine and revealed its existence in his address to the Navy Day dinner last October 27th.'

Mainwaring's head had begun to ache and he pressed the tips of his fingers to his temples. It didn't help, so he took them away again and went on, 'Of course the latter had nothing whatsoever to do with the running of double agents which is our main task, but it's a very telling example of what can be achieved by carefully planned deception tactics even though our best friends were the target. I'm sure you'll agree with that.'

'Certainly I will,' Grant said, 'but . . .'

'But it still doesn't answer your point,' Mainwaring broke in. 'Don't worry. I'm getting there slowly. The thing is that the degree to which we can manipulate the enemy is limited by the amount of information the agents he believes he has operating in this country could reasonably be expected to acquire. If we exceed that limit – well, that would make anyone think, wouldn't it? With Pemberton, however, apparently a highly placed officer on a military planning committee, we can push the horizon very much further away as, obviously, he will have access to information no spy could ever hope to get his hands on in anything but the most fragmented form. Agreed?'

'Yes.'

'Very well,' Mainwaring said for the second time. 'For the moment put aside thoughts of the Gestapo and what they might or might not achieve, and assume that the *Abwehr* accepts Pemberton as a recruit. His imaginary committee will be concerned solely with our eventual return to mainland Europe in force which, according to the planners, is unlikely to take place in less than two years. Pemberton will spend that period telling them of our thinking and of our actions and, as in the case of double agents, much of what he says will be both true and verifiable. Again in fragmented form, the majority of double agents will confirm what he says with varying degrees of detail and accuracy. The minority will ostensibly get it all wrong and will almost certainly be assumed to have fallen victim to our cover stories. Then, the enemy's confidence having been gained, and we may have to sacrifice some lives to win his trust in Pemberton, we hand the Germans a bill of goods which will leave them stranded in the outfield. With luck it will take them days to relocate their forces in the right place, and by then it will be too late.'

His head throbbing, Mainwaring pressed his fingers against the corners of his eyes again and Grant made use of the pause to say, 'Sir, except for Pemberton's new part in it, I really know all this.'

'You weren't aware of the reason for putting Pemberton in to bat,' Mainwaring told him, 'and until you were it was pointless attempting to discuss the risk factor with you.'

Throughout what had been a virtual monologue, Clayton had scarcely moved, but now he sank lower in his chair and said, 'Why don't you go and borrow some of your secretary's aspirins, Edward? I'll explain why we do not believe that we have been foolhardy.'

Mainwaring smiled gratefully and left the room.

'Ian.'

'Yes, Peter?'

'Don't call him "sir". He doesn't like it.'

'Oh. Thanks for telling me.'

There was a long silence and Grant waited patiently, aware for the first time of the ticking of the clock on the mantel and the sound of traffic in the street below, until Clayton saying, 'About Pemberton' dispelled them.

'Yes?'

'The risks to him are great and to us small. He is aware of both those facts and knows precisely what he's doing. I tested him myself by suggesting that he blew Lohengrin in isolation if the pressure became too much, but he refused to accept that. His point, which I had hoped he would make, was that he had been Parsifal's controlling officer too and that he would certainly reveal the fact under drugs or torture. Consequently, *in extremis*, the story he will tell is that von Neustadt was apprehended by us shortly after his arrival, that he revealed the identities of both Parsifal and Lohengrin under interrogation, together with the appropriate clearance phrases for both of them, and that he was subsequently executed. We then staged his shooting at Eastbourne as a cover story, which happens to be true even if the alleged reason will have changed.'

Mainwaring came back into the room then, but neither man looked at him and Clayton said, 'Put yourself in the place of an *Abwehr* interrogating officer and tell me what you would infer from that.'

'It's neat enough as far as it goes,' Grant told him. 'If Pemberton breaks and talks, only Lohengrin's organization and that being operated on behalf of the dead Parsifal will have to close down. In addition, the uncovering of those two agents being placed at von Neustadt's door should, by implication, strengthen the position of the rest of them.'

'As far as it goes, you say?'

'Yes, it ignores the fact that Pemberton must know a great deal more.'

'Well, he's not a fool,' Clayton said. 'Obviously he's aware that Lohengrin and Parsifal cannot be the only pebbles on the beach, but he doesn't actually know of any others, and what he doesn't know he can't talk about. In fact, if he tried to express an opinion in that direction it would almost certainly be disbelieved on two counts. The first, that all men reach a stage under pressure when they will say anything they think their inquisitors want to hear, and that renders their statements valueless. The second, that what Pemberton may have guessed to be the truth would be inconceivable to the Germans. They'd discount it as the ramblings of a broken man, or look upon it as an attempt by us to undermine their faith in their own espionage network.'

As though he had been contradicted, Clayton added almost angrily, 'For heaven's sake, man, *we* can hardly bring *ourselves* to believe the magnitude of our coup with all the facts before us! What chance have they got?'

'And Lohengrin?' Grant had spoken the words quietly, his tone seeming to suggest that he had asked the unanswerable question, but he still amplified it by going on, 'He could destroy Pemberton in one sentence.'

'Which would be most unfortunate for Pemberton,' Clayton said, 'but it wouldn't do us a great deal of harm beyond the loss of an excellent case officer and a useful double agent. The points already made to you would still apply and Pemberton would admit to the uncovering of the two agents by wireless fixes on unauthorized transmissions leading to his own mission, a mission designed to unearth more of them by his infiltrating the German Secret Service. Lohengrin could add little other than the names of a couple of his fellow spies now dead and known by the Germans to be dead.'

Grant sat for a moment longer, looking thoughtful, then stood up before saying, 'I'm obliged to you both, and pray that you have read the German mentality correctly.'

Mainwaring spoke for the first time since his return to the room, 'We think we have. Before you joined us, we tried deliberately to expose one of their people in our care. The man wasn't much use to us and we made him a test case, trailing our coats by breaking all the rules in an attempt to discover their procedure in such circumstances. I can only assume that they refused to believe he had been turned, because they didn't bite. They're still paying him, still asking him all the usual questions and he's still working for us.'

'Extraordinary,' Grant murmured and walked out, the thoughtful expression fixed on his face.

*

Pemberton nodded to Frischauer, ignored his outstretched hand and looked at the second man present. Again a hand was extended towards him, this time horizontally from the shoulder.

'Heil Hitler!'

'Really?' Pemberton said. 'Well, fuck you and Hitler both.'

The man gazed at him woodenly and Pemberton guessed that he had not understood the words. Frischauer raised a quizzical eyebrow.

'You won't live for very long if you say things like that in this country, Colonel Pemberton.'

Shrugging, 'Demagogic crap,' Pemberton muttered.

Frischauer sighed, pointed to a chair and said, 'Perhaps we start again. This is not the most auspicious beginning. They tell me from Lisbon that you are aggressive, but so much I had not expected. Why should you be so?'

Shrugging again, Pemberton walked to the chair and sat down. He didn't reply to the question. It was weird, he thought, to be sitting in this darkly panelled room, looking at German uniforms, at swastikas, at a picture of Hitler on the wall. It was weirder still to hear the sound of air-raid sirens coming through the heavily curtained windows and Frischauer saying, 'Ah, the Royal Air Force adds its welcome to mine.' Weirdest of all was the knowledge that he was facing a man he had been in wireless communication with for many months and that only he was aware of the fact.

'Yes,' Pemberton said. 'They're the people Goering was stupid enough to say would never cross the boundaries of the Reich. Bloody fool.'

Propped on the edge of his desk, Frischauer watched him curiously. The other man stood, watching him too, his face still wooden. Pemberton felt a bead of moisture dislodge itself from his left armpit and trickle down the side of his chest, felt too the quivering of his nerves and prayed that neither manifestation of his intense anxiety would become visible. The silence dragged on until, finding it unbearable, Pemberton broke it by asking, 'Who's this man?'

'He is only for making sure that you do nothing foolish. Lisbon are warning us, as I tell you.'

'Oh for Christ's sake!' Pemberton said. 'What do you expect me to do? Kill you and walk home?' When Frischauer made no reply, Pemberton added, 'It must be obvious to even a square-head like you that you're in no danger from me, but you'd better warn him that if he comes near me I'll take it as an unfriendly act and kick his shoulder-blades off.'

Anti-aircraft guns began to bark then, making the glass of the windows rattle and there was the distant crump of exploding bombs.

'Do you wish to go to the shelter, Colonel Pemberton?'

'How the hell would I know? It's your air raid, not mine.'

'We stay here for now, I think.'

'Anything you say.'

'What I say,' Frischauer announced in a louder voice, 'is that for an admirer of our system you are behaving in a most strange fashion!'

'An *admirer* of your system?' Pemberton said. 'I *hate* your stinking system!'

'Then why are you here?'

'Oh, for Christ's sake!' Pemberton repeated. 'Get that idiot Pelham in here.' He half rose from his chair, looking towards the door, then subsided again and went on, 'I told him what to tell you about me. Didn't you read his wireless messages?'

'*Herr* Pelham is busy. You tell me, please.'

'Oh, very well. I came here, as you must know, to offer my services to your Intelligence establishment with a view to achieving a swift cessation of hostilities between our two countries. Neither side is prepared to surrender and by the time you are it will be too late.'

'By the time *we* are?' Incredulity in Frischauer's voice.

Pemberton nodded offhandedly. 'Yes. We're going to smash you, make no mistake about it. Italy first, probably, then you. The writing is on the wall. You'd better start reading it.' More bombs fell, still distant. He gestured towards the window and added, 'Before long there will be a thousand of our planes over Germany at the same time with a regularity that will reduce this country to rubble, and Goering will be no more able to stop them than he has tonight's visitors.'

Frischauer smiled and said, 'I'm sure the *Reichmarshal* will be fascinated to hear what you have said, but enough of your frightening us to death. You tell me that when *we* have surrendered it will be too late. For what it will be too late?'

'For stopping the Russians.'

'Ah so. You are the anti-Bolshevist.'

'I'm glad your memory's coming back.'

'Please to explain the connection.'

'Surely it's obvious,' Pemberton said. 'The effort required to defeat you will be colossal. Our planners have no illusions about that, but it *will* be made and it *will* succeed. The tragedy, which so few of my countrymen seem to recognize, is that it will all have been for nothing.'

Still smiling, 'Why is this?' Frischauer asked and Pemberton replied angrily, 'Can't you see it either? We shan't have the strength left to hold the Russians! By tearing each other to bits our countries are making them a present of the whole of Europe!'

'So we should unite against the common enemy?'

'We must!'

'This is what you English call a capital idea,' Frischauer said, 'but it is not new. Already the *Führer* has said it many times.'

'Then he's got something right for once.'

'And for this idea you will betray your country?'

'To save the world from the Mongol hordes I would do anything!' Pemberton told him.

There was a long silence after that. Frischauer appeared absorbed in contemplation of the high polish of his boots, his face thoughtful. Pemberton could feel the eyes of the other man on him, but did not look in his direction. Outside, the guns had fallen silent and the windows no longer rattled. Neither fact registered on Pemberton's mind and he sat motionless, aware of his muscles locked in tension, aware of his shirt clinging to skin now slick with sweat, aware of the heavy thumping of his heart. That bit about saving the world from the Mongol hordes sounded pathetically puerile when memory repeated the words back to him. Right for the occasion? He hoped so. 'Don't be afraid of a little theatricality,' Clayton had said. 'They'll understand that more easily than British reserve. Very theatrical race, the Germans. You know, all those banners, and strutting like turkeys, and shouting *"Sieg heil"*. Strange people.'

The sirens sounded again, but lost in his mental rambling, Pemberton didn't hear them until Frischauer said, 'Ah, your friends go home. Now we shall eat and amuse ourselves. Perhaps then you like our system better.'

'I didn't come here to amuse myself,' Pemberton answered. 'If I can't see somebody in authority tonight, I'd like to go to bed. It's been a long day and I'm tired.'

'Already you see somebody in authority,' Frischauer told him. 'More later for the questioning. You will have no difficulty to stay awake where I take you. Come.'

Frischauer pushed himself away from the desk and left the room. Pemberton sighed, rose and followed him with the expressionless man at his heels.

Outside the door, 'Colonel Pemberton of the British Royal Army,' Frischauer said. 'My secretary, *Fräulein* Hildegarde Mohr. You go with her, please.'

The girl smiled, less mechanically now, and that made Pemberton smile back. He followed her, thinking how pretty she was, then turned and glanced at the nameless, expressionless man.

'Aren't you coming too, Fritz?'

Frischauer answered for him. 'No. I think you are not after all dangerous.'

It was a rather luxurious bedroom she led him to. It had a bathroom attached to it and civilian clothing was tidily laid out on the bed.

'The Colonel thought you would feel more comfortable in "civvies",' the girl said.

Pemberton blinked at the colloquialism, at the perfect accent, but before he could speak she asked, 'It isn't really called the Royal Army, is it?'

'No, just the Army. What remarkable English you speak.'

'I was educated at Roedean and Girton,' she said. 'Could you be ready to leave in half an hour?'

He nodded and watched her graceful progress towards the door. When it shut behind her he switched off the light and parted the curtains just enough to reveal the steel mesh covering the glass of the window. Its presence made much more sense to him than the conversation with Frischauer had done. He closed the curtains, switched on the light and undressed, glad to be rid of the *Lufthansa* uniform and damp shirt. After he had showered, he dressed in the clothes provided for him, finding that they fitted well enough. Lisbon, he supposed, had informed Berlin of his approximate size as well as of his aggression.

When he had finished there were still fifteen minutes to wait and he thought about searching the room for hidden microphones, decided that it would be a pointless thing to do as he didn't intend to say anything, and thought about Hildegarde Mohr instead. Apart from Claire, she was, he concluded, the most desirable creature he had seen for a long time. Frischauer and the late Major Dressier, who had so envied his superior's afternoons with her, would have agreed with him.

She returned in precisely thirty minutes and he followed her back the way they had come, admiring her legs. It was an easy thing to do, but Pemberton did it with dedicated concentration, then allowed his imagination free rein about the rest of her. It was, he found, a pleasant and temporarily effective method of tricking his mind, of preventing it from dwelling on what would happen to him if he made a mistake, or Lohengrin reverted to his original allegiance.

'We go to a club I know, off the *Kurfürstendamm*,' Frischauer said.

'All right.'

'Behave yourselves if you can,' Hildegarde Mohr said, and Frischauer nodded, smiling.

Both in civilian clothes now, the two men stood, ten minutes later, in a small queue of others similarly dressed in the foyer of the club but, despite their apparent anonymity, the man in white tie and tails at the tasselled rope barrier seemed to know who everybody was.

'*Herr Kapitän.*'

'*Herr General.*'

A languid hand gesturing them past the barrier.

'*Guten A bend, Herr Standartenführer!*'

Be particularly polite to the SS, Pemberton thought. Then it was their turn.

'*Herr Oberst.*'

Frischauer nodded, took Pemberton by the arm and led him into the club.

There was a lot of red plush, gilt mirrors, some twenty tables and a miniature stage. Nearly all the tables were already filled, mostly by men, but with an occasional woman here and there. A table, close to the stage, was vacant and a waiter conducted them to it.

'*Bringen Sie mir eine Flasche Kognac und die Speisekarte,*' Frischauer said, and like a conjurer the waiter produced menus from beneath the tail of his coat, then went to fetch the brandy.

'You like women?' Frischauer asked.

'Naturally.'

The German laughed and said, 'Perhaps these are not so natural, but you like, I think. First you must choose your food.'

'You choose it. I can't read the language and wouldn't know what the dishes were if I could.'

'Very well.'

They drank brandy and beetroot soup with a raw egg broken into it. Following Frischauer's example Pemberton stirred the mixture and watched the egg swirl into the form of a spiral nebula. The result tasted excellent, but he didn't like the main course. Heavily spiced sausages of several kinds, sauerkraut and a type of bean so hot that he choked and gulped brandy to cool his mouth.

Frischauer laughed again, 'Hot, no?'

When he could speak, 'Hot, yes,' Pemberton said.

They were finishing a fruit flan chosen from the sweet trolley when the lights dimmed, went out. Silence as intense as the darkness descended on the room, then Pemberton heard movement on the stage beside him and the soft rolling beat of a kettledrum. Obscurely, he felt a growing unease which had no connection with his ever-present anxiety. At the table behind him a woman sighed tremulously. The kettledrum continued its monotone roll.

A spotlight pierced the darkness, holding arabesques of tobacco smoke in its beam, impinging on a naked man, his wrists manacled in front of him, a heavy wooden triangle at his back with a metal hook at its apex. More lights sprang to life, illuminating the girls, four of them, two to either side of the man, clad in double-breasted leather greatcoats, tall collars turned up, hems almost touching the insteps of their high-heeled jack-boots. Pemberton felt ice forming in his stomach and pulsing outwards to chill his skin, glanced at Frischauer, seeing his slack mouth and beads of sweat forming on his forehead. Looked back at the girls, two in brown, two in black, highlights moving on the leather like oil on water, whips hanging from their belts. Searched incongruously for a word to describe what little could be seen of their expressionless, exotic faces beneath the peaks of military-style caps, finding 'robot' and then 'android'.

Hearing the man speaking stumblingly, his voice quavering. Asking Frischauer to interpret. Being told that it was a confession of black-market dealings and that he had chosen this in preference to hanging. Watching two of the girls grasping the man, turning him round, forcing the manacles over the metal hook on the triangle, spreading his legs apart and strapping his ankles to its base. Looking at naked female flesh because the greatcoats were backless from the armpits down, and only the shoulders and the belts at the waist were holding them in place. Listening to the drum's soaring crescendo, to the crack of a whip, to the man's gasping cry. Seeing the stark white welt across his back suffuse with pink. Hearing the woman behind him groan and repeat the same words over and over again and Frischauer saying breathily, 'The bitch at the next table wants them to do it to her!'

There were seven welts on the man's jerking body and he was screaming when Pemberton smashed open the door marked *Herren* and spewed the borsch, the sauerkraut, the sausages and the flan onto the floor. It was a long time before the sounds from the restaurant ceased and he returned to it. The man hung by the wrists, head drooping, motionless, his back, buttocks and thighs hatched in red. Just as motionless the girls stood as first they had, their shaded eyes seeming to despise the air above the heads of the diners, the whips back on their belts. The spotlights faded, died.

'Perhaps now he wish he hang,' Frischauer said and Pemberton realized with utter revulsion that so great had been his host's absorption that his own absence from the table had gone unnoticed. When the restaurant lights came on there was only a rash of blood spots on the boards of the stage to show that anybody had ever been there.

'Amusing, no?' Frischauer asked and by so doing came very close to death. Pemberton sat, muscles tensed, the middle knuckle of his right hand protruding, locked there by its fellows and his thumb. He heard only the subsiding moans of the woman at his back, saw only the area of sweat-dampened hair just below and behind Frischauer's ear which was his target. It was only the sudden burst of applause from an audience released from a sadistic trance which saved him, saved Frischauer, saved Lohengrin, saved the mission.

Avoiding the question, trying to keep his voice steady, 'How very fortunate that that exhibition was scheduled for this particular night,' Pemberton said, saw Frischauer's start of surprise and listened to him saying, 'It happens each night. There are always undesirable elements for correction. You wish one of those girls, yes?'

'I wish one of those girls, no,' Pemberton told him. 'I want to go to bed.'

Frischauer looked surprised again.

Chapter Twenty-Two

Pemberton took his second shower of the night, spending ten minutes under it as though disgust was a material thing he could cleanse from his body. It made him feel no better and he dried himself, put on the pyjamas somebody had left ready for him, then lay down, not bothering to turn off the bedside lamp because he didn't expect to sleep.

If he had expected one thing more than another it had been the tactics of confusion and disorientation that he and Professor Morris had employed, but all that had happened had been a near-pointless exchange with Frischauer and his own exposure to a viciously sordid spectacle. All? The vivid memory of the terrifying women and their screaming victim brought the taste of bile welling up in his throat again, but he swallowed repeatedly, forcing it down, forcing the mental images from him, because they had no relevance, no point. Pemberton cursed softly, blasphemously, and looked at his watch. Its hands stood at 2.17.

Anticipate, anticipate, he told himself, but could think of nothing more original than that manifestation of the police state, the hammering on the door in the darkest hour before the dawn. It came at 2.24.

'*Geheime Staatspolizei! Gestapo!* Open!'

The door swung inwards to crash against a chest of drawers behind it.

'Go on,' she said. 'Admit it. I scared you half to death, didn't I?'

She looked adorable, Pemberton thought. Short blonde hair gleaming like a burnished helmet, violet eyes sparkling, the completely plain white satin nightdress with its plunging neckline, moulding her breasts, sharp hipbones and thighs. The door closed as quietly as it had opened noisily.

'Did Frischauer send you, Hildegarde?'

An emphatic nod of the head, no prevarication at all.

'Yes, but I would have come anyway. I caught a glimpse of you when you came back from the club and you looked so distressed. What happened? It's only a high-class brothel, isn't it?'

'Something like that,' Pemberton said. 'They had a cabaret act I found rather disgusting, that's all.'

Hildegarde Mohr nodded again, watching him, then, 'Do you want me to go away?'

The urgent need for human contact in this awful city swept over Pemberton, followed by a tidal wave of sexual desire for the delectable girl, a desire fuelled by months of longing for Claire Helier, a desire he didn't try to fight because he knew he could not.

'No,' he said.

She smiled without coquettishness, raised her hands to the back of her neck to release the bow of the halter there and shimmied the clinging material of the nightdress down her body until it lay in a pool at her feet. Then she walked to the bed.

Their first contact was violent, short-lived, but after that came a period of exquisite gentleness, a time of exploration and wonderment for Pemberton. She was a friendly and imaginative lover, meeting his demands, not demanding herself, holding his head softly cushioned to her breasts during the times when he lay quiescent, half asleep, half awake, always aware of her presence. Small compassionate noises blended with amused whispers of protest when he wanted her yet again. It was a quarter to eight when she kissed him lightly, slid off the bed and stood beside it.

'I must go now. You have to appear before the Court at nine.'

'Ah, is that the programme?'

She gave another of her emphatic nods and looked as excited as a child when she said, 'Oh, I am so looking forward to tonight! I can hardly bear to wait!'

Pemberton smiled at her, puzzled. 'What happens then?'

It was as though she hadn't heard his question and for several seconds she stared absently at him before saying, 'It's difficult to recognize a girl wearing full stage make-up, with her face framed by a high collar and a Gestapo cap tilted over her nose. I was the taller one in black. Tonight I'll be wearing pale blue leather. I'm sure you'll like it. It's most becoming.'

'Why are you telling me this?' Pemberton's voice suddenly harsh.

There was nothing childlike about her any more when, eyes very wide, features set in hard lines, she said, 'Your friend Pelham talked yesterday, so you'll be making a stage appearance this evening. Your scene involves an execution, not correction.' She paused before adding, 'See you on the triangle at midnight.'

For a moment the violet eyes lost their focus and her body quivered, then Hildegarde Mohr stooped quickly, grasped her nightdress and walked out of the room, the glistening garment trailing behind her like a bride's train.

*

The room was vast, almost a hall, and a table stretched across one end for nearly its entire width. Talking amongst themselves, thirty men, nine in civilian clothes, the rest in a variety of uniforms, sat behind it. One of them was Colonel Frischauer. Pemberton stood facing them, his gaze fixed on a huge portrait of Hitler flanked by two red banners reaching from ceiling to floor with the black swastika set in a white circle and crowned by an eagle emblem at their centre. He thought, sardonically, that it was all very impressive.

He was very tired, but steady enough now. As it was meant to do, the chilling ending to his night of love had smashed through his defences like a battering ram, leaving him prostrate on the bed. In his mind, he was already secured to that terrible triangle, hearing the drum beat increasing in tempo and the soft excited panting breaths of the girls, feeling his flesh cringe in anticipation of the first lash and wondering how long it would take him to die.

Pemberton had wasted fifteen minutes living that nightmare before, for the third time, his legs carried him to the shower and he washed the sweat from his body. There, common sense and his training came swiftly to his aid, inducing a wave of self-contempt which cleansed him more than any amount of water. It had been cleverly done, the mounting tension of the awful evening with Frischauer, the ecstasy of its violent release and the tenderness which had followed in the arms of a pretty woman, the sudden display of poisoned fangs when she turned from goddess into viper. Yes, cleverly done and enough to make a spy abandon hope and confess his sins – if it had made sense.

It hadn't made sense. One didn't sacrifice a source of potentially invaluable information on the altar of perversion for the gratification of an audience devoted to the pursuit of vicarious sadism. No, one did not do that. One milked the source dry to the very last drop, and that was a process which could extend over a period of many weeks. From that it followed logically that he would not be meeting Hildegarde and her friends on the triangle for, as Clayton was fond of reminding him, the Germans were an eminently logical race.

His progress towards balance had faltered there with the thought that he might yet go under their whips that night as part of the process of softening him up, but he had discarded it. Frischauer had told him after the performance that almost half of those who chose what was described as correction from the girls in preference to the gallows, died anyway from shock, fear or heart failure. They couldn't afford to risk that with him. Somebody had given Hildegarde Mohr the wrong lines to recite and that, in turn, had given Pemberton hope for himself and hope that Lohengrin had said nothing at all.

He looked away from Hitler's painted regard and looked at the long row of men. They were still talking, referring to files, making notes, ignoring him. His watch told him that he had been standing there for eight minutes. That it was all part of the routine he knew perfectly well, but tiring of the game, he turned to his right and walked to the row of chairs apparently taken from his side of the conference table and placed against the wall there. They were identical except for the one at the centre, a solid oaken thing with arms and the eagle-swastika motif on the high headrest. He chose that, hefting it above his head, carrying it back to where he had been standing and setting it down with a thud. Then he sat on it. He had their attention now.

'I don't recall anyone inviting you to sit.' The words came from the man directly opposite him, wearing the uniform of a *Wehrmacht* general, bemedalled, sitting in a chair the twin of the one he had selected, English excellent, accent thick.

'Obviously an oversight,' Pemberton said. 'You are forgiven.'

'You will address me as *Herr General*.'

'I'll do that when I'm sure that we are on the same side. Not before.'

The general peered at him over the tops of his spectacles. 'But you know we can never be that. You have already been informed of your impending execution and the form it will take, have you not?'

'If,' Pemberton said, 'you are referring to threats issued by Frischauer's whore, I don't believe them any more than you do.' He saw Frischauer flush and that encouraged him, although he didn't know why it should. He decided to rub it in and added, 'Never mind. She enjoyed telling me about it so much that it gave her an involuntary orgasm. I rather suspect that Frischauer is incapable of helping her that way.' Somebody laughed, a sound quickly stifled, and Pemberton realized that he had made a good German joke. Frischauer's face turned from red to white.

'What did you hope to achieve by coming here, Pemberton?' The general cocked his head to one side and light glinted on his spectacles, obscuring his eyes.

Pemberton sighed theatrically. 'Oh no you don't,' he said. 'I've explained all that to Pelham and he has told you by wireless and probably in person by now. I've also explained it to Frischauer and he must have repeated what I said too. Can't we move on to new ground?'

'I'm waiting, Pemberton.'

Sighing again, Pemberton began to talk, painting a picture of himself as a chauvinist aware of his country's limitations, and a patriot whose patriotism allowed him to see the necessity for short-term submission to a foreign power in order that the future of his country be assured. He blocked the canvas in with specious theories on grand strategy and hoped that he had achieved a portrait of a traitor with a mission, the righteousness of which he had no doubts about at all. The reaction he obtained was nothing more than a quiet hum of conversation which, he supposed, was made up of those who understood English explaining what he had said to those who did not. The general sat unmoving, his gaze fixed on Pemberton's face.

'I bet you blink first,' Pemberton said.

The general steepled his fingers, pressing their tips to the underside of his chin, before saying, 'You really are a fatuous fellow. I believe you English have a saying "to die laughing". Will your humour stretch that far when I tell you that *Herr* Pelham has revealed you to be an officer of British Intelligence?'

'I don't know where he got that idea from,' Pemberton replied, 'but he's absolutely right.'

It *was* the general who blinked. 'But you have informed us that you are a member of a military planning committee.'

It was time to show anger. 'Oh God,' Pemberton said, 'is that uniform yours, or did you borrow it for the occasion? Of course I'm on a planning committee! Look, let me try to put it simply! A planning committee makes plans! Most plans have a cover plan to mislead your espionage organization about our intentions! Military Intelligence makes the cover plans! That's my job! Is that reasonably clear, or shall I say it all again? What the hell do you do over here? The days when you could blunder around all over Europe virtually unopposed have gone, you know! You're on the defensive now! Don't you want to know where you are going to be hit next? Wouldn't you like to have forewarning in due course of where the knock-out punch is coming from? Oh, why can't I be allowed to talk to somebody with some conception of what's going on?'

The spate of words left him trembling and he was thankful for that. His nerves, never far from the surface since leaving Lisbon, had needed an outlet and his outburst gave him a reason for letting them show.

'You're nervous, Pemberton.'

'Of course I'm bloody well nervous! Wouldn't you be, telling the lion you want to help and sticking your head in its mouth to prove it?'

'You mentioned our espionage organization. What do you know of that?'

'Bugger all,' Pemberton said.

'What does that mean?'

'It means I know nothing. Well, I've read in the papers that we've caught a few spies and strung them up. As I've told you, my job is to mislead them, not catch them.'

'As you would hope to mislead us, no doubt, if we were to employ you.'

'Well, you'd have to be pretty stupid not to think of that possibility,' Pemberton answered. 'All I ask is that you judge me by results. You don't have to believe what I tell you, but you'll be damned fools if you don't.'

A man in civilian clothes seated next to the general whispered something to him. The general nodded and turned back to Pemberton.

'Kindly give me an example of a recent operation in which you have been involved, one of which we are now aware.'

'The Bruneval raid,' Pemberton lied and marshalled the facts he had been given about it in his mind.

'So? Who was it carried out by?'

'That won't get you anywhere,' Pemberton said. 'You can't check on it because you didn't take any prisoners, but I'll tell you anyway. It was "C" Company of the 2nd Battalion of the Parachute Regiment. They jumped from RAF Whitley bombers and were evacuated by sea. What you can check on is that they took three prisoners; two of the soldiers guarding the radar station and a radar operator.'

'What else did they take?'

Pemberton frowned and closed his eyes tightly before saying, 'I'm not a scientist, but I did read their report. Wait a minute.' He pinched the bridge of his nose with forefinger and thumb, released it, opened his eyes and went on, 'They took the receiver and transmitter, the pulse generator, whatever that is, and something called an amplification – no, a frequency –

no, an intermediate frequency amplifier. That's it, I think. Anyway, they took the whole bag of tricks.'

'And the object of the raid?'

'Oh, the boffins – er, the scientists wanted to know what stage you had reached in radar development in some band or other. 53 metres, centimetres, millimetres, something. I don't know. None of it means anything to me.'

The general turned his head to his left, said, '*Herr Professor* von Hippel?' and a civilian five places away from him nodded ponderously.

'You seem to have your facts right,' the general told Pemberton, 'but it is possible that they were given to you before you left England, so be good enough to make us a present, as a gesture of good will. Tell us what the English have in store for us next. I mean something rather more specific than air raids.'

'Of course,' Pemberton said. 'There's a huge dry dock at St Nazaire in the west of France. It's the only one on the Atlantic coast big enough to take one of your capital ships like the *Tirpitz*. During the next few days, depending on the state of the tide and the moon, that sort of thing, an old destroyer called HMS *Campbeltown*, escorted by motor gunboats and a commando force, will attempt to make its way into the Loire estuary and ram the dock gates. *Campbeltown*'s bows are crammed with high explosives, so there should be quite a bang when she goes up and that will put paid to the dock for you. I suggest you grab a telephone and warn your defences down there.'

Nobody grabbed a telephone but there were a lot of raised eyebrows and for the first time someone other than the general spoke directly to Pemberton.

'Please to say again more slower.'

When Pemberton had repeated the information the man in the uniform of a rear-admiral said, 'Not last night but the one before, the destroyer *Campbeltown* is ramming the St Nazaire dock and exploding. The dock gate is badly ruined.'

Pemberton shrugged, murmured, 'I'm sorry,' and made a helpless gesture with his hands. The news was no surprise to him. At Lisbon Airport the MI6 man called Beresford who had watched him and Lohengrin board the plane had had his jacket slung over his left shoulder to tell him that the raid had taken place and that, consequently, he was free to make his useless gift to the Germans.

'What more can you tell us?'

Turning back to the general, 'Nothing specific,' Pemberton said. 'I've been away too long and targets change on the basis of air reconnaissance, information received from resistance groups and our own agents, and the weather plays a big part. Well, you know all that, but in the long term I'd keep very much awake in Norway if I were you. Always be alert in Norway. We haven't been doing all that probing for nothing.'

'Ah yes. The massive training of mountain troops.'

'Precisely.'

'Perhaps I was a little hasty when I described you as fatuous, Pemberton.'

Pemberton shrugged again.

'Assuming for a moment that we are prepared to employ you, what remuneration are you seeking for your services?'

Presented with another opportunity for a display of anger, Pemberton took it, less because its effectiveness as a tool against the enemy had been agreed between Clayton and himself, than for the reason that the fear-induced adrenalin loose in his system needed to be consumed.

'To use your own word,' he replied, 'in order to be fatuous it is not necessary to be offensive!' His voice rose as he spoke furiously on. 'My name's George, not Judas, and if that reference escapes you let me make a practical point! I will *not* place myself in the position of accepting greasy bank notes from the greasy pocket of some Teutonic oaf in a public lavatory on the third Tuesday of each month, or whatever the standard procedure is! It would place the whole enterprise at risk and you can't get more fatuous than that!'

For the first time the general smiled, then he said, 'I'll say one thing for you, young man, nobody can accuse you of being ingratiating. Perhaps you can think of some other form of reward should it ever become due to you.'

'That's easy,' Pemberton said. 'The first piece of hard Intelligence you get from me resulting in a significant German success, put Frischauer on display in a club I know of.'

He was rewarded by a barking laugh and the words, 'You hear that, Frischauer? The Englishman wants your she-cats to stroke you. We must think about that. We really must.'

Frischauer grinned, but there was no humour at all in the rictus-like contraction of his facial muscles; his eyes flickered wildly and it occurred to Pemberton that the man had just been threatened. That, he thought, was extremely interesting and he wondered if Frischauer could be suspected of whatever crimes had led to the downfall of the late Major Dressier. The possibility of the continuing existence of suspicion, of active distrust amongst the members of the German Intelligence establishment encouraged him. Then the general was addressing him again.

'Pursuing this hypothesis that you may one day serve the cause of the Third Reich, how would you propose to communicate with us? By radio?'

Pemberton shook his head. 'All the Morse I know is SOS and Beethoven's Fifth.'

'Beethoven's Fifth? What has that to do with Morse?'

'Tune into the BBC any time,' Pemberton said, 'and you'll find out. Those deep tones from the Fifth Symphony spelling out the Morse letter "V" to tell you the British are coming and the Americans with them. I wouldn't be able to sleep at night with that message booming inside my head.'

'You take great pride in the nation you propose to betray, Pemberton.'

'Of course. We're better than you. If we had listened to Churchill during the thirties and built up the RAF, the Battle of Britain wouldn't have been just a major German defeat, it would have been the end of the *Luftwaffe.*' He paused before adding, 'Well, perhaps not. I imagine you would have had the sense to stop the assault after forty-eight hours. That is if you had dared to start it in the first place. Anyway, you need us, just as we need you. We've already shown you that the Italians are no use to you as allies. They couldn't fight their way out of a paper bag.'

'Cruel, but accurate,' the general said. 'So you visualize an English surrender not involving the occupation of your country, in return for which you would join us in fighting the Bolsheviks. Is that correct?'

'In broad terms,' Pemberton replied in a patient voice, 'that is the general impression I have been endeavouring to convey both before and since my arrival. As you seem to be experiencing some difficulty in grasping the concept perhaps you'd like me to write it down for you.'

'How did you come to be recruited by *Herr* Pelham?'

Pemberton, readying himself to elaborate a spurious global plan by which the British Empire was left intact and Germany retained all of Russia while permitting the Allies to use bases at its far-eastern end for an assault on Japan, was caught unawares by the sudden change of direction.

To gain time, 'Hasn't he even told you that?' he asked.

'Just answer the question.'

'We first met at an anti-communist gathering months ago,' Pemberton said. He spoke reflectively, as though trying to cast his mind back. 'I don't remember who spoke to whom first, but a friendship developed over the weeks and we began to meet regularly.'

'At this gathering?'

'Sometimes, but more often at a pub.'

'A what?'

'An inn.'

'I see. Wasn't it extremely risky to be seen in the company of these people? Surely such groups are kept under surveillance by your MI5.'

'Special Branch probably,' Pemberton said. 'No, I don't think it was. We always met in different houses and I imagine that Pelham felt the risk worthwhile to keep you informed of the strength of anti-communist feeling in Britain.'

'I meant for you as a serving officer.'

Pemberton shook his head. 'As an officer of Military Intelligence? Certainly not. My cover story would have been that I was trying to infiltrate the organization. That would have been considered highly commendable by the short-sighted fools who decide our policy towards the Soviet Union. As it happens, nobody ever asked me, so the point doesn't arise.'

'And eventually *Herr* Pelham proposed that you come here. Correct?'

'In a very cautious and roundabout way, yes.'

'Wait outside,' the general said.

*

The Court adjourned after twenty minutes, leaving only the general and the man wearing civilian clothes who had whispered to him still in the great room.

'Do you think he's insane?'

'Not in the clinical sense,' Admiral Canaris said. 'For him to believe that his professed goal is obtainable indicates that his grasp on reality leaves just about everything to be desired, but I don't think that matters to us so long as he's sincere in his views. They're the stuff that traitors are made of. Misplaced idealism always is.'

The other nodded. 'That's true enough, but one thing still worries me. After the girl left him this morning she watched him through the observation port and has stated that he had the appearance of a very frightened man. His rapid recovery from that condition and his truculent attitude towards me suggest a degree of experience and training hardly typical of an ordinary regimental officer.'

'I agree with you,' Canaris said. 'We must never lose sight of the possibility that he has been planted on us by the British. Conversely, to forego what may prove to be one of the most important sources of Intelligence of the war would be insanity itself. I incline to the view that he is what he claims to be, largely because of his knowledge of the naval assault on St Nazaire. There's no possibility of his having been told of the success of that raid in Portugal. The morning after it had taken place he spoke only with Horst Eckart and Pelham before the plane left Lisbon.'

'A secret sign perhaps?'

Canaris looked at the general from under his eyebrows. 'Manfred, you're a suspicious old devil. Don't let us hamstring ourselves on the altar of improbabilities. We don't *have* to believe anything the man tells us. We simply listen, analyse and judge him by results. Now let's have him back in. I have a meeting with the *Führer* at eleven.'

With Pemberton seated again in the big wooden chair, 'We have decided,' the general said, 'that it would be of no particular advantage to us to execute one enemy lieutenant-colonel. You will not, therefore, be entertained by Frischauer's women, which, no doubt, will be a disappointment to your bed-mate of last night. Instead you will be returned to your home country whence you will communicate to us all such information as you consider will assist the cause of the Third Reich. Details of how this can best be achieved will be worked out between you and my staff over the next few days.'

'I can't spare a few days,' Pemberton told him. 'It's imperative that I get back to Lisbon within twenty-four hours or I'll miss the ship I came out in. I'm supposed to be on a fortnight's climbing holiday in Scotland and if I'm late getting back from that – well, overstaying leave is a very serious offence for an officer. It could lead to a court martial and then where would our scheme be?'

'Don't worry about that, Colonel Pemberton. We shall be sending you home by a much more direct route.'

'Very well, *Herr General*,' Pemberton said and saw the other smile faintly in acknowledgement of the formal mode of address.

Chapter Twenty-Three

By their own lights they were very pleasant to Lohengrin in Berlin, treating him with the respect due to a hero and an awe once reserved for the Delphic oracle. He hated it. To be introduced as a man with the courage to serve the *Führer* in the very heart of the enemy's camp distressed him both for the inaccuracy of the words and the fulsomeness with which they were spoken. Unused to such talk, his senses much more in harmony now with British attitudes, he found it tastelessly extravagant and recalled the visit of a stranger to the house on Southdown Road. 'Hello, Ace. How's our bloody old spy these days?' he had heard Pemberton say before the door closed on the two men. That he had liked, and with the memory had come the realization of the extent to which he had become two people.

Patriotism lived in him still, and with it pride in what his country had accomplished, was continuing to accomplish, in the face of formidable numerical odds, but his certainty of victory had deserted him. The mastery of Europe once seemingly inevitable was less so now. The sight of the constant stream of ambulances carrying the casualties brought from the East Front by the returning troop trains bore witness to that. So too did the astonishing resilience of the British, their self-confidence, their unquestionable ability. Those attributes he had seen for himself and they made him fear for Germany. And now the Americans were coming. Of those people he knew little, but there were an awful lot of them and he knew in his heart that if the tide had not already turned they would turn it.

By the end of his first full day in the city he was no longer convinced even of the desirability of victory because he disliked what he saw, disliked what he felt, and could dispel neither sensation by telling himself that he was rationalizing his own treachery. There was something sick about the people; a sickness whose symptoms he saw in the arrogance of the masters and the servility of the underlings, in the blank faces and machine-like movements of marching soldiers and, most of all, in the look of glazed adoration which appeared in too many pairs of eyes at the mention of Hitler's name. He supposed that he should have been prepared at least for the last, but was not.

But his unease came from something deeper than the visual evidence of idolatry, deeper even than the proof of a persecution which he did not yet guess to be genocide provided by the boarded-up fronts of Jewish shops. It had its origin in the air of decadence pervading Berlin, a catering to the pleasures of the flesh which put him in mind of the dying years of the Roman Empire. Unaware of and exposed to nothing remotely resembling Pemberton's experience, the nightclubs his hosts insisted that he should visit until the early hours of the morning shocked him nevertheless. To him the seemingly endless lines of women, their bodies clad in exiguous parodies of military uniforms, their legs only in black stockings and shoes with cruel heels, were a total negation of sex as enshrined for him in Claire's gentle femininity. Hating them all for degrading her by the association of gender, he shook his head with increasing anger at repeated suggestions that he choose a companion for the night from amongst them.

'Try two,' somebody said. 'It's quite an experience. Werner here had three at once on Saturday and couldn't walk straight until Tuesday.' Everybody laughed, Werner managed to look simultaneously proud and sheepish, Lohengrin declined again.

By the time the last club was reached, the party had dwindled from sixteen to five, like a combat group under heavy fire, its members falling victim to the female enemy. Dimly lit, the place had curtained alcoves around its walls and the air was heavy with smoke from opium pipes. The entertainers were exotic, beautifully gowned – and male. A solitary disgruntled staff officer accompanied Lohengrin back to his hotel, asking him what he *did* want, receiving no reply. From then on he was left to his own devices at night.

The days were different. Then he saw not only the pampered staff officers, but decorated veterans from the East Front, the Battle of Britain and the Atlantic war as well. They, as often as not, were quiet, old-young men with tired watchful eyes, who smiled rarely, but meant it when they did so. For them he felt affinity because they reminded him of home. Home? Where was that? There seemed only one truthful answer. He *had* been thinking of England, but home wasn't necessarily there. His liking for these daytime men showed that. Home wasn't a geographical location any longer, it was wherever Claire might be.

Resenting the feeling of brotherhood instilled in him by the combat soldiers because, unknowingly, they held up his guilt before his eyes, he turned his mind from them and thought only of his companions of the night. It was they and their kind who held the power, it was they and their kind who had to be obliterated, it was they and their kind who made his treason clean. Not far beneath the surface of Lohengrin's awareness lurked the knowledge that self-absolution after the event with no accompanying penance would not survive even his own examination. He didn't delve for it then.

When they had asked him everything they wanted to ask him, and he had enlarged on everything he had already told them by radio, they put him on the plane for Lisbon. He felt enormous thankfulness when its wheels left the runway at Gatow, and gratitude towards Admiral Canaris, who, he had been told, had personally authorized that the flight be routed through Minden so that *Herr* Pelham could talk with his father for half an hour.

During the short journey to the town to which his father had been traced, Lohengrin, relieved to have left Berlin behind, glad to be meeting again a parent he hadn't seen for years, thrilled by the coming reunion with his wife, had only one immediate concern, and that was for Pemberton. As he had been ordered to do by London, he had counselled extreme caution on the part of his German superiors in their dealings with his potential recruit. He'd seen an opportunity for a major Intelligence coup and grasped it, he had told them, but could offer no guarantees. They had nodded wisely and congratulated him on his own caution in absenting himself from England while the Englishman and his motives were closely examined.

It was only when the plane bumped down onto the small Minden airport that Lohengrin realized that he would not be returning to England if Pemberton had not passed whatever tests they had put him to. The now obvious fact pleased him for he had grown to like Pemberton very much.

*

They blindfolded Pemberton for the drive to Tempelhof, put him in a seat in a windowless section of a plane and blindfolded him a second time before it reached Cuxhaven. There he was taken aboard a U-boat and allowed to see again. He didn't like what he saw. Where it was visible at all the curved steel of the hull barely cleared the top of his bowed head. That was constricting enough, but made more so by the maze of pipes and valve wheels, of cables and junction boxes, which covered most of it in varying degrees of thickness which made movement hazardous to the scalp.

To either side of him, more valves, more pipes, cables, levers, gauges, indicators, dials, pressed in on him. Reason told him that they were doing no such thing, but reason wasn't very convincing this day. He didn't like the smell of sweat, cooking and machine oil either, or the roar of the big diesels which set the whole mass vibrating about him. It got a little better when somebody pushed him into a tiny compartment away from the press of bodies and he could sit down and wonder how so many men could live and work in such surroundings.

It got very much worse when the U-boat moved from the calm waters of the harbour into the North Sea. Its corkscrew motion affected his stomach in a way that the rolling and pitching of the Portuguese freighter had not, but that worried him less than having constantly to protect himself from the many sharp objects waiting to stab at his lurching body. Physically fit as he was, Pemberton found himself tiring rapidly and it was an enormous relief when the gyrations eased, stopped.

'Is better under water, *nein*?'

He looked up at the man with the white cover on his cap. All the other caps he had seen had been black and he supposed that white was for ready identification.

'Yes,' he said. 'Are you the captain?'

'*Ja.*'

'When do we get to England?'

'In tomorrow's night,' the man said, nodded and went away, leaving Pemberton, his feeling of relief gone, with nothing to do but listen to the hull groaning in protest at the enormous pressure of the sea outside and to watch water trickling down from flaws in the steel. The hull was not groaning in protest at anything, the pressure was not enough to crush a swimmer, let alone a submarine, the steel was an excellent product of the Krupps organization and the moisture was condensation, but Pemberton's imagination gave the lie to those facts. Claustrophobia, which had only brushed him before, had him in its grip and his body added its own quota of moisture to the damp air. He sat grimly waiting for the trembling to start. It did not, but that gave him no comfort because he could see it lurking in the shadows of the next sixty seconds, waiting to pounce. Pemberton started living his life in one-minute sections, unable to project his mind further than that.

In ones and twos, men, officers he supposed, came into the compartment, said '*Guten Morgen*,' looked at charts, wrote in books and went away again. Somebody brought him food, but he couldn't eat it. He tried to sleep but couldn't do that either. When the captain came back he asked for a lavatory, was taken to a space he could barely get into and was told to touch nothing. 'You go. I dispose,' the captain said. With agonizing slowness Pemberton's minutes dragged themselves into hours.

Aeons later, 'Is dark. We go up,' the captain informed him, clipped orders were given, high-pressure air roared into ballast tanks and they were back on the heaving surface. The diesels coughed, rumbled into life, the corkscrewing motion returned and Pemberton was sick on German property for the second time in three days, but it was not until four-thirty in the morning that he knew with absolute certainty that he wouldn't live to see another day. It surprised him a little to discover that he was past caring about that and hoped only that death would come quickly.

Death announced its approach to him in the form of shouted commands, figures in foul-weather clothing dropping down a vertical steel ladder from the conning tower, the sound of the diesels abruptly cut off and the thud of a hatch slamming shut. Silence and stillness followed until the captain looked at him and said, 'The English frigates come. Perhaps now it will be noisy.'

Death drew closer with a flail-like sound growing in volume, passing directly overhead, beginning to recede. All the men that Pemberton could see were staring upwards, wide-eyed, frightened. He did the same, wide-eyed, terrified, but there was nothing to look at but the pipes, the valves, the cables, the junction boxes and the frail steel supporting them.

Death arrived with a series of concussions so appalling that Pemberton thought his head had split open. With it, it brought instant darkness, a whipping of the hull which threw him from his seat to a deck alarmingly tilted and a persistent whining in his shocked ears. Only when dim emergency lighting came falteringly to life did Pemberton concede to himself that he was still alive, although how death had missed him he had no idea at all.

A bump from what he imagined to be the forward part of the U-boat set the hull oscillating again, then the angle of the deck decreased, levelled, and everything was still, everything was silent except for the whine now fading from his ears.

'Water most shallow,' the captain said to Pemberton. 'We lie on the sea-bed in great quietness and they go away perhaps. We are hoping this is so.'

To Pemberton the words seemed to come from a long way off. He nodded and levered himself up from the deck, hoping so too, hoping it very hard indeed, his indifference to death evaporating as though it had never been. After half an hour of nerve-racking apprehension the frigates were heard to depart, the U-boat lifted from the bottom and men went about the tasks of repairing minor damage, sweeping up broken glass, replacing cans of food and other objects which had burst forth from their stowing places. Pemberton's tension eased, but only marginally, because there was still another day of claustrophobic torture to be endured.

Somehow he endured it, but he felt light-headed and his legs were rubbery when he clambered up the conning tower ladder onto the bridge. Men had to help him over the side of that, support him as he groped for the rungs leading down to the U-boat's streaming upper deck. It was very dark and he didn't see the rubber dinghy at all until they lowered him into it. There, other hands were waiting to grasp him, to thrust him down until he was sitting in six inches of water swirling about in its bottom.

Ten minutes later Pemberton staggered through the last of the surf and collapsed on the coast of Kent not a hundred yards from the spot where he had watched Lohengrin keep his rendezvous with the German courier so very long ago. If the two sailors in the dinghy said anything to him before they paddled out to sea, he didn't hear them. He didn't hear anything much at all until a voice shouted, 'Halt! Who goes there?'

At that he lifted his head off the sand, saw the gleam of a shielded torch and called tiredly, 'What the hell do you mean by halt? I'm lying down, aren't I?'

Silence, then someone saying, 'Doesn't *sound* like a Jerry,' and another answering in a lilting voice, 'You shut your bloody trap, Fred. I'm in charge of this patrol, look you, and I'm taking no bloody chances. I told you I seen a boat. Bloody spy, I shouldn't wonder.'

A chill which had nothing to do with the clammy cold of his soaking clothes spread through Pemberton's body. The merest rumour of a boat, his connection with it and the attendant publicity that would bring could jeopardize the entire operation. It was, he thought bitterly, the worst of bad luck that these men should have seen anything in such poor visibility, that they should have been at this particular spot, at this particular time at all. For a moment his tired mind continued to wallow in self-pity, then he took hold of himself, thanking God for a readily identifiable accent and the form of words that went with it.

'For Christ's sake, you raving Welsh twit!' Pemberton shouted. 'Come and help me up! I'm bloody near drowned!' He had coarsened his voice to an approximation of cockney and hoped that that would do. Again there was silence, then the torch and crunching footsteps advanced towards him across the sand.

'Raving Welsh twit, is it, boyo?'

He looked up at the soldier, dimly seen behind the torch. 'Well, I'm sorry, mate, but . . .'

'Who are you?'

'Able Seaman Jim Ashley, Merchant Navy.'

No, he said, he hadn't got his papers on him. Fell out of his pocket in the water probably. No, he said, he wouldn't tell them what ship he was from. Ship sinkings were secret in war time. Yes, he said, of course they'd seen a dinghy. The fucking thing had sunk under him twenty yards out, hadn't it? It took them only a minute to establish that he was unarmed, harmless and too exhausted to walk without help. Twenty minutes later he was at a country house, standing in front of a major of the Argyll and Sutherland Highlanders, wondering pointlessly what the Welshman who had found him was doing in a Scottish regiment, wishing that the man wasn't still at his back.

'Well, Ashley,' the major said. 'What are we going to do with you?'

'Got a message for you, sir,' Pemberton replied. 'From my captain, sir. About the sinking. Anybody who got ashore was to tell it to an officer and nobody else, sir.'

'I see. All right, Jones. You can go.'

Pemberton turned and watched the soldier leave the room. When he faced the major again he found himself looking at a levelled service revolver.

'You're no able seaman, Ashley. If that's your real name. Who are you?'

Ignoring the question, resuming his normal voice, 'Can you make a telephone call from here without going through your own switchboard?' Pemberton asked.

'I can.'

'Then will you please do this? Call Scotland Yard and ask for Special Branch. When you get them ask for Detective Chief Superintendent McGill or Detective Inspector Lovelock. One of them is always there. Say who you are and where you are and that "Zulu", calling himself Able Seaman Ashley, is waiting for collection at the nearest police station, wherever that is.'

The major gazed at him curiously for a moment before saying, 'Hmm. I can't see that that does anybody any harm.' Then he picked up the phone, dialled 'O' and asked for Whitehall 1212. Only when he had finished talking did he put his revolver back in its holster.

'They're sending a car,' he said, smiled suddenly and added, 'Look, I realize why you want to go to the nearest cop shop. It's the obvious place for us to shove you off to. That point having been taken, would it be a gross breach of security if I offered you a drink and the loan of some dry clothes before you go?'

'No, it wouldn't, so long as you're doing it for a shipwreck survivor called Ashley,' Pemberton told him and smiled in his turn.

Dawn was close when a small anonymous car drew up outside the police station and its small anonymous driver signed a receipt for Pemberton. It took Pemberton less than a hundred yards to decide that the driver was quite the worst handler of a car he had ever encountered. The car, its gears screeching in protest at every change, appeared to agree with his assessment.

'Stupid machine,' Clayton said in a quietly reproving voice, then continued, 'Obviously they've employed you, on approval as it were, otherwise you wouldn't be here, but I suspect that you've been put through the mill.'

'It was a nauseating example of terror through example and threat,' Pemberton told him. 'That hard-soft-hard routine. It nearly worked too, but I'd better start at the beginning. When I . . .'

'Go to sleep,' Clayton broke in. 'You look terrible.'

Pemberton slept nearly all the way to London, waking briefly at intervals to ease his cramped body and legs, at others when the gearbox shrieked in anguish. He didn't mind. It felt quite remarkably safe in the little car with the short tubby man at his side. It felt even safer, but slightly ridiculous, when they reached Clayton's flat and he was sent straight to bed. There he slept without a break until Clayton served him breakfast at twenty to six in the evening.

'You're being very kind to me, sir.'

'I'm just trying to look after what I hope is a national asset,' Clayton said. 'Get some of that inside you, then tell me if you think you are one.'

The tray across Pemberton's stomach bore a plate of fried spam, fried dehydrated potato and boiled cabbage. There was a bowl of canned pineapple cubes on it too and half a bottle of burgundy. He worked himself into a more upright position on the bed and began to eat. Clayton watched him owlishly and Pemberton wished that he would stop doing that because he didn't want him to see that his hands were trembling. When he poured burgundy from the bottle its neck rattled on the glass and some of the wine spilled onto the tray. He muttered angrily to himself and heard Clayton say, 'Don't worry about it. It's only to be expected.'

Uncertain whether having his condition recognized and accepted made him feel better or worse, Pemberton concentrated on eating the awful wartime food. Very little of what he had been given to eat between his arrival in Berlin and his return to England had stayed in his stomach for long enough to do him any good. That he should have been extremely hungry was obvious, but he was not, and only the fear of appearing ungrateful for his host's amateur culinary efforts enabled him to swallow four more mouthfuls. Then he put his fork down on the plate.

'All right, now tell me all about it,' Clayton said. 'And I do mean all. You know well enough how important the smallest detail can be.'

The telling took an hour and a quarter and not once was Pemberton interrupted. He ended with the words 'Then you arrived in that mechanized pram, sir,' and was rewarded with an indignant look and Clayton saying, 'Well, really! One doesn't collect a stray able seaman from a police station in a chauffeur-driven Rolls, you know. That would undoubtedly excite comment and – Oh, you're teasing me of course. People are always doing that.'

Briefly Clayton appeared to puzzle over why people should always be doing that, then his face cleared and he said, 'I really must commend you on your fortitude under a series of extremely trying circumstances. You have laid the foundations which should enable you and the double agents to carry through the greatest deception plan in military history. It will take time and great patience on your part to obtain the confidence of the enemy, but we are already very much in your debt and . . .'

He stopped speaking, sighed, then went on, 'Oh, dear me. I do believe I was embarking on something resembling an oration there. No doubt you would prefer a bath and a shave to listening to that. The bathroom's through that door. Help yourself to anything you need.'

Pemberton watched while Clayton took the tray and scurried from the room like a harassed waiter, then he got off the bed and stood cautiously upright. Just as cautiously, he moved towards the bathroom, troubled by the discovery that his legs were as unsteady as his hands.

Chapter Twenty-Four

'I told you not to come back, *not* to come back, to stay away and be *safe*,' Claire said in her growling cat voice. '*Why* did you come back? *Why* don't you ever listen to anything I say? Oh God, I'm so pleased to see you. I've missed you terribly. I think I'd have died if you'd found a girl over there you liked more than me. You should have arrived yesterday. What happened? I've been sick with worry. Oh, my love, welcome home!'

She peppered his face and body with darting kisses like punctuation marks and Lohengrin lay still, watching her, not speaking, wishing to halt neither the flood of words nor the shower of kisses. It was early morning before they said anything to each other which made any sense.

'Was it truly dreadful, darling? Did anything awful happen?'

'No, nothing awful. They tried to treat me well, offering me women and – and things. I didn't like that. It was all so sordid. Some of the people are pretty ghastly. In fact a lot of the people are pretty ghastly, but then there were others I liked. It was all a bit confusing really. The nice ones were like pleasant people anywhere, but the others were – ugh! Worse than the bad ones here. I can't explain exactly.' Lohengrin paused, then said, 'But there was one awful thing.'

'Oh my love! What?'

'They treated me like a hero of some sort. That made me bitterly ashamed.'

'Ah, don't,' Claire whispered and tightened her arms around him.

'I can't help it, my sweet. I'm a shameful person. Most of the time I can drown myself in you and forget it, but at other times, particularly when my nose is rubbed in it, I . . .' He let the rest of the sentence go.

'You should have stayed there as I told you to do,' Claire said, but she said it without conviction.

'It wasn't all you. You would have been enough, but there was something else.'

'What sort of something else?'

'My file at MI5. They were going to deliver that, or an edited version of it, to the *Abwehr* office in Lisbon if I'd stepped out of line in any way. That would have been a death sentence if ever there was one.'

'Oh, the fearful bastards!' Claire said. 'God, how I hate us!'

They lay for a long time after that, holding each other, not speaking until Claire broke the silence by saying, 'I think something awful happened to George Pemberton in Berlin. Do you know anything about that?'

'No, we didn't see each other after the plane landed there. He must have come back by some other route.'

'Yes, he got here about a week ago. He's been very quiet and withdrawn in a strange way. Sort of different, somehow. I'm worried about him. He's such a nice man.'

'I didn't think he looked very well when I met him downstairs last night, but he told me that everything had gone according to plan.'

'He told me that, too,' Claire said. 'Did you see your father?'

It had been a depressing meeting in the tiny passenger terminal at the Minden airstrip. Emotion had been present, but found no expression in the stilted words they had spoken to each other. To Lohengrin, his father appeared much older than he had expected him to be; older and shrunken and nervous too, as though he felt threatened by the thoughtful kindness of an authority not renowned for displaying any such thing. He had cast frequent anxious glances at the big official car placed at his disposal for the meeting and looked with awe at the plane diverted for the benefit of his son. It had been clear to Lohengrin that such consideration was totally outside his father's experience and sadly obvious that it made him somehow suspect in his parent's eyes.

'Wunderbar, wunderbar,' had been the only thing the old man who was not really old at all would say in reply to queries about his welfare and his avoidance of eye contact when he spoke served only to emphasize the inaccuracy of the statement. Unable to make verbal contact, and in no position to do anything constructive if he had been, Lohengrin had been thankful to return to the plane.

'Yes, I met him at a place called Minden,' he told Claire. 'He was in great form.'

'That was happy for you, darling. Um – darling?'

'Yes?'

'Did they mention Wolfgang von Neustadt in Berlin?'

He could feel the sudden rigidity in the body pressed to his side, the tautness of the arm across his chest.

'Yes they did, Claire, but they only wanted to know what was said in this house and how he appeared to be. There didn't seem to be any doubt in their minds about his being killed in Eastbourne as the newspapers reported it.'

There was a desperate urgency in Claire's voice when she said, 'Make love to me, Frank! Make love to me *now*! Drive him out of my head! He's been there ever since you left! *Please* make him go away for a little while!'

*

Standing, covering his nakedness with manacled hands, trembling uncontrollably, eyes slitted against the circle of searing brilliance with the nimbus of lesser light surrounding it. The slow roll of a kettledrum, the muted baying of the diners coming from the blackness beyond the light and his own voice repeating 'Ich bin ein englische Spion' over and over again as he had been ordered to do. Phantoms to either side of him in the darkness betrayed by glimpses of shining leather, gleaming skin and mocking eyes, himself the only solid thing in a howling desolation of fear. The baying taking on a pulsing beat. Hands, black-gloved, materializing, becoming real, closing on his bare arms, gripping, turning him, lifting his wrists towards the hook. The click of metal on metal, straps tightening around his ankles with a terrible finality and Hildegarde's voice at his ear saying 'Enjoy your fleeting hour upon the stage.' The drum-beat and the growling of the people swelling, his skin, his whole being cringing, the . . .

Pemberton's body arched, jerking him awake. There had been no pain. It was not possible, he supposed drearily, to dream pain. With ever increasing dreariness, he had been supposing that for nine consecutive nights and was becoming more and more fearful of falling asleep lest the nightmare should repeat itself.

Professor Morris hadn't helped. Required by Clayton to describe to 'The Puppet Maker' everything about the attempts to manipulate him, he had reluctantly done so. Morris's reaction had been contemptuously dismissive. 'The bloody fools got it the wrong way round and gave you time to think,' he had said. 'What they should have done was make you the star, have the women *take* you from the table, deal with you on the spot, then hand you over to the Gestapo for expert interrogation while your wits were still scrambled.' And that was how the dream started now: the four imperious figures advancing on the table where he and Frischauer sat, dragging him to the stage, stripping him. Sometimes his struggles to escape from their clutching hands woke him and he was grateful for that, but it did nothing to counteract the growing belief that his reason had been permanently affected by what he had witnessed. Sighing, part in tired desperation, part with irritation at himself, Pemberton swung his legs over the side of the bed. His head had begun to throb and he thought about taking some aspirin, but couldn't remember if he had any and seemed not to have the energy to go and look.

'Pull yourself together,' he said to the darkened room, stood up, then sat quickly down again because the floor tilted beneath his feet. He wondered what had made it do that, but not for long because his mind drifted away to the club off the *Kürfurstendamm*, settling, for once, not on the stage but on the table at his back. He had looked at the occupants when he and Frischauer had got up to leave and saw them again now more as three-dimensional images seated before him than as a product of memory. The man young, fat, balding, with a small rosebud mouth and slug-trails of running sweat marking his powdered jowls. The woman who had groaned with pleasure thin, forty, good-looking, dressed for erotic effect, scarlet fingernails like talons and the corrupt eyes of a fallen angel with an awful hunger in them.

'There's been nothing like you on this earth since the Rome of the Emperor Caligula,' he whispered to the couple, but they appeared not to hear him and faded from his sight before he could say anything else. Almost immediately, he forgot them and thought about Caligula. He'd made his horse a consul, hadn't he? Did Hitler have a horse? If so, would he make it a *Reichsmarshal*? That would be a joke. '*Jawohl, Herr Reichsmarshal* Horse!' Very funny, that. Perhaps Frischauer had a horse too, but that wouldn't help him. He was going to kill Frischauer after the war, horse or no horse. Oh yes, it was aspirins he had been going to look for. Somebody would give him . . .

Came found Pemberton at eight in the morning, half on and half off the bed, flushed, muttering to himself, unconscious.

*

The six days during which he was nursed by Claire were a bittersweet experience for Pemberton, but they brought him tranquillity and an ephemeral happiness. Nothing basically wrong, but complete rest essential, the local doctor had said. Do what Mrs Pelham tells you, the local doctor had said. Working too hard or perhaps it was too many late nights, the local doctor had said, and laughed jovially.

Another doctor, armed with intelligence and a high security clearance, came from London to examine him and listen to what he had to say. He laughed too, but there was no humour either in the bark of sound or in his word, when he said, 'What the hell do you expect? You people should be locked up.' He prescribed a sedative which, for forty-eight hours, left Pemberton conscious of little other than Claire, upright but floating. Sometimes her head seemed almost to touch the ceiling. It was nice, he thought, watching her do that, but it was nicer still on the third day when her feet were back on the ground and he could talk to her, listen to her admonitions and be fussed over with a kitten's fierceness. The nightmare didn't return.

Carne, Newland and Harry came to see him, bringing a bottle of whisky they had somehow persuaded the landlord of the 'Angry Saxon' to part with and were expelled from the room for their pains by a blonde fury. Clayton arrived from London, was granted fifteen minutes with the patient, then despatched back the way he had come. Not until the sixth day was Lohengrin permitted a visit.

'Bad, was it?' he said.

Pemberton had thought a great deal about what he was going to tell Lohengrin, had decided that the whole truth would have the most salutary effect on him, but was not ready to live the experience yet again in words. After Clayton, he had to repeat his tale to Professor Morris and two sets of debriefing officers.

'They sent me back by U-boat and we got depth-charged,' he replied. 'I suppose it wasn't all that dramatic, but I appear to have a bad case of claustrophobia which made it distinctly unpleasant.'

'I believe you. Still, you're looking very much better than when I saw you the other day.'

'That's thanks to your wife. She's been babying me outrageously.'

Lohengrin nodded, smiling, then the smile faded and he said, 'I wish they hadn't given you *der Wurm* as a code name. So tasteless of them.'

'What the hell does it matter what they call me? I don't give a bugger.'

'Well, I do,' Lohengrin told him. 'It's insulting to you. They should call me that. I'm the one who turned.'

The words, bitterly spoken, made Pemberton frown and he breathed in deeply, seeking courage, before saying, 'Oh no you don't! If you're going off on that tack again I'll have to tell you what happened in Berlin. Now listen to me.'

Increasingly whey-faced, Lohengrin heard him out, then his cheeks suffused with colour and he said defensively, 'Your people weren't all that gentle with me, you know.'

'They didn't use women on you. Not in that way.'

'Oh, don't give me that holier-than-thou stuff. Don't tell me you haven't got women prepared to do just that if the psychological moment was right.'

'I'm not, because I'm sure we have, but we don't do it in public for the gratification of third parties.'

Pemberton saw Lohengrin wince and listened to him say, still defensively, 'What's so special about employing women?'

'Coming from you, of all people, that's an extremely strange question,' Pemberton said.

Lohengrin flushed again, stood up and moved to the door. When he reached it he turned and murmured, 'I'm so sorry. It really is obscene, isn't it?' He paused, his eyes uncertain, bewildered, then added, 'I have to go now. Claire said I mustn't stay too long.'

Chapter Twenty-Five

'The Marquis of Trent is here, Prime Minister.'

'Have him come in,' Churchill said. 'Ah, there you are, Edward. Come in. Come in. You look well. How are "Trent's Transfixers"? It's a long time since I saw the lovely creatures.'

'They're well enough, thank you, Winston.'

'Good. Sit down and tell me what brings you. You and I haven't met face to face since I asked you to accept the services of American officers on the staffs of General Eisenhower and Admiral Stark. How are they coming along?'

'Very well indeed,' Mainwaring said. 'They're quietly constructive men with an excellent grasp both of the problems we face in balancing on this tightrope and of our long-term aspirations in deception. In fact, they have been rather less inclined to press schemes for immediate military advantage than our own fighting services were in the early days.'

'I'm glad to hear it, but not surprised. President Roosevelt promised me that they wouldn't rock the boat. Now, what can I do for you, Edward?'

Mainwaring looked at the pugnacious face before him, its forward-thrust lips emitting cigar smoke, its eyes watching him unblinkingly over the tops of half-moon spectacles. Some face, he thought, and that reminded him of the prime minister's reply to Hitler when he threatened to wring England's neck like a chicken's. 'Some chicken! Some neck!' Churchill had said.

'Seven months ago,' Mainwaring began, 'with the help of a German agent under our control, we arranged for one of my officers to be recruited by the *Abwehr*. He was taken to Berlin, questioned in a rather cursory fashion, apparently accepted as a genuine turncoat and employed by them. His claim to exceptional usefulness rested on the pretence that he was a member of one of the military planning committees and since then he has been sending across information by wireless through the man who is supposed to have recruited him and by secret writing and microphotography.'

He saw Churchill nod and went on, 'Our problem has been that his function is not the same as that of the double agents. All the Germans can reasonably expect from them is observation, analysis and the occasional scoop, which gives us plenty of latitude for feeding the enemy our standard mixture of fact and misinformation at times of our own choosing. In this man's case we are limited to fact, as he is supposedly in possession of it.'

'How have you contrived to provide them with that without inflicting damage upon us?'

'Mainly by providing it too late for them to react to it, Winston. They accept the principle that commando raids are often mounted and executed at very short notice for security reasons and that weather forecasts can result in an operation being advanced. Only when a raiding party is known to be in action does he tell them about it, providing precise details of its composition and objectives.'

'Thus confirming that he has access to vital information, if not to a truly efficient method of communicating it. I see. What does he use his invisible ink and microphotographs for? They're much slower methods.'

'Imaginary plans for the invasion of Norway, mostly,' Mainwaring said. 'We appear to have them hooked on the idea that that's where we'll invade and that obliges them to maintain unnecessarily large forces there, as you know. He can always tell them that those plans have been cancelled when our true objective can no longer be concealed.'

'All right. Go on, Edward.'

Mainwaring pulled at his lip before saying, 'He came under suspicion recently for his failure to forewarn them of the Dieppe raid. It was a pretty sizeable affair and they couldn't believe that, in his position, he knew nothing of it. We got around that one by telling them that it was planned and carried out by the Canadians, not us. In view of the large numbers of Canadian troops involved it sounded plausible and it seems that we have been believed.'

'He might just as well have forewarned them of it, considering the tragedy it turned out to be,' Churchill said. For a moment he sat staring at the smoke curling up from his cigar, then looked sharply up at Mainwaring. 'You've come to ask me for a sacrifice, haven't you, Edward?'

'Yes, Prime Minister.'

Churchill picked up his cigar, brandished it like a stick and rumbled, 'Oh no you don't. I won't have you salving your conscience at the expense of mine by addressing me as "Prime Minister". Passing the buck, the Americans call it. As you're intent on asking me to make the Nazis a present of British lives, you can do it under the name you've always called me by, without reference to seniority.'

'Sorry, Winston.'

'So I should think. This fellow of yours, is he truly the key? Can we . . .? No, don't answer that question. You wouldn't be here if he were not. Go and talk to them at Combined Operations. I'll tell Mountbatten you're coming and why.'

'Thank you,' Mainwaring said. He stood up and left the room quickly, thinking that, even for the emotional man he was known to be, he had never seen Churchill look so miserable.

Two weeks later, 'Fox Force' made an unopposed landing on the island of Walcheren off the coast of Holland with orders to destroy fuel dumps and a radar station. A quarter of a mile inland it came under heavy fire from three sides from what appeared to be a battalion of infantry supported by artillery and tanks. Caught in open country, hopelessly outnumbered, casualties mounting, his escape route to the sea rapidly closed, the force commander surrendered.

The following evening, Pemberton received a radioed message of congratulations from Berlin and the landlord of the 'Anglo-Saxon Arms' noticed that the normally abstemious officer drank rather a lot.

*

Between October 1942 and the end of January the following year, two major events stood out like beacons. In Egypt the British 8th Army struck at Rommel's legendary *Afrika Korps* with such devastating force as to send it reeling back with barely a pause to Tunisia, more than a thousand miles to the west. For the first time a German army had been routed and with its defeat the threat to the oil fields of the Middle East, and even to India itself, had been lifted. The landing of Anglo-American troops under General Eisenhower in Morocco and Algeria sealed the fate of the Germans in North Africa, but came almost as an anticlimax to General Montgomery's hurtling pursuit through Libya.

In Russia the German 6th Army was ground into the rubble which had once been the city of Stalingrad by overwhelming Soviet strength. Field-Marshal Paulus and sixteen of his generals were taken into captivity with what was left of their commands. If further evidence had been required that German military infallibility was a myth, it had been given.

Bewildered as he was by conflicting loyalties, both events affected Lohengrin deeply. He had come to accept that the only road to salvation for him lay through a negotiated peace; a solution, he had persuaded himself, which would somehow expunge his guilt. That that course was to be denied him was obvious now. What for a long time had been writing on the wall was emblazoned across the sky in letters of fire and it had not needed the joint demand for the unconditional surrender of the Axis powers issued by Churchill and Roosevelt from Casablanca to show him that.

And the Americans had barely joined the fighting yet. It was true that they had begun their own air raids across the Channel independently of the RAF, but that meant nothing in relation to their physical presence in Britain. Throughout the length and breadth of the country, in villages and small towns, they had grown to outnumber the inhabitants and in the cities they were everywhere too. There was no longer any question in his mind that when they and the British moved in full concert, Germany must fall. It was only a matter of time before the final day of reckoning between him and his conscience came.

With increasing grimness Lohengrin continued to build on his betrayal, transmitting the coded messages Pemberton told him to transmit, replying to the constant stream of questions coming in from Berlin in whatever way Pemberton instructed him. He knew the meaning of the cipher groups he sent and knew too the reason for his being permitted to know. It was psychologically better for a turned agent to be fully involved in what he was doing, to have seen the things he was describing and to have been to those places he claimed to have visited. It was physically safer for him as well, in case he should again be required to visit his paymasters in Lisbon or anywhere else, for then he could speak with the conviction of experience and avoid the pitfalls of fantasy.

Most of the information he provided was true within the limits of what Pemberton considered to be normal fallibility, some of it was subtly slanted towards misinterpretation, a small fraction of it was lies plausible enough to be explained away as human error should they ever be detected. Lohengrin understood. At the cost of gaining very little immediate advantage, his credibility was being enhanced, his reputation secured, so that the big lies he would eventually tell would be believed. That the big lies would relate to the Allied invasion of Europe was not a very difficult conclusion for him to arrive at.

Only the meaning of the messages he transmitted on Pemberton's behalf in his capacity as *der Wurm* was withheld from him. He lay in bed one night wondering about the most recent of those he had tapped out on his Morse key two hours before, then forced it out of his mind for the pointless conjecture it was. Sinking towards sleep, his uncontrolled mind drifting between despair about the fate of the pleasanter majority of his countrymen when the Invasion came to them, and the effort to remember what was the exact relationship to him of the field-marshal with his family name of Paulus who had been defeated at Stalingrad, Claire's voice brought him sharply back to full wakefulness.

'What did you say, darling?'

'I said to make us a baby,' Claire repeated and nuzzled his shoulder with her nose.

'Yes, I thought you did, but we've been through all that and decided that it would be an irresponsible thing to do in wartime.'

'You mean you decided,' Claire said. 'What I want to know is why I can't have a baby when everybody else in the country is being irresponsible. That's what I want to know.'

The bitterness which flooded over Lohengrin was strong enough to taste and he swallowed repeatedly to rid himself of the sensation. He wanted to tell her there were occasions when depression made him regret the weakness which had led him to besmirch her beauty by contact with his treachery. He wanted to tell her that he could never bring himself to compound the felony by inflicting his shame on another generation. 'What did you do in the war, daddy?' 'I was a traitor, son.' It didn't bear thinking about, so he tried not to think about it and didn't tell her anything.

'Say something, Frank. Give me one good reason why I can't have a baby.'

Feebly, 'The rationing, darling. It might be undernourished and be born with rickets. It wouldn't be fair to . . .'

'Oh, fiddlesticks! Nursing mothers get concentrated orange juice and cod-liver oil and all sorts of stuff. They've got all that very well organized.'

Lohengrin remained silent and there was a long pause before Claire said quietly, 'It's because you don't want a murderess to mother your child, isn't it?'

Appalled, he sat sharply upright and shouted, '*Christ!* Why must women *always* get it wrong? You're no murderess! You did what you had to do and saved both our lives doing it!'

'No, it wasn't like that,' Claire told him. 'He could have killed me if he'd wanted to, but he didn't because I was a girl. He just stood there and let me calmly and coldly shoot him down.'

'Oh don't be so bloody stupid!' Lohengrin said, then gave a small shaky laugh and added more quietly, 'You didn't coldly and calmly do anything. You shot up half the room, including me. It was just his bad luck that he got in the way.'

'Hmm. Then why can't I have a baby?'

'Don't push it, Claire. Please. I can't explain now. Later perhaps, not now.'

'Later you'll explain, or later I can have a baby?'

'Please, Claire darling.'

'I'll get another man to give me one if you won't.'

Coldly, 'Perhaps that would be best.'

There was another long pause before Claire said, 'I told them at my interview that they would turn me into a whore. I was wrong. They didn't, *you* did. That's what I am. Your whore, not your wife.'

For the first time since they had met she deliberately turned her back on him.

The totality of his selfishness confirmed, his last reason for living gone, Lohengrin called on the local doctor next day. He looked haggard after a night of utter loneliness within a foot of the woman he loved, the woman whose dim shape he hadn't taken his eyes from until, shortly after dawn, she had risen and left the room without a word. The doctor agreed that he certainly appeared not to have been sleeping well and gave him a prescription. He kept the pills the chemist provided in a shoe, one of a pair he never wore, and put those from the next prescription with them. And the one after that. It was necessary to make absolutely sure. It was necessary, too, to do it the tidy way, not to leave anything messy, not to cause more distress than he had to.

Throughout this period Claire was gentle, and contrite about what she had said, but it wasn't the same. It wasn't the same at all – until she found the pills. It hadn't occurred to him that she would take it into her head to clean the unused shoes hidden at the back of the closet. She called him to the bedroom, then stood with her hands on his shoulders, her face pale but calm.

'It was fathering a child that worried you so, not who its mother was.'

Claire's words had been a statement, with no trace of interrogative inflexion in them. Lohengrin looked at her blankly, then at the chair with the shoes, the tin of polish, the brush and the cleaning rag on it. After that the window seemed to absorb him for a moment before he glanced at the pile of pills on the handkerchief spread out on the bed. Only when he had looked at all those things did he nod in forlorn agreement.

'Ah, my only love. What have I done to you? What *haven't* I done to you?' Her arms slid around his neck and she drew his head down to her shoulder. Too tall for his body to accept the contortion asked of it he let his legs fold under him and knelt with his face crushed to her breast. That made breathing very difficult, but he didn't mind. His beloved friend had come back to him.

Pemberton noticed the change in Lohengrin and was thankful for it. For some weeks he had been worried about him, concerned about his lethargy, his increasing indifference to what was going on about him, his lack of appetite, but responsibility in that direction rested with Claire and he hadn't interfered. Then, quite suddenly, everything appeared to be all right again and he could stop reminding himself of what had happened to Parsifal. He would not have been thankful at all had he overheard the conversation between Claire and her husband that night.

They were sitting on the bed, side by side, holding hands, when Claire said, 'You know, I hadn't expected any of this to happen when I was given you as my first assignment. Isn't that a funny word to describe you as? I wasn't supposed to fall in love with you. I was just supposed to get you in a right old emotional muddle, they call it "entrapment" I think, so that that horrid Professor Morris could get you in a worse one that you couldn't get out of, but then I went all weak at the knees about you and simply had to tell somebody, so I told Gail and . . .'

'The girl you wanted to be bridesmaid who couldn't make it?'

'Yes, my very best friend. I've had a crush on her for absolute years. Anyway, I told her and she was absolutely furious with me and gave me the biggest talking to of my life. Oh boy, you should have seen her! Oh boy, you should see her anyway! If you think I'm good-looking you should see her! She'd blow your socks right off and . . .'

'Stop it, darling.'

Claire began to cry silently and Lohengrin disengaged his hand so that he could put his arm round her.

When the little spasm ended, 'Sorry, sorry,' Claire whispered. 'I was just talking.'

'I know, my love.'

When she began to speak again, she did it slowly, calmly, as though the points she made had been itemized on some mental list. To Lohengrin she sounded older, almost mature.

'Frank,' Claire said, 'the day I came to see you at that clinic after I had shot you, you asked me what you were going to do and I told you what you mustn't do was go away from me again. Then, very stupidly, over the past weeks I went away from you, didn't I? That was wicked, but I didn't have any idea how wicked until I found out today that it had made you decide to go away from me for always, to go away from everything for always.'

He felt her shudder and tightened his arm about her, but her voice was still calm when she went on, 'Gail would have seen the danger at once, but she's always been the clever one. I'm really an awfully silly bitch, darling. Despite everything you've told me about shame and drowning yourself in me and – and everything, I hadn't understood how intensely you felt about the shame part. Not until today when I worked out why you wouldn't give me a child. It all came to me then.'

'Claire, I . . .'

'No, let me finish, my dear. You see, I don't believe I knew what shame was. I didn't feel a twinge of it when I seduced you before I fell in love with you. That was just a big kick which made me feel very important and patriotic because I'd succeeded in doing what they had told me to do, and proved that I was pretty attractive.'

'Don't tell me that you needed proof,' Lohengrin said, but Claire ignored him and talked on.

'I didn't even feel it when I suggested that you stay in Germany and be safe. That was treason, you know, and makes me just as much a traitor as you. So does not telling George Pemberton about those pills.'

'Have you thrown them away, Claire?'

'No,' she said. 'I crushed them up so they aren't recognizable and put them – I put them in a safe place, not in a silly old shoe.' Sighing she added, 'So there we are, my love. If you find that you can't stand it any longer and decide to go away for always, I'm coming with you.'

'Now you're being hysterical, Claire.'

'Do I sound hysterical?'

'No, darling, but I can't accept all this discovery of shame stuff you're talking. You felt it very strongly when von Neustadt was shot.'

'No, I didn't,' Claire replied. 'I felt the most appalling guilt. It's quite different. Some guilty things you can feel jolly pleased about, not that I ever could about that one, but shame is much worse. You can never *ever* feel pleased about it. I know that now. Shame is what I've done to you. Shame is my murdering our baby by not letting it be born because it would destroy you if it was born. That's what shame is, and if we can't help each other bear it I'm not going to stay behind to find out if I can carry it alone.'

When he made no reply she stood up and said, 'Come to bed now. We've both had enough of today.'

Chapter Twenty-Six

'You're looking rather under the weather, sir. Is something wrong?'

Clayton blinked at Pemberton, half smiled and said, 'Something very nearly was. The entire edifice we've built up over the years almost came down like a house of cards. I had to order an execution to prop it up yesterday. It's a bit illogical to worry about such things with everybody killing everybody else as fast as possible, but I'm not a fighting man and if I were I'd draw the line at assassination. Chap you stayed with in Lisbon actually. The head of their *Abwehr* office.'

'Horst Eckart?'

'That's the one,' Clayton said. 'It seems that he had come to the conclusion that Germany would lose the war and decided to change sides. He approached our man Beresford out there and promised to give us a complete run-down on *Abwehr* organization and personnel in return for a safe passage to England and British citizenship. Obviously an accident had to be arranged for him rather quickly.'

'Obviously,' Pemberton agreed. 'If he had ever got here the Germans would have had to assume that he'd blown half their agents in this country, we'd have had to be seen to arrest them and bang goes the whole deception plan.'

'You should be on the Committee,' Clayton said. 'I had to explain that to one of the members who thought that accepting Eckart would be a great coup for us. Still, never mind about that, or my squeamishness. They're not what I asked you to come and see me about. Come over here.'

Pemberton followed the tubby man to a side table with an oblong of parchment on it. He thought it was probably a map turned face down. Clayton fingered it for a moment, doing it delicately as though it were some substance liable to spontaneous combustion, then gave Pemberton a look of agonized embarrassment before saying, 'Considering the secrets you've been made privy to since your return from Berlin it seems ridiculous to talk to you about secrecy, but I am required to inform you that what I am about to reveal to you is known to very few people anywhere. It's one of the great secrets of the war and – well, I won't labour the point.

Suffice it to say that it has been deemed desirable that you be made aware of the broad strategic picture to enable you to do your job to the maximum effect in your capacity as *der Wurm*. Clear?'

'Perfectly, sir.'

Clayton nodded and reversed the map. It showed the whole of the British Isles and the north coasts of France, Belgium and Holland. It showed two Allied orders of battle, one true, one false. It showed army groups real and imaginary. It showed the Invasion beaches, two sets of them.

'How soon, sir?'

'Next June, probably,' Clayton said. 'That plan is tentative at the moment, but I am told that it is likely to harden very much along those lines. Study it. Take your time.' He turned away, sat at his desk and began to write.

Pemberton studied it. He studied the planned grouping of armies in the Midlands, the west and the southwest. He studied the largely imaginary army locations in Scotland, the east and southeast. He studied the routes of hundreds of miles of railway line under construction to carry troops and equipment to the ports of embarkation, and the routes of railway line there was no intention of building. New airfields intended, new airfields pretended, hundreds of both. He studied them too, together with tank and transport parks, ammunition and fuel dumps, food stores and repair shops, factual and notional.

When he had studied all that, he looked at the dotted lines connecting the ports of Britain to the coast of France. Along those coloured green the assault ships and the men-of-war would sail to the Cherbourg peninsula. Along those coloured red, leading to the Pas-de-Calais, they would not. It was all very simple and extremely complex.

'Sir.'

'Yes, Pemberton?'

'These phantom armies will have to be seen to exist for the benefit of enemy air reconnaissance. That means dummy tanks, planes, landing craft. Dummy all sorts of things.'

'Precisely,' Clayton said. 'That is being taken care of. What is more, they must be heard to exist too. We're currently thinking in terms of creating, as it were, some ten non-existent divisions, and ten divisions would make a great deal of radio noise with all their wireless telegraphy traffic. That's presenting us with a major manpower problem, but we shall solve it.

Indeed, we *must* solve it so that the Germans can monitor the transmissions. There's no such thing as a silent army these days.'

Nodding, Pemberton asked, 'How about imaginary divisional and regimental insignia? The double agents will need to report on those in the normal course of their duties.'

'We have artists designing them now. They'll be distributed to the appropriate case officers, including yourself, from time to time as the formations notionally assemble.'

Pemberton nodded again and asked another question. 'Will there be a diversionary raid on the Pas-de-Calais area on D-Day to back all this deception up?'

'No,' Clayton told him. 'We can't spare the shipping, but the Germans will think there is. It's only a gleam in some boffin's eye at the moment, but apparently bombers dropping aluminium foil and flying elliptical orbits which gradually close on the French coast will give the same pictures on radar screens as an advancing fleet of ships. An electronic bluff in other words. It should convince the enemy of what we hope we shall already have persuaded them to expect anyway and gain us invaluable hours. Reinforcements rushed to Calais and Boulogne can't hurt us in Normandy.'

He paused for long enough to remove and replace his spectacles, then added, 'So now you know the scope of the misinformation you will be required to pass to Germany over the coming months. The whole team of double agents will support what you say by providing isolated details strictly within our usual limits of what they could reasonably be expected to acquire, but the big leak will be yours to make. You'll deal with me direct on the timing of each phase. Any recommendations?'

'Yes, sir. That nobody in B.I.a. Section makes a single, solitary mistake, at least until D-Day plus ten.'

'Amen to that,' Clayton said.

*

Even scarred as it was with sandbagged anti-aircraft gun emplacements, search-light positions and barrage balloon winches, Edward Mainwaring thought that St James's Park was still one of the prettiest places in London. He liked walking beside the lake best and always took a paper bag of stale bread with him to feed the water birds.

'The white duckling at the back isn't having much luck,' Clayton said.

Mainwaring nodded and lobbed the last crust towards it, but a large mallard reached the morsel first. He shrugged, crumpled the empty bag and put it tidily into his pocket before saying, 'Losing the initiative can be disastrous.'

'It never had it, Edward. The mallard was too quick for it.'

There was a soot-stained piece of bread wedged in a crack in the pavement near Mainwaring's feet. He prised it free with the ferrule of his umbrella, picked it up and threw it towards the small duck. The mallard got there first again. Mainwaring turned and strolled along the bank, followed by Clayton and the ducks gliding across the smooth surface of the water.

'I was talking about us,' he said. 'All the years of plotting and planning and building. Now there's so little to do but wait. I feel like a man with all his fingers and toes stuck in holes in a dyke, praying that the pressure won't increase.'

'I adopt a more active mental posture,' Clayton told him. 'I see myself on a high-wire, juggling oranges. With a figure like mine exercise is essential, so I'll leave the dyke to you.'

'Oranges. Now there's something I haven't eaten in a long time. And bananas. It's strange to think that there's a generation of children growing up that has never seen a banana.'

They walked on, talking trivialities, two middle-aged men with lives in their hundreds of thousands in their keeping. Each knew that the other was intensely nervous. Each knew that the months ahead would be an eternity of agonizing apprehension. Each knew those lives would be saved. If the fragile dyke of deception held. If a foot didn't slip on the wire. If nobody dropped an orange.

*

Lohengrin did not so much drop an orange as try to cast it from him. It had been one thing to read of the turn of the tide in the newspapers, or to hear the surge reverse its direction in the measured tones of BBC announcers. Italy had surrendered, the Russians were counter-attacking in colossal strength, the U-boats which could have ended the war had suffered a devastating defeat in the Atlantic. Both the printed and the spoken word told him of these things and, for the last, he had the evidence of his own eyes in the ever-increasing numbers of American servicemen arriving unhampered, unscathed from across the ocean, bringing their tanks, their guns, their planes with them. Grimly he had continued to tell Berlin of the movements of those and British troops in whatever fashion Pemberton required of him.

It had become a different matter entirely to see with his own eyes genocide in the making. No memories came to him of the burning of London, of Coventry, of Plymouth and Portsmouth and Liverpool and so many other cities as he watched the massed air assault. Even in bed at night there was no escape from the thunder of planes, and, in a continuing downward spiral of depression, he blamed himself for their presence.

In the mornings the tight formations of the United States 8th Air Force held the stage, dragging condensation trails behind them on their way to the Continent. They held it again in the afternoons coming back, those that came back. The air wasn't clear of them before RAF Bomber Command took over the task of annihilation, filling the sky from horizon to horizon, those that returned assailing his ears with their passing until the dawn. Then the Americans began the cycle again.

The news of the destruction of Hamburg stunned Lohengrin and the realization of the sustained, calculated ferocity of the attack continued to jerk increasingly at his nerves after the first shock had passed. Only gradually did the story become clear as the reports of pilots were studied and their aerial photographs analysed. He would have liked to have blamed the Americans for the holocaust but could not because it was the RAF which had done this terrible thing. For several consecutive nights, bombing groups, often in excess of a thousand planes, had struck at the city, raining high explosives and phosphorus upon it until the expression 'fire storm' was born.

So many, so intense were the conflagrations, so great was the heat, that the oxygen in the air was totally consumed and buildings not levelled by explosives fell to the hurricanes screaming in from all sides to replace the air the fires had eaten. The fires gulped down that new fuel and grew. People who had survived the explosions and the fires died of asphyxiation, robbed of breath by the raging flames.

It took time before knowledge of the full extent of the catastrophe reached England through neutral Sweden, the knowledge that Hamburg had suffered the greatest disaster of any industrial city in the history of the world. Most of the population exulted. Lohengrin sank deeper into shame and despair. This was not the blitzkrieg in which he had once taken pride. This was Armageddon.

Common sense and Claire's gentle love gradually restored a sense of proportion to him. He saw that the death of even such a major city was overshadowed by the devastation of the Russian front, but that did nothing to ease the guilt he felt at the lies he had told Berlin about RAF losses. That these were very considerable was common knowledge, but he had been required by Pemberton to paint a blacker picture, a picture of bombers by the dozen lost in the North Sea on their way home to England which had not been lost, a picture of bombers by the score so damaged that they crashed on landing when they had not crashed. Lohengrin persuaded himself that had he not told those lies the anti-aircraft defences of the Reich would have been strengthened and Hamburg and other cities could have been better protected. To a not insignificant degree he was right, for on the strength of his messages, and those from others like him, some fighter squadrons had been transferred to the east to stem the Russian onslaught, but he was spared confirmation of the success of his deceit.

Lohengrin threw down his orange on receipt of a message from Berlin. Harry had left the room, leaving him to decode it for himself, leaving him with Claire, leaving the wireless transceiver still on, still warmed up. Claire watched her husband at work, saw his jaw tighten and his face lose its colour, saw his hand leap to the transmission key.

'Darling, no! Never without Harry!'

He seemed not to hear her and she threw herself towards the set, grasping the electric lead, tearing it free as Harry came back into the room.

'What's up, miss?' Harry always called her 'miss'.

'I'm so sorry, Harry,' Claire said in a flat, calm voice. 'I just tripped over this flex and broke it.'

'Oh, that's nothing, miss. It's not broken. I'll plug it back into this socket here. There we are. You finished for tonight, sir?' Harry always called Lohengrin 'sir'.

'Yes, thank you, Harry,' Lohengrin said.

In their bedroom, 'What on earth were you trying to do, darling?' Claire whispered.

'I was trying,' Lohengrin told her, 'to tell Berlin to ignore all my signals, past, present and future. You shouldn't have stopped me.'

'But why? Why now particularly? We've been through all that. Please don't say because Harry wasn't there for once. He'd have heard the key clicking, you know.'

'I had to try.'

She stood for what seemed a very long time looking at his pale, set face, waiting for him to say something more. When he did not, 'Why?' she repeated.

Lohengrin said, 'I saw men in Berlin wearing them. Rather nice men, not like some I met who weren't wearing them. Nice men. They looked awfully tired. They'd fought in Russia, or France, or at sea, or in the air. Decent men. You'd have liked them.'

'What are you talking about, my love?'

'What?'

'Darling, I don't understand what you're saying. What decent men wearing what?'

'Oh,' Lohengrin said, took the decoded message from his pocket and read it aloud. 'By order of the *Führer*. In recognition of your courage and loyalty to the Third Reich you are awarded the Iron Cross, Second Class. *Heil Hitler*.'

He put the paper back in his pocket, gave his wife a twisted smile and added, 'At least we can be thankful it's only second class.'

The night was a sleepless one for Lohengrin, a period of assessment spent flat on his back, almost motionless, his gaze rarely moving from one particular spot on the darkened ceiling.

That his spontaneous reaction to the receipt of the evening's signal had been the act of an imbecile was not something he needed to assess, it was simply a fact. For all that, it, and Claire's own reaction to it, had brought home to him the certainty that he was tired of belonging. He belonged to the National Socialist Party, for a period he had belonged to Professor Morris, now he belonged to Pemberton and, above all, to Claire. The last, the sweetest imaginable captivity, he had known to have been the final act in the shattering of his identity, but he had rejected the knowledge. Now he faced it, and throughout the long hours of darkness the catalyst of the award of the Iron Cross blended with enforced passivity to produce a volatile mixture.

By the time day had done its poor best to announce its arrival through the heavy black-out material covering the window, the mental chemistry had completed its work. As though acid had etched copper, he saw a path which could lead him back to himself, a path which would avoid suffering for Claire if he trod it carefully – if he was lucky.

Lohengrin had decided to earn his medal.

Chapter Twenty-Seven

The turf bordering the lane consisted more of daisies and dandelions than grass, but the square section Lohengrin cut carefully with his spade came away easily enough. That made him frown because it was the chalk an inch below the surface which had prevented the roots of the weeds from penetrating any deeper. It was the chalk too which seemed to make a nonsense of the signs screwed to fence posts every thirty yards. 'Danger! Mined Verges!' they read. He frowned again in worried exasperation, wondering if the signs were a bluff, because it would be difficult to bury mines in chalk. Then the worry left his face leaving only the exasperation as he muttered, 'Oh, come on. Somebody's probably invented the pickaxe.'

Abandoning the spade he fetched a trowel from the car and began probing the ground, shuffling slowly to his left on hands and knees. A quarter of an hour passed before the blade of the trowel came into contact with something that didn't feel like chalk. It took him almost as long with hands which wouldn't stop trembling to uncover sleeping death in the guise of what looked like an inverted grey dinner plate. Despite the chilly October afternoon, Lohengrin was sweating heavily as he looked along the lane in both directions, then up at the hillside and down at the sea. Rabbits, gulls, the breeze and, high above, the ever-present planes. Nothing else.

He hadn't really expected anything else, because for over three days he had watched the lane for several hours and nobody had come along it. Sighing tremulously, he took up the spade and levered the mine free of its bedding of soil and chalk, then carried it to the car. With the sinister disc covered by sacking, turf and assorted pieces of farming paraphernalia he filled in the hole the mine had left and resumed his search. Two more mines had joined the first when he heard the sound of footsteps and jerked his head to the right in time to see an army officer stroll round the bend in the lane fifty yards away. Nerves taut, fighting off a despair strong enough to produce a feeling of nausea, Lohengrin went on cutting bits of turf.

'Hey! You! What the flaming hell do you think you're doing?'

The officer wasn't strolling any longer and Lohengrin pushed himself back from his kneeling position to squat on his heels and watch his hurried approach, then, 'It's all right,' he said. 'There aren't any mines here. There isn't enough soil to bury them in.'

Face both angry and suspicious, the man with the insignia of a captain on his shoulders stood over him now. 'As it happens you're dead wrong and quite likely to have ended up dead too if I hadn't come along, but never mind that! I asked you what you thought you were doing!'

'I'm taking samples of soil for analysis,' Lohengrin told him. 'For the Ministry of Food. Here you are.'

The other took the identity card, looked at it and handed it back. 'All right, but why here, for Pete's sake? You can't expect to grow anything on these narrow strips, can you?'

Lohengrin shook his head. 'No, but it's the best place for testing the acidity or alkalinity of this hillside.' He waved an arm at the green slope rising above them as if the captain might not have noticed it before adding, 'The rain leaches the salts from the soil and the greatest concentration ends up here at the lowest point.' Plausible? Not very, he thought, but possibly good enough for a soldier, even an officer. If only the man would turn away.

'I thought everybody knew that chalk was alkaline.'

The statement brought sweat to Lohengrin's forehead again and he imagined that he could actually see the mines hidden on the floor of the car. He drew the back of his hand across his eyes to remove the moisture and to dispel the vision. The action left a streak of mud above his eyebrows.

'It's a question of degree,' he said. 'I've got a portable testing kit in the car, litmus paper and all that, but it isn't accurate enough. I'll have to take samples back to the lab.' He paused then added, 'You see, they want to grow linseed. It makes good cattle fodder after the oil's been pressed out. The oil's excellent too. Lots of uses. You probably used it on your cricket bat at school.'

The mention of a cricket bat seemed to disarm the captain.

'Indeed I did. Cigarette?'

'Thanks.'

Lohengrin stood up and took one from the proffered packet, then immediately wished he had not because it was difficult to keep his hand steady, but it was all right.

They smoked and talked for a little, leaning against the car while Lohengrin's nerves screamed at him.

'These mines – any risk of detonating one if I accidentally prod it with a trowel?'

'Oh no. I was exaggerating the danger a bit. Of course, you might if you gave it a bloody great clout, but they aren't anti-personnel. They were put there in 1940 to stop enemy tanks using this track.'

'That's a relief,' Lohengrin said.

'Yes. Well, I'd better be off. Good day to you.'

The captain turned to go and in one unbroken movement Lohengrin grasped his spade and swung its edge against the side of the officer's head, then stood looking dully down at the corpse. Despite the gaping skull-wound there wasn't much blood and he supposed that meant that the heart had stopped instantly.

Seven miles to the north, with the body of the man he had killed hidden in a bramble-covered ditch five miles behind him, Lohengrin was still repeating to himself that there had been no choice. He had been examined at close quarters, along with his car and identity card, under circumstances which had made it necessary for him to deflect suspicion from himself. Had his questioner lived, the connection between unexplained explosions and who was responsible for them would have been swiftly made. No, there had been no choice at all, but reiterating the fact didn't make him feel any better.

Lohengrin drove carefully on to strike his first small blow for Hamburg, for Germany, and above all for himself. He knew exactly where he was going and knew as well that he had to go there now before his courage ran out of him. Wishing that the autumn fields were less barren, he consoled himself with the thought that the innocence of mid-afternoon would provide him with cover, because it was an unlikely time for a sabotage agent to operate.

*

'It's a 4-6-0 "Pacific"!'

Alf gave his brother a scathing look and said, 'You're daft, you are. It's an ordinary 4-4-0 "Atlantic".'

Wilf glanced at him defensively and muttered ''Tisn't' without conviction. At eight, Alf was nearly two years older than he and could tell a railway locomotive's type head-on without having to count the bogeys and driving wheels which was pretty rotten of him when he knew all the makes of cars and aeroplanes by sight too.

'Get ready to jot down the engine number when I sing it out.'

'A'right.'

The train was approaching fast now and Wilf watched it appreciatively, enjoying the growing sound, the steam escaping from the big external cylinders and the smoke streaming back from the squat funnel. He licked the end of his pencil in readiness just as flame flashed briefly in the dusk.

Southern Railway Atlantic-class locomotive number 17984 lurched, then continued its careering progress at an angle of twenty-five degrees to the track before toppling onto its side. A windowless mail van followed it and the remaining nine coaches jerked, jolted and screeched to a halt, still upright, in a zig-zag formation across the north- and south-bound lines. Troops poured from the wrecked train.

American servicemen reached the engine first and dragged the unconscious driver and fireman from their cab, then carried them to safety, clear of the hissing steam. In the steam itself an officer stood looking down at the remains of the bodies of two children. He was saying, 'Oh Jesus, Oh Jesus,' over and over again. A sergeant ran towards him calling, 'You okay, Lootenant?' but all the lieutenant would say was 'Oh Jesus.'

*

The rain sweeping in from the Channel glistened like silver threads on a vibrating loom in the headlights of the circle of cars, trucks and ambulances. Derailed carriages glistened wetly along their lengths, except for one so steeply canted skywards that its end was lost in the gloom above the pool of luminance. Men, mostly uniformed, moved amongst the wreckage, calling to each other, their voices drowned periodically by the blare of a loud-hailer. From somewhere a woman was screaming.

'What's the casualty situation so far?'

'Fifteen dead, sir. Twice that number injured. Nearly all of them from the second train. The first lot got clear with only cuts and bruises before the north-bound train ploughed into the wreck. Except for the two boys, that is, but they weren't passengers. There are still people in there, of course. Well, you can hear them. Cutting equipment and arc-lamps are on their way from Newhaven and Lewes and they're sending heavy lifting gear down from London.'

The chief constable nodded and watched a prostrate figure taken from one of the carriages and carried away into the darkness before asking, 'What was the period between the two incidents?'

'Four minutes, sir,' the police superintendent told him.

'Hmm. I wonder if it was planned that way. Two for the price of one, as it were.'

'I'd certainly have planned it that way if I was an enemy agent or a fifth columnist, sir. Always assuming this was sabotage.'

'I think we must assume that it was,' the chief constable said. 'It'll be hours before they've cleared enough of this shambles to enable the track to be examined and we can't afford to wait that long before we take action. What have you got so far to indicate what it might have been?'

The woman's screams were fading now, barely audible above the roar of the rain on the roof of the car. Frowning, the superintendent took a notebook from his pocket, held it towards the light from the dashboard and began to read aloud.

'Troops in the first carriage think they may have heard a bang immediately prior to the derailment, but it was followed by such a racket that they can't really be sure which came first.' He looked at his superior and said, 'That's a contradiction, of course, but I understand what they mean, and they were separated from the engine by its own length plus the length of its tender and of the mail van.' Returning his attention to his notebook he went on, 'Both the engine driver and fireman suffered severe concussion resulting in retroactive amnesia and can't remember anything for some minutes before the crash, so they can't help us. I did consider the possibility of the two boys having placed some heavy object across the lines, but the school exercise book we found near them is full of engine numbers and . . .'

'Quite,' the other broke in. 'Railway enthusiasts don't wreck trains, or if they did they wouldn't be stupid enough to stand there and be crushed. Go on.'

'Well, that leaves the RAF, sir, and they are adamant that no enemy aircraft has succeeded in crossing the south or east coasts during the past twenty-four hours. They say that even if a fighter-bomber had managed to slip under the radar net it would have shot up the train with cannon fire, not attempted to drop a bomb right in front of the engine. Either way the passengers would have seen or heard it. Other people too. It was a clear day before this downpour started.'

'Which makes it likely, as trains don't just fall over for no reason, either that somebody loosened a length of rail or placed an explosive device on the track.'

'That's what I think, sir.'

'All right,' the chief constable said. 'I don't know of any way of identifying rail looseners, but we can try our hand at apprehending someone illegally in possession of explosives. Get on to the army and ask for assistance in setting up road blocks all over the county. You'd need transport of some sort for a job like this, so we'll stand a chance of netting whoever it is if he tries again.'

'It's a big operation, sir.'

'And this is a big mess,' came the reply.

As if to underline the statement, the arc-lamps brought from Newhaven were switched on and bathed the scene of devastation in violet radiance. The steeply canted carriage cast purple shadows in several directions like an indecisive sundial and men shielded their eyes against the sudden glare.

The chief constable gestured with his hand and added, 'Imagine this happening all over the place when the invasion starts rolling. It'd be catastrophic. Let's get cracking before MI5 asks us why we're sitting on our backsides.'

*

Lohengrin did not try again. He had had no intention of doing so until he knew if his first attempt had been successful and to what extent. Then there would be more observation, more careful planning to be carried out before he took further action. For all that, they netted him within fourteen hours of the chief constable issuing his instructions, but the net was to prove faulty.

The BBC made only brief reference to a rail disaster in Sussex in which twenty-three people had died. It was a minor incident in the scale of things, and there were more important matters to report to the world. The national press gave it a few column-inches, but the local paper, reduced by rationing to the size of a news-sheet, devoted most of its front page to the story. Lohengrin read all about it over breakfast, looked at the accompanying long-range photograph which was good of the rain but showed nothing else readily identifiable, and wondered how he felt.

There was sadness, particularly for the children, but turning his thoughts to Hamburg quickly dispelled that. Only God knew how many children had died in that holocaust. There was satisfaction, but no elation. There was, as well, a grim determination to continue with his campaign. The day outside the house sparkling, washed clean by the night's storm, offered a new beginning.

'What's on the agenda, darling?'

Lohengrin looked at his wife. 'I've got to be at the experimental farm near Eastbourne by ten.'

'Oh, may I come with you? I've never seen it and it's such a lovely day.'

'I'd like it very much if you would,' Lohengrin said. There was nothing else he could say, and anyway, he meant it both for his own pleasure and because the campaign would be jeopardized if he were inexplicably to neglect his job for the Ministry of Food.

*

The standard of cooking in the crowded little house always dropped dramatically when Claire was away, and Pemberton looked unbelievingly at the unrecognizable mess on his plate which represented lunch, wondering whether Sergeant Newland or Harry was responsible. He concluded that with such similar techniques the answer could only be established by asking them, and he had no intention of doing that.

Reluctantly he began to eat, telling himself that this was the price he must pay for being temporarily spared Claire's disturbing presence. That pressure on him didn't occur at weekends, for then he and the others withdrew to their rented rooms to give the couple some semblance of normality in their married lives. The arrangement also gave Pemberton the opportunity to be seen to be doing what he was ostensibly supposed to be doing, for, as the likelihood of a German invasion of Britain receded, vanished, the plausibility of his cover as an expert on anti-tank defences had receded and vanished with it. Now he was allegedly in charge of the construction of tank parks and boarding ramps in preparation for an invasion going the other way. The tale had satisfied the landlord of the 'Anglo-Saxon Arms' and, through him, a sizeable proportion of the inhabitants of Seaford.

By the time Pemberton abandoned his lunch at a point where he believed he had eaten enough not to give offence to the cook, his thoughts had turned back to Claire. Now he felt deprived of her presence rather than spared it, and the change had nothing whatsoever to do with the quality of the food. No longer newly-weds, it was touching to see husband and wife grow ever closer to each other, quietly happy when they were together, vaguely uneasy when they were not, but he could have done without that call on his emotions. He left the table undecided whether he preferred her presence or her absence.

*

The experimental farm didn't interest Claire in the least, but she was very happy there. It was so good to see Frank doing ordinary dull things like prodding soil and looking at plants through a magnifying glass. It was even fun to listen to him arguing amicably with the manager, using a lot of words she didn't know the meaning of. Frank seemed to enjoy it all too, a different Frank to the man agonizing about fathering a child or becoming desperate over being awarded some silly medal. Those incidents had troubled her deeply and after the second she had telephoned Gail for advice, only to be told by the sergeant on duty at the house off Sloane Street that Her Ladyship was abroad, in the Mediterranean, he had thought. Gail's not being there when she was most wanted had upset Claire even more until the realization came that the problems were not such as could ever have been discussed between them; not if Frank was to retain his fragile grasp on liberty.

They left the farm at four and drove home through country lanes because it was prettier that way and there was plenty of time before the evening wireless call from Germany. Cock pheasants ran at their approach, not bothering to fly, and rabbits flicked white tails at them before vanishing into the ferns growing at the edges of the woods to either side. A long sinuous creature undulated across the road in front of the car, moving very fast. 'Oh look! A stoat!' Claire said. 'I do hope it doesn't hurt the rabbits!' Lohengrin smiled.

The Army had made its plans very quickly, but there was an immense number of roads to be identified on the ordnance maps, thousands of men to be detailed to cover them and much transport to be provided to place them in position, so that the trap could be sprung at the same moment right across the county. Not for years had the movement of troops excited comment, so that factor had given the brigadier in charge no cause for concern, but to have closed sectors piecemeal could have alerted the fugitive. The loss of time he had felt to be a minor consideration because a sabotage agent needed a base, a store for his explosives, close to his area of operation, and was unlikely to stray far from it. 'Commence search of all vehicles at 1615 hours,' the order read.

When, a hundred yards ahead, a soldier stepped onto the road and raised his hand, Lohengrin slowed the car and stopped it beside him. A second soldier with a corporal's stripes on his arms joined the first.

'You chaps want a lift into Seaford?'

'No thank you, sir. Would you and the lady mind getting out? We have orders to search all vehicles.'

Claire giggled and said, 'You'll have your work cut out searching this one with all that junk in the back. If you come across a comb, it's mine. I lost it months ago.'

'We'll see what we can do, miss. Now, if you don't mind.'

The corporal, a rifle in his right hand, gestured with his left and they got out of the car. Claire turned to her husband and made a comical face of enquiry, then stood very still when she saw how white he was.

'What's this, sir?'

'It's a theodolite. Be careful with it. It's Ministry of Food property.'

'Ah.'

The tripod with the little telescopic attachment on top was placed on the grass verge. Graduated surveyor's poles followed it, and a leather-covered reel of measuring tape. A sack-cloth plumber's bag with rope handles was upended, its contents scattered onto the roadside: a trowel, a ball of twine, secateurs, a small oil-can wrapped in a rag, a pair of garden shears, a square wooden box with a lock.

'What's in 'ere?'

'Bottles of chemicals and some test-tubes.'

'Open it, please.'

Lohengrin's fingers trembling as he selected a key from his ring, inserted it, turned it. The corporal moving closer to look at the contents of the box and saying 'All right'. Claire watching the scene, wide-eyed, frightened now by her husband's agitation, apparently unnoticed by the soldiers, but so obvious to her. A glance into the car showing her the jumble in the back down to the level of the rear seat, and the private soldier's hands lifting a filled sack with 'Bone-meal' stencilled on it.

'Corp!'

The urgency of the cry and the double metallic click as the corporal forced a round into the breach of his bolt-action rifle reached her almost simultaneously and fractionally before understanding struck her, as though a photographer's flash had exploded in her brain. What the man had seen she did not know, but she knew with absolute certainty what it was used for, what it had *been* used for.

Since the shooting of von Neustadt, Claire had never again carried the gun Gail had given her, but it made no difference. The garden shears fell open when she picked them up by one handle and the single blade encountered no resistance when she drove it upwards into the soldier's back. He fell forward, half in and half out of the car, twitched once, made a strange gargling sound and lay still. Claire stared down at him, muscles locked, frozen, only vaguely aware of a heavy thud nearby.

'It's all right, darling. Let go the shears now.'

Lohengrin had to say it twice before she heard him, before she saw her white-knuckled hand still gripping the wooden handle. She whimpered then, pulled the blade out of the dead man, turned and hurled the shears far into the deep bracken.

'Oh, it's a pity you did that,' Lohengrin said, but the words did not register with her. She was looking at the corporal lying in the road with the theodo-something beside him. All three legs of the tripod were broken and so, she guessed from the angle of his head, was the corporal's neck. That had been very quick of Frank.

'Are you all right, my dear?'

'No, Frank, I'm not all right. What an awfully silly question.'

He nodded and said, 'Well, at least you're making sense. Wait here.'

So Claire stood where she was, only her eyes moving as she watched the bodies carried to the wood, then their caps which had fallen off and their rifles. After that, Frank took two grey things to the wood one at a time. They looked like the breastplates she had worn in a play at school when she was being a warrior princess. That had been a super costume because there wasn't much else to it except for a short skirt and metal shin guards and a helmet with wings on it and the other girls' fathers in the audience hadn't taken their eyes off her and . . .

'In you get, darling.'

All the other stuff was back in the car, she saw, and wondered why she hadn't noticed Frank doing that. It didn't stay there very long though, because two other soldiers stopped them and took it all out again, then put it back themselves. When they had looked under the seats, under the bonnet, under the car and in the boot they stuck an important piece of paper on the windscreen and said they were sorry for having troubled 'sir' and 'miss' and waved them on. They saw a lot more soldiers before they got home, but they didn't search the car because of the important piece of paper, so that was all right.

Claire was safely in her bedroom before she began to shake.

*

'How did you guess? Was it second sight, or female intuition, or something like that?'

'Of course it wasn't,' Claire said. 'I haven't got any of those things. It was looking at you. I've seen you when you've been in a muddle before, you know, and it was easy to tell that you were in a very bad one today. Then when that soldier shouted I sort of guessed what it was all about and knew that you would be taken away and hung, I mean hanged, and Gail had told me to protect you, as if I needed telling, and I love you, and that's that.'

They were sitting side by side on the bed, as they had in the past at times of stress, holding hands like children. And that's what she looks like, Lohengrin thought, a child, an adorable child. With no make-up, her long fair hair fastened at the nape of her neck by an elastic band and one of his pyjama jackets covering her almost to her knees, she could have been taken for sixteen.

'I'm so sorry,' he whispered. 'So very sorry. You see, I'd done so very much worse than just fail as a wireless agent. I'd actually been made to . . .'

He stopped talking when her grip tightened and she jerked his hand, then listened to her saying, 'Oh, for goodness sake, I know what you were actually made to do. I was a big part of it. You were trying to redress the balance, that's what you were trying to do. That's an important expression, isn't it? Redress the balance? You redressed it as a matter of honour. I understand all that.'

'You were never meant to know, Claire. You were certainly never meant to be implicated and you wouldn't have been if I'd hidden those mines in a better place.' Lohengrin paused before adding almost to himself, 'If only I could have found those shears.'

'Yes, I did rather make them a present of us, didn't I? I suppose you wiped those mine things and the rifles clean.'

'Yes.'

'What a truly stupid bitch I am.'

'I'd be in prison now but for you, Claire.'

'Hmm.'

There was silence between them until Claire gripped his fingers hard again and asked very quietly, 'How long, Frank?'

Speaking slowly, thoughtfully, 'Not sooner than noon tomorrow,' he said. 'Nothing will have started until it was time to relieve those men and they were found to be missing. Then they may or may not find them in the darkness. If they do they'll stop everything until daylight for fear of destroying evidence when they search for what the press likes to call the murder weapon. You know, footprints and bits of thread caught on brambles and – well, they'll find the shears quite soon after first light because they'll have a lot of searchers, but they'll still have to be processed for prints at Eastbourne or somewhere and that'll take a bit of time.'

Lohengrin fell silent and stared broodingly at the floor for so long that Claire had to say 'Go on, Frank' to bring him back to himself.

'What? Oh, sorry. Well, if there's somebody bright in charge he'll have the photographs of the prints driven immediately to London for checking by Special Branch. After that it'll only take a telephone call to the police here, or perhaps they'll keep it private and just tell George Pemberton.'

Claire lifted the hand she was holding and pressed it to her cheek before saying, 'I'm so glad there's no question of me being left behind now.'

Chapter Twenty-Eight

Other than what she had been taught at school, and she had forgotten most of that, Claire knew nothing of religion, but she thought it would be polite to report to God and tell Him what she intended to do, and St Peter's where she had been married seemed an appropriate place for that.

The church was empty except for a woman with a mop swabbing the aisle and Claire sat down in the back row of pews and waited for her to finish. When she had done so and gone clanking away with her bucket, Claire told God all about it, right from the beginning. God didn't say anything and nothing happened at all until a rather handsome young man with a white surplice over his cassock came in and said the early service doesn't start for an hour yet can I do anything for you? and she said no thank you very much I'm just being peaceful and he smiled at her and said that's what the place is for and disappeared through the door where she and Frank had gone to sign the register. After that she waited for a few more minutes, but God still didn't say anything, so she got up and went home.

Frank was alone in the house when she got there, as she knew he would be because it was Sunday. With his work for the Ministry of Food finished for the week, and no wireless communication with Germany scheduled, he wouldn't be needed until Monday unless there was some unforeseen emergency. That was as certain as it could be, because Harry had taken bits of the wireless transmitter away with him last night as he always did so that it couldn't be used until he brought them back again. What was also certain was that there were only a few hours left until noon.

'Hello, my love,' Lohengrin said. 'Oh, you do look so pretty.'

Knowing that she was the only pretty thing left in his life, she had been particularly careful to appear so this day.

'I know. Sexy too. Do you feel sexy?'

Without waiting for a reply she grasped his hand and led him towards the stairs. Near the top she felt him hesitate, then follow again at her gentle tug. In the bedroom she stripped quickly, left him taking off his own clothes and walked to the bathroom. It was some minutes before she returned with a glass of cloudy liquid in her hand.

'Drink this, darling. It tastes foul, but it will make you feel nice.'

He took the glass from her, his eyes on hers, asking an unspoken question, then drank at her slow nod.

The bath was much fuller than the wartime austerity regulations permitted and water slopped over the side when Claire lowered her body onto Lohengrin's. More followed it at the urging of her hips. They looked steadily at each other, not speaking because everything had long been said.

He was growing sleepy now from the drug, Claire saw, and she quickened her movements until his breathing shortened, deepened. When she felt him begin to jerk beneath her she pressed down on his shoulders so that his head slid underwater and held him there. He didn't struggle at all.

'Don't be lonely, my love,' Claire said. 'I shan't keep you waiting long.'

They had promised each other to do it together, but she had decided that she must punish herself first. God hadn't told her to, but she felt sure that that was what He would want.

In the bedroom, dressed again, she stood looking at Mr Hotchkiss squatting on top of the chest of drawers. 'Grumpy old bear,' she said, and reached out to caress the furry muzzle with the back of her hand.

*

The soldier on sentry duty at the bottom of Southdown Road watched appreciatively as the pretty blonde girl approached, her hair swinging at every stride. He had seen her often and built many fantasies about her. Today, he thought, she looked even more special. Sort of gentle and proud.

'Lovely morning, miss!'

'Isn't it?'

A sweet smile and she was past him. He turned so that he could watch her retreating legs just as she scrambled between the strands of the wire fence surrounding the golf course.

'Miss! Come out of there! For Christ's sake, can't you bloody well read?'

The girl's voice floated back to him as she began to run and he hurled himself at the fence, hanging half across it, pleading with her to stop, shouting commands, shouting obscenities.

The exploding mine didn't make a great deal of noise.

*

Pemberton, who had never seen action, had never seen a soldier cry before. The sight confused him because it seemed unnatural and, because he was dead inside, he had no inclination to join him at it. 'Take it easy.

Take it easy,' he said and patted the man's shoulder in what he imagined to be a most unmilitary gesture, then looked away from the sight of someone struggling to find his voice.

It was amazing, he thought, how quickly a crowd could gather. Police, soldiers, sailors, airmen, civilians, an ambulance and its crew. None of them was doing anything but stare. None of them would do anything until the squad with the mine detectors arrived.

'Sorry, sir. I'm all right now.'

He looked at the soldier. 'Well done. She climbed through the fence. What then? You told me she said something.'

'Yes, sir. Well, I hollered at her, sir, and she started to run and she said – and she said . . .'

Pemberton waited patiently, looking over the man's shoulder.

'Sir, she said "It's all right, Mr Hotchkiss. It won't hurt very much." Sir, I dunno why she said that. My name isn't Hotchkiss.'

His gaze rested for a moment on the pathetic bundle which had been Claire Pelham then, 'No,' Pemberton said. 'No, of course it isn't.'

He turned away and began to walk slowly up Southdown Road.

*

Clayton returned from a meeting at the Home Office shortly after noon to be told of the double tragedy by his secretary.

'Oh, dear me,' he said. 'Does His Lordship know?'

'Yes, Mr Clayton. I felt he should be told at once.'

'Thank you for that, Jane. Get Colonel Pemberton on the line, will you?'

'Yes, sir. Sir, Commander Reeves is in the outer office. He says it's important.'

'Right,' Clayton said. 'Send him in and hold that call for the time being.'

When he was seated the Special Branch man spoke for several minutes and ended by saying, 'With two of your people involved I thought I should come straight to you with all that so that you can tell me how you want it played.'

'I'm very glad you did,' Clayton told him. 'I take it you're quite certain that Mrs Pelham was involved in the killings and that Pelham was responsible for the Sussex train sabotage.'

'There's no doubt at all about the first. The fingerprints speak for themselves and they were seen together by various witnesses yesterday. I gather that the wife wasn't somebody easily overlooked.'

Clayton nodded and Reeves went on, 'The evidence on the sabotage is circumstantial, but it has been established that the first train was derailed by a mine, two more mines were found by the corpses and – well, I ask you!'

'Quite,' Clayton said. 'Keep Mrs Pelham out of it, please, Reeves. You know what Pelham was, and it will look better from the German point of view if it appears that she killed him when she found out what he'd done, then killed herself. Can that be arranged?'

'Oh, I don't think it needs arranging,' Reeves replied. 'That must have been just the way it happened. I'm surprised I didn't work that out for myself.' He smiled without any trace of humour, stood up and walked from the room.

Less than a minute later Clayton followed his example, went along the passage and found Edward Mainwaring standing in front of his fireplace, staring at the three silver-framed photographs on the mantel above it, the camera portraits of his wife, his daughter and his ward. The words 'two down, one to go' formed unbidden in his mind. He winced and moved to Mainwaring's side.

'I'm sorry, old friend,' he said.

In an almost American gesture, Mainwaring put an arm across Clayton's shoulders and thumped him twice, then turned away and sat at his desk. Settled in his chair, he linked both hands behind his head before saying, 'It was a suicide pact of course.'

'Of course.'

'What do you suppose triggered it?'

Knowing that he was failing in his duty, not yet clear in his mind if it mattered, not caring too much if it did, 'I haven't the remotest idea,' Clayton lied.

'I'm glad Claire died,' Mainwaring said.

Clayton turned his head slowly and stared hard at Mainwaring, wondering what he knew, what he had guessed, feeling infinitely sad for him.

Mainwaring saw the intensity of his chief assistant's regard and went on, 'Oh, don't get me wrong, Peter. All I meant was that the child chose a precarious way out. It was an anti-personnel mine she trod on. That could have left her alive, but with no legs. I don't think she would have liked that very much. She was very proud of her body.'

Relief flooded through Clayton and when Mainwaring said, 'Ah well, meanwhile the war goes on. How's Pemberton?' he replied, 'Stunned. Stunned, but steady. It's been a multiple shock for him. Losing Lohengrin as well as Parsifal must have hit him hard and he'll be blaming himself for both. Particularly Lohengrin. Mutual bonds had been forged there, the kind of bonds we like to see develop. Then, of course, there was . . .' Clayton stopped talking and made a helpless gesture.

'Love for the unobtainable,' Mainwaring said. 'Love for Claire. It's greatly to his credit that he never let that become obvious. I wish for his sake, as much as anybody's, that the verdict on her could be made anything other than murder of her husband followed by suicide, but it must be that for public consumption, for German consumption. It's the only safe way of closing the file on Lohengrin.' He paused, then said, 'Pemberton is of immense value to us. You told me he was steady. How steady?'

'Too steady, according to Carne.'

'Then you must shake him. You must release the tension.'

'I intend to, but I have to talk to you about the choice of instrument.'

'Now don't you start trying to protect me, Peter,' Mainwaring said. 'Recent events have changed nothing. You must use the best instrument we've got. I know you'll find a way.'

*

'Her Ladyship's expecting you, sir. Straight up the stairs to the top floor and the flat door's facing you.'

Clayton thanked the sergeant standing behind the desk in the hall of the house off Sloane Street and followed his directions. When he reached his destination he paused for a little while to recover his breath, then pressed the bell.

She looked pale and rather stern, Clayton thought, but otherwise exactly as he remembered her.

'It's good of you to see me, Lady Abigail,' he said.

She stood aside to let him in, then took his hat and coat and placed them on a chair. He looked around him at the gracious room, a room which fitted her to perfection, wishing that he was somewhere else.

'Isn't that a Cézanne?'

'Yes, and that's a Manet over there. Do sit down, Mr Clayton. May I give you a sherry? I'm afraid that's all there is.'

'You're very kind.'

He took the glass she gave him, sat when she did and watched her cross her legs. They were ridiculously long legs.

'I don't know where to begin,' he said, and his voice carried genuine agitation.

'Begin,' Gail told him, 'by lying back in that chair instead of sitting on the edge of it like a ramrod. When you've done that, drink some sherry and look at my legs some more. They're very therapeutic legs. After that, just let it come.'

The only surprise that Clayton felt was that her words did not surprise him. He had forgotten this aspect of her and chided himself for not remembering one of the main facets which made her so very good at what she was required to do. He relaxed, and the comfortable feeling he had spoken of to her what seemed so very long ago came back to him. It increased when he saw that the stern set of her features had softened without assuming any trace of condescending compassion.

'By the way,' Gail added, 'there's no need to talk about Claire. We'll take that as said.'

Clayton inclined his head. 'Thank you. In that case it will only be necessary to refer to her indirectly. It's your resignation I came to see you about.'

Her expression did not change, and for a moment he thought it was a trick of the light that made her eyes blazingly green, then realized that it could not be so because her head had not moved at all. Slowly the brilliance faded.

'It's no use, Mr Clayton,' she said. 'I once embarrassed you, or perhaps hurt you would be a better way of putting it, by describing myself as a government harlot, so think of me as a courtesan if you find that any easier to stomach. Well, whether you do or not, I'm an ex-courtesan now and that is final.'

She raised a hand as Clayton started to speak and went on, 'No. It was a difficult decision to justify in my letter of resignation, so I didn't attempt it, but I'll explain it now so that you can understand that there's no point in your arguing. You obviously know that I was sent to Algiers at the request of the Navy to do a patch-up job on a couple of their people, don't you?'

'Yes, but . . .'

'Wait. I fell in love with the second of what are humorously known as my "subjects" there. That has never happened to me before. Of course, you don't sell soiled goods to the person you love, so I sent him away, but the damage had been done and I'd drawn my own teeth. To be a truly successful courtesan you don't act the part, you are the real thing, or as close to it as you can think yourself into being. That's impossible for me now and . . .'

'Lady Abigail!'

'Yes?'

'Please don't distress yourself any further. I am not without my sources of information, and what I have not been told I have surmised. It's part of my reason for being here.'

'Oh?' Gail said, and frowned suspiciously.

'Yes. There's a man I want you to meet.'

'Oh my God! Haven't you listened to a word I've been saying?'

Ignoring the question, 'I'm not asking you to go to bed with him, I'm asking you to meet him,' Clayton said. 'He's a nice man, a key man in our invasion plans, who has been through a bad time.'

Her face furious, Gail whipped out of her chair with such speed that Clayton thought he was about to be attacked, but all she did was stride to the Cézanne and stand glaring at it. Her sherry glass had toppled and amber liquid was spreading across the top of the coffee table by her chair, dripping to the carpet. Clayton made no move to do anything about it.

'He's been through a bad time,' Gail told the painting, 'Isn't that *amazing*? Isn't that *unique*? Now he's cracked up and wants a mother-substitute, and out of all his harem the only one our Mr Clayton can think of is little Gail, so forget everything you've tried to explain and trot along like a good girl, darling. This man *needs* you!'

The movement of her head was as quick as a bird's when she turned it to look at Clayton over her left shoulder and he saw that the eyes were burning with green fire again.

Before she could go on, 'He hasn't cracked up, as you put it.' Clayton said, 'and he needs you less than you need him.'

'Than I need him?'

'Lady Abigail, you returned to this country from the Mediterranean eleven days ago and you haven't been outside this flat since.'

'That's not much of a testimonial to your sources of information. They could have told you that downstairs. Also, since my resignation, it's none of your business.'

'We try to look after our people,' Clayton said, 'and I also confess to an interest of an avuncular nature. The double burden of an unhappy end to a love affair and the tragic death of someone who was virtually a sister is not one I would wish any woman to carry alone, particularly one I hold in affectionate admiration.'

Gail's body had followed her head to face him now and her voice had lost its sharpness when she spoke.

'You're being very sweet, Mr Clayton, but you must let me sort out my own problems. I've had rather a surfeit of men over the past two years and, things being as they are, I'd obtain no emotional catharsis whatsoever out of being thrown at some stranger.'

'I think you just might,' Clayton replied. 'Won't you please sit down and let me tell you who he is? You see, you have certain things in common.'

'Oh, very well,' Gail said tiredly. 'Let me mop up this sherry first.'

*

When the front door of the house on Southdown Road opened to Gail Mainwaring's knock, she found herself looking at a slender, grey-eyed man in his middle thirties. All of him was dusty, from his uniform shoes, to his bare forearms, to his sandy hair. She liked what she saw.

George Pemberton looked back at heart-wrenching beauty and felt instant suspicion, suspicion which blossomed into resentment.

'Yes?'

'I'm a friend of Claire Helier's – I mean Claire Pelham's and I mean I *was* a friend.'

'Oh, of course,' Pemberton said. 'The most beautiful woman in London.'

'She was awfully pretty, wasn't she?'

Pemberton frowned. 'I meant you. I've just recognized you. The Lady Abigail Mainwaring, the most beautiful woman in London. That's what the society papers call you, isn't it?'

'Well, you don't have to sound so bloody tough about it,' Gail said. 'It isn't my fault. May I come in?'

'Must you? I'm right in the middle of closing the house down.'

'Oh God. I'm sorry,' Gail whispered and added almost inaudibly, 'I loved her too, you know.'

She turned away then to take the few short steps along the path to the road.

'Wait! You'd better come in!'

Doing as she was bidden, wishing he would stop barking at her, she moved into the living room and stood looking around at the male muddle;

one curtain on the floor, the other still suspended by a solitary ring, piles of books in inconvenient places, a carpet draped over the banisters.

'What did you mean when you said you loved her too?'

Gail glanced curiously at him. 'Simply that. She was my kid sister in everything but blood.'

'I didn't mean that. I meant your saying "too". It means "as well as" in that context. As well as whom?'

'Oh, Colonel Pemberton,' Gail said sadly. 'You *are* Colonel Pemberton, aren't you?'

'Yes. I'm George Pemberton.'

'Then surely you're not going to deny her now.'

She watched the pleasant face crumple, then slowly regain its composure.

'I'm very sorry. Is it public knowledge?'

Shaking her head, 'No,' Gail said. 'Just to a few. They think you did very well under intolerable circumstances. There wasn't anything they could do about it because Frank Pelham had come to depend on you as well as on Claire.' She smiled gently at him, gestured at the room and added, 'Of course, you're making it public now. You're doing all this without help from choice, aren't you?'

'Thank you for understanding. I'm in a bit of a muddle inside, knowing that I should have seen it coming. They were so happy with each other, and jealousy didn't let me see anything beyond that. Anyway, I wanted to be alone and to . . .'

'Yes, of course.'

There was a long silence before Pemberton asked, 'Why did you come here, Lady Abigail? Having met you, I know it can't have been out of morbid curiosity.'

'No, it wasn't that,' she told him. 'Certainly not that. I thought that you and I might find it a happy thing to be alone together for a few days. I thought perhaps . . .'

'Oh no you don't!'

She had been staring at the window with its single curtain hanging like a flag in still air, but the angry command brought her head round to meet his furious gaze.

'I've been in this business a long time,' he said, 'and I know the form. Some stupid bastard gets himself upset for one reason or another, so they throw a pretty girl at him. There, there, come to mummy and she'll kiss it better. That's what killed Claire, you know! What did they tell you about me? That I had lost my edge? That I was coming apart at the seams? Don't bother to tell me! I don't really care too much, but I'll tell you this! You try the seduction routine on me and I'll smack your bottom so hard you'll be arrested for glowing in the black-out!'

Gail felt the muscles in her cheeks tugging at the corners of her mouth, but fought the smile down.

'Colonel Pemberton.'

'Yes?'

'I was only thinking of walking. The Lake District is a very pretty place. It might be rather pleasant to get away, to get ordinarily, physically tired.'

'Euphemisms, euphemisms,' Pemberton said.

'It doesn't have to be a euphemism for anything.'

'With the most beautiful woman in London? You must think me very simple.'

'No, I don't think you're that. I think you're very self-centred.'

For the first time Pemberton noted harshness in the perfectly modulated voice, noted too the green blaze which Clayton had witnessed, then listened to her saying, 'I'm a bit muddled inside too. I was responsible for Claire joining the Service. I told her what to do and a lot of how to do it. I gave her the gun she killed the German with. I suggested the marriage be permitted. I killed Claire as surely as if I'd shot her. I was hoping, given time, that you who loved her could be persuaded to forgive me all that. There's some first person singulars for you!'

Without warning, Gail sat down. It wasn't a graceful movement. It was as though her legs had collapsed under her while her back remained rigid, so that she was sitting bolt upright on a packing case, looking at the floor, hands folded on her lap. Her face held no expression, but tears formed on her lashes, hesitated there, then spilled over and trickled down her cheeks.

'Oh, for God's sake, woman!' Pemberton shouted at her. 'Don't sit there dripping like a blasted poached egg!'

Slowly her head came up, seeming to leave her chin behind as her mouth gaped in astonishment, then, *'Woman! P-poached egg!'* she stuttered. 'I – I . . .'

Pemberton watched the haunting eyes begin to smile, the mouth follow them, and heard her say, 'I think I like you, Colonel Pemberton. I really think I like you. Will you come walking with a poached egg?'

For a long moment he continued to scowl, then sighed softly and held out his hand to her.

'Yes,' Pemberton said. 'Yes, I'd like to do that.'

EPILOGUE

It was eight months since Pemberton had walked with a goddess, talked with a goddess and lain with her throughout eleven nights of passionate tranquillity. Because it was precise, there was nothing contradictory for him in the description, although to explain the paradox would have been beyond his powers. The passion had departed with her, but the tranquillity she had left with him like a blessing. He had been careful not to question the miracle, accepting it as just one of those things that goddesses do. She was married now, The Lady Abigail, to the naval officer she loved, and that made Pemberton very content. Knowing that she could never be his, but she having given him so much, it was a happy thing for him to know that her heart's desire had been achieved.

It was eight months too since Pemberton had stood, as he was standing now, on Seaford Head, looking down towards the street where he and Carne and Newland and Harry had lived. And Lohengrin. And Claire. He would never forget them, his friends and partners in the great game, the game which had been won the week before. There was much confusion still, much misery to endure, much fighting and dying to be suffered, but the great game was won. The Americans had made that certain when they stormed ashore in Normandy on beaches designated 'Utah' and 'Omaha'. On 'Omaha' they had been cut down in swathes, faltered, fought on and prevailed. They prevailed on 'Utah' too. The British, with Canadians and Frenchmen at their side, had made it even more certain. They had fought D-Day's first waterborne battle, smashing their way across beaches called 'Sword', 'Juno' and 'Gold', to take the bridges over the River Orne and the Caen Canal.

Just inland from the British beaches stood the 21st *Panzer* Division, formidable, menacing, static. It remained static for vital hours because *der Wurm* had said the Normandy landings were a feint, a diversionary raid, and the reports from German agents in Britain bore him out. The *Panzer Lehr* Division and the 12th SS remained static too, held back from the battle by the orders of the *Oberkommando der Wehrmacht*. When the 21st *Panzers*, battle-hardened veterans of the *Afrika Korps*, eventually rumbled forward to drive the British back into the sea, they had found the streets of Caen piled high with rubble from Allied bombing and could not pass through the town to engage the invaders.

Far to the east, close to the Pas-de-Calais at the narrowest point of the English Channel, waited Field-Marshal Erwin Rommel's main strength, the massive German 15th Army. It waited because *der Wurm* had said that that was where the Invasion would come, and electronic evidence more persuasive than any number of agents could provide had borne him out again.

Soon, Pemberton knew, the Germans would understand, soon they would move, but soon was already too late. His imagination carried him to the Normandy coast and showed him chaos turning into a semblance of order, madness becoming method, as troops, tanks and guns poured across the captured beaches to join the assault forces. It showed him too the largest armada the world had ever seen hurling salvo upon salvo of steel and high explosives at enemy positions far inland.

He didn't need his imagination to show him what else was being hurled at them. Below him the sea was alive with ships from the Newhaven staging area. Wherever he looked, the Spitfires, the Typhoons, the Mustangs, the Thunderbolts, the Lancasters, the Liberators, the Fortresses, criss-crossed the sky at altitudes from a few hundred feet above his head to almost the limit of vision. Beneath his feet the turf trembled at their passage and the air all about him quivered in sympathy with it. They would strike in Normandy at targets too distant for the naval guns to reach. They would strike at the 15th Army to preserve for as long as possible the fiction that the Pas-de-Calais was the true invasion area. They would strike at other formations that the people of B.I.a. had been able to persuade the German High Command to position at the wrong place at the wrong time.

Pemberton knew all that and knew as well that it all meant very much more than immobilizing the enemy Fleet in Norway, more even than tricking the United States into war with a forged map, for this had been the ultimate deception. This was retribution for all the years of death and misery and privation. This was the final reckoning. This was victory.

Vaguely embarrassed by the grandiloquence of his thoughts, Pemberton made his way down the hillside to Seaford, glad that Lohengrin could not hear the atmosphere thrumming its message of doom to his country. As he crossed the bottom of Southdown Road he glanced towards the house where they had lived, said a last goodbye to him and wished him well, wherever he might be. He said goodbye to Claire too and told her for the first time that he loved her.

His pilgrimage done, Pemberton walked towards the railway station, and the little train with the saddle-tank locomotive, telling himself that one day he would find a girl like Claire and ask her to marry him. One day he would do that. One day. Sometime. Somewhere.

If you enjoyed *Lohengrin*, please share your thoughts on Amazon by leaving a review.

For more free and discounted eBooks every week, sign up to the *Endeavour* newsletter.

Follow us on Twitter and Instagram.

Printed in Poland
by Amazon Fulfillment
Poland Sp. z o.o., Wrocław